DS 06/21

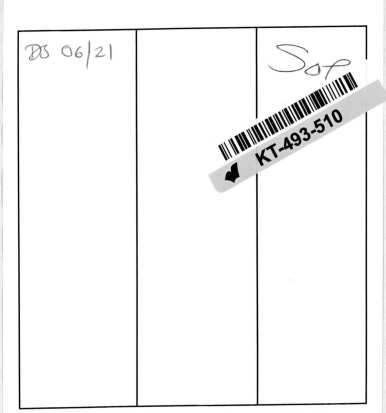

KT-493-510

This book should be returned/renewed by the latest date shown above. Overdue items incur charges which prevent self-service renewals. Please contact the library.

Wandsworth Libraries
24 hour Renewal Hotline
~~01159 293388~~
www.wandsworth.gov.uk

Wandsworth

Also by Beth Lewis

The Wolf Road

BETH LEWIS

BITTER SUN

b

THE BOROUGH PRESS

The Borough Press
An imprint of HarperCollins*Publishers*
1 London Bridge Street
London SE1 9GF

www.harpercollins.co.uk

This paperback edition 2019
1

First published in Great Britain by HarperCollins*Publishers* 2018

A catalogue record for this book
is available from the British Library

ISBN: 978-0-00-814553-8 (PB)

MIX
Paper from
responsible sources
FSC FSC‴ C007454
www.fsc.org

This book is produced from independently certified FSC™ paper
to ensure responsible forest management.

For more information visit: www.harpercollins.co.uk/green

For Neen

*

He walks broken. Barefoot in the dust. Middle of the road, asphalt shimmering in the heat, he walks like one of the returning soldiers. The ones with plastic legs. Limp. Shamble. Limp. Shamble. He's too young for the jungle so he's here. On the long road to town, rimmed with cornfields. The stalks heavy with gold on one side. Mangy and rotten on the other. A good year and a bad year, shoulder to shoulder.

He's forgotten his name.

Smoke streaks across the asphalt from burning fields. Driving away the blackfly and maggots, refreshing the soil with ash. Next year will be better, they'll say. Next year we'll forget this ever happened.

He's forgotten his home.

His t-shirt flicks in the breeze. Scarlet smears across his chest and arms, diluted to pink and brown at the hems. Thick blood thinned by dirty water.

A car slows, then swerves when the driver sees the blood. Foot down hard on the gas. Gone into a cloud.

The dust coats his skin and prickles his eyes but he doesn't feel it. The road is too long, stretching endless. Sharp gravel digs into his bare soles. Threatens to cut.

His head sways side to side with every step, a metronome without its tick.

The blood, on his arms, his stomach under his shirt, his legs down to the knees, feels tight and sticky.

He's forgotten his family.

A horn blasts behind him. A truck sidles alongside. He never heard it coming. A man leans across the empty passenger seat and winds down the window.

'Hey, you.'

He wavers at the sound of another person.

'Hey, don't I know you?' the driver says. 'Are you all right, son?'

The voice, the life, pulls him. He turns but doesn't see. His vision blurred by grit and glaring sun and exhaustion. He opens his mouth but the words seem to come from another throat. The air to make them from another chest. The brain to form them from another head. An innocent head. Three simple, perfect words float off his tongue and into the truck.

'I killed her.'

PART ONE

Summer, 1971

PART ONE

1

It was a heatwave summer when I was thirteen. A record breaker so they said. Momma, my sister Jenny, and me lived on a small farm a mile from town. A house of faded white-wash boards and a three-step porch in an ocean of cornfields. Oak tree in the yard with a rope hanging off its fattest limb. Used to be a tyre on it, one from the front of my pa's tractor, but it broke last year and he was long gone by then so the rope frayed and rotted and turned grey.

Momma had let the farm overgrow in the six or so years since he left. Gone to the war, she said, and never told us more. She said the land was his and the house was hers and she didn't give a rip about our cornfields, stunted and choked with ragweed. She made our money elsewhere, though I was never sure where. I did my best to keep the fields tidy, the corn planted and harvested, but it was only me working so the haul was always small. Still, last harvest I managed to sell the crop to Easton's flour mill for a good price and bought myself a new pair of boots and Jenny a jump rope.

It was a Friday, a few weeks before school let out for summer, that we found it, me, my sister and our friends Rudy and Gloria. Larson had dressed up to the nines for Fourth of July on Sunday, all ticker tape and flags and red, white and blue. There would be a parade, floats and cotton candy and corn dogs, then the fireworks would light up the sky. Every year Al Westin set up a shade outside his grocery store to give out free ice cream cones to the younger kids and the Backhoe diner threw open its windows and played Elvis and Buddy loud onto Main Street.

Larson was one of a hundred small towns in the middle of the Corn Belt though it was on its way to being something more. Just last week a 7-Eleven shot up in the trodden-down, boarded-up laundromat, giving the place new life and a brisk trade that upset Al Westin. We're a flyover town in a spit-on state, Rudy always said. But that was his daddy talking. Larson was full of good people who smiled on the street and wagged a finger if you dropped a gum wrapper. There was a carnival every year, the school just got a gleaming new yellow bus and the church had a fresh, young pastor who took the class for snow cones after Bible Study when it was steaming hot. We're a big-heart town, Mrs Lyle from the post office would say.

Eight in the morning, before the sun revved up its engine, Jenny and me walked the mile to school. I carried her book bag while she skipped ahead and sang and then screamed when I chased her and when I caught her we laughed. Momma didn't much like us going to school. She said it made pansies of men, made their heads soft and their hands limp. Too much holding a pen, she said, not enough holding a woman.

But school was our sanctuary, a place full of friends and

learning, and there was Miss Eaves. She taught geography two hours a week, after lunch on a Monday, last on a Friday. Best part about the class was me and Jenny took it together. Jenny was a year younger but the middle school wasn't big and both years fit in the same room. We had desks next to each other. We passed notes.

Jenny loved all those countries, languages, people, currencies; pesos, francs, dirham, lira, exotic to the ear. She was obsessed with the pictures of buildings older than anything in Larson, older than anything in our United States, and her enthusiasm was infectious. That class opened up our world, made us four want to get out of Larson, get out and see it all. Though for me, that desire to up sticks stayed in the classroom, for the others, it was constant, like breathing. I loved that class for the lessons on soil and agriculture and how they grew rice in China or coffee in Brazil. I'd be running the Royal farm one day so I sucked in anything and everything that might be useful.

Miss Eaves hushed the class, clicked her fingers for us to sit down. We called her Miss but she was a missus four times over, skin and bone but somehow soft. Jenny liked her. She said Momma was all odd angles and sharpness but Miss Eaves was a cloud of cotton candy, sweet-smelling like inhaling powdered sugar. The skin on her hands was folded and sagged like a bloodhound's cheeks. She had been a big woman once, she'd told me after class once, but lost it all when her fourth Mister went off to war in '68. Said she couldn't eat without anyone to eat for. Momma called her loose and unnatural, four Misters and no babies? What kind of woman is that?

Everyone else in class was goofing off, Jenny giggling with Gloria and Maddie-May, Rudy shooting spitballs at the back of Scott Westin's head, but I was quiet. I didn't have the energy to horse around. It'd been too hot to sleep for the past week and we didn't have one of those fancy central air units like in Gloria's house. Jenny and me shared a room and a bed up in the attic where the heat stuck. We made shadow puppets and butterflies with our hands and made them dance. I told stories of far-off kingdoms, and she'd pretend to be the princess while I roared as the dragon. Momma never woke to tell us to keep the noise down. Whiskey was her bedmate and not much could rouse her. When we were too tired to play, Jenny would ask for a story, then drift off to sleep when I was barely halfway through.

That Friday, with the world turned up hotter than the Backhoe fryers, flies circled and swooped on the ceiling. We made fans of our exercise books and shifted desks to escape direct sunlight. Poor Benjy Dewitt who sat closest to the window got scorched, blisters bubbled all up his left arm. Sweat and steam rose off us, turned the chalk dust to paste and smeared ink. Even Miss Eaves was struggling. Mid-way through a talk on volcanoes, when the breeze died and the classroom started to smell keenly of sweat, she stopped, threw her notes aside and said that magic word, 'dismissed'.

'Get out, the lot of you, go cool down,' she said.

When we didn't move, she clapped her hands together and shouted, 'Hustle, hustle!'

Let out early. On a Friday. The class erupted and spilled out of the room, out of the school. Me, Rudy, Gloria and Jenny didn't tell our parents. Momma wouldn't care but Rudy's dad would make him clean car parts in the salvage yard and Gloria would have to practise her piano and painting an extra few hours. I had a dozen jobs to do on the farm but we had a free hour or so to spend together and I wasn't going to waste it on chores. We just wanted to run, arms wide like we were flying. We'd be like ducks taking off from a pond, powering their feet, getting lift and height and then up, up, up, into the blue, soaring higher where nothing mattered and nothing could touch them. That was us. That was summer.

The four of us were gone, out into the sun and through the fields to the Roost. A place that was ours and ours alone. It was a wooded valley, our dip in the world, with a narrow but deep river running through it, thick with laurel and brush and creeper vines, grown dense and high like the sides of a bird's nest. In the Roost we'd built a shack, our Fort. We'd added to it since we were six and seven and now it was a grand structure. The roof was a square of sheet iron Rudy lifted from Briggs' farm when the old man pulled down his cattle shed. Walls were a dozen new planks left over from when they repaired the post office after Darney Wills, sodden drunk, ran his father's truck through the front window. Then we had a broken doorbell and handle, all ornate gold scrolling on the edges, Gloria got from her father when they replaced it last year. That gave us a touch of class, we all said.

We always covered the path down to the Roost with branches. It was a narrow opening between thick shrubs and trees so was easily concealed. It was far off the roads, in the middle of fields, but we wouldn't take any chances. It was Rudy's idea to keep it hidden. This is a peachy spot, Johnny, he said, and we don't want any old yahoo knowing about it.

But that Friday, the branches were thrown aside.

'Did we . . .' Gloria started, no doubt meaning to say,

'Did we cover the entrance the other day?' but we all knew we had.

'You think someone . . .' Jenny trailed off too.

Gloria picked up a branch, held it like a baseball bat. 'Do you think they're still down there?'

'I can't hear anything,' I said, and found a stick too.

Rudy picked up a branch shaped like a club and rested it on his shoulder.

'Jenny, you stay up here.'

My sister scoffed and grabbed a stick of her own. 'Hell to that. I'm coming too.'

Rudy grinned and saluted, knocking his heels together like he was in front of the Queen of England.

Rudy tested out the weight of his club, swiping at nettle heads until he cut one clean off.

'Ready?' he said and we nodded. 'No mercy!'

We barrelled down the hill into the valley, Rudy hollering out his war cry like some mad general, me right behind, branch up and catching on the trees, the girls behind me screaming.

We charged to the Fort, expecting intruders to leap out and flee in terror or put up a fight at least, but the Roost was empty. Rudy stopped dead and I crashed into him, knocking us both into the dirt. A moment, a beat, while we realised we were alone and unhurt and had just yelled our throats sore at nothing, then we all four collapsed into howling laughter. We frightened nobody but the birds.

'Check it out,' Gloria said, the first to get up, dust herself off, and look around.

The Fort's roof was bent, our door swung on one hinge. Inside was strewn with leaves and muck, the blanket we often sat on snagged on a nail and ripped. Someone had been here. Suddenly the laughter vanished and my chest tightened. But who knew about this place? Maybe a bum? One of those hobos who rides the rails and sleeps under trees like in the movies? Or some other kids from school, maybe Patrick Hodges or the Lyle boys, thinking this was unclaimed land? Did the fuckers wreck the place when they realised it was already taken?

It was a violation and we all felt it. The unrelenting, unending heat wasn't enough, the world wanted us punished more. Maybe it was taking revenge on Rudy for stealing a pack of cigarettes from his father, or Gloria for skipping her piano lesson and making the teacher wait, maybe on Jenny and me for not being better at washing linens or placating Momma when she was in one of her tempers.

'We should repair it,' Rudy said, kicking a board over, insects fleeing in the light. 'Soon as. Pick that up, clear it out and go get a rock to beat out the dents. It'll look stellar again in no time.'

Everything was stellar to Rudy. Didi's blueberry pie was stellar. Clint Eastwood, man, him and Telly were stellar. Swimming in Barks reservoir, now that's stellar. Rudy was the oldest by four months and that was enough to make him our leader. A flash of his straight-as-a-die teeth and a flick of his sandy blond hair, cut like a movie star's, and you can't say no.

I picked up the board he'd kicked. One from the post office. It was heavy, covered in mud, and he bent down to help. To most in Larson, Rudy was the bad kid, the prankster, the you-won't-amount-to-anything boy from the Buchanan family of cons and thieves, but to me and Jenny and Gloria, he was goodness made bone and skin.

The girls set about tidying the inside, repairing the

blanket, setting the cobbled-together table and mismatched chairs and tree stumps right. I found a heavy rock for knocking the dents out of the roof.

'We'll need more nails, and a hammer,' I said.

'I'll get some from McKinnon's hardware,' Rudy said. 'Got a few bucks saved up from cutting his grass last summer.'

Rudy hoarded money, his Larson escape fund. Even Jenny had a few nickels under her pillow. Seemed like every kid had one, except me. I had money saved up but it wasn't for a bus ticket, it was for old man Briggs' second tractor. He'd promised to sell it to me when I had the cash and could reach the pedals. I was one-for-two but that kind of money is hard to come by around here. I'd have it though, one day, you can bet your weekly on it.

We straightened up the roof and rehung the door and by that point, the sun and heat had eased and we'd forgotten that anyone else had ever been here.

Rudy and Gloria were over by the lake when Jenny came out the Fort saying she was hungry.

'I'm craving some fishes, Johnny.'

I smiled at the way she said 'fishes', the way her mouth puckered up at the *sh* sound.

'Get the poles,' I said. 'Perch'll be running about now.'

Jenny jumped and clapped and rushed back in the Fort to get the poles. They were nothing much, just saplings and line, but they were ours and they kept us fed. Friday meant Momma would be in Larson, at Gum's Roadhouse, shooting pool and tequila. No dinner on the table. No one looking for us. Sometimes we stayed out here all night, lit a fire, slept in the Fort, watched the sunrise over the fields.

Summer before last we'd dammed and diverted the river

a few hundred yards upstream from the Fort where the land dipped in a natural, deep curve. It was Rudy's idea. Everything was Rudy's idea and no matter how sky-high crazy, they always felt like good ones. It'll be our own private swimming pool, Johnny, he'd said, ten times better than Barks because it'll be all ours. And it was up to me to make it work. I'd read a bunch of library books to make sure we got it right. It'd taken us months, all over that winter. Even when our hands were frozen and we had to dig out the planks and rocks from under a foot of snow, we kept building. By last summer it was full and we called it Big Lake. The water was clear and you could see all the details of the forest floor, like you were looking at a carpet through a glass table. In winter it froze solid and we'd ice skate and try to play hockey and fail. It was a thing of beauty, I always said. A place trapped in time, like when they flooded whole towns to build their hydro-dams. Houses and streets and rusted-up cars, all held as they were before the water came.

Last year, Rudy and me hung a rope on a strong laurel branch. Shame on us but we were too chicken to swing into the water, too stuck to run and fly and let go then get that sickening moment of falling and *splash*. What if there were rocks we hadn't seen? Or sticking up branches that'd skewer us dead? I wasn't the best swimmer in the world and everyone knew it so never expected me to go first, but even Rudy was afraid, though he joked it off. Jenny stood close by me, said she didn't want to get her dress wet and, despite the heat, despite the cloying, sweating hotness of the world, all we did was dip a toe.

Except Gloria.

None of us were looking for her to be the bravest, the first. We took it as certain that she would go last, she was a girly girl, rich family type. But before Rudy could turn around and tease her for it, Gloria was sprinting. A blur of red dress and red hair as she ran for the rope, kicking up brown leaves, sending them skimming the water. I remembered her swinging high, letting go, shrieking and disappearing into the lake, then popping up like a mermaid, hair dark red and stuck to her head, laughing and calling us all sissies. From that day on Rudy said you can never be sure with Gloria. Momma thought the same when I told her the story. She'll grow up to be a quicksand woman, Momma said. Careful of that one, John Royal, she'll have you running circles you don't even know about. Be the death of you, she will.

Gloria always did what nobody expected.

So that Friday when we were fishing for perch in Big Lake, it was Gloria, wandering, not fishing because she thought it was boring, who found it. Tangled in the roots of a ripped-up sycamore, half-sunk in the flooded wood.

'Come look,' she shouted, stick in her hand for prodding. 'Get over here the lot of you.'

Rudy, on the other side of the lake, ran.

Jenny trailed behind me. 'But the fish, Johnny.'

'It'll just take a minute. Hook's in the water anyways.'

Gloria pointed with her stick. It was just out of arm's reach, the thing in the roots. But it wasn't a thing. The closer I got the clearer I saw. Rudy stopped running. He saw it too. Gloria's face was frowning and pale. Rudy looked back at me with hard eyes that said, *keep Jenny back*. It wasn't real, it couldn't be, not here. It was grey skin and hair once blonde like Rudy's. It was bloated but not unrecognisable. Gloria's stick left impressions in the skin.

It was a woman and she was dead.

2

We didn't tell anyone about the body, at least not at first. A mixture of fear and fascination silenced us. It fizzed inside us, this knowledge, this secret, so colossal and strange we thought it would crush us if we put one toe wrong, one word in the wrong ear.

The four of us stood silent and staring for I don't know how long. Just as dusk was settling and the starlings began their wheel, we decided to pull the woman out of the water and roots and lay her alongside a fallen tree trunk. We thought it kinder, to have something at her back, some comfort.

The woman, in my head I named her Mora, for the sycamore tree, was the first I'd seen naked. Mora's were the first breasts, the first swatch of hair between the legs, the first bullet hole.

Gloria couldn't look at her. Jenny couldn't stop.

Rudy swore in a whisper and leaned into me. 'What do we do?'

But I didn't have an answer.

'Who do you think she is?' Jenny said but nobody wanted to guess.

'We should tell Sheriff Samuels,' Gloria said and I heard a tremor in her voice. Usually so steady, her tone, rich like knocking on oak, shook at the sight of death. Rudy was quiet, a deep frown clouding his eyes, as if were he to concentrate hard enough, he would bring a storm rolling across the cornfields.

'Not yet,' I said. It was a terrible secret, I realised. One that could change everything, and I didn't know what to do. I wanted to run home, to Momma. She'd know how to handle it, what to say, she always knew best, but I was rooted. Momma wouldn't be home this time on a Friday night and, besides, how could I explain it?

Jenny stepped closer, looked at Mora as if she'd come upon a rat snake taking in the neighbour's dog. The serpent's jaw dislocating and reshaping itself so unnaturally. Something that small ingesting something far too big, you can't help but watch, a jumble of curiosity, revulsion, an urge to help surpassed by a want to know if it would succeed in its swallowing. I'd never seen that expression on Jenny's face before. Something happened to her that day. Changed her from the girl who would lazily kick her feet in the river, breathing in the sun and scent of evening primrose, to a girl who couldn't sit still, as if she had electricity running through her, twitching her muscles, itching beneath her skin.

'Why's she naked?' Jenny asked.

'Maybe she was swimming,' Rudy said.

'Swimming and then got shot,' I said.

Maybe they didn't see the bullet hole. Maybe they

thought it was something else, something innocent, and this poor woman had simply drowned while taking relief from the sun. Maybe it was and I saw a gunshot where really there was a hole made by a branch after she was already dead.

I bent down and lifted a lock of hair from Mora's face. Everything about her was grey. Her hair, between my fingers, was wet and coarse, grainy with silt. It didn't have the softness of living hair, it hung wrong, it looked wrong. She was deflated, absent of rushing blood and air. It was human as I've never seen human.

'Johnny,' my sister's voice, a frantic beat. 'Johnny, look.'

The dead woman's chest moved.

I yelped, stumbled backward, hit my elbow on a rock. Gloria gasped and Rudy swore and Jenny's eyes widened.

A spike of fear pressed against my stomach. Same place on my gut as the hole in hers.

'She's alive, she's alive, oh God oh God, do something,' Gloria said, tugging on Rudy's arm, backing away.

Mora's chest rose then fell in a strange breath. Her eyes didn't open. Her hands didn't move.

'We have to tell someone,' Rudy almost shouted. 'We have to get help.'

Her chest rose again but lower, not high beneath the rib cage. A bulge formed at the top of her abdomen, it shifted, squirmed. The breath was not a breath.

I pressed my back against the fallen tree, scrambled up.

'Jenny, get back,' I said.

But she'd bent over, put her face inches closer to the movement.

A shape formed in Mora's skin, defining itself against the weight of her flesh like an arm stretching out beneath a heavy blanket. My pulse echoed in my ears and chest, drowned out everything but the soft squelching sound of the body. Nobody moved. Gloria still clutched at Rudy's arm and he at hers. Jenny still stared, bent slightly at the waist, her top lip hooked up in pleasured disgust. I backed up, moss and bark flakes sticking to the sweat on my t-shirt, resisting the urge to grab Jenny and run.

The pink edging the inside of the hole in Mora's stomach pushed and turned outward, a black something appeared. Wet and shining, it forced itself free, a thin sinuous tube. I felt sick, I wanted to hurl up my breakfast, my lunch, those few biscuits I'd eaten after class, I wanted to be empty. My head told me it was an eel or catfish, my eyes said demon, devil, alien.

Jenny backed away as the creature wriggled free of the hole and flopped, writhing and slick, on Mora's stomach.

'Kill it! Kill it!' Gloria screamed.

'Quiet,' I said, harder than I should have. She was so loud, so shrill, I feared her call would bring parents and police down on us and we'd have to explain all this.

The eel spasmed and jerked and fell into the leaf litter inches from my feet. I jumped onto the log, Rudy and Gloria cried out, ran halfway to the Fort, Jenny shuffled backward but she was slow. The eel flicked itself, landed on her bare foot. She shrieked as if stung, the spell of the body broken, and kicked out.

I lunged for her, pulled her close to me, wrapped my arms around her shoulders. The eel landed far from the water, then as if sensing its distance, increased its convulsion.

We all looked to Rudy but he was up on a tree stump, squealing worse than Jenny.

The eel flicked toward us and Jenny and Gloria screamed afresh.

'Kill it!' they yelled.

Do something, Johnny boy, get your head together and goddamn do something.

I grabbed a stick, hooked it beneath the eel's body and flicked it in a long, squirming arch into Big Lake.

A breath. A beat. A splash.

'Let's get out of here,' Rudy said, finally climbing down from his perch.

I looked at him, big brave Rudy Buchanan, shaking like a sissy with a spider on his hand. Rudy would take down a bully in a single punch but he was quaking in his shorts at a fish? I tried not to laugh.

'It's just an eel. What are you so afraid of?'

He glared at me. 'It came out of a *dead body.*'

'Johnny, come on,' Jenny said. 'We should be getting home.'

We shouldn't. We didn't have a curfew and Momma wouldn't be wringing her hands for us. But when I looked around at my friends, my sister, I saw them all shaken. In truth, I was shaken too but one of us had to keep it together or we'd all be screaming on tree stumps.

I'd gotten rid of the eel but the body, the girl, she lay where we'd dragged her and all humour drained from my mind. It changed the day. Turned the blazing sun cold. Jenny's face showed raw confusion at what we'd found, what it meant. I saw the same in Rudy's eyes, in Gloria's. Hooked lips and frowns.

I usually had the answers but today, I was as lost as them.

The four of us left the Fort in shuffling silence. We emerged from the trees and the sticky evening heat pressed against us. I suddenly missed the cool, sheltered air of the Roost but couldn't face going back down there. Not now, maybe not ever.

'We have to tell the sheriff,' Gloria said. 'They have to find out who she is and who did that to her.'

'Cops won't do anything,' Rudy said. 'There's all sorts going on in this town they don't know about. Shit, if they did, Samuels would have a heart attack.'

Gloria scowled at him. 'I think a murder is a little more important than your dad's chop shop.'

Rudy sneered and mimicked her voice. Gloria punched him in the arm.

'What will they do to her?' Jenny asked, looking back toward the trees, toward the valley and our lake.

'Take her away,' Rudy said. 'Put her in a morgue. Find her parents, I suppose.'

'I'm going to tell the sheriff,' Gloria said.

'We'll get in trouble,' I said, a knot forming in my chest. 'We moved her.'

'Yeah, we will,' Rudy said, his finger bouncing in the air. 'He's right. We moved her. They'll think we did it.'

'Don't be stupid.' Gloria's scowl deepened.

'All the detective books and cop shows say you don't touch the body, Gloria, and you definitely don't move it,' I said. 'Maybe we should wait until Samuels finds her himself?'

Rudy pointed at me, his arm straight out. 'I like Johnny's plan.'

'It's a stupid plan,' Gloria said. 'I don't care what you say, I'm going to tell Samuels.'

Rudy grabbed the back of his neck with both hands, his elbows stuck out like sails. 'Just wait, yeah? Just a day.

Maybe do one of those anonymous tip-offs and leave us out of it.'

His voice turned small. 'They'll think I had something to do with it. They'll lock me up, Gloria. I'm a Buchanan. I got bad blood, remember, and everyone in town knows it.'

Jenny put her arm through Rudy's, held his hand and pushed her cheek against his shoulder.

'You're not bad,' she said. 'We'll all tell Samuels the truth. You didn't touch her and if they think otherwise, they'll have to go through us to get to you. Right, guys?'

'Right,' Gloria said and took Rudy's other hand.

I completed the circle, put my arms over Jenny and Gloria's shoulders, pulled the four of us into a group hug.

'We're like a flock of birds, aren't we?' I said. 'We stick together and we protect each other from eagles and *eels*, hey?'

I prodded Rudy's stomach and he told me to shut up.

'A flock. I like that.' Jenny patted my back. 'We've got a Roost after all.'

Rudy finally smiled. 'You and your birds, Johnny,' he said, just as quiet, then shook his head. 'If only we were, huh? We could all fly the hell out of here.'

'We will, one day. All four of us,' Gloria said, then checked her watch. 'I've got to go. Daddy's taking me to the fairground in Bowmont tonight. Mom is at one of her Clarkesville society dinners and thank God she didn't make me go to that. I'll win you each a teddy bear.'

Gloria broke the circle and Rudy went with her, to see her home like he always did. Then he turned, walked backward a few steps.

'We're a flock, yeah?' he shouted, the wince, the curl,

the confusion still on his face, though he tried to put a mask over it. He smiled, flapped his arms like wings. '*Ca-caw, ca-caw,* Johnny. See you guys tomorrow.'

They waded through Briggs' wheatfield toward town, waist-high in gold, as if their torsos were floating free. We walked everywhere. Jenny and me didn't have bikes. No money for scrap metal that does a job your legs can do just fine, Momma always said. Rudy was fixing up a broken, rusted-up Schwinn but getting nowhere, and Gloria had a pink Raleigh she refused to ride because we couldn't ride with her.

I let myself smile as I watched my friends. My flock.

Jenny fidgeted by my side. The calm she'd had with Rudy and Gloria had gone with them. She glanced at me, then away, then down at her feet.

I couldn't move. Behind, the Fort and the body. Away to the left, my house, empty and sweltering. Right, Rudy, Gloria and the cops. Ahead, nothing but fields and sky. The sun burned rich orange and bled into the clouds. A swarm of starlings, black spots on gold, pulsed between power lines.

'I'm hungry,' I said. 'There is still some chicken from yesterday's dinner.'

'How can you be hungry after *that*?' she asked but I shrugged.

Jenny squinted at me, like she did when I said something stupid. Momma did it too. Where Momma might yell at me, Jenny just turned away, sighed through her teeth, and stalked across the field. The path home was well trodden, we made shortcuts of the fields, they were our highways and backways, free of grown-ups and rules.

'Shouldn't we go straight to the police?' she asked. 'Feels wrong to just leave her down there.'

'I know but we agreed. We'll go tomorrow. I guess we just try to forget about it for tonight.'

We walked together, silent, until we came to Three Points, a triangle of land made by three crisscrossing irrigation streams. Momma said it'd been there since they split up the land between us, Briggs, and Morton down the track. She said that idiot Briggs couldn't count right and ended up short on one side. Caused a rift between the families for years and the swatch of land remained unclaimed. It was twenty strides end-to-end and covered in grass green as a lime candy straight out the jar. No matter the weather, no matter the heat, Three Points stayed alive. It was a rule, one of those known somehow by everyone in town, that you could say or do anything on the Points. It didn't belong to anyone so no one was watching, no one was listening.

Jenny slowed and stopped in the middle of the island.

'Do you think someone in Larson killed her?' she asked.

I'd thought about it while we were walking but pushed away the idea almost as quickly as it came.

'I don't want to think about what that would mean.'

'What about the Fort? Could the person who wrecked it have killed her?' she said; her voice had an edge of fear to it, a tremor I recognised. Her eyes darted left, right, into the trees, over the fields. 'Could . . . could they still be around?'

I put my hands on her shoulders. 'No. Whoever did it is long gone. And even if they aren't, you've got me and Momma and we won't let anything happen to you.'

The tension in her eased, her shoulders dropped. 'I know *you* won't, but her? She'd probably offer me up to the killer for a bottle of bourbon.'

It needled at me when she spoke of Momma like that.

I'd tried for years to be peacekeeper between them, but the barbs kept flying, the hate kept growing and resurfacing no matter what. Now my days were all about maintaining the uneasy calm.

'Let's go home,' I said, straightened up and took Jenny's hand. 'Momma won't be there anyway.'

Twenty minutes and two more fields brought us to the edge of our yard. We both stopped and Jenny's grip on my hand tightened, turned my knuckles white and sore. Faded red truck parked skewed against the side of the house with two deep tyre scars in the dirt. Fresh dent in the door. The frayed rope on the oak branch swayed but not by the breeze. Momma always flicked the rope with her finger when she got home. Her mindless habit.

The sound of footsteps throbbed from inside the house. One-two, one-two, a stumble, a crash, the picture frame in the hall, dropped and broken twice this month already. A low moan, something monstrous in it, thick and slurred. A clatter of metal on enamel, the pan that cooked yesterday's chicken, pushed into the kitchen sink.

Jenny sighed. 'Looks like you were wrong, Johnny.'

3

There weren't many reasons Momma would leave Gum's before midnight on a Friday. It likely wasn't to give us a new pa this time, as I couldn't hear anyone else in the house. A Pigeon Pa, Jenny called them. They fly in, shit all over the place then fly out again, none the wiser. Momma alone in the house meant Ben Gum, owner of Gum's and one of our years-ago Pigeon Pas, had cut her off. When that thought hit us both, Jenny's grip on my hand turned iron.

'I don't want to go in there,' she said.

'It won't be so bad. She's just drunk. You know what she's like when she's drunk. You go straight upstairs and I'll bring you dinner.'

Jenny kicked at the dirt. 'Like that'll help.'

I tried to stifle my sigh. 'Just try not to sass her.'

We could turn around, run back to the Fort or go to the west field and sleep between the corn while Momma slept off hers. That would be better than seeing the anger and snarl on Jenny's face a moment longer. But we stood by that rope swing too long. The crashing inside stopped for a sickening moment. Then the slam of the back door flung wide, the screen's rusted spring whining. Then the slapping steps of her shoes on the dirt. Then the voice.

'There you are, my babies,' Momma said, slurred and breathy. 'Look at you both, skin and bone. You hungry, my babies?'

Momma's hair, thin curls turned white-blonde instead of gold like Jenny's, flared wild on her head, like a storm brewed on her skull. And it did. On it. In it. She was a tornado, my momma.

'Hi, Momma,' I said and nudged at Jenny to say hello but she wouldn't.

'Come inside now.' Momma swayed on her spindle heels and spindle legs wrapped up in tight blue jeans, her red camisole cut a half-inch too low.

She caught herself on the side of the house. 'I'll fix you both a plate. Get in, get in.'

She pounded her fist on the whitewashed boards with every word, then hurled up her arm, half sick of us for being there, half gesturing which way to go.

I felt my sister's heartbeat thrumming through her hand. I took a step toward the house, tried to pull Jenny with me but she wouldn't move. Her face set in a dark frown. A prickle went up my back, I knew what was coming.

'Please, Jenny,' I whispered but she shook her head.

'Not when she's like this,' she said.

Momma saw Jenny's expression and matched it. All her slur and swagger disappeared and she turned pin-sharp. Momma stood tall and straight, her back like rebar, and set toward us. Careful steps turned ragged fast. Red whiskey heat rose in her cheeks and filled up her throat, turned the sweet words sour.

'Look at you,' she sneered down at Jenny. 'That dress. Showing off those legs. You're so dirty. Get in this *fuhking* house. I made you dinner and you'll damn well eat it.'

Then she was in front of us, her hand on Jenny's arm, pulling her toward the porch. Her eyes, blue and bloodshot, flared up bright despite the dark, red lips pulled back, lipstick on her teeth, smeared on her chin.

'Let me go!' Jenny tried to pry Momma's fingers but her grip was iron.

'I am your mother and you will mind me.'

Jenny's shoes cut furrows in the dirt, her nails dug into Momma's wrist. 'I wish you weren't. I hate you! Let me go!'

Momma recoiled like those words were a slap across the cheek. I put myself between them, one hand on Momma's hand, the other on Jenny's, tried to prise them apart.

'She didn't mean it, did you, Jenny?' I said, keeping my voice level, calm, anything not to throw gas on the fire.

'I meant it,' my sister snarled. 'I wish you weren't my mother.'

The sharp sobriety in Momma crumbled and her slur returned. 'You ungrateful little witch.'

She yanked on Jenny's arm again, harder, fiercer, I thought it might pop out the socket. I was invisible to them. They sniped through me, around me, trading hurled stones and scratches one for one.

Momma's elbow dug into my side, pushed me, and suddenly her and Jenny were away. Momma dragged her around the house. Jenny cried out, scratching, swearing and saying the most awful things about our mother, calling her ugly, fat, a bitch, and all sorts else. I squeezed my eyes shut for a moment. The noise, the hate, it all hurt too much to hear. Then I followed them around the house, begging them to stop but they wouldn't. It felt like they never would.

At the step up to the back door, Momma finally let go and Jenny fell, landed hard on a rock, but Momma didn't see.

'You stupid, stupid girl,' she hissed and went to grab her but Jenny scrambled away and I was between them again. Behind me, Jenny whimpered, clutched her knee.

'Momma, please.' I took her by the shoulders and held her wavering gaze. Same as Jenny, the best way to calm them both. 'Jenny's just tired, she doesn't know what she's saying. She doesn't mean it.'

Momma's eyes, red-rimmed with drink, welled with tears. 'She breaks my heart, that girl, just breaks my heart.'

'I know. Please go inside, Momma. I'm so hungry and I'd just love some of that chicken. I'll talk to her, okay? She's sorry, she's really sorry and so am I. Please?'

Keep it calm, John Royal, keep the eye contact, keep the tone light, keep the platitudes coming.

Momma wasn't Momma when she was drunk. She was a beast of ups and downs and harsh words she didn't really mean. At least, I hoped she didn't. I prayed neither of them did, else what hope was there for us?

'She needs to learn respect,' Momma said, voice like a dry kettle on the heat. 'She needs her momma's teaching, she can't be dressed so loose.'

'I know, Momma. I know.'

Momma put her hand, soft and warm and trembling, on my cheek. 'You're such a good boy, John. My perfect boy.'

Her hand fell away and her gaze drifted. 'You look hungry. I'll fix you a plate.'

Then she went inside and let the screen door bang. The only sound left in the world was Jenny's anger, her sharp breaths and tiny scratches of her nails in the soil. I went to her, knelt down beside.

'Jenny,' I said, soft as cotton, put my hand on hers. 'Are you all right? Let's go inside now.'

Tears mixed up with dust, streaked down her face. Her hair, gold blonde and perfect, was rucked up and twisted. She shook. Hands on her knee, a trickle of blood down her shin.

'We have to,' I murmured, distracted, eyes on the blood. The image of the girl, the body we found, hit the back of my eyes.

Jenny wiped her face hard with the heel of her hand. A bruise blossomed on her arm.

'No. I won't go in there.'

And she broke, wept hot tears into her hands. I wrapped my arms around my sister and sat until her sobs eased and the last of the evening light faded to night. I teased my fingers through her hair, tamed it down best I could without hurting her. A speck of rage grew in me that Momma had let this happen and Jenny had let this happen and a few stupid words had blown up into a fight that would linger for days. I wished I could say to Jenny, it wasn't all Momma, was it? You said some nasty things too. You hurt her feelings too. You made her cry too. Why can't you both just get along? Why do I have to be stuck in the middle all the time? But I clenched my jaw, swallowed down the blame, and tried to soothe my sister.

'It'll be worse if you don't go in,' I said. Then, as if it made it all right, 'You know she's only like this when she's drunk.'

I met Jenny's eyes, raw and blazing. 'I meant every word.'

She slapped away my hand and scrambled to her feet.

'Please, Jenny, just come inside,' I said but she wouldn't hear it.

'You go, Johnny, you go be with her, she's got your stupid chicken.'

Before I could say I'd share, she ran. Just turned and ran.

'Jenny!' But she was away, into the night, into the fields.

I whipped around to the house and to those three steps up to where my mother waited, wrapped in her own hurt. I heard her move inside, the clinking of glass as she poured another drink. Those sounds mixed with the rustle and crackle of Jenny's footsteps running through dry grass.

I was stuck in the back yard, between Momma and sister. I didn't stand a chance of catching up with Jenny but I knew where she would go. She was like those starlings, darting and weaving, the best runner in our class. Mr Escott, our phys-ed teacher, said it was a good job I could read and work a corn huller because I wasn't much good for anything else. The rest of the class had laughed. I'd stared at my skinny arms and legs, my too small gym shorts, and watched the others cross the finish line.

'John?' Momma said, gently from the back door. 'Come on inside, baby.'

She smiled, that full smile that lit up her face and eyes, rosy and glowing with whiskey. The snarl and sneer was gone, like it had never been. A flipped switch and there was my momma again, reaching for me.

'Dinner is on the table.'

This wasn't the woman who'd said those things to Jenny and dragged her across the yard. It just wore her face, spoke in her voice. It was the drink. It was the sickness. Not my momma, not really.

I went inside and sat at the kitchen table. Jenny would be fine. I'd never been able to truly calm her after a fuss like that, I'd never be able to get her to come home if she didn't want to. Besides, if she was still riled up the fight would start fresh soon as she walked in the back door. It was best for them and me to wait it out, let the anger subside and then find her, cradle her, let her sob it all out onto me instead of watch her beat it out of herself. I knew where she'd go, I'd find her.

Momma sat down beside me at the kitchen table, smoking a Lucky Strike. She reached to me, brushed my hair back, then flicked out her ash into a chipped cup.

'How was your day, baby?'

'Fine.' It wasn't fine. We found a dead body. But I wasn't ready to say that. It was still too mixed up in my head.

Momma went quiet as I ate. Her eyes flickered every now and then, like she was thinking of something, wanted to say it, but chickened out. She bit on her lower lip. Jenny did that when she was worried.

'Is your sister all right?'

'I don't know. I guess,' I said. 'She will be.'

Momma stubbed out the Strike and rubbed her forehead, tucked her hair back, laid her hand over her neck, fidgeted like she had ants crawling all over her skin.

'That girl makes me so mad sometimes, the way she talks to me. If I'd have spoken to my mother like that, ooh she would have kicked me out of her house so fast it'd make your head spin. You heard what that girl said, didn't you?'

She shook her head, finally her eyes went to mine, eyelids

drowsy with drink. 'You'd never talk to me like that, would you, baby? You're my prince. What a good boy you are.'

She cupped my cheek with her hand. Soft skin. Sweet smell of tobacco and old perfume on her wrist.

'My temper sometimes, I don't know,' she said, waving her arm, dismissing it as nothing.

Then she snapped back to me. 'Oh! I almost forgot.'

Momma went to the family room, to the cabinet behind the couch. She pulled out a package wrapped in brown paper. A rectangle, about two inches thick, tied up with string.

'I got this for you,' she said, skipping back over to me and setting it down on the table. She moved my still full plate and pushed the package closer.

'I saw it in the thrift store on Lexington a month ago and I thought, my John will just love that, so I had them wrap it up and then I went and forgot all about it, can you believe it?'

A fire lit in my chest. A present. For me? It wasn't Christmas and my birthday was way back in March and we didn't have the money for throw-away spending.

'What is it?' I said. I traced the edges with two fingers, felt a ridge on the right side and a fizz of electric went through me. A book.

Momma made a dopey face. 'Open it and see, dummy.'

I untied the string and ripped the paper away in one tear. My eyes went wide and my mouth dropped open and I couldn't quite believe it.

The cover, a pale beige cloth, said, *Birds of North America*, then smaller at the top, *A Guide to Field Identification*. Below, three vivid, multi-coloured birds perched on a bright green branch.

'Do you like it?' Momma said, her hands clasped below her chin. 'You used to love watching the crows steal the corn and you're always out gawking at those starlings.'

'I love it,' I said.

I flicked through. Pages and pages of exact, perfect drawings and information on habitat and nesting and migration. I couldn't stop staring. Some birds I recognised immediately. Wrens. Tanagers. But there were so many more. So much more to learn. I wanted to devour it then and there and go searching for them in the fields and trees.

'Are you sure, baby?'

I looked up at Momma, her eyes on me like she was nervous. Scared she'd got me wrong, that I'd hate it, hate her, but I never could. I went to her and threw my arms around her neck.

'Thank you, Momma. I love it. I love you. It's the best thing.'

She hugged me back, hard, and held on for a few seconds before releasing me. She grabbed my face in both hands and kissed me on the forehead. 'I love you too, my little prince.'

Then she let me go, said something about her programmes, and disappeared into the family room. A moment later I heard the television blare out *The Partridge Family*. I cleared my plate while pawing through my book. Stopped when I got to the cardinal. A striking red bird, Jenny's favourite. We'd seen one, a year or two ago, when we'd gone camping with the Bible Study class down at Fabius Lake.

A sharp prick of guilt hit my chest and I closed the book and took it upstairs, hid it under my side of the bed. I didn't want to tell Jenny about it. She'd be upset that Momma hadn't got her anything and it would spiral into another fight. As I came back downstairs, I listened for Momma's movements but just heard David Cassidy's warbling, then I snuck outside.

I found Jenny down at the Roost, staring into the tiny ripples on Big Lake. With her golden hair and in her pale yellow sundress, she shone in the dark.

'I knew you'd come after me. Eventually,' she said, but she didn't seem sad or angry, just glad I was there. Her voice was calm as the lake, quiet as the water. She stared, trancelike, as if red-eyed on Mary Jane. Blood streaked down her shin so I ripped a swatch out of my t-shirt and dipped it in the cold water.

'Here,' I said, 'let me clean that.'

The blood diluted and ran down to her foot, soaking pink into her bobby sock. Jenny didn't look at me or seem to notice what I was doing, her eyes fixed on a point across the lake.

'It's so quiet here,' she murmured.

Only chirping crickets and the soft lapping of water. No shouting or screaming or hurt feelings. No whiskey slur in Momma's voice. Just us and our breathing and the darkness. It was like the feeling you get when you duck underwater, everything muffled and thick. The water holds every part of you, keeping you buoyed and enclosed, safe, for a time. You know the world is still out there but it can't touch you except when you come up for air.

'Do you think she's lonely?' Jenny said and I wondered if she meant Momma.

Then I saw where she was looking.

Something shifted in that moment. Jenny turned to me, our eyes met. The moon and starlight broke through the canopy enough to highlight the water, define the shapes of the trees, and her, pale against the black. Jenny took my hand and we went to Mora.

'It's so strange. She looks like she's sleeping,' I said, and felt something squirm inside me.

You shouldn't be here, Johnny boy. It's a goddamn dead body and you're, what, visiting with it?

My dinner, chicken and mashed potatoes and carrots, churned and swirled in my stomach.

'We should go home,' I said.

Jenny knelt beside Mora and pulled me down. 'We can't leave her here alone. Look at her, she's beautiful.'

She picked a scrap of dead leaf from Mora's forehead and flicked it aside.

I don't know how long we knelt there, staring into those dead eyes. I'd never seen a smile like that on Jenny's face before and it scared me. That change, that jitter in her bones that Mora sparked had fanned to a dark flame and I didn't know what it meant. I checked around us, suddenly aware of what this picture might look like to anyone watching. And a creeping cold in my bones that whoever did this to her, this poor girl, could still be around. But it was empty, silent, I saw everything through moonlight, all silver and black and not quite real. This wasn't quite real. How could it be?

'Death is special, isn't it, Johnny?' Jenny said. 'It's like the way the Pastor Jacobs talks about God. Death is a kind of god. It's terrible and powerful but if you treat it right and have faith, it's love. Behind the fear, death is love, isn't it, Johnny?'

I swallowed burning bile.

Jenny lay down beside Mora and I had no choice but to lie down too. I couldn't leave my sister here, alone, with a killer on the loose, and she wouldn't go home yet. So I stayed, despite the nausea, despite the strange, sour smell, despite the gnawing pain in my head.

But Jenny seems calm, John.

She seems happy.

And that's good enough for now.

Jenny fell asleep quicker than she had in weeks but I couldn't. I lay on the ground, stones and twigs poking into my back, replaying every word of the argument until the movie reel reached the gift Momma gave me. The bird book. Light beige cloth. A dozen shades of blue, red, green, every colour filled my head, blotted out the pale white body beside my sister. I fell asleep in those colours, to the sound of cooing birds and gently ruffling feathers.

Jenny and I woke to warm sunlight and a fuzzy voice on a radio. I opened my eyes, squinting. We didn't have a radio at the Fort. Could have been a dream or some kind of birdsong, I didn't know. Then it came again. Then a close, clear, hundred-per-cent real voice said something back, *bzzt* ten-four. My eyes adjusted to the sun and my insides turned to snow. Jenny woke too and immediately tensed and clutched my arm.

Standing over us was Sheriff Samuels and a dozen of his deputies. The way they looked at us. Their eyes wide, their mouths set in grim frowns. One was chucking up his breakfast far off and I hoped it wasn't in Big Lake because it would make swimming gross.

Samuels made Jenny and me get up. Made us stand there and wouldn't talk to us. Would barely glance our way. Most of the deputies looked away. A few of Larson's lookie-loos up at the top of the valley were fixated. In front of the police tape, far upstream, Rudy and Gloria stood with a skinny cop taking notes. They weren't looking at us. Maybe didn't see what the cops saw. Maybe saw everything. Jenny and me got one last look at Mora before they laid a tarp on her.

That's when the rumours began, starting almost before they took us down to the station. Murmurings of 'freaks' and 'perv kids' floated through the valley. The radios crackled and came alive, descriptions of the scene were repeated, again and again. Responses came: you shitting me, Miller? Say what? There were kids with the body? Jesus Christ, the missus'll never believe that. And so it went. Through the fuzzy connection, the news of what the sheriff's men found by the lake spread to all of Larson.

4

They put Jenny and me in the back of Deputy Miller's patrol car. An old Plymouth with rust blooming at every join and a cage between us and the front seats. Three bolts were missing from the left side and I reckoned I could kick out the rest, get into the front, get us free and clear if I needed to. The radio crackled. A shotgun stood upright, locked to the dash. Ripped seats spewed out dusty yellow foam. A bare spring pressed into my back. Make sure you got a plan, John Royal, my momma once told me, if you're ever snatched by the pigs. Make sure you've got your story right in your head and, if you don't have a story, make sure you tell your lie before the other guy tells his.

I held Jenny's hand. We had no need for a lie but adults sometimes see a different truth in what kids tell them.

It was barely past eight but the sun was spinning up its wheels, getting ready for another record high. Miller had left the windows open front and back but there wasn't a breeze. The air inside the car was thicker than outside, full of dust and old cigarette smoke, so dense the fresh air couldn't get in. Criminals aren't fit to breathe clean.

Jenny squeezed my hand. 'I'm scared.'

'We haven't done anything wrong.' I turned to her, smiled. 'They just want to ask us some questions because we found her. That's all.'

The heat rose with the sun, ticked up a degree or two every minute, multiplied by ten for sitting in a metal box. The sweat popped from my skin. My shirt, my legs below my shorts, the backs of my arms, stuck to the seat. We'd been in the car half an hour. Another half and we'd be fork-tender. They'd be able to pull us apart with a spoon.

I hung my head out the window, breathed out the dust and in the scent of the elders. Thought about all the chores I had to do on the farm. Weed the west field, tend the corn, check the fences near Morton's boundary, and a dozen others. In the trees, a wren or maybe a warbler sang, undisturbed by the scene on the ground. Birds don't care. We're big, slow lumps to them, always looking up while they're looking down.

'John,' Jenny tugged on my shirt, pulled me back inside the oven and nodded out of her window.

Emerging from the track down to the Roost, we saw them. The skinny deputy with Rudy and Gloria. The cop had hold of Rudy, tight by the arm, like he was chief suspect and they'd caught their man. Gloria walked freely alongside. Rudy had a black scowl on his face, red-eyed and resigned to the treatment. He's a Buchanan, I imagined the sheriffs saying, course he's got something to do with this mess.

'Hey,' I shouted, climbing over Jenny to get to the window. 'Hey, you guys. What's going on?'

Gloria jogged over, got halfway before the deputy barked

at her but she kept running. 'They want to take our statements. That's all.'

She came right up to the window as the skinny deputy put Rudy into another car. He called her again but she paid no attention.

'I thought we were going to wait,' I whispered, 'we were going to tell them together.'

Gloria looked down, wincing apologetic. 'I know, I'm sorry. I got home, changed and went out with Daddy but Mandy had my laundry. She asked why my dress was so muddy and why it smelt so strange. She kept asking and asking and it just all came out.'

'It's okay,' Jenny said and reached out, took Gloria's hand.

Gloria took the comfort for a moment then frowned. 'They've made a real mess down there.'

'Miss Wakefield,' the skinny cop shouted from the other car.

'See you at the station,' Gloria said, then ran over to the skinny cop who opened the car door for her. She got in the back seat with Rudy.

Rudy waved, held up his hands and shouted, 'They didn't cuff me this time!'

The skinny cop banged on the roof to shut him up, then got in, cranked up the engine. The tyres chewed the ground as they tried to get a grip, chunks of dirt flew up behind. A flock of birds exploded from the nearest tree. Skinny cop punched the gas and the car popped out of its dustbowl, skidded over the grass. He swerved, wild to the left then the right before getting control, then snailed the car onto Briggs' farm track. They disappeared into a dust cloud and left Jenny and me staring after.

It was another half hour of swelter before Samuels and Miller trudged up the valley. Samuels with his light blue shirt turned dark from sweat, red-faced like a cartoon pig, said something to his deputy. Took out a handkerchief, wiped his forehead, his cheeks, under his chin, back of his neck, then started again from the top. Miller, loose roll-your-own hanging out his mouth, dropping flakes of tobacco and ash, hitched up his belt and spoke around the joe, puffing out smoke and losing more strands.

Samuels' round little eyes met mine. I felt headsick from the smell of the car. Headsick from the smell of death and dirt on my skin. Headsick from the mutterings of 'freak' and 'perv'. From the grim, disgusted looks. And from Jenny. From that strange, serene expression she wore last night when she lay down beside the body.

Gloria and Rudy would be at the station by now. Answering questions. The skinny cop would be telling everyone what they found. The rumours of weird kids sleeping next to a body would spread through Larson like locusts through corn. Come on, sheriff, waddle that gut over here and take us to the station, get this over with. But Samuels kept staring. Kept wiping.

Samuels nodded along to something Miller said, chins appearing and disappearing with every bob of his head. Rolls of flesh. A shiny, pink ocean of it, wave after wave, nod after nod.

'What's taking so long?' Jenny threw herself against the back seat and pulled her knees up, tucked into her chest. The red scratch livid on her shin.

'I don't know,' I said. 'But they're going to ask us a lot of questions.'

'So? We didn't do anything wrong.'

I shifted on the leather seat, arms and legs sticking. 'They won't see it that way.'

'They're idiots.'

'They are. But we need to agree what to tell them.'

'What's to tell?' Jenny's arms tightened around her knees. She did that when she was embarrassed, held herself close like she would split apart if confronted. Momma used to do it too, before Pa left, before the Old Milwaukees and the whiskey, but Momma didn't get embarrassed any more. No sense in shame, John Royal, she said, shame comes from other people and who gives two sweet fucks about other people?

Jenny elbowed my side. 'Johnny?'

'Sorry.'

A few more deputies appeared at the top of the valley, crowding behind Samuels. One, his uniform soaked through with sweat, held a handkerchief over his mouth like he was going to hurl. Samuels turned to him, patted him on the shoulder, and the cop turned and retched into the dry grass.

Jenny nudged me again. 'What do we tell them?'

'We tell them the truth but we don't say anything about you and Momma arguing. That's family business. We say we were worried about foxes or dogs getting to the poor woman before the police could come so we went down there to keep watch. We fell asleep. That's it.'

'That's not the truth, Johnny.'

Outside, Samuels' voice boomed. 'Wrap it up, boys.'

He slapped Miller on the back and lumbered toward us.

'It's close enough,' I whispered. 'You remember it?'

Jenny nodded, arms tightened up around her shoulders.

Samuels and Miller both got in the car, the axles groaning under their new weight. The sheriff inched the Plymouth out of the field. As soon as we got onto the track, he put his foot down. Fresh air flooded the car, prickled my skin, blew away the stink of cigarettes and leather. It would take about twenty minutes to get to the station. Jenny held my hand as I hung my head out the window.

The wind and sun pulled at my eyes, stung tears from them. I let them blur, enjoyed the haze. The world had become too real. Too stark and bright white, all sharp edges and hard stares, and I didn't know what would be waiting when we arrived at the station. For a few more minutes, at least, it was just a car ride.

I heard a rumble of a big engine on the road behind and turned against the wind, hair flicking in my eyes. I blinked the tears away but the haze didn't lift. The heat transformed the asphalt to water, shimmering, wavering like a mirage, made the car almost invisible. The car, a light blue or grey, kept its distance, too far away to see its details, but close enough to hear the engine, feel the thunder of it in my chest. I could tell a car's badge from a glance but nothing much else. I knew it was a Ford but didn't recognise it from around town or school pick up. This was a back road, a shortcut into Larson locals used. Outsiders didn't know it. My chest vibrated with the roar of the engine, like I stood too close to a booming speaker. The shimmer grew. The grey paint job, so pale, like no colour I'd seen, didn't reflect the light, seemed to absorb it. Seemed to pull the colour out of the world, suck it up and devour it.

'Johnny?' Jenny's voice.

The grey car swerved, took a right and disappeared.

'John! My hand.'

I turned to my sister. I'd been clutching her fingers, my knuckles white.

5

Samuels parked at the back of the station and led us through the cops' entrance. Thoughts of the grey car faded and all but disappeared with one step through the door. Just someone lost on a back road, nothing strange, the heat playing tricks. Get your head on straight, John, this is about Mora.

A blast of frigid AC hit me, hardened my skin, turned my outsides into a shell. Too hot to too cold, one hell to the other. Samuels took us through a mess of desks used by the deputies and junior officers. One wall was glass and looked out onto a corridor spotted with doors. Some marked IR 1, IR 2, some unmarked. Interrogation rooms. Observation rooms. Cuffs. Locks. Would there be a spy mirror like in the movies? Once they get you in, you don't get out.

Samuels walked us into reception. Brown carpets dotted with orange triangles made my stomach churn. The receptionist, Mrs Drake, watched us. Everyone knew Mrs Drake.

The witch woman, one in every town. Old, thin, with a loose grey bun on top of her head, arcs of escaped hair framing her face like claws. A mole on her jawline sprouted white whiskers. Her eyebrows arched.

She touched a crucifix around her neck. The deputies at the Roost had radioed all about what they found the Royal kids doing. Freaks. Was she looking for signs? Horns erupting out our foreheads? Forked tongues? Would everyone in Larson look at me and Jenny like that from now on?

The churn in my gut turned to a tide, swelling and burning up my throat. I imagined it fizzing through my flesh, turning me to mush on the inside. What was Samuels going to say? Would he take Jenny away into one of those rooms? She'd be scared. My sister would be scared and I wouldn't be able to help her.

'Sit,' Samuels grunted, pointed to a row of chairs by the front wall. I hadn't noticed them, nor who was sat on the far end, head down, under the leaves of an overgrown pot palm.

'Rudy!' Jenny dashed over.

He looked up as Jenny sat next to him. 'What took you guys so long?'

I nodded at Samuels who leant against the reception desk.

'He drive as slow as he runs?' Rudy asked.

'You betcha,' I said, took a chair beside my sister. 'Where's Gloria?'

Rudy slouched so far in the chair he was almost lying down. 'She's in there.'

He pointed to a glass-walled office. Through the blinds, I could just make out Gloria and, beside her, filling the room, her father. Her knees bounced, her head bowed and staring, look of shame on her face like she'd disappointed her father, rather than angered him. Mr Wakefield was nice, a lawyer who worked all the time but he took Gloria on trips, bought her pretty dresses, played Frisbee and tennis in their back garden, knew how to laugh. Not like her mother. Gloria might as well not have a mother for all the attention she paid her. She's more like a distant aunt, Gloria said once.

'What's going on? Have they spoken to you yet?' Jenny asked. I kept my eyes on Gloria, hoping she'd look this way. See us. Know she wasn't alone.

'Nah,' Rudy said. 'Been waiting for Poppin' Fresh over there to get back.'

Samuels glanced over like he heard us, said something to the receptionist, still clutching her necklace, but didn't take his eyes off us.

'What are they talking about?' Jenny whispered.

'He's telling the Drake to get your mom down here.'

'What about you?' I asked.

Rudy gave a tight smile. 'My old man is on his way. The Drake said he sounded worried on the phone and would rush right down but you know that's crap. Hell, I'm just enjoying my last few moments of living before he gets here.'

I shuddered at the thought of seeing Rudy's dad. The notorious Bung-Eye Buchanan. I crossed my fingers Jenny and me would be gone before he arrived.

I glanced at Gloria but could see only Mr Wakefield. Grim look on him. Arms folded over his chest. Black moustache set in a straight line. White shirt, beige suit-jacket on the chair behind him. Called out of work, even this early on a Saturday. No wonder Gloria looked so upset.

Samuels, still at the reception desk, took out a handkerchief, swept it over his face and the back of his neck. It
came away limp. I could see why people called him a joke.
Bad genes made him too pale for a place like this. Waxy
white skin and blotchy red cheeks, he couldn't run a
hundred yards without wheezing. He was mashed potatoes.
He was rice pudding. All starch and sugar stuffed into a
straining blue uniform.

'Stay put,' the sheriff said as he strolled past, small black
eyes tagging us, one by one.

As he opened the door to the office, Mr Wakefield surged
upward and his voice, like a warning siren, too loud, shrill
edge to it, filled the room.

'About goddamn time, Len.'

Mr Wakefield's eyes locked on us, narrowed at Rudy. He
paused, just a second, then, as calm as he was angry a
moment before, said, 'I'm sure you have good reason to
call me in here on a Saturday. How can my Gloria help?'

Samuels closed the door and the sounds muffled. Gloria
sat rigid the whole time and me, Jenny and Rudy had no
idea what to say to each other. My attention flitted from
Gloria, her now smiling father, to the Drake, dialling,
tutting, then resetting the telephone.

She tried a few more numbers. Momma was known to
go to Gum's and spend the night there when she was too
sauced to drive. The Drake asked for our home number and
I called it out to her. I gripped my hands together in my
lap, prayed there'd be no answer, prayed Momma wouldn't
be woken by the phone and storm down here, still sodden,
and take it out on Jenny the moment we were alone.

After the third try, the Drake crowed, 'Where's your
mother? She int home or drinkin'.'

She was home, I knew, just sleeping it off. Wake the dead more likely than waking Momma on a Saturday morning.

'Why don't you try the church?' Jenny said. 'Don't the Gardening Society meet on a Saturday morning?'

I flinched at the cruelty in Jenny's voice. Momma didn't set foot in church, and the Gardening Society? Mrs Ponderosa and Momma hated each other, old classmates, beauty queen rivals. A stolen boyfriend here and there and the whole town knew it. Those women say Patty Royal is about as likely to rise early on a Saturday to talk God and rose bushes as a snake growing legs.

The Drake stared for a moment then picked up the receiver and dialled.

Jenny smirked. Rudy nudged her. They sniggered.

'Stop it,' I said and Jenny looked stung. I almost told Mrs Drake to ignore her, Momma would be sleeping is all and wouldn't hear the ringing, but the call connected before I could.

'Yes, hello, pastor,' she said, and turned away, cradled the phone, spoke quietly so we couldn't hear.

A few minutes later, the Drake put the phone down and the reception went quiet. No more dialling. No more clipped, disdainful remarks. Just muffled voices from the office. Samuels and Wakefield. Not a peep from Gloria.

I rested my head on the wall. Watched the clock. Jenny and Rudy chatted about something, school maybe or plans for after. Getting out of Larson, how, when, where to? Pretty much all Rudy and Jenny talked about when they were together. I'd heard it all before. LA. Movie star. A million bucks and a beach house. Won't it be great, Johnny, you can all come on vacation and we'll go swimming in the ocean. Fat chance, bucko, I thought, I've got all the swimming I need here in Big Lake and Barks reservoir, who wants the stinking, salty ocean when you've got good, rich Mississippi run-off? Good enough for my fields, good enough for me. Can't grow corn in salt, after all.

The office door opened. The muffle cleared.

'Thanks for coming down,' Samuels said, one hand on the door, one held out to Gloria's father.

Mr Wakefield shook it. 'Anytime, Len, anytime. Glad to hear nothing more will come of this. Gloria is a good girl, despite her choice of friends.'

Gloria scowled at her father but he didn't notice. I smiled at her tiny defiance, that's our Gloria. Then my smile faded. What had she told them? Was she in trouble? Was it our turn now?

Mr Wakefield's eyes squinted again, moustache curled on one side. 'Up for re-election this year, right, Len?'

He spoke slowly, as if each word was heavy and full like a water balloon Samuels had to catch.

'I am.'

Mr Wakefield nodded, released the sheriff's hand and took his jacket from the back of the chair. The three of them stepped out of the office. Gloria kept her head down, her gaze away from us, only occasionally looking up to her father. My teeth clenched. I felt Jenny shift through the chair.

'Good luck with it, Len, you know you've got my vote,' Mr Wakefield said. 'Let's hope that poor girl and this whole sorry affair is put to bed as soon as possible. We can't have anything derailing your campaign. An unsolved murder is a bitter pill for voters to swallow.'

'I wouldn't worry about that, Mr Wakefield,' Samuels said, smiling tightly. 'This one's a nasty case for sure, but cut and dry all the same. It'll be easy to wrap up.' Samuels clapped Mr Wakefield on the shoulder.

Mr Wakefield folded his jacket over his arm, kept that smile and that squint. 'That's good, Len. Real good.'

I looked at Jenny. Something sparked in me. Did they know who did it? Who killed Mora? Easy to wrap up. Maybe they already had suspects. Maybe they already had a guy in custody, behind one of those closed doors, and we were just witnesses. They just needed us to fill in some blanks so they could nail the bastard against the wall.

I leaned in to Jenny, these new thoughts burning through me. 'Everything is going to be okay.'

She tried to smile but I knew she didn't believe me.

Mr Wakefield put his hand on his daughter's back. 'Time to go, honey.'

Gloria finally looked at us, opened her mouth to speak, but her father made a soft *zzt* sound and guided her toward the door.

Before they got halfway, the door opened and Pastor Jacobs strode in, straight to reception.

'Morning, Mrs Drake. How is your Walt doing? I hear he's finally got that '39 Lincoln up and running?' The pastor's thick voice, heavy and rich enough for a church, filled the reception area.

'Up, running, and bleeding us dry,' she said.

The pastor laughed, said something I didn't catch but it must have been sweet as the Drake's cheeks lit up red.

'You called about John and Jenny Royal,' he said.

He saw us a second later, said his thanks to the Drake and walked over. He passed by Mr Wakefield, the man stuck in his spot since the pastor walked in. Their eyes met. Held. Then broke apart.

'Well,' Mr Wakefield said, then turned back to Samuels, ignored the pastor. 'If there's nothing else, Len. We'll be going.'

Samuels shook his head. 'I'll be in touch if there's any follow-up.'

Mr Wakefield left, Gloria trailed behind. No more parents, just the pastor. A swell of relief rose up in me. If Momma had burst through that door, we'd be ear-clipped and screamed at. We'd feel it worse when we got back to the farm. My kids, Momma would say, don't end up in the sheriff's station. My *fuhking* kids don't go playing with dead bodies, I raised them right, I raised them good. And on and on and on. Jenny would get the worst. She always did.

But it was Pastor Jacobs, here, now, for us.

He knelt in front of Jenny, between Rudy and me, all concern in his eyes. 'You two okay?'

We nodded.

'How about you, Rudy?'

'Yes, sir,' Rudy replied. 'They called my old man.'

Jacobs made a face. 'They got through, huh?'

'He'll be here soon, I reckon.'

Jacobs patted Rudy and me on the knee. 'You hang tight here a minute, let me find out what's going on.'

He strode to Samuels. Low voices but sharp. I caught words like *parental supervision,* and *questioning minors,* a barked *unacceptable.*

A film of sweat covered the pastor's forehead, a huge slab of light tan skin made worse by dark hair cut too short. It was swelter outside and the poor man had to wear his black shirt buttoned up to the throat. He had a square jaw and stubble but somehow always looked neat and well-presented. He'd only been our pastor for two years, shipped over from somewhere out east, and right away shook things up. The young radical, some of the old ladies from the Gardening Society called him. Mrs Ponderosa said he was a dish and if she was ten years younger. Ladies like to think kids aren't listening but we are. They file into the church hall after we clear out from Bible Study. They gossip. We linger. We hear it all. Mostly they say Pastor Jacobs is nice. Friendly. He even gave a good sermon on one of those few Sundays Momma got us up and dropped us off at service. You go to your church, John Royal, and I'll go to mine. Then she'd gun the truck toward the interstate.

Jacobs broke away from Samuels and came back to us, stood right in front of Jenny again. 'He just wants to ask a few questions. You feel up to that? I'll be right there with you.'

Jenny looked at me. Rudy looked at me.

'Yes, sir,' I said, all my nerves and worry gone.

'Good.' Seriousness cracked, relief shone through. 'Jenny, would you like to go first?'

She nodded and Jenny, the pastor and Samuels went into the office. Door closed. And me and Rudy were alone. He hopped into Jenny's empty chair.

'This is messed up, isn't it?' he said.

'Sure is.'

Rudy shuffled in his seat. 'Spill, Johnny. Why'd you go back to the Roost?'

'Doesn't matter. It's stupid.'

'Try me.'

I sighed through my nose. A little lie, that's all it would be. I couldn't really explain what Jenny was thinking last night because I didn't know and Jenny would hate me to be telling tales about her, even to Rudy.

'Momma was drunk,' I said and he nodded. 'We didn't much want to be at home, figured we'd sleep down at the Fort like normal. But it was weird there, you know, with the body. I was afraid animals would get to her before the cops so we stuck around. I don't know, we just fell asleep.'

Rudy nodded along with me as I spoke. 'Makes sense. I thought about doing exactly the same. Perry, man, he was being a Grade-A asshole last night, kept flicking his cig ends at me, still burning too, the fucker. Crushed a beer can on my head an' all. I could've gone for a night under the stars. Should've. Felt hinky though. You're braver than me, Johnny.'

Then he started talking about something else. Riding in the cop car or what would happen when Bung-Eye got here. I wasn't listening. I had all my attention on Jenny. Through the window, sitting where Gloria had sat. Pastor Jacobs had his hand on the back of her chair, angled himself toward her, head going from her to Samuels and back.

'Johnny, earth calling Johnny.' Rudy waved his hand in front of my face.

'What?'

'I was saying I hope they question my dad.'

'Why?'

He laughed but only half because nothing to do with Bung-Eye was wholly funny. 'Because if anyone knows anything about some dead girl, it's him. Shit, that bastard probably did it and dumped her there himself.'

'That's dangerous talk for a place like this,' I said, lowered my voice. 'Your dad would whip you bloody if he heard it.'

Rudy threw up a hand, slumped back in the chair. 'Screw him. Like he'll even show up. I'm going to be here all day.'

The office door opened and Jenny stepped out. No tears. No red eyes. No fear tensing up her body. She was okay.

'John? You're up, buddy,' the pastor called and I went. I'd tell the truth, at least most of it, and what's there to fear in that?

Jenny took my seat next to Rudy. Her feet dangled and she kicked them back and forth like she did in the river, lazing on the bank, face turned to the sun. All calm now.

Inside the office, I took the chair across the desk from Samuels. The pastor rested his hand on the back of it like he had with Jenny. Like he would his own child, if he had them.

'Am I in trouble?' I said because nobody else was speaking.

Samuels' too-small eyes darted between me and the pastor, landed on me. 'Should you be?'

'Come on, Len,' the pastor said, looked at the sheriff like he was looking at a tiresome child. I liked him more and more.

Samuels picked up a pen. 'All right, let's start with an easy one. Why were you on Hayton Briggs' land?'

'Mr Briggs' name is Hayton?'

Samuels straightened, cocked his head to the side. 'That funny to you, boy?'

I shrank. 'No, sir.'

'No, sir, it ain't. Now answer the question.'

'We were just you know, hanging out. The Roost – I mean Mr Briggs' valley – is just where we go sometimes. It's not farmland, so Mr Briggs doesn't mind. I don't think he minds.'

'Uh-huh,' scribble on the notepad. 'What were you doing down there yesterday?' Same tone. Round, piggy eyes blazing.

'I . . . we were just going for a swim, some fishing too. It was hot, you know.'

'And which one of you found the body?'

'Gloria. It . . . she . . . was tangled up in the sycamore roots.'

'And whose bright idea was it to move her?'

I opened my mouth, gaped. Couldn't remember. 'All of us. We all decided it would be . . . nicer for her.'

Samuels looked up from the paper, to the pastor, then back down. He wrote something else.

Pastor Jacobs put his hand on my shoulder. 'You're doing fine, John. Just tell the truth.'

Samuels shot a look to Pastor Jacobs.

'Tell me something, kid,' Samuels leant on the desk, blue shirt straining against his bulk. 'Why didn't you and your friends tell anyone about it until the next morning? Why didn't you march straight down here and knock on my door and say, sheriff, we've found a body? Huh?'

My eyes darted around, trying to land anywhere but Samuels. 'I don't know.'

'You don't know?' Samuels sat back in his chair, one hand on the desk, tapping the pad with the pen, growing a field of black dots with every strike.

'Most people,' he said, 'would call 911 when they witness a crime. You know what kind of person don't call 911, boy?'

Nerves bunched up and crackled inside me. All sense of calm gone. I knew where this was going. I tried to swallow down a dry lump in my throat but it wouldn't budge.

'Guilty people,' Samuels carried on. 'See, I don't get why you and your friends wouldn't have said something. Makes me think you four have something to hide. Now, I can't see Miss Wakefield or your little sister doing anything to that girl, but you? The Buchanan boy? Well now, that's a whole 'nother ball game.'

'Sheriff, I don't—' Pastor Jacobs started but Samuels held up his hand.

I opened my mouth to say, no, you're wrong, but nothing came out.

'Why's your shirt ripped, son?' the sheriff said.

The question came out of nowhere and stunned me. My t-shirt. Ripped? I looked down and saw a swatch torn out.

'That's blood right there.' Samuels pointed with his pen to a small smear of reddish brown at my side I'd not noticed. 'If I test that, is it going to be the dead girl's blood?'

All words stuck in my throat except one. 'Jenny.'

'John?' Pastor Jacobs put his hand on my shoulder and snapped me out of it.

'It's Jenny's blood. She . . . she fell over and cut her leg. I tore a piece off my shirt to clean it up.'

'Well ain't that convenient,' Samuels was relentless. 'We found you by the body, with blood on you. Can you see what that looks like? Maybe you slept down there to make sure no one else found out what you done? That sound about right to you? You and the Buchanan boy plan it together? Was he going to come back in the morning and watch her today? Were you going to bury her?'

'No!' I leaned forward in my chair. 'This is crazy. I didn't do anything, neither did Rudy. We just found her in the lake. That's it. We didn't do anything. We found her like that. Jenny has a cut on her shin, go check for yourself.'

My heart beat frantic in my chest and my eyes jumped from Samuels to Jacobs and back and forth and to that stupid notepad and those lies he was scribbling and I wanted to lunge at them, rip them up and make him write the truth.

'Len,' Pastor Jacobs said, firm enough for the sheriff to lean back in his chair and raise up his hands in mock surrender.

'We have to explore all kinds of theories, son, you understand.' He paused for a moment, then asked, 'Do you know the dead girl?'

'No,' I said, just as firm as the pastor. 'Never seen her before. Who is she?'

He ignored my question. 'You live in that farm, huh, the old Mitchell place before they upped it and headed east, right?'

I nodded.

'That's about a mile from the valley. Were you "hanging out" down there on Monday evening?'

Monday.

Monday?

My mind emptied of anything useful. The day was blank in my head and Samuels was staring and waiting, his brow scrunched up, blotches of red blooming on his neck and sweating. My crackling nerves stung, wrapped around my bones and tightened. It was only a few days ago. Come on, Johnny boy, get your head together, the sheriff is going to throw you in a cell if you don't.

'It's okay, John,' Pastor Jacobs said, leaned into me. 'I can't remember what I had for breakfast this morning. If the sheriff here asked me, I'd be looking just like you are. I find it helps to start at something you will remember, like, what was your last lesson at school on Monday?'

Samuels sighed, muttered something about wasting time. I thought back, the grey block of time in my head coloured, came into focus. Monday. Mr Alvarez.

'History,' I said.

'Good,' the pastor smiled. 'So after the bell went, what did you do?'

'Uh . . .' then it hit me, a freight train of a memory. All my words came out in one long stream.

'We watched football practice after because Rudy always says he wants to play running back for the Lions when we start high school so he needs to study the plays. He's going to be so famous, he says, people would be all, "Superstar Mark Easton, who?"' I smiled, then caught the red glare from Samuels. Get to the point, that look said, or its bars and biscuits for you tonight.

'After practice, the four of us went to Gloria's house. Mandy . . . that's Gloria's housekeeper, she'd lit the grill and was in a pretty bad mood.'

Samuels raised both eyebrows. 'Why's that?'

I pictured Mandy, in Gloria's back yard, hands on hips next to the flaming grill, plate of charred steak on the patio table. She filled up my flicker reel. As soon as she saw us, she threw up her arms, shouted that she'd had enough. Mandy was always fit to burst, full of hot anger. She was an Ozark mountain woman sprung right out of the stone, impossible to soften and you wouldn't want to.

'Mandy said that Gloria's dad had asked for steaks for dinner for him and some of his work friends and he wanted it on the grill, ready for when they got back at six sharp. She'd done it but he hadn't shown up and it was past seven. Gloria said he was probably caught up with a case. Sometimes, Gloria said, when her dad's law firm gets a big case, he can forget the time.'

Samuels scribbled it all down. 'How long did you stay at the house?'

'A while. Mandy let us have the steaks. Then we watched *Bandstand*.'

'When did you leave?' Samuels sighed out the question, getting impatient, writing it all down as if it would be useful one day.

'Nine. Maybe a bit after.'

'Had Mr Wakefield returned by then?'

I shook my head.

An exchange of looks between pastor and sheriff. A few seconds of silence.

'Is . . . Did I say something wrong?' I asked.

Like a click of the fingers, Samuels changed direction. 'So what were you and your sister doing down at the – what's that you kids call it?' he checked the paper, 'the *Roost*, last night?'

Everything in me clenched, talons around soft marrow.

'Nothing.'

'Nothing?' Samuels said, leant forward. 'You were found sleeping beside a corpse, son. You really sitting in my office, trying to tell me that's nothing? I'm the sheriff here, I'll be the one deciding what's nothing. Now you answer my question. Why in God's name would you do something like that?'

I wanted to tell him he wouldn't understand. He wouldn't get it. I didn't get it. Only Jenny really knew, but I had a lie. I just hoped it matched Jenny's.

'John, are you okay?' the pastor said.

'We were making sure nothing happened to her. Animals, you know.'

'Sorry, son, but that smells like bullshit to me.'

'It's true!' Wasn't it? Was that what Jenny had told him too? Oh God, what if she hadn't? My bones felt like they'd crack under the tension, my muscles split and frayed like old rope.

'Come on, son. You were all but spooning that girl. Did you get some kind of thrill out of it? Did you like being that close to a naked girl?'

'Enough,' the pastor shouted. Samuels stopped. I opened my eyes and he threw the pen onto the desk. 'That's enough, Len. He's just a kid.'

'I need answers to my questions, pastor, and you'll do well not to interfere.'

'Not to questions like that,' the pastor said, as fierce as the sheriff, matching him for volume. 'John didn't have anything to do with this girl's death and you know it. Yes, maybe he and his sister did something a little strange, but that's not what this investigation is about. This isn't a witch-hunt. He told you why they were down there, so did Jenny, and they're both telling the truth. You got your explanation so we're done here.'

I stared at both men. Stunned. I hurt on the inside, bruised and shaken, but Jenny had told the right story and the relief soothed me like ice water on a burn.

'If you say so, pastor,' Samuels said in that careful, heavy tone Mr Wakefield had used.

'I say so.'

'Well I guess you and your sister can go.' Samuels threw the pen down. 'I'll be calling on you, John, if I have any more questions.'

'And I'll be here too for any follow-up interviews, right, sheriff?' the pastor said and stood up, motioned for me to follow.

Samuels didn't see us out. Didn't shake the pastor's hand like he'd done with Gloria's father. Jacobs closed the door behind us but stopped me from joining Rudy and Jenny.

'John. Are you all right? Samuels was out of line.'

First time in a long time anyone had asked how I was. It softened the bruises, returned my sense of calm. 'He's just doing his job I guess. I'm okay.'

'No offence, bud, but I'm not buying it. You're pale as potatoes, as my mother used to say, and I don't think you've begun to understand what you've been through. Seeing a dead body, that can mess with your head. I'd like to talk to you some more about it, if you want to. I know how close you are with your mother and sister, and your friends, but sometimes it helps to speak to someone else. Someone outside your group.'

I glanced over to Jenny, still chatting away with Rudy. I thought back to last night and how she'd acted down at the lake, the way she'd looked at Mora's body. That strange fascination in her eyes. For the first time in my life I didn't understand my sister and that scared me. Maybe talking would help. The pastor knew his stuff and had God on his side. If anyone could help my head sort out this mess, it was them.

'I think I'd like that.'

'How's Tuesday? I'll write you a note to get you out of your last lesson,' he winked.

Study hall. 'Yes, sir, that'll be fine. Thank you, again, pastor. For sitting with Jenny too. She'd have been scared on her own and I hate her being scared.'

'Anytime,' he said, looked at me like he was watching a bird with a broken wing take flight.

I went back to Jenny and she jumped up. 'Can we go?'

'Yeah. Rudy, you coming?'

Rudy shook his head. 'Not until dear old Dad comes to get me so I can have my turn in the little glass room. Won't that be just stellar?'

Rudy slid down the chair, folded his arms and stared at the far wall. Wide eyes. He was trying to keep it together but fear always shows. It's a black shape behind tissue paper. Rudy was all tissue paper when it came to his father.

'See you later?' I asked. Later meant after dinner, down at the Roost, with a couple of Camels and Gloria's portable radio.

'Wouldn't miss it,' Rudy said. Something in his tone made me think he wouldn't come. Made me think I wouldn't either.

'Don't worry,' the pastor said and sat two chairs down from Rudy. 'I'll keep an eye on him until his dad arrives.'

Jenny and me said our goodbyes and left the station. Stepped out of cool central air into thick heat and the smell of Main Street. Exhaust fumes and greasy steam from the Backhoe diner, the occasional floating scent of flowers from Al Westin's grocery store. Noon sun prickled my scalp and the top of my nose and I didn't realise how dry my mouth and skin had become. Shrivelled up in the cold, false air.

Jenny took my hand when we got half a block from the station. Already slick with sweat. 'That was scary.'

Before I could respond, reassure her, I caught sight of a battered Chevy tow truck driving too fast up Main. I knew that truck. A rusted hook swung from a cable off the boom. The hood was faded yellow but the rest of it was blue. On the door was the chipped decal, half missing from a replacement back panel. Buchanan Auto Salvage. Inside, Rudy's father sucked on a can of Budweiser, eyes on anything but the road.

'Shit,' Jenny said, watching the truck, and this time, I didn't snap at her for cursing.

The truck swerved across Main, cut up a station wagon. Its horn echoed down the street. Bung-Eye flipped the driver the bird and chucked the empty can out the window. Then the truck passed us. Bung-Eye's good eye found us. The heat disappeared from the sun and chills went up my back. He pointed out the window, right at us, and formed his hand into a gun. *Bang*, he mouthed and winked his milky, dead eye.

Then he took a left and disappeared into the back of the sheriff's station.

I shook off the chill. Shook off that look in his eyes. That look that said, I know who you are. I know what you've been doing.

'Should we go back?' Jenny said.

'No, we shouldn't,' I said and she didn't argue. I didn't want to be in the same room as that man. Everyone knew Bung-Eye and knew to stay out of his way.

Rudy didn't come to the Roost that evening but we all four met up at the Backhoe first chance we could. Sunday afternoon. The diner windows were thrown wide and the streets lined with people watching the parade, waving flags, blowing whistles, cheering as the Fourth of July floats slid down Main Street. The high school marching band following behind the last float – the Larson Lions, decked out in blue and gold uniforms and shining helmets – tooting 'Oklahoma' and twirling batons. The fireworks were set to go off from the football field at nine but the four of us didn't feel much like banging the drum.

Rudy showed off a shiner and a limp from his father so Gloria bought us two milkshakes to share as apology for telling Mandy about the body. Our momma, when she found out, didn't much care, never even scolded us. I felt for Rudy, always did when he turned up bruised. Momma could make a slap sting to high heaven and her words could crack bones, but Bung-Eye was something else, some horror kicked right out of Hell for bad behaviour. We got through it. We didn't talk about it, not really, and that was for the best.

It didn't matter, not in Rudy's big-picture thinking, because it wouldn't last. The four of us were on a fast track out of Larson, that's what Rudy, Gloria and Jenny kept saying. Few more years and it'd be *sayonara* to all those fists and snipes. Only snag in Rudy's great escape plan was me. I didn't want to leave.

The diner was jammed. The four us squeezed around a two-person table, Jenny and Gloria sharing a chair, Rudy on a stool.

Gloria said something but it was lost in the noise from the band passing.

'I said we should do something!'

'About what?' Rudy shouted back.

We leaned over the table, heads almost touching, the only way to be heard.

'You know . . .' she said, leaned further in, 'about *her.*'

'What can we do?' I asked. It felt wrong to be talking about this. Here.

The person who killed her was probably in this diner, or on the street, or in the parade. I choked back a mouthful of milkshake.

'We could . . .' Gloria's words were lost as a dozen mill workers poured into the diner singing and spinning football rattles.

Behind them, Gloria's mother appeared in a tight red dress. The mill workers whistled, spun their rattles faster. She ignored them. Her eyes found Gloria and she waved, holding a paper flag, her hand laden with rings and bangles.

'I've got to go,' Gloria said, stood up then ducked back down to whisper. 'Come to my house tomorrow after school, I have an idea.'

6

School on Monday buzzed with talk of the body. Whispers filled the halls and corners of the yard at recess. Even the teachers were gossiping between classes. The four of us were attacked with questions soon as we stepped through the doors. What's a body like? Did you touch it? Does it smell bad? Who was she? How'd she die? And on and on. The worst though, was the one they murmured behind our backs, the one that changed the way they looked at us; did they kill her?

Through the day, the rumours swarmed, gained life and solidity, they grew into full-blown accusations and theories that, somehow, Jenny and me had killed the girl, dumped her body and then gone back to admire our handiwork before the cops found her. At the final bell, the doors to school flung wide and we poured out onto the front lawn where parents would be waiting. Some kids ran but slowed down to pass me and Jenny. They stared. I stared back.

'Freaks,' someone shouted and everyone laughed. A collective roar of giggling and jeers. Freaks, losers, weirdos.

'Johnny, let's go,' she said, grabbed my arm.

Then I saw little Timmy Greer, runt of the class, try to make his name. He picked up a rock, wound back his skinny arm and hurled it at Jenny. I grabbed her, turned her away, and the rock struck my back. I cried out. The little shit had power. But the pain disappeared when I saw, across the lawn, away from the doors, Rudy and Gloria staring at us. They'd left by the side door, right where Gloria's locker was.

Another rock hit the back of my leg and with it a chilling cry, 'Killer!'

That stung the worst, the first time it'd been said out loud, given breath and life. Then Jenny screamed as a rock caught her shoulder. They all joined in. Laughing and shouting.

'Freak!'

'Perv!'

'*Murderer!*'

Tears burned my eyes. They threw stone after stone and Rudy and Gloria didn't move, like they didn't believe what was happening. Neither did I.

Jenny dropped to the floor and me on top of her, covering her, protecting her best I could. It was hail. It was storm. Crack after crack. Sticky feel of blood in a dozen places. My head, my hands, my legs. Make it stop. Make it stop. Every time Jenny yelped, heat rose in me. Rage. Anger. The rocks kept coming, handfuls of gravel from the path, every strike cut my breath short.

Then mercy. The voice.

'Stop it! Hey! Cut it out!' Rudy. Charging in. A god in middle school. 'Leave them alone!'

The laughing kept going but the rocks stopped. Caught doing something wrong, the pack scattered, a few parting shots but nothing hit hard. Just another school day done. An act of violence giggled through, it's okay to throw stones when the targets are freaks and weirdos. Ain't that right, Mom and Dad?

Make me a bird, I thought, that I may drag them all sky high and let go. Who would be laughing then?

Rudy helped me up. Gloria helped Jenny. My face stung in a hundred places. Jenny had cuts about her arms and legs but, mercifully, her face remained untouched.

'They're saying all sorts about you both, the bastards,' Rudy said. He tried to sound older, like a pa telling off his boy, but the worry on his face at the blood on mine gave him away.

'I heard,' I said, my ears ringing with *killer, murderer,* my eyes boiling with tears. 'They don't know shit.'

Gloria picked out a piece of grit from Jenny's arm with one hand and held her hand with the other.

'Mandy will clean you both up,' she said.

On the walk to Gloria's house, a mansion by Larson standards, she asked the question I'd been dreading.

'Why did you go back to the body?'

I stared at her, stunned, and then my eyes darted to Rudy. His were lowered. He knew I'd think he told her and he hadn't. Unless he had and they didn't believe me.

Jenny, limping from a deep gash in her knee, answered.

'Because it was a hundred times better than being in that house.'

The harshness in her tone shocked me and our friends. I don't think either Rudy or Gloria knew how bad it was for Jenny until then. In truth, neither did I. Sharp, drunken words were one thing but since when was a cold dead body better than a warm bed? Better company than a real live mother? I swallowed down grit and tried to understand it but I couldn't.

Gloria put her arm around Jenny, Rudy didn't say anything, he didn't have to. He'd spent nights in the Fort on his own when his dad got heated. Better a dirt floor than Bung-Eye's backhand or belt.

Rudy put his arm around my neck, a friendly headlock. Gloria and Jenny walked in front, entwined, their heads resting together.

They never asked about that night again. Plenty of people did, over and over, rumours sprouted like weeds after the first rain, but between us four, there was nothing more to be said.

We waited in Gloria's kitchen. One single room bigger than my whole house. Gleaming white and red tiles, like a picnic blanket draped on the walls. Mandy tutted and shook her head at our injuries. Rudy leant against the cabinet holding but not drinking his glass of lemonade. Ice clinked. Condensation beaded and ran. Gloria fretted in the corner, pacing, talking about mess, impatient to tell us her big idea, only to be hushed over and over by Mandy. Jenny sat with Mandy at the table, getting cleaned up while the woman muttered about who did it and why and if Jenny were her daughter, oh you wouldn't be sniffling over nicks like this if you were my girl, she said. I waited my turn, standing awkwardly in the middle of the tiled floor, like a statue put in the wrong place.

Mandy had all but raised Gloria and the pair had a tense, parent–child relationship the like Gloria never had with her real mother. Mandy was the one telling her to pick up her shoes, clean her teeth, eat her cabbage. Real Mother dressed Gloria in bows and made her twirl. I doubt Gloria's mother knew a thing about her daughter other than what colour dress best matched her eyes. Mandy didn't care about any of that. She was ruddy-faced, skin scorched and bloomed from years over a steamer iron, her thin blonde curls made lank from the heat. Her body was a pillow lined with steel. Tree-limb arms, stump legs and hips spread wide from six babies of her own.

Jenny hissed, cried out.

Mandy dropped a chunk of stone onto the table. Red, ferrous streak in the granite. My sister's blood. My blood.

'Hush your whining, whey girl, just a scratch,' Mandy said. Thick, Ozark accent. Straight down from the mountains Mandy came, like an avalanche.

Jenny sat at the kitchen table, leg on the big woman's lap, while Mandy dabbed and cleaned the cut on Jenny's knee. Deep. About an inch long. Every time Mandy took a cotton wad to it, took off all that red so the edges of the cut were clear, Jenny's blood would well up again, spill down her leg, drip onto the floor.

'You ain't got no sticky in you,' Mandy said, talking more to the blood than my sister. 'Idiot body of yours, needs the sticky to gum all this up and stop the running. Here,' she handed Jenny a folded-up kitchen towel, 'hold this against that hole long as you can while I tend your shoulder.'

The mound of cotton wool, clean and white on one side of the table, shrank and transformed into gore. Wool stained red and wet, slapped every time Mandy threw a used piece on the wood. Despite her grumblings, she was gentle.

Carefully sluicing away the grit, responding to Jenny's wincing and yelps. Every time I heard Jenny's pain it was an electric shock through me, a tiny charge that made me want to leap forward.

'Lemme see that hole,' Mandy said, placed her hand over Jenny's and pried the ruined cloth away from her knee. The old woman smiled. 'Ah, there it is, the sticky done gummed it up. No more running away with you.'

Jenny smiled along with Mandy's words, the music in them, so quick and up and down and lulling. Gloria said she'd sung her lullabies as a baby and my insides turned green. I didn't know any lullabies. Momma wasn't the singing type, unless it was on a table in Gum's or humming Patsy Cline in the bath.

Bandaged up, limping but mostly undamaged, Jenny was on her feet. She took the untouched lemonade from Rudy and drew down half the glass.

Then it was my turn with Mandy and her thick, hard hands.

'You telling who did all this to you chickies?' she said as I pulled my ripped-up shirt off over my head and sat down.

Gloria stopped pacing and locked eyes with Rudy and Jenny. Then me. A minuscule shake of her head. Mandy was a talker, we all knew, and no one liked a snitch.

'We were up at Barks,' Rudy said before I could think of a lie. 'The cliff side, you know Fisher's Point? The Evel Knievel twins here got too close to the edge. Scared the shit out of us.'

'Hush your nasty tongue,' Mandy snapped, 'don't be cussin' in my ears.'

Rudy met my eyes, winked. If there was anything Mandy hated more than a torn sock she had to darn, it was foul language. Piss, shit, fuck, all would shut her up quicker than a drunk can pop a bottle cap.

Dozens of small cuts and bruises covered my back and shoulders, but none as bad as Jenny's knee. It took Mandy most of an hour to clean me up. Wet wool, dab dab, then the sting of Bactine. It pulled tears from my eyes and I couldn't stop it, I tried, but it was tiny spikes all over my body, stabbing, piercing, deep down into my muscles. Be a man, John Royal, I heard Momma's voice in my head, but it hurt, all kinds of hurt. Each spike was a reminder of the stone that made it, the hand that held the stone, the kid that threw it. Classmates. Friends.

'You all done, mister man.' Mandy gathered the soiled wool in one arm and the bowl of red water in the other.

'Shoo shoo shoo,' she said until Gloria moved away from the sink. 'Go on now, go play outside.'

Gloria wasn't allowed boys in her room. The only place me and Rudy could be with her was outside.

The house was a great whiteboard castle with red shutters and columns at the front pulled straight out of a Roman history book. Gloria said her father had the shutters repainted every year. Nothing like a fresh coat of paint to make you forget the troubles of the past year, he said. Sand them down, paint them over, good as new, it's like those rain storms never happened.

The house sat in private gardens, surrounded on three sides by thick trees. Rose bushes ringed the front grass. A gazebo in the back. The back lawn was pristine, as if nobody had ever stood on it. Table and chairs on the patio. Pots of plants that had no business growing in this part of the world dotted all over. Going to Gloria's house was like going on vacation. We'd be brought lemonade. We'd be cooked dinner. Me and Jenny never wanted to leave but Rudy never wanted to stay. He shuffled and fidgeted until we were outside. A bad kid in a good house never quite felt comfortable, he'd say. He always said he was bad. Bad stock, bad blood, bad name. A Buchanan through and through. A name isn't anything, I told him once at the edge of Big Lake, you can change it like you change your shoes. You can be anybody. He liked that but he didn't believe it.

On the far side of the back lawn, the trees crowded, came together like secret agents protecting the president in one impenetrable line. We weren't allowed on the lawn, Gloria's mother was particular and Jerry, her gardener, would take the blame if we rutted the grass. We went slowly, Jenny still limping hard on that right leg, across the flagstones to the edge of the trees and through. Gloria strode ahead, kept telling us to hurry.

The Roost and Fort weren't our only spots. A wall encircled Gloria's property way back into the trees. There was a break in the brick from when a beech dropped a branch two winters past. Too expensive to repair, thank you very much Gloria's father. It was our exit. Doorway to our secret.

One step outside that wall and Rudy was Rudy again. A stopper pulled out of his back and the poison air hissed out.

'Come on, Jenny,' he said softly and helped her over the broken wall.

Rudy settled Jenny on the ground then held out his hand for Gloria, as if asking the lady to dance.

We sat with our backs to the outside of the wall, dried-out leaves beneath us, bright green life above us. No matter the steaming summer day, beneath the canopy our skin prickled and cooled, natural air conditioning.

'So I've been thinking,' Gloria started but Rudy held up his hand and shushed her.

'No serious talk before a smoke. You know the rules.'

Gloria huffed but didn't argue. Rules were rules.

Rudy took a crumpled pack of Camels from his back pocket and a matchbook from his front. He tapped out a joe and lit it up. Only one between us. They were precious, worth far more than money.

'Took these off my old man,' he said, took a drag and passed it to me. 'He won't notice. If he does, he'll blame Perry. Big bro is always swiping off the bastard.'

I breathed in the smoke, let it fill me up and heat me from the inside. Then out, in one long delicious breath. I didn't smoke much and Jenny never touched it. Both of us too scared Momma would smell it and show us Pa's belt. But when I did partake, it was old man Buchanan's Camels, lit with a proper match, not one of those gas lighters. Rudy was particular about that, which meant we were too.

I passed the butt to Gloria who took a short puff, followed by a cough. She never quite got the hang of it. We didn't bother offering it to Jenny, she always said no.

But today, Jenny snatched the joe right out of Gloria's hand. Took a drag. Too long, too deep. Blasts of grey smoke, one, two, cough up your lungs, then she spat. Rudy's eyes bugged. Gloria cough-giggled. And I just stared.

'Momma will smell it on you,' I said.

In response, Jenny took another pull. The orange tip blazed.

'Don't care,' she said, coughed some more.

The buzz was back in her bones. She shifted, tried to get comfortable on the ground. Raised her cut leg, rested it on a flat rock, then decided not and drew her knees to her chest. Rudy plucked the joe from her fingers and showed her how to hold it, how to breathe it in.

If anyone should be showing my sister how to pull on a joe, it was me but I didn't move to take over. I was still wary of Jenny, still confused by her behaviour, felt like for the first time in our whole lives, I didn't know my own sister.

Gloria refused another drag, tapping her foot with impatience.

Rudy noticed and, with a smile, kept the conversation away from her.

'Heard you're seeing the pastor tomorrow,' he said to me.

'Heard right.'

'What are you going to talk about?' he asked, ground the butt out on a rock and tucked the end in his shirt pocket. Rudy didn't litter. He said it made the world ugly.

'The body I guess,' I said.

Rudy laughed. 'Watch he don't quote Bible at you. Did that to me once, some Sunday. He took me outside after, asked me where my old man was. I said he was working but you know that's a lie.'

Nobody quite knew what Rudy's dad did, one job one winter, another through the summer, selling, buying, this and that. Can't quite put your finger on it. Ask around Larson what Bung-Eye Buchanan was up to and they'd walk the other way. One of those Town Truths everybody knew, like the secret of the Three Points.

'Pastor Jacobs took me round the side of the church, away from people, then squatted down beside me like he was readying a shit. He asked me if I knew where my dad was this Sunday. When I said no, Jacobs, he said,' Rudy shuffled, raised up his hands, took on the pastor's mannerisms, 'he said, "Rudy, one day you'll tell me the truth. The more you lie, the longer the devil's roots grow inside you. Proverbs teaches us that *a false witness shall not be unpunished, and he that speaketh lies shall perish.*"'

Rudy laughed, Jenny said the pastor was a creep. I bit my tongue.

'I won't forget that,' Rudy said, 'long as I live. Every time he sees me he asks about my old man, he's got some kind of obsession with him,' another laugh. An almost beautiful sound but for its sour edge, a strawberry picked too early.

'He asks after your dad too,' he said to Gloria and she sighed, arms crossed over her chest.

'Maybe he's got a thing for old Wakefield,' I teased, 'wants to hold hands and kiss him.'

Rudy made smooching sounds and Gloria punched him in the arm, called us both gross.

'Sorry, sorry,' he said, 'must be Mrs Wakefield. That red dress she had on at the parade raised a few eyebrows.'

Jenny laughed; it sounded hot and strained from first-time smoke. 'Not just eyebrows. Gloria's mom walking down Main Street in those dresses of hers raises a whole lot else, especially with Mayor Wills.' She wolf-whistled and grinned wide.

'That's the least of it going round town about dear Mother,' Gloria said with another sigh.

'Your mom's got more lipsticks than a New York tranny, and the jugs to match.' Rudy slapped his knee and filled the forest with laughter. Birds fled their perches and I waited for Gloria to skin the boy alive.

'You're a jerk, Rudy Buchanan, you know that?' she said.

'But you love me still.' He puckered up and planted a fat kiss on her cheek. A red blush spread over them both.

'I hereby declare it, Gloria's got half my heart,' then he jumped up and grabbed Jenny's hand, kissed it. 'Jenny has the other half and Johnny has my whole butt!'

Then he pulled his shorts down, showed off his backside. We all screamed and fell about laughing.

Rudy the charmer. Rudy the handsome prince. Rudy had more hearts carved into trees around Larson than anyone, at least that's what he said. But it was never a brag. He could say, I'm the best-looking guy in three counties, and you'd nod along.

There weren't any girls in Larson carving a heart around my name.

'Enough bullshit, you guys. Can we talk about what we came here to talk about?' Gloria said. 'Rudy, tell them what you told me earlier.'

Rudy went quiet, all the joking gone. 'After you guys left the Backhoe yesterday, I stuck around. After the parade, everyone went to the football field for the fireworks. That's when Samuels and that skinny one, Robin or Roberts, whatever, came in for their two-dozen doughnut snack. That sheriff, man, two bites and poof, no more doughnut, now you see it,' Rudy waved his hands like a party magician, 'now you don't.'

'So what?' I said. 'Samuels is a lard-ass, that isn't a secret.'

'Shut up. Point is the place was empty and they didn't see me at the next booth, just minding my own with my chocolate shake. They were talking hush hush but I could hear them.'

'What did they say?' Jenny asked, rapt.

Rudy leant forward, like we'd be overheard out here. Ears in the trees, eyes in the leaves.

'They were talking about when they found the girl,' his

eyes flicked to me. 'Robin said the doctor who examined the body said she was maybe sixteen or seventeen.'

Four years, if that, older than us. I felt a lump grow in my throat. Gloria nodded along to the story.

'Shit,' I said, 'that it?'

'Messed up, huh?'

'Do they know who she is yet?' Jenny asked.

'If they did, it'd be all round town,' Gloria said.

Jenny shuffled closer to me, awkward with her leg. She scratched at a smear of dried blood on my t-shirt. 'I can't believe they don't know her name.'

'It's awful, just awful,' Gloria said.

'She's just . . . nothing,' I said. 'Without a name they can't do anything. They can't tell her mom or dad, or have a funeral without anything to put on the headstone. But it's just a couple of made-up words, they could give her a new name if nobody claims her.'

'Names are everything, Johnny,' Rudy said with a scowl. 'Those made-up words are all some idiot needs to brand you a no good thief or a pussy. Sure you can sign a piece of paper and change it, but that's just like putting on a pair of pants. You still got an arsehole underneath. Bet some folk in town think all sorts about the Royals, especially now you've been sleeping with dead bodies.'

Rudy, all flashing smiles and eyes, threw a twig at me. I threw one back.

'Shut it, Buchanan.'

Gloria snapped her fingers like old Mr Frome did when we were horsing about in biology class. 'Shut up both of you. Rudy, keep going.'

He stuck out his tongue at her then carried on. 'The sheriff said the doctor reckons she'd only been in the water two or three days but dead for four or five. At the most.'

'How did she get in our lake? Who knows it's even there?' Jenny said.

'She must have been dumped elsewhere and, like . . . dislodged her upstream.' Gloria raised her hands. 'Samuels hasn't got a clue.'

'Get this,' Rudy said. 'Samuels said something about paint. He said they couldn't find a match to the green paint they found on her back. Did you guys notice any paint?'

We shook our heads. We hadn't seen her back. We'd dragged her and laid her out face up. Maybe she'd been lying in spilled paint that mostly got washed away.

'It gets worse,' Gloria said.

Rudy leaned in, pointing and stabbing at the air with a twig for emphasis. 'That lardo's too lazy to even go looking for her. It'd take too much time away from stuffing his face. Samuels said, word for fucking word, "Let's check the missing person notices, if there ain't nothing there, fuck it." Fuck it, he said.'

Disgust transformed Jenny's face. 'He's going to give up? That was a bullet hole, right? Someone killed her, didn't they?'

Gloria punched the ground. 'Exactly.'

'How can nobody care?' Jenny rested her head on the wall, puffed out a sigh.

None of us had an answer to that. It deflated us. Maybe some cop in Mora's town was fretting, wringing his hands and sticking her picture on a pin board while our cops were scratching their balls.

Gloria stood up, brushed off her skirt. 'That's why I asked you here. We are going to solve the murder.'

'What?' I asked. This was the big idea? The plan she couldn't talk about in the Backhoe?

Gloria nodded. 'We have to find out who she is and who hurt her. Someone has to.'

'Stellar!' Rudy jumped up.

Jenny's eyes widened. 'I'm in.'

'If Samuels can't find out who she is, what makes you think four kids can?' I said. I didn't want to go digging, I didn't want to see pictures of Mora, I didn't want more rumours circulating. I didn't want to see what that would do to Jenny.

'Samuels isn't looking,' Gloria said. 'He's just ticking boxes. If he really wanted to find out what happened, he could. Everyone in this town knows everyone's business.'

'She's right.' Rudy stuck his hands on his hips. 'Someone will know something. People don't talk to cops.'

'People don't talk to kids either,' I shot back.

Then Jenny pushed herself up. 'We have to, Johnny. She can't be nothing. She can't be nobody.'

'This is stupid.'

Jenny folded her arms, just like Momma did when she was about to shout. 'It's not stupid. You're stupid. What kind of people are we if we do nothing?'

Bad people. Just like Samuels. Just like whoever did it. I clenched my teeth. Three pairs of eyes on me. Waiting.

'Fine. *Fine.*'

Rudy let out a whoop. 'Let's do this! What's first?'

The question was directed at me.

'Oh right, you want *me* to solve the murder?' I glared at them, at Jenny.

'You're the practical one, Johnny,' Gloria said, nudged my shoulder with a smile.

The others had the ideas, I worked out how to make them happen. It was me who drew up plans, with a stick in the dirt, for constructing the Fort, me who worked out how to dam the river and make Big Lake. Now it was me they looked to again. Identify a dead body, solve a murder, catch a killer. Easy as that. Jesus.

I rubbed the back of my neck, slick with summer sweat. 'In the books the detectives always go back to the beginning.'

'Where's that?' Jenny asked.

'Where all this started,' I said. 'Big Lake, of course. We should follow the river upstream and see if we can find the place she was dumped. Maybe we'll find something the cops missed.'

'When?' Gloria asked, looked at Rudy and Jenny.

I stole a look at my sister. She was almost trembling, her fingers working in the dirt, clawing thin furrows, raking at broken leaves. She didn't seem to notice her nails darkening with mud. After the rock fight, and now Jenny itching in her skin to investigate a murder, I didn't have the heart for searching tonight. But I couldn't say, *my sister is going mad, I need to get her home.*

So I made an excuse. 'It's too late now. We're out of daylight. Tomorrow, after school. I'll meet you outside when I'm done with the pastor. Jenny and me have to get home now.'

Jenny frowned, went to argue but thought better when she saw my expression.

'Momma will be waiting,' Jenny said.

'Tomorrow then?' Gloria nodded.

I sighed out the word, 'Tomorrow.'

*

Jenny and me left Rudy and Gloria as the sky turned gold.
Must have been close to eight when we cut through the
forest onto the back Barton road, the dirt track that ran
behind Wakefield land. Word was the road led all the way
to Paradise Hill, through the scrubland east of Larson.
There were all kinds of hidden roads around here, all kinds
of paths you could take and never be seen. We turned west
on Barton without having to think. You don't go east.
Another one of those Town Truths.

We went slow because of Jenny's leg.

'I don't want to go through town, Johnny,' she said,
halfway along the track.

'Me either. We can loop up to the railway line, cross up
by the Hackett place.'

She held out her hand for me to help her. I took her
weight, just as blood began to seep through the dressing
on her knee. I hurried us, the starlings would soon be
flocking.

This route home would take us an hour longer than
going through town but it was worth it. The Hackett land
had a hill, a rare and precious feature in Barks County. It
was the Island, salvation in a sea of wheat. Our path took
us right up and over.

From the top of the Island the land swept down onto a
flat plain. The view always reminded me of that moment
when you lift and flick a blanket to lay it neatly on the bed.
The moment it curls upward, the perfect, effortless curve,
made by the air and the weight of the cloth.

The top of the hill gave one of the only full views of
Larson for miles. The white, bulbous water tower dominated
the east side of town, the Easton grain elevator rose up in
the north, and spiked in the centre of town, the wooden

church spire. Then Larson spread out in squares, Main Street and Monroe and Cypress, until it gave way to swaying corn and fences, hemming us in. But up here, on the Island, it was as if the world had fought back and drove a fist up through the rock and soil, made this little piece unworkable, unchangeable, left it for the wildflowers and meadow grass to flourish. I stood at the top with my sister and breathed in the higher air, like I was breathing in a taste of another world.

'Johnny,' Jenny grabbed my arm, 'Johnny look, the birds.'

I turned to where she was pointing, down the slope, far off to where the field met the road. There, above power lines and fences, a great flock of starlings pulsed in the sky. Dark specks wheeled across the field, outstanding against the colour of the evening. They dipped down to the top of the wheat then surged upward as one. A rolling boil of wings and thrumming bodies. It was gasoline flicked into water, the swirling pattern of it changed with every blink, every ripple.

'I love them,' I said.

'I do too.'

'Why did you go back to the body?' A sudden burst of nerves grew in my gut. Why did you say that, Johnny? Where did that come from?

You know where.

Jenny turned to me, cheeks reddening, squirming embarrassment in her eyes. 'I . . .'

'I'm sorry. I just . . . I need to know.'

Her jaw clenched. 'I wanted to see . . .' tears rolled down her cheeks, every word was forced, 'I wanted to see what would happen to me if a fight ever . . . if she drank too much . . . I don't know. It was dumb. Forget it.'

She turned away from me and back to the birds.

I hated what she said, it hurt some primal part of me and my instinct was to round on her. How can you say that? How can you think that? She loves you. She loves you more than you realise. You'll see. But I stood still, silent, and a deep sadness washed over me. I took my sister's hand and held it tight.

The flock danced for ten or so minutes then settled on a nearby stand of ash trees, foregoing the pylons and fence poles, instead filling the branches. A great big screw you to human handiwork.

With them settled, and unmoving, the sky was dull again, the land just flat and my sister seemed calm inside, smiling like the girl I knew. We started down the hillside, another mile and we'd be at the edge of Royal land.

7

When we got home the house was quiet. Momma's truck was parked where it should have been instead of skewed in the middle of the yard. The dent from last week knocked out by some friend in town. Moths swarmed around the porch light and, inside, only the family room lamp was on.

I opened the front door to the yeast stink of beer and a gentle, rhythmic snoring from the armchair. Jenny, still angry at Momma, made quickly for the kitchen. She poured a glass of water with a couple of ice cubes from the freezer box, then hobbled upstairs. She didn't care about making noise. Momma wouldn't wake. I got myself a glass of water and, once Jenny was safely upstairs, I went to check on Momma. The TV fizzed on a blank channel and a line of smoke trailed up from the armchair.

Momma lay with her head on her shoulder and half a Marlboro burning to ash in her fingers. An empty six-pack of Old Milwaukee tall-boys on the floor.

'Hi, Momma, I'm home,' I whispered, trod lightly to her,

picked the butt out of her hand. The pillar of ash collapsed onto the floor. An hour later and they'd have been scraping charred Momma off her chair.

When I shut the TV off she stirred. Didn't open her eyes but knew I was there.

'Hi, baby,' she said, slurred and thick with sleep.

'Hi, Momma.' I took her empty hand in mine. 'Let's get you up to bed.'

'Mmhmm.'

She let me pull her to standing. Put her arm around my shoulders and leaned hard on me but I could take it. She was my momma, my bones were built for carrying her. I don't think she opened her eyes the entire way down the hall, up the stairs, into her room.

'You're such a good boy, John Royal,' she said as I sat her down on the edge of her bed. 'You're my best thing.'

I knew Jenny could hear, right above us, and I knew Momma's words would be like those stones hitting her all over again. The selfish part of me didn't care and was still upset at Jenny for acting so strange so I didn't try to hush Momma.

I kissed her on the forehead and guided her head to her pillow. It was too hot for blankets but I draped a sheet over her up to her waist. Momma always said she couldn't sleep without her ass covered, even if she was sleeping in jeans.

As I turned to go, Momma found my hand. Eyes still closed, she shuffled over in bed and pulled me down beside her. Arm over me, her heat on my back, her breath on my neck. Smell of beer and sweat but I didn't hate it. It was Momma smell.

'I love you, John Royal. My best thing,' she murmured right up close to my ear.

Jenny couldn't have heard that.

'I love you too, Momma.'

Then she squeezed me tight and we lay like that. Her breathing soon turned deep and slow, her arm became dead weight over me, pressing me down into the mattress.

A creak from the upstairs floorboards said Jenny rolled over in the bed we shared. I was giving her room, I thought, to stretch out her leg and not be bothered in the night. I fidget. I kick out sometimes. If I caught her knee with my heel I'd never forgive myself. Really, it was for the best I sleep down here.

It was hot as Hell that night and Momma's sauced-up body heat doubled the sweat on me. But I didn't move. I must have slept because I remember waking up. Momma's snores in my ear and the blue dawn light in my eyes. And Jenny. Standing in the bedroom doorway, blazing. The bandage on her leg was red through and a river ran down her shin. Then she was gone and her footsteps, uneven with the limp, trailed off down the stairs. I closed my eyes, took a deep breath of Momma, then, despite myself and all my will, I drifted back to sleep.

When I woke again Momma was gone. Sound of running water rushed up from the kitchen. I sprang out of bed, sticky and hot, and ran upstairs. No Jenny. Her leg needed attention, I needed to help her before her and Momma got into another fight. Where was she?

Downstairs, into the kitchen, and there. With Momma. I froze. Momma had filled up a basin and got some clean bandages. Jenny sat up on the kitchen table, wincing through a smile, while Momma redressed the wound.

'Morning, sleepyhead,' Momma said when she saw me.

She pinned the fresh bandage to Jenny's knee then, to

my shock and Jenny's too, dipped her head and kissed it better.

'You'll have a hell of a scar to show, sweetpea,' she said, not a hint of slurring or hangover.

I couldn't move. Jenny and Momma, getting on, kindness and pet names. It was like I woke up and stumbled right into the *Twilight Zone*. That one with Barry Morse and the player piano that made people act strange when a roll was playing. I almost listened for the music. Don't question it, Johnny, you'll spook them.

'Go on now, both of you,' Momma said, 'get ready for school. I'll drop you both in.'

Jenny and me looked at each other then to Momma. Surprise must have been clear as glass in our faces because Momma clicked her fingers and said, 'Go on, get.'

'Thank you, Momma,' Jenny said and I think she wanted to hug her then but something stopped her. Years of memories maybe, a survival instinct or something like it. Instead she slid off the table and we both got ready for school.

Momma drove us. Dropped us by the front doors.

'Have a good day, babies,' she said, hanging out the car window.

'Yes, ma'am,' we both said, climbing out the truck.

'Be careful of strangers, you hear? After they found the poor girl by the lake, you don't know who might be a killer in this town.' Her eyes fell on Jenny. 'The thought of anything happening to my babies . . .' She shook her head, almost welled up, then waved to us and drove away.

I could count on one thumb the number of times Momma drove us to school. When she was gone, I couldn't speak. This wasn't the other side of the coin, this was a whole new coin on the spin.

'What . . .' Jenny started.

'I don't know,' I said.

'She was . . .'

'I know. What did you say?'

Jenny shrugged. 'She found me in the kitchen trying to change the bandage and, maybe the blood freaked her out, I don't know.'

Whatever this new Momma was, we didn't want to jinx it. We didn't say anything else about it, just went to class, and carried the tender feeling with us.

8

All through school, ignoring the gossip and sharp looks, the question after question, the shouts and stifled giggles at the cuts on my face and arms, two thoughts rolled around in my brain. First, what I'd say to Pastor Jacobs and second, how the hell I was going to solve a murder. Come three o'clock, when I finally got to the church, my head emptied of anything useful. I even thought about asking the pastor how to identify a dead person but quickly shook it away.

I didn't like Pastor Jacobs' office, tacked onto the back of the church like a toenail ripped but hanging on. The tang smell of damp and the uneven floor set my stomach rolling the moment I walked in. Momma told me it was a trailer from Paradise Hill a few miles out of town, that trash land where the junkies and dirty women lived in double-wides. They say the previous owner, one of those fire-and-brimstone congregants, donated his home in his will. The man slipped away in his armchair, Momma said, it was a week before they found him, took them a month of airing and four deep cleans to get the smell out.

'Where was it?' I asked.

The pastor, still standing at the door after letting me in, said, 'Where's what?'

'The armchair.'

I scanned the room, looking for some sign of it, four depressions in the carpet from the corners, a stain maybe. Jacobs lowered himself gently into his chair, a big leather thing a kid could get lost in. He rolled up the sleeves of his black shirt, adjusted his stiff white collar. His eyes darted across the map of cuts on my face but he never asked about that.

'Ah, the rumours,' he said instead, warmth in his words, 'I've heard several so far. A man was murdered for a pack of cigarettes and wasn't found for a month?'

Something in me sunk. Had Momma just told me a beer-soaked tale she'd heard at Gum's?

'Mrs Ponderosa from the Gardening Society said a jealous wife poisoned her husband in this trailer. Left him and ran away with the Clarkesville sheriff who covered up the whole thing. Or maybe the old guy killed himself, I can't remember. Probably he just died of disease or age, if he died at all. Which did you hear?'

I felt stung, foolish, still standing in the doorway. 'Momma said the man died in his armchair.'

'The Paradise Hill church man. That's a good one,' he smiled and it was a real smile and that sting of foolishness in me disappeared. 'Personally, I prefer the one about the man who killed his neighbour over a can of dog food. You hear that one?'

I shook my head.

'I'll tell you sometime.' He gestured to the wooden chair on the other side of his desk. 'Grab a seat, son.'

I did and the strangeness of the trailer faded. It was just a room. Just an office, painted and decorated to the best it could be. Despite the damp smell and the heat my chair was comfortable. The pastor pulled off his white collar and dropped it into his desk drawer.

'Don't tell anyone I did that,' he said and winked at me. 'I'm meant to be on duty and in uniform at all times.'

'Yes, sir,' I said, unsure who I would tell anyway. Momma? God?

He was younger than I thought. I saw that now he was in his own place, relaxed as he could be in that black shirt. The deep lines and shrunk-back hair seemed more from hard living than long living. He studied me, tapping a pen on his desk, like he was working out how best to ask about Mora and us sleeping down at the Roost with her. The longer he was silent, the more my nerves fizzed.

'Johnny.' He paused. 'Can I call you Johnny? Do you prefer John?'

Nobody had ever asked me that. Momma and Jenny and Gloria and Rudy called me Johnny but never asked if I liked it.

'John is fine,' I said and he smiled.

He wasn't the same as the other day in the station. There was none of that victorious lion I'd seen with Samuels, he was calmer, relaxed. That feeling of safety came back and a deep sense of calm settled over me like a blanket on a cold night. I had my farm and my pastor and my God, and that's a mighty army to have at my back.

I sank into my chair. 'So . . .'

'So,' he said, fingers playing on the desk, not catching

my eye like he didn't know where to start, what to say. The clock ticked on the wall and, outside, I could hear two women chatting on the sidewalk.

He felt it too, I could tell, the awkward silence, so he half laughed and blurted out, 'You're not in trouble, okay, John?'

I smiled, wanted to laugh a little at his nerves but I guess it was the first thing he thought of. Grown-ups say stuff like that when you're so deep in shit you can't swim your way out.

'I know,' I said and he went back to tapping his fingers.

My eyes went to the wall behind him, scanned a poster showing off the birds of Barks County, a Dodge car calendar stuck on April, and a map. The whole world laid out flat, every country a new colour, with strange lines and numbers all over it.

He followed my eyes to the posters, the chair creaked as he turned. I thought he'd explain the map. Miss Eaves did that when she saw a student staring, she'd go, 'Good eye, that's the Mississippi delta', and launch into a talk about drainage basins and steamboats. Pastor Jacobs didn't.

I kept staring, averting my eyes every time he tried to catch mine, suddenly thinking this was a mistake, I should be home working on the farm or in study hall with my friends. The calm ebbed away. I hoped he would take the hint and let me go, stick true to his *you're not in trouble* words and forgive me for saying I'd come here. While I waited for him to speak, in my head, I reeled off the names of the birds on the poster. Such wonderful names, they rolled around my brain like snowballs. I knew them all without looking at their labels. Golden Plover. Kestrel. Redstart. Baltimore Oriole. Green-Winged Teal. And that one, the

Lincoln Sparrow, I'd learned from the book Momma gave me. Name them all, Johnny, and a hundred more until this hour is all used up.

'Hang on,' the pastor said and his change in tone made me look at him. 'We're not doing this right, are we?'

Jacobs stood. He wasn't that tall but with the trailer's low ceiling, he was a smiling giant, ballooned into the space.

'It's hot as the devil's shit in here,' he said and whipped his hand to his mouth. 'Don't tell anyone I said that.'

He looked like a schoolboy caught with his hand in the jam, giggling, red-faced.

'Come on,' he said. 'Let's go for a walk.'

He swerved around his desk and past me, flung open the door, but there was no cool relief, only more swelter, more heat, and the buzz of insects attacking a butterfly bush.

'You know, John, the summers here are something else.'

As we walked, he took a white handkerchief from his pocket and wiped his forehead. The sheen returned a second later.

'You shouldn't do that,' I said, then clamped my mouth shut. Don't go telling a grown-up what to do, Momma said, especially a pastor, or he'll put you on a fast track to Satan.

He glanced down at me, dabbed the cloth on his upper lip. 'Do what?'

'Wipe it away,' I said, pointing up to his forehead. 'It won't get a chance to cool you down if you get rid of it.'

I'd told Jenny the same last summer. I'd wanted to tell that joke Samuels a few days ago. Sweat's there for a reason, the body knows what it has to do, we just have to listen to it.

'Is that right?' Jacobs said and I saw that kindness in his

eyes I'd seen in the station. 'I'll bench the handkerchief from now on. Thank you, John.'

I swallowed. Unsure how to respond. But when I looked up at him again he wasn't the looming giant sending me to Hell, he was a man who helped me and my sister by fending off the sheriff. He was a man who listened and the more I talked, the more he seemed to listen.

But I wasn't sure I knew what to say yet. I still hadn't unravelled it all in my head yet, not Mora, not Jenny, not the way it made me feel, because I didn't know how it made me feel except sick. Except scared. But not of a dead body. Of my sister. Could I really tell him that? Could I let him think bad of Jenny?

Royal business stays on Royal land, Momma said. But my mind kept flipping. One moment, I'd have spilled my guts the second he asked, in the next I'd clam up and want to get the hell away from him. Maybe Pastor Jacobs was only talking to me because he was a gossip like the kids at school and wanted answers, not because he truly wanted to help. The heat, the man, the conversation, all combined inside me. Sharp fluttering filled my insides. Felt like birds on my bones.

Out of the back of the churchyard, we crossed into the fields. A path cut through the wheat and led up to Barks reservoir. Older kids went swimming there after church on Sundays. Momma said it was too deep for me and Jenny, we'd drown no question. Now I've told you that, Momma said with a smile, it means that if you go there and you die, I won't be crying over either of you.

'Look, John, check out that beauty,' Jacobs said, squatting down beside me, arm on my shoulder, pointing.

A hawk, a northern harrier, one of my favourites, hovered

above a spot in the middle of the field. Held there, as if on a wire straight from God. The bird stared, tiny movements of its wings kept it level in the breeze.

'You see that white patch on its tail?' Jacobs said and I knew he was about to tell me what it was. I kept quiet, let him tell it.

'That's a northern harrier. He's spotted a mouse.'

So intent, measured, patient, and yet, with one turn of his wings, he could strike, quick as a bullet out of a gun. We watched for a few more seconds, then, as the pastor shifted, muttering about his bad knee, the harrier dove. Into the gold wheat, gone for a second, then up into the air, a twitching tail caught in its talons.

Jacobs clapped. 'Just magnificent.'

The hawk landed at the top of a tree and ripped apart the mouse. I couldn't take my eyes away. In seconds, tear, crunch, gone. That was all it took, a strike, a shot, and the mouse was ruin and wreck just like Mora. One second, one bullet, and she was a body, not a girl.

'That's a hell of a bird,' Jacobs said, standing up and leading me away, back to the path.

'The British just named a jet plane after it,' I said and the pastor looked at me, one eyebrow raised. I clammed up. Momma always said no one likes a smart-ass.

'They did, huh?'

I nodded, waited for him to question me like Momma would have. Where did you hear that? Was it that teacher who told you?

'Well,' Pastor Jacobs said, 'that doesn't surprise me in the least. It's a beauty.'

And he smiled at me and accepted what I said and that was new for me and it felt good. Really good. I kept my eyes on the harrier until we passed through a stand of trees and into the next field. Jacobs kept quiet for a while as we walked, until the hawk was far out of sight.

'As much as I'd love to,' he said. 'We aren't here to talk about birds, are we?'

Cold flooded up my bones. He picked a length of wheat and twirled it in his fingers like those baton girls at school.

'Do you want to talk about it?' he asked.

'Not really.'

'That's all right. We can talk about something else for now. But eventually, we'll tackle the big stuff.'

The Mora stuff. The Jenny stuff. Black worms squirmed in my gut. It felt strange to be out there with just him, despite wanting to, despite agreeing to it. I felt exposed, like walking bare-ass through nettles and poison oak. The rest of Larson was in school. Rudy, Gloria and Jenny were in study hall without me, talking about the Civil War and President Lincoln and some amendment. We had a test on Friday and I didn't know my dates and I was here instead of there.

I squeezed my eyes shut, balled up my fists at my sides, kept walking, hoping Jacobs wouldn't notice. Jenny needed me. She always forgot how to spell Gettysburg. Why did I have to miss school, miss her? I suddenly hated myself for agreeing to these stupid sessions. Nobody else was out of class, just me. Just the freak John Royal. And when this hour was up I'd have to go back there, to the Roost, to the lake, to that depression in the dirt where the body lay and I lay.

'John?' Pastor Jacobs put his hand on my shoulder. It felt wrong, too heavy, too hard, like an iron bar pressing into my skin. Then he knelt down on his bad knee, stared

right into my eyes, just like in the sheriff's station. Did he
see a soul? Was that what pastors did?

'This was a mistake. I shouldn't have come here. I need
to be at school.'

My breath caught, heart galloped. I needed to get away.

'Calm down, count to ten with me. Come on, nice and
slow, one-one-thousand,' he nodded at me and I took a
deep breath, repeated the number. 'Good. Two-one-
thousand, three-one-thousand . . .'

All the way to ten-one-thousand. The redness cleared.
My fists relaxed. Breathing came easier. Gloria knew how
to spell Gettysburg. She would tell Jenny. She would make
sure she remembered. I was in a field, the sweet smell of
the wheat, on a well-trodden path turned to dust by
hundreds of running feet. A picture of Jenny running
through the dark corn flashed behind my eyes, then finding
her pale and staring down by Big Lake.

'Do you get upset like that often?' Jacobs said.

'No,' I said. 'Just when . . .' *when I'm scared of my sister for
wanting to sleep next to a dead body*, 'when I need to help
Jenny and I can't. We have a test.'

'Next time you feel panicked, before you do anything
else, count to ten, just like I showed you. Will you do that
for me?'

'Yes, sir. I will.'

The calm edged back, slowly, as if afraid to show its face
all at once. I couldn't help Jenny now, out here, while she
was back there. Something ached inside me at the realisation. Sometimes I wouldn't be there. Sometimes she would
be alone. Like she was alone at Big Lake before I found
her. What had she done before I got there? I shivered in
the heat.

'You can call me Frank, you know,' he said. 'I've never felt much like a "sir".'

I nodded and tested the word. 'Frank.' It felt strange on my tongue. I'd never heard anyone else, young or old, call him that. I smiled. 'Yes, Frank.'

We carried on toward Barks but he didn't say anything else. Maybe my panic had scared him, made him think I wasn't worth helping, and now he wanted to use the hour up as quick as he could so he could be rid of me. John's fine, Mrs Royal, I don't need to see him ever again.

As we walked, I prayed not. I wanted to feel what I'd felt in the station, like I had a guardian, something like a father who wouldn't fly away. Frank – the name sounded odd, even in my head – wanted to talk about Mora but he was dancing about the subject. I'll talk about it, I decided, if that's what it takes. I'll talk, but only to you. I stared up at him, waiting for the questions, studying every bit of him.

He wasn't an old guy, not really, though everyone is old when you're thirteen. Much older than Momma, but she'd forced us out too young she said. His hair was still rich brown, he didn't have all that many lines around his face, not like old man Briggs – *Hayton!* – or Mrs Lyle from the post office. Momma said Pastor Jacobs had a jaw that could lever open a paint can. That's how you can tell a man is from good stock, John Royal, Momma said, I should have had you by that pastor so you'd have a jaw that could take a hit. I had a weak chin, Momma said, it'd crack like a peanut shell under a good right hook.

We reached the southern edge of the reservoir. The beach was bigger than it should have been for this early in July. The summer was too hot, too long, drying us all up to husks and draining the reservoir too quickly. A few kids playing hooky splashed about, laid out on towels, a blue cool box full of Cokes between them. I swallowed down dust and ached for one of those Cokes. Hiss and pop of the cap and wonder in a mouthful, fizzing down my throat.

'Think they'll share?' Frank nudged me, sweat shining on his forehead. He didn't take out his handkerchief, didn't wipe it away, not even with his sleeve.

He squinted against the sun to make out the truant faces. Then he shouted, 'Mark Easton, is that you? And Tracy Meadows? You kids have a free period or should I be calling parents?'

The four of them, all juniors a few years up from me, spun around. The two on the beach scrambled up, dusted off the sand, Mark and Tracy. The two in the water ducked down so just their heads showed. One of those in the water was Darney Wills. He wrecked his father's truck in the post office when he was fifteen but he was on the football team and his father was mayor of Larson, so nobody much cared. Accident. Just kids larking about. No one got killed, after all.

I stepped behind the pastor as we walked down onto the beach. Wanted to hide from them. The two on the beach whispered, laughed, pointed.

'Hey there, pastor,' Mark Easton, the boy on the beach, called out. Even Mark Easton didn't call him Frank. A tiny bud of pride blossomed in my chest.

Frank got close, me trailing behind. I wanted to speak up, say let's get the hell out of here, but we were too close now. Contact made. Questions asked.

The girl, Tracy, looked right at me, not even a glance at the pastor. I was a sideshow. Rumours grew up fast and strong in Larson, then went rampaging through town in hobnail boots, leaving marks, making holes, twisting and expanding every time a new idiot jumped on its back. The girl nudged Mark. I wanted to bury myself in the sand, let me get eaten by those hawks, let me be ripped up and devoured. All better than those looks and whispers.

Mark joined Tracy in staring, smiling, a look out to that beast Darney Wills and whatever poor girl he'd dragged into the water.

'You should all be in class,' Frank said, 'and you sure don't look sick.'

'Aw come on,' Mark, said, 'we've only got a week of school left, finals are done.'

'I tell you what, you give me one of those Cokes and I'll forget I saw you.'

'Deal,' Mark said, reached down into the cool box. So slow, his eyes always on me. Stop it, stop looking at me. I wanted to be home. I wanted the farm, the isolation of the fields, the silence of the corn.

Pastor Jacobs accepted the bottle, twisted the cap and handed it straight to me. I took it but didn't drink it, not in front of them. In the water, Darney stood, started wading to shore. The girl still cowered beneath the surface.

'Coach Ray got you back in practice for the summer?' Jacobs asked Mark.

'Yes, sir.'

'You boys best keep that defence tight next season. God loves football but he loves a state champ more.'

Darney whooped on his way from the water. 'We'll destroy Trenton next year, pastor.'

Mark smiled, held Tracy's hand. Mark was a modest hero to the town, never brash like Darney or wild like Perry Buchanan. He was all things to all people. The Light of

Larson they called him. Football star. Baseball star. Star grades. Star smile. Star fucking attitude. My teeth ground together the longer I was near him. Larson treated Mark like a god, as if touching him or getting his attention would somehow bless their narrow lives. He was like a son to me, they'd crow, and everyone would listen slack-jawed and gawking.

Mark Easton, the boy with a hundred fathers. John Royal, the boy with none.

Until now. I looked at the pastor.

They kept talking, Mark and Pastor Jacobs. Mark showed off his throwing arm and his form. The pastor lapped it up and I felt my insides shrivel.

'You boys work hard this summer,' Frank said.

'Yes, sir,' Mark said. 'We'll sure do our best to get to playoffs next season. Maybe you can have a word with the man upstairs for us.'

Jacobs nodded, winked, told the four of them that he didn't want to catch them there again during school hours. I strode ahead, every step away was one less clenched muscle, one less tight heartbeat. I looked back once. The four of them were on the beach, talking, looking, smaller and smaller until we turned and entered the fields again.

My mood lightened the further away we got. The day's heat cooled and clouds grew over the sky. A few spots of rain hit my forehead, puffed up dust on the path. My teeth clenched. Rain. Nothing worse for corn than too much rain. I checked the sky. No black storm clouds bleeding their load, no taint of ozone in the air. Just a shower.

And with that, the rain stopped, beat back by the sun. Frank wiped his forehead with his handkerchief and I with my sleeve.

I gave the Coke back to Frank, untouched, and, after frowning at it, he couldn't resist long. He gulped down a quarter of the bottle and handed it back to me. I took a sip. Wonder. Fizz. Cold on my tongue. Soon the bottle was empty and Jacobs let me keep it to return to the store for the nickel. I held onto that bottle like it was a gold bar.

'You got nervous around those kids,' Frank said halfway through another field.

I didn't say anything.

'People like to talk in this town, don't they?' he said.

'There's nothing else to do.'

He let out a small laugh. 'You're not wrong there. But hey, those guys are gone now. Just you and me. The talk will die down eventually. I've heard some of it myself. Like the kind of questions Samuels was asking you.' He paused, raised an eyebrow to see if I knew what he meant and the gossip echoed in my head, *I heard John Royal killed that girl.*

I flinched and tried to smile.

'Don't you worry,' he said. 'Everyone knows you didn't do anything.'

I'd have to prove it. Rumours were as good as a signed confession in this town. I clutched the bottle. A mix of feelings inside me, like when you throw too many colours together and get muddy brown. I was full of different measures of relief and embarrassment and sadness and guilt for thinking bad of myself and Jenny for what we did and something close to admiration for this pastor, even a dash of enjoyment at being here and talking to someone who talked back to me like a grown-up and painful anger that anyone thought I could have killed Mora. All those colours churned up in my stomach and made me feel sick.

'You know,' he said after another long silence. 'I saw a dead body once, when I was about your age. My father.'

He waited for my reaction but I didn't know what it should be. I barely remembered my real pa. I wished I'd seen him dead, at least then I'd know for sure where he was.

'He died of liver cancer when I was twelve,' the pastor kept going. 'Back in Virginia, where I'm from.'

I turned to him then. I knew where Virginia was. Miss Eaves quizzed us on all the states. I didn't do all that well, though Jenny and Gloria aced it. Jenny would have been fifty for fifty but she mixed up the Dakotas. The pastor didn't have the voice of Virginia. Virginia was tobacco and moonshine and you could hear both in their words. Frank spoke carefully, each syllable said as it was written down, didn't cut off any ends or soften his Ts. I wondered if he was lying but as soon as I thought it, guilt shot through me. Frank was a man of God and the Bible and people like that don't need to lie. I wasn't sure, at thirteen, if I truly believed in Heaven or Hell but I believed in Pastor Jacobs. Believed his goodness and accepted his help, his attention. Bathed in it, soaked it in.

'John, are you listening?'

I nodded and he resumed. The body looked like his father but it wasn't truly him. His soul was with God. Death is just a journey. He looked so peaceful at the end. My head filled up with pictures of Mora, forever sleeping by Big Lake. I saw the way Jenny had looked and smiled and calmed, the electricity in her bones dulling for a time, like the lights in a thunderstorm, dimming and flickering out, then flaring wild when Samuels woke us. Seeing the body brought my sister peace, like seeing his father had given the pastor peace. Hadn't it?

'Why were you in the valley?' Frank asked and I only then realised we were almost back at the church.

'It's where our Fort is.'

'Why were you there so late?'

I shrugged. I couldn't say it, not out loud, not to a grown-up, not yet.

'Do you sleep there often?'

'Sometimes.'

'When things are bad at home?'

'No,' I said quickly. To a question like that, a moment of hesitation meant yes. I wouldn't let him think badly about my family. Things weren't roses and cream but that didn't mean he could take guesses and think the worst.

Jenny thought the worst, thought Momma would hurt her one day.

I shuddered, and shook my head.

'Momma sometimes gets a temper. It's just the drink, that's all. It doesn't mean anything. It's always forgotten about the next day.'

I was telling myself, and Jenny, as much as I was telling the pastor.

Jacobs nodded, picked another length of wheat from the field. 'Does she hurt you?'

'She just shouts sometimes is all. She gets mad at Jenny if her dress is too short or if she gives back-talk or sass, but Momma just tells her off.'

She'd never really hurt her, I knew it like I knew my name. I'd agreed with Momma a few times in the past. Jenny's dresses and shorts were sometimes too high on her legs, especially after we'd been swimming. She had Momma's lip that was for sure and didn't have to be drunk to use it. Besides, Momma was being kind, tending wounds and kissing foreheads and driving us to school. Any hurt or darkness was gone for now.

I put aside thoughts of Momma, changed the subject back to Mora, which suddenly felt more comfortable. Besides, Gloria would kill me if I didn't find out all I could.

'Do they know the girl's name yet?'

Jacobs narrowed his eyes at me before answering. 'No. The sheriffs are doing all they can to find out who she is.'

'I don't think she was from Larson. We'd know her face.'

Pastor Jacobs tilted his head to the side like he was considering what I'd just said. 'You're right. Cross your fingers and toes, John, we'll catch whoever did it.'

'Do they have any ideas? Could it have been someone from here?'

'I'm not all that sure. But they're working on it. We have to let the sheriffs do their job and keep out of their way.'

I scuffed my shoes in the dirt, didn't move when he started walking again.

'What's the hold-up?' he asked.

I looked up at him, squinting against the sun. 'They don't really think I did it, do they?'

He dropped down for a third time onto his bad knee. His black pant-leg turned orange with the dust. 'No. They don't. And if anyone, Samuels, Miller, *anyone*, accuses you, they'll have me and the big man,' he pointed to the sky, 'to deal with.'

His eyes were wide and I believed every word. I nodded, thanked him, and helped him to his feet. I walked beside him in silence, my cheeks and insides glowing.

We reached the back of the church and Frank checked his watch. 'Time flies, hey? We're done for today, you're free.'

Too soon. An hour a week wasn't enough to spend with your father.

Whoa there, John. Frank isn't your father. He's a friend, that's all. You'll come back next week and he'll be happy to see you and you'll see him at church on Sunday and at Bible Study and that's it.

At church with a hundred other people.

Stop it. You have Jenny and Momma to take care of.

Yes.

Yes. Time to go back to Jenny.

Frank stepped up to the trailer door, then turned back to me, held out his hand for me to shake. Always smiling.

'See you next week, John, we'll talk some more. Maybe we'll see another harrier, hey?'

Wait. One more minute. 'Can I ask you another question?'

His hand hung from the door handle. 'Fire away.'

'Why did you help me and Jenny at the station? You could have left us until Momma showed up.'

'Nobody could get a hold of your mom. I believe everyone deserves to have someone in their corner. You're a good kid, John, and you can always come to me.'

'Thank you. And thanks for waiting with Rudy too. His dad can get real rough, you know.'

Pastor Jacobs smiled again. 'That's my pleasure.'

He stretched out his arms and inhaled deeply, gazing over the church green, onto the streets and folk strolling toward the school to pick up their children.

'This town,' he said, then looked down at me, wide grin on his face. 'And all its people, they're my flock, John, and it's my job to be a good shepherd to them all. You youngsters, I have a fondness for. You're our future and your spiritual and emotional wellbeing are top of my chore list. I've got to set your souls on the straight, bright path.'

He laughed, shook his head. 'Listen to me, babbling, giving you the hard sell. See you next week.'

He ended our first session with a nod and I turned, started toward school.

As I was walking away, Pastor Jacobs called out, 'Don't forget to count. When you get worried, just count.'

'Yes, sir – Frank. I will.' And then he was inside his trailer and I was on my way, lighter than I'd felt in a long time.

At the front of the church, as I was crossing the lawn to the sidewalk, still strewn about with red, white and blue ticker tape, I stopped. Heard it almost before I saw it, a low rumble. An idling car. On the corner of Munroe and Main sat a pale grey Ford. My stomach turned cold and I knew it was the same car, the one I'd seen driving behind Samuels' patrol car when we found Mora. I saw it clearly now. A Mustang, old one by the look of the paint job. Momma called them pony cars for pony boys. But that grey, so pale it stole the sun, dulled the glorious summer light to nothing. The windows were like mirrors against the light but I thought I saw a shadow of a driver. My insides began to squirm. I felt, deep in my gut, it was watching me. Waiting for me.

The Ford crawled forward. Toward the church, toward me. The sound of its thick, clunking engine filled up the street and my ears and I backed away, until I bumped against the church wall. My Lord, protect me, I thought, Pastor Frank protect me. Some sinister force, some energy, bled from that car and I wanted to run but my legs were iron rods, unbending, unmoving. It didn't seem real. The heat haze followed it, made it shift and I thought I was seeing things. Seeing ghosts. But ghosts weren't real. Just memories people were afraid of, right, John?

The car slid level with me, the shadow inside, I felt its gaze, not its eyes because I couldn't see them. It was a shape. Dark and formless against the sunlight. I wanted to call out but my throat was dry.

The engine roared and the car sped away. Gone, and like that, the ill feeling went with it.

All the air blasted out of me and I wanted to laugh. It was just a stupid car. Probably Darney Wills on his way home from Barks trying to scare me.

I shook off that cold strangeness and let the summer sun heat me back up, let it prickle my skin as I walked. The light feeling returned and I found myself smiling.

Just a stupid car.

Before I went to school, I took the Coke bottle to Westin's grocery and Al Westin gave me a nickel. I bought an apple for Jenny and polished it on my sleeve all the way to school until it was glossy red and gleaming. I met her outside with Rudy and Gloria and she squealed at my gift. Hugged me and we shared it, bite for bite.

'How was your talk with the pastor?' Jenny said, chewing. A bubble of juice burst at the corner of her mouth.

'Boring,' I said. 'He quoted Bible at me the whole time.'

'Told you!' Rudy laughed.

'Can we go now?' Gloria said.

I tried to argue, say we should get home, I had chores, Jenny had chores, but in truth I wanted to spend as much time with the loving, concerned version of my mother as I could. I wanted Jenny to. I wanted her to feel the love I felt every day and realise how wrong she'd been. But the three of them had their minds and hearts set on solving Mora's murder and I was silenced. So I was almost gleeful with relief when we reached the Roost and found one of Samuels' deputies standing guard on the path. A van parked at the edge of Briggs' field said there were more cops around.

'Tomorrow?' Gloria whispered from where we hid in the bushes and we all agreed, then parted ways to head home.

But the deputies stood watch for the rest of the week, all through the weekend, and we couldn't get close. For Rudy, Gloria and Jenny it was a week of frustration, for me, it was joy. I'd worn a smile all those days. Every day was full of hugs and cooked meals, kisses and stupid, wonderful games. Momma taught us Blackjack and Euchre, she put Jenny's hair into long pigtails, and even got us a quart of mint-choc-chip ice cream. We ate it right out of the tub. Three spoons and no leftovers.

But no good thing can last.

On that Friday, the last day of school, Momma went to Gum's and didn't come home until Sunday. When she did, she was a tornado, shouting all sorts about Jenny and her hair and her dresses and how she'd have men after her and how it was all her fault Momma didn't have a man and had lines on her face and nobody wanted her. Jenny gave back as good as she got and the pair of them screamed so loud the glasses in the cupboard shook.

I held Jenny while she cried all Sunday night. She kept saying over and over, I wish she was dead, I wish I was dead. Every word between them both was a knife to me. I balled my tears up and forced them down into that dark pit inside me. I was rot in a tooth, all fine on the outside until one day it's not and the tooth shatters and the black, foul guts of it spill out. You can have moments of joy, John Royal, but you can't have years, you can't have months, or weeks. You get moments, so savour them.

The first no-school Monday, ten days after we found the body, the four of us finally met at Three Points and began our search for Mora's killer.

9

It's the yellow I remember clearest. The tatters of police tape, like army banners left behind after the battle. Torn, stamped into the earth, but glaring up at me. There were a thousand footprints leading to the Roost. None of them mine or Jenny's or Rudy's or Gloria's. They were all from the sheriff, deputies, men in white coveralls and hoods, photographers, journalists, the coroner. Our Roost was invaded. Our private piece of Larson ripped up.

We stood at the edge of the trees at the top of our valley. The sky was sombre and overcast but still sweltering, the feeling of storm-static in the air. Our well-worn, narrow path was now a wide scar of dried mud. The invaders had trodden water from Big Lake and the stream up the slope on boots and trouser legs, left it to bake hard in the sun. They'd brought her up this way, Mora, probably in one of those black bags. I could see it, the boot prints of the men carrying her, the weight of her pressing them deep into the mud. They would have hauled her to the gate a few hundred yards east, toward town, the closest you could park a van or ambulance. The slice of flattened grass showed their path.

'This is messed up,' Rudy said.

Nobody would take the step, break the barrier.

The sun beat hard on our foreheads, noses, backs of our necks. It was still early, just past ten, but the heat didn't care about the time. All four of us lived half our lives outdoors. Our skin was tanned calves' leather that didn't burn any more, just darkened in the summer, lightened in the winter, like the waxing and waning of the moon. But in this summer, this heatwave, this swelter, with every searing lungful of dust-thick air, our bodies suffered. I felt the sun's damage on the back of my neck, the telltale prickle of a burn, but still I couldn't move. I didn't want to see what they'd done to our Roost, our Fort, our lake. I didn't want to see what they'd taken and what they'd left behind.

'Didn't think you boys would be so chicken,' Gloria said. She took the first step. Disappeared into the trees, down the bank.

Then Jenny.

Then Rudy.

Down the slope, into the shade of the valley.

'Johnny.' Jenny's voice, rising up from the river. 'Get down here. Now.'

I stomped down the incline, kept my eyes on my feet, not to stop myself falling or tripping but to not see what the invaders had done. I felt the change before I looked up. The sound of the valley was wrong, like it was wider, bigger, almost an echo chamber, where it had been enclosed and soft. The rumble of a tractor two fields over, tinny chirp of birds, a breeze bringing the smell of a clearing fire – all aliens landed in our seclusion.

'Jesus.' Rudy raked back his hair like he wanted to rip it out. 'Jesus!'

With one look up, every happy memory shredded and blew apart in the wind. Our valley was the threshing floor after harvest, the yard when a fox got in the garbage, strewn with debris and things that didn't belong. Latex gloves and balled-up evidence bags. Styrofoam coffee cups and napkins from the Backhoe diner. More police tape. The ground, leafless, grassless, beaten by the invaders so thoroughly the weeds had fled or been killed. The banks of the narrow stream were indistinct and the floor had become a solid mass of uneven, dry-mud ridges and kicked-up clods.

The four of us trailed deeper into the Roost, to our Fort and Big Lake. Fear filled me up with cold despite the heat. Would the Fort even be there? Would that bastard Samuels have knocked it down, kicked the walls out of spite or a joke? A laugh with his deputies. Stupid kids, what kind of structure is this?

But there it was, intact, mud sprayed up one wall and the door flung wide, but standing. The ground around it and up to the shore of Big Lake was ruined but our dam was there, our Fort was there, and it was as if the trees knew it. They crowded in, hugged the air close, the sounds and smells from the outside world lessened and eventually I stopped noticing them. The cold inside me evaporated and all the tension in the four of us went with it. Smiles. Patting shoulders. Bright eyes.

'Thank God for that,' Gloria said and wrapped her arms around Rudy.

He gave a cheer, Jenny grabbed my hand and squeezed. We were us again and we remembered why we came.

The area around Big Lake where Gloria found the body and where the four of us dragged her was almost unrecognisable. The log we'd laid her next to was rolled over and out of place, the sycamore roots were pulled up, chopped up, and lying in rows on the bank, a tangle of yellow tape discarded beside.

The lake itself was transformed into an expanse of brown water.

'They must have had divers in, kicked up all the mud,' Rudy said, tapping me on the shoulder, flapping his finger toward the water. 'Read about this lake down in Colorado. Hiker found an arm washed up on the shore so they got boats and guys in breather masks. They found, like, five dead people down there.'

'Sounds extreme for a lake like ours,' Jenny said.

'It's deep though, isn't it?' Rudy carried on. 'Maybe there are more under there. Who knows what they found? Maybe they found my flick knife you douchebags threw in.'

'Yeah and maybe they'll see your initials on the handle and come and arrest you.' Gloria stuck out her tongue.

She hated knives and had been the one to snatch it off him. She'd hurled it right into the middle of Big Lake. Jenny clapped and I smiled but it was a shame to lose it. At least, it was a shame for Rudy to lose it. He thought he was James Dean with that knife in his hand. He tried to get it back, went swimming for it every day for the next week but never found it.

I did.

The same day Gloria threw it. Rudy had stormed off and Jenny and Gloria went picking wildflowers to make the Fort more homely. I groped around in the mud until my fingers closed around the handle. I never told anyone, not even Jenny. Jenny wouldn't understand why I'd want a knife. Why I'd kept it hidden behind a brick in the crawlspace wall. Why I'd spent a whole night down there after I found it, cleaned it, dried it so it wouldn't rust. I was marvelling, staring at the shine on the blade, admiring the mechanism, *click*, *flick* and ready for action. It was mine and my own secret and no amount of sulking and sniping from Rudy would make me give that up. I'd tried to scratch his initials out. But he'd carved them deep and I could still see them. RB right there in the black handle.

'Here, look,' Gloria called from the far side of Big Lake.

Jenny skipped over the dammed stream to join her. Rudy, beating a stick in the bushes near the Fort, did the same.

I stared into the muddy water. It must have been days since they dredged the lake but the silt hadn't settled. My chest seized at the thought that it never would. How could it? Now that it had seen what it had seen, been violated by divers and police, rakes and sticks drawn across its soft bed like fingernails down a back. That glass-clear lake of a few weeks ago, one with a carpet of leaves and twigs, was ruined. I picked up a stone, dropped it in the water. A brown ripple and gone. Swallowed up.

'Johnny!' Rudy shouted. Snapped his fingers at me like he would a mutt. 'We ain't getting any younger over here.'

He put on a cowboy voice from that William Holden movie I hated. We'd snuck in the back of the picture house in Clarkesville to see it. Come on, Johnny, Rudy had said, tugging on my shirt, Hell-on-Healey – Bill Healey, the owner of the picture house – won't catch us this time, you'll see, and Rudy was right. Scared me bright white all the shooting in that movie. Rudy called me sissy for days, along with God knows how many variations; royal sissy, queen sissy, Johnny King of the Sissyboys. That voice he put on brought those stings back, like coming face to face with a nettle patch after you'd fallen in once. You feel pain twice, Momma says, once with the cut, then again with the memory.

'What?' I said.

That selfish, black part of me was glad then that I'd taken Rudy's knife.

'Tracks.' He waved me over. 'Leading along the river. Come on.'

Jenny and Gloria looked at me, half-smiling, twitching almost, raring to go. Those cop shows called it a lead. We had one. We had to follow it. The stings faded, made Rudy my friend again and not a bully I wanted to clock in the mouth but never would.

Gloria pointed down a path that hadn't been there before, called me to hurry up.

'Sorry,' I said and leapt over the stream, ran to them. 'It's just, you know, they wrecked our lake. Makes me mad is all.'

'And a woman is dead,' Gloria snapped, like a snake strike. 'I think that's more important than some stupid muddy water. For Christ's sake, John.'

Rudy whistled. 'Mellow out, Gloria. We know why we're here.'

Gloria huffed and barked something about the path and where it might lead. Now I had caught up, Jenny threaded her arm through Gloria's to calm her down. The girls walked ahead, Rudy and me a few steps behind, giving them space. Gloria was all red in my eyes. Red hair. Red cheeks. Red dress. A warning. STOP. DANGER. Those snakebite words of hers throbbed through me. The weight of the poison made me drag my feet.

Rudy put his hand on my back, gave me a pat. His mouth puckered up in one of those sad smiles. You got burned, Johnny boy, he said without saying it.

'Yeah, yeah,' I muttered and Rudy's pucker widened to his movie-star grin.

Gloria looked at me over her shoulder. A little nod, a little smile, and the tension was gone.

The girls walked on, arm in arm, pointing here and there, at a footprint, a discarded glove, a crushed soda can. We emerged from the valley, beneath clouded sky. The path became a rope strung through the four of us, tugging, dragging, and soon we were running. We crossed a strip of fallow land turned to dust in the heat. Then a cornfield, the stalks looming an easy three foot over our heads. The policemen's path spread between the rows, like they'd taken a giant rake to it to till up clues.

'Check it out,' Rudy called from two rows over, 'they dug something up.'

We converged around a hole. An arm's length round and the same deep.

Then I noticed the dog tracks. Dozens of them. Darting off in every direction.

'What do you think was in there?' Jenny said, hushed, but that electricity was still there, sparking behind her eyes.

Rudy reached down and felt around in the dirt. His fingers dug furrows, searching for anything the idiots might have missed.

'What would make them even dig here? In this spot?' Gloria said, glancing side to side like a rabbit on the road.

'The dogs must have smelt something,' I said.

I kept my eyes on the hole, each new claw unearthed just another line of brown. Dust fell through Rudy's fingers as he threw out handfuls. But it was just a hole. A dog could have dug it weeks before we even found Mora. It could have nothing to do with her or the search.

'This is useless,' Gloria said, standing up, brushing her dress. 'We should keep going.'

'There are dog tracks leading further into the field.' I pointed. Gloria nodded. We were partners again.

Rudy threw away a handful of dirt and smacked his palms together. 'Sir yes sir,' he said and jumped up. He jerked his hand in a mock salute and left a smear of brown across his forehead. Nobody told him.

'What was in there?' Jenny said, as if to herself. She squinted at the hole, trying to pick out something, anything, that might give us an answer.

I helped her up as Rudy and Gloria followed the dog tracks.

Jenny grasped my hand. 'There's something in there, Johnny, I can feel it. Something buried.'

A quiet electricity raced through her and into my arm. Her grip tightened. There was compulsion behind her expression, a yearning pull I could feel through her and it scared me.

She looked back at the hole. 'They found something horrible in there. I know it. That's why they won't look for Mora's truth.'

Jenny's eyes were wild, blood-red spiderwebs pulsed at the edges. 'They found something worse.'

The strange horror slammed into me, the feeling that made me almost afraid of my sister. I didn't know this version of her, the version that went back to Big Lake and

slept beside a dead body. This frantic version kneeling over
a hole, seeing evil in the dirt. *You're losing her.*

'Okay,' I said, soft and calm like how I'd talk to Momma
on a bad day. 'It's okay, Jenny. It'll be okay. Rudy said
once that gangsters bury drugs and cash in fields like this.
Maybe that's what happened here, the dogs smelled a
haul of pot and started digging. Nothing to do with her.
Right?'

Jenny frowned, like my words were a puzzle she couldn't
solve.

'Come on, let's go find the truth, together,' I said.

The sparks in her dulled and my sister came back, inch
by inch. She nodded and lessened her grip but didn't let
me go. I didn't want her to. Rudy and Gloria waited for us
to catch up then the four of us set off again together.

We were quiet for a while. Rudy found a stick and swiped
at dried corn leaves hanging low off the stalk. They made
a noise like ripping paper with every hit. That sound, mixed
with the last of the chirping cicadas, set the rhythm for our
steps. The corn stalks towered above us, and the sky was a
thick, heavy grey. It was as if we'd stepped through the
wardrobe but Narnia was dead and dry and covered in ants.
They latched onto our shoes, crawled up our legs and
nipped our shins. Clouds of midges invaded our nostrils
and ears, stuck to our sweat like it was amber on tree bark.
I stopped thinking about the path, the tracks we were
following, I didn't even notice if they were still there.
Nothing else existed in the world, just this cornfield, just
us. Jenny's hand in mine, radiating heat all through me,
but I wouldn't let her go.

Then the light changed. Ahead the air felt clearer and
in a few more steps we came out on a dirt road. Blinking,

emerging from the relative darkness of the field, we stood in a row along the edge of the road.

'No more tracks,' Rudy said, too quiet, too distracted, and for good reason.

Across the road a series of fields, dirt ploughed to deep furrows, stretched for another mile or two, until they met a group of low buildings. The fields swerved to avoid the property, curved around it and resumed straight lines on the other side. Even the land didn't want to touch or see or know what was in there and I couldn't blame it.

We knew those buildings. We knew the dried-up dirt they sat on, the farmland turned salvage yard, ringed with a chain-link fence and a vicious yellow dog only one man could control. Everyone in Larson knew that property and everyone knew to keep their distance.

Buchanan land. Buchanan rules.

'I didn't realise we'd come so far,' Gloria said, glancing at Rudy.

I let go of Jenny's hand and crossed the road. A stone in my chest dropped to my stomach. The tracks reappeared. Big, deep footprints in rich earth kept damp by irrigation channels. Two sets, two deputies, led in one distinct line to those buildings. Rudy saw them too.

'Still want to go searching for a killer?' I said.

'Come on.' Rudy strode toward his home, and didn't even look back to check we were following.

I'd been in Rudy's place only once, the day after last Christmas. His brother, Perry, and Bung-Eye hadn't been home in days. Rudy spent Christmas day on his own in that house without a crumb of food. Same as the year before and the year before that. Me and Jenny had tried to get Momma to invite Rudy over but we were having a family Christmas. Me, Jenny, Momma, and whatever Pigeon Pa she had that month. Just family, Momma said. Bullshit, I'd thought, and tried to tell her Rudy was family but she wouldn't listen. Gloria tried to invite Rudy over too but her parents wouldn't have a good-for-nothing Buchanan in their house. When she pushed harder, she was sent to her room without supper. I snuck over to Rudy's place with a bag of turkey and day-old bread rolls and we had our own Christmas. That was the first time I saw Rudy cry.

I'm getting out of here, Johnny, he'd said, I ain't like them. I never will be. Come with me. I've got money saved up. He took a worn Greyhound bus timetable out of his back pocket. Thirty-six bucks, Johnny, that's all it'll take to get us to LA, I've got it all planned out. We can get out of this shithole together. You and me, Johnny, just you and me.

I'd nodded, said yes, but just to make him feel better. I think he knew that deep down I didn't want to leave Larson but sometimes hanging onto a lie lets you get through the day where the truth would end it all. We ate turkey sandwiches and watched black and white Christmas cartoons on Bung-Eye's TV set. It was another two days before Bung-Eye and Perry came back and when school started a week later, Rudy showed off a black eye as his Christmas present.

The chain-link fence around the Buchanan land was more symbolic than functional. Full of holes big enough to dance through, it served as a test to curious folk. Sure, you can walk right through that missing panel, go for it, take one step across the line, see what happens.

'What now?' Jenny said.

'We have to go in.' Gloria stepped forward but didn't

touch the fence. 'Don't we? Maybe your dad knows some-thing.'

'Maybe he killed her,' Rudy said in a dead tone.

We were all thinking it, of course we were. Nobody jumped to defend Bung-Eye, there was no point. They say he broke a bartender's nose for giving him a quarter instead of a nickel in change. You could hear the crunch from the other side of the bar.

'Is your dad home?' I asked.

'I don't think so. Him and Perry had business in Bowmont last they told me. They'll be gone till tomorrow.'

Gloria hooked her finger on the fence. 'Is it true he's been in prison?'

'In and out like a fucking yoyo. He says they keep a cell open for him in Red River.'

'I heard it was drugs,' Jenny said.

Rudy scoffed. 'And the rest. Guns. Flipping cars. Beating the crap out of people. You name it, he's done time for it.'

'Should we have a look around?' I said.

I didn't like talking about Rudy's father, as if saying his name too loud would summon him right to us.

'The trail led here.' Gloria ducked through the hole in the fence before any of us could grab her.

'We either follow the trail to the end,' she said, standing tall inside Buchanan land. 'Or we give up and are no better than Samuels.'

Jenny glanced at me, held my eyes for a moment, then she was gone, on the other side with Gloria. Rudy and me stayed where we were. We knew what was waiting inside that mess of buildings and junk.

'There's nothing there,' Rudy said but it was weak. 'I would know about it.'

'Would you? Do you know what's in all these barns?' Gloria said and Rudy didn't have an answer. 'A girl is dead and nobody cares. Why are you letting a broken fence and a bunch of rumours stop you?'

I went through the fence and Rudy followed. With dragging steps, he led us between the maze of buildings. The main house, the giant faded red barn beside a rusting grain silo, two single-storey outbuildings, and a grimy trailer up on concrete blocks with a deep, black fire pit in the yard. Stacks of crushed cars stood sentinel every corner, towering six or seven high, then a row of them like the Great Wall of China stretched the length of the property. Piles of scrap metal and exhaust pipes and wheels grew at the base of the stacks but this wasn't a junkyard you could visit to pick up a spare set of rims. This was Buchanan property, down to the last broken washer.

The thing that struck me hardest was a strange, heavy smell in the air. It should have been the harsh tang of oil and rust and burnt tyres, the base notes of a place like this, but it was sweet, sickly, almost herbaceous. It got into my head, my nose, turned my stomach, but lessened the further we went from the stacked cars. It left a dull ache in the back of my head.

'It's so quiet. There's not even any birds,' Jenny said.

Except for our footsteps, the only sound was a soft, machine hum from somewhere deep in the compound. No flies, no buzz of mosquitoes or cicadas, it was as if the insects were too afraid or sensible to cross that fence line. We reached one of the squat outbuildings. A line of bullet holes pocked the wall.

'Target practice,' Rudy said and pointed to broken glass

at the base of the wall. Beer bottles and jugs. Green, brown, clear. Indiscriminate destruction.

'What are we looking for?' Rudy swung his arms around. 'There's nothing here.'

'What's in the barn?' Gloria asked, heading toward the doors.

'It's his workshop,' Rudy said, 'just car parts, tools, useless farm crap my dad doesn't use. Perry said the other day there's a brand new Dodge Challenger in there and they've been working on it for a few days. He said the old man won it in a card game but I call bullshit.'

He tried to keep it light, but he couldn't hide the nerves. Rudy didn't want to go in the barn but that made Gloria practically run for the doors.

She didn't get to them. She didn't even get across the yard between buildings. She froze mid-step at the end of the bullet wall.

'Gloria?' Jenny said and went to her.

Gloria whipped around and grabbed Jenny's arm, yanked her away.

All I could see in Gloria's eyes was white. Bright white. Jenny's expression told the rest. It was the face she wore when Momma was drunk.

Fear filled up my blood and turned it solid in my veins. My heart couldn't pump it. It thudded against my lungs and drove out all my air. Then I heard the voices. The deep, rough sounds of Rudy's brother and father, all drawl and horror like they would spit out demons with their chewing tobacco.

They were coming. Footsteps crunching on dirt, kicking a stone, grinding out a cig butt. They shouldn't even be here, they were in Bowmont, right? Right, Rudy? Jenny was too far from me. Gloria pulled her out of my sight, behind a stack of crates. Rudy gripped my arm and dragged me around the other side of the bullet wall.

I tried to wrestle free, get to Jenny, but Rudy was too strong. I tried to shout but he slapped his hand over my mouth and hissed to shut up.

Jenny. Jenny. Jenny. Like my heartbeat.

'You want to get caught?' he whispered right in my ear. 'Jenny and Gloria will be fine. They'd never hurt a girl.'

He said it so sternly that I had to believe him.

I nodded and he let his hand off my mouth.

'What are they doing here?' I mouthed the words.

Rudy shook his head and held his finger against his lips. We pressed our backs to the wall of the outbuilding. I was sure my heartbeat would vibrate through my spine, into the wood and shake the glass windows. *Buzz-buzz, buzz-buzz,* here I am Bung-Eye.

They weren't talking any more but the footsteps got louder, closer. They rounded the other side of the building, painfully close to those crates and to Jenny and Gloria. My heart thundered afresh. I closed my eyes and Frank popped into my head. If he was here he'd save us, he'd talk to Bung-Eye and calm him down. But he wasn't here. What would he tell me to do? Pray? Dear Jesus, if you've got any good in you, you won't let a thing happen to Jenny, ay-men.

I chanced a look around the corner of the building. Perry and Bung-Eye. Standing a few feet from the crates, not moving, not really talking, just waiting. I couldn't see Jenny or Gloria. For all the rumours and stories centred on Bung-Eye Buchanan, you form a picture in your head of him. Ten-foot tall, bearded, brick-built and full of temper maybe, but not Bung-Eye. Clean-shaven and his hair always combed and oiled to a neat quiff. Shorter than average and made up of bone and sinew rather than fat and muscle. He was a snake, not a dog, and all the deadlier for it. The glass eye, milk-white and unblinking, gave him the name and a dozen versions of the story for how he lost it. Ask him one day and it was a bar brawl, ask him a week later and it was a shaving accident. He was all cracked leather and denim, biker patches and black boots. Perry was a carbon copy of his father, just with two working eyes and a newer jacket.

Rudy yanked me back, whispered that I was stupid.

Even Momma had stories of Bung-Eye Buchanan. He was sweet on her when they were kids, sharing sips of hooch behind the high school bleachers. She was the Cornflower Queen back then, and rode a float down Main Street with a crown of blue flowers. He was the bad boy and still is. A dangerous, beautiful man, she called him.

Rudy's back straightened. The rumble of a truck engine on the far side of the Buchanan property.

''Bout time,' Perry Buchanan shouted as I heard the truck come to a stop.

The door opened, then the sound of boots on the ground. A man said, 'Where is it?'

No reply but I heard more footsteps then the unmistakable sound of the barn doors sliding open and closed.

The silent starter pistol fired. Jenny and Gloria dashed past the end of the building before me and Rudy could even look around the corner. They didn't stop, didn't see us, must have thought we were already at the fence and gone. Shock replaced fear in my blood but I still couldn't move. I watched them run, red and blonde hair streaming behind them, dresses billowing like sails, arms and legs a blur of tan skin. They were around a stack of cars and out of sight and me and Rudy went to follow when we heard the barn door rattle open.

We slammed our backs against the wall, didn't breathe, didn't dare.

'We have a deal?' said Bung-Eye.

They exchanged a few more words. There must have been two men arrive because two engines fired up. The truck first and the other a low rumble I felt deep in my bones. It was too loud to be real, too perfect, like the MGM lion roaring over and over under the hood.

'The Challenger,' Rudy whispered, a hard frown on his face.

I'd thought it was a joke. Another Buchanan bullshit tale. We both risked a look, just to check we weren't hearing things.

The truck backed away from the barn door and there she was. A brand new Dodge Challenger, sky blue with shining chrome trim, a white stripe straight up the hood onto the roof, looked like it had never seen a road. They revved the engine and the rumble ran right through me, made the windows shake.

'That's a beaut,' Rudy breathed. 'If I'd known it was in there, I'd have taken it for a spin, right down Main Street.'

The Challenger turned out of the barn and edged down the track toward the road. Something lit up at the edge of my memory. I'd seen a car like that, somewhere. I squinted against the gleam of the chrome, tried to see it clearer. It couldn't have been in a movie because that model was right off the lot. Was that April on Frank's Dodge calendar hung on his office wall? No, wasn't a car like that, it was *that* car, the white stripe, the chrome trim, but it was different too.

How many could there be in a town like Larson? But the smoky memory refused to clear. Maybe it was just from a photograph in a magazine Al Westin had shown me. That man could talk cars until sun-up.

The man from the truck appeared and handed over a fat paper bag.

'It's all there,' he said.

Perry took it, opened it to peer inside and gave the bag a shake.

'I trust you,' Bung-Eye said, gave him a dead-eye wink. 'And I know where you live if it comes up light.'

The man got back in his truck without another word and followed the Dodge off Buchanan land. Bung-Eye took the bag from his son and felt the weight, like he could tell the value from that alone. He stuffed it against Perry's chest and hocked up a fat gob of spit. It hit the ground with a puff of dust.

'Ain't much for the trouble,' he sniffed.

Perry dug his hand into the bag and pulled out a handful of notes. 'Shit, that car didn't cost us nothing.'

Rudy and I watched without moving. I felt him shaking against me – this close to his dad and brother, spying on them, his fear was a stink on his skin. If they caught him, I couldn't imagine what they'd do.

'You a retard, Per? You get horse-kicked when you were a boy?' Bung-Eye said and clipped the side of his son's head. 'If Samuels could do his job half as well as he can put away a dozen jelly-filled, that car would have cost us everything.'

Perry nodded but didn't seem to be listening. His eyes were on the money, rubbing it between his fingers, trying to count but not getting very far.

Bung-Eye pulled out a pack of Camels and lit one up.

'Damn. That cocksucker didn't have to kill her.' He shook his head and threw the full joe as hard as he could, like anger or grief made the cig taste bad. 'She was a good girl.'

Perry turned solemn. 'Should have wrecked the fucker's car. Sent it to him and Samuels in boxes.'

I looked over my shoulder at Rudy.

'They knew the girl,' I whispered but he was ahead of me. His face was set in familiar anger, another reason to hate his name and the blood pumping in his veins. His family was involved. Somehow. Whoever killed Mora must have given over that car to keep the Buchanan boys quiet. They must've flipped it and sold it within a couple of weeks for a quick buck. Done and dusted, hands clean of any wrongdoing. Can't prove nothing, sheriff, ain't never seen a car like that and I'd remember. That was the Bung-Eye way, deny, deny, deny.

Rudy clenched his fists, his body coiled up. I'd seen it before. He had his dad's temper, he would lash out. He would kick and punch and spit at the nearest tree or building or the ground if he thought he could hurt it. Where Rudy would kick a tree, Bung-Eye would kick Rudy. He wasn't his dad, not through-and-through.

I grabbed both his arms, tried to pin them against his sides, but he pushed me off. I tripped backward and hit the wooden wall. The thud rang out like a bell on a clear night.

A second. A heartbeat.

Bung-Eye shouted, 'Get your gun, Perry.'

Rudy and me sprinted out from behind the building. Both men roared Rudy's name and gave chase. It was thunder and rage, a stampede coming down on us. I gave everything to my legs. Don't stop, don't ever stop, run to the ocean, run to the moon, just don't stop. We were gaining ground, the bulls were tiring, the smoking the drinking the age all catching up.

We were twenty feet clear. Then thirty. Perry pulled ahead of his dad, closed the gap but we could make it. We just had to get to the fence. We'd be safe at the fence.

Forty feet and change. Just had to keep going.

Rudy yelped. His knee buckled and he disappeared beside me.

He hit the ground hard and rolled. Perry was on him in seconds. Then Bung-Eye. They had their prize. They didn't chase me.

'Run, Johnny!'

Rudy tried to pull himself free but Perry had his arm. 'Keep going!'

Bung-Eye's voice roared behind me, chased me like thundering hooves. 'I know you, John Royal! You mind your fucking business. You come on my land again and I'll kill you, boy, you hear me? I'll find you and I'll fucking kill you.'

I ran, oh God, I ran. Jesus forgive me. I had to get to Jenny. I had to know she was safe. I told myself they won't hurt Rudy, not really. They'd kill me if they caught me. He said so. They wouldn't kill their son and brother. That was blood. That was family.

Rudy cried out. I saw it all over my shoulder. Every sickening second. Rudy delivered a fist to Perry's balls so hard the man doubled and dropped and brought his little brother's face down with him. Bung-Eye didn't break stride. He grabbed Rudy's wrist, lifted it, and stamped on his son's forearm.

Rudy's bones snapped. A sound like a gunshot across the fields. Searingly loud. So final and irreversible. Then he screamed. It shook the ground. Shook me. Turned my insides cold and dark.

And I kept running.

Coward. You fucking coward, John Royal.

10

When Rudy's arm snapped, so did our great plan to solve a murder. Our little crime-fighting club fizzled out and Mora's killer was no closer to caught. I felt shame, mostly, that I'd failed Rudy and together we'd failed that poor girl. Then I felt embarrassment that we'd ever thought four kids could make a difference. What a joke, Johnny boy, one day on the job and you see how much of a joke you are. Jenny still talked about Mora all the time. Who she might be, what she might be like, who might have hurt her and why, always why.

We didn't see Rudy for the rest of that summer. I checked the Fort almost every night but he was never there and he didn't come calling to the house like he usually would. He wasn't at Sunday church or Bible Study and he was never down at Barks for swimming. I went over to the Buchanan place once but with Bung-Eye's warning still ringing in my ears, I daren't get too close. They'd repaired the fences and Perry'd put that yellow dog on a longer leash. I couldn't even get to the front gate. Jenny tried to call on Gloria but Mandy shooed her away. Miss Gloria is at camp, gone all summer. That woman's a tiger protecting secrets when she's sober but give her a couple of frosty Buds and that tiger turns kitten. Momma saw her down at Gum's. Gloria and her daddy had some terrible fight after she told him what happened. Mandy didn't hear details but heard the name Buchanan and 'dead girl' clear enough. Next morning Gloria was packed off to camp on Lake Michigan.

No Gloria. No Rudy. Felt like I'd lost my right arm and my left leg and was now this misshapen thing, hobbling through the days, aching all over. No drive to keep the promise we made to find the killer. I knew it wasn't Bung-Eye, though he was a part of it, and that made me even less inclined to carry on. Jenny kept throwing out theories and suggesting next steps I always made an excuse not to take. If the most evil man in Larson hadn't killed Mora, then there was someone even worse in our town. Who, what, could be worse than Bung-Eye Buchanan? Didn't take me long to realise it wasn't worth finding out. Getting Rudy hurt like that, maybe one day getting Jenny or Gloria hurt like that, it would never be worth it.

I told Jenny that when we were grown enough to make a sheriff listen and stand a chance against Bung-Eye, we'd start digging again. We wouldn't stop until we dug up the whole truth. That's a God's honest, hand-on-heart, kick-me-if-I'm-lying promise.

It worked for a while, then she stopped talking about it.

The heatwave of '71 got itself in the record books. Hottest. Longest. It broke in September, just before harvest. The clouds rolled in from the south in fat clods and let loose, soaked the fields. We didn't see our friends except in school.

We didn't go out and play. You'll get too muddy, Momma said, and I'm not doing your laundry every night, think we're made of money? Why don't you just burn a ten-buck note instead?

I'd even forgotten about the pale grey Ford. Forgot about the feeling it gave me when I saw it, the tingle down my back, the squirm in my gut. Put it to the back of my head and left it there. By October I'd stopped flinching when I heard an engine on the road.

Then, as if that car sensed I'd moved on, I saw it again. On the last Sunday in October. Halloween. Once, and only for a few seconds, driving along Main Street while Jenny and me were in the Backhoe. It didn't stop or slow, just passed by, but it chilled me. I nudged Jenny, asked her if she'd seen it but she looked at me like I was crazy. Seen what, Johnny? Nothing is what. It was gone before she even turned but it set a cold in my bones that took too long to shake. A cold like I'd seen something I shouldn't, something not quite of this world that nobody else could see.

Three times was not a coincidence. Was it following me? Haunting me? I had to tell someone and there was only one person I could talk to.

'Do you believe in ghosts?' I asked Frank at our Tuesday session. Early November had brought a chill to the air. He brought out the space heater that day, turned the trailer office into a sauna. Over the previous month, the sessions had become less about counselling and more about hanging out. That's what it felt like. Two buds, talking, maybe playing a round of rummy. He never let me win but I did once and it was the greatest feeling. He bear-hugged me and gave me the deck so I could keep practising at home.

'Ghosts?' he frowned, shuffled the deck and dealt another hand. 'What makes you ask?'

I picked up my cards. 'No reason. Just, you know, that woman we found in the summer,' I shrugged, tried to keep the tone light. 'Made me think about things, death and spirits and stuff.'

He nodded, fanned his cards and rearranged the order.

'It's natural to think that way after experiencing something like you kids did. But I tell you, John.' He picked up a card and put down a three of spades. 'Ghosts? They're just storybook tales designed to frighten. When a person dies God takes their soul to Heaven or sends it right to Hell. They say ghosts are souls that stick around to make trouble. That would mean God missed them in his sorting and God doesn't miss, John. God does not miss a thing.'

I took the three, added it to my three of diamonds, and put down a seven. We'd played so much, we did it all by reflex now, we could talk without really paying attention to the game.

'Are you sure? I saw . . .' I started, paused, unsure where to go.

'What did you see?'

Suddenly I felt foolish. I shifted around the cards in my hand, even though they didn't need it. 'Nothing, it's stupid.'

'Hey. Nothing in this room is stupid. You should know that by now. What did you see? Spill it, kid.'

I smiled. Tried to. Shrugged off my discomfort. 'It's nothing really. Just . . . well . . . a couple of times now I've seen this car.'

He looked up from his cards. 'A car?'

'An old Ford, Mustang, I think. It's got this weird paint

job so I recognised it. I've seen it a bunch of times around town.'

'Did you see who was driving it?'

I shook my head. He put down an eight of clubs and I picked it up, tucked it into my hand beside a nine and ten of the same suit.

'What's weird about the paint?'

'It's this light grey colour, but it's not shiny or anything like . . .' *like the brand new blue Dodge, gleaming in the sun.* 'Like new cars. It's this faded grey, seems like it sucks in the sunlight. I don't know.'

Frank nodded along, eyes on his cards, and didn't speak for a while. The silence set a squirm in my belly.

'Like I said, it's stupid. Just a car.'

'You should stay away from it, John.'

'Why?'

'Strange things happen in this town. Have you noticed? That woman you found, now this car. And no driver? A pale grey the sunlight doesn't touch. A *Mustang.*' He shook his head, tapped the edge of his cards, his eyes darting left to right and back and forth. Quiet. He bit down on his lip and then looked at me, right in the eye, startled, as if he'd forgotten I was there.

'Revelations, John,' he said, nodded along with himself, put on his hard sermon voice. 'Revelations 6:8, do you remember your Bible studies? *And I looked, and behold a pale horse: and his name that sat on him was Death, and Hell followed with him.*'

Those words – *pale horse* – cinched up my muscles, tightened around my heart and throat and brain. I knew the passage, all the kids did. The end of days stuff is like the Bible's action movie, all fire and explosions. We all read it again and again, acted out the parts, vied to be a horseman, but I hadn't matched those words to real life. Now they stared me in the face. Pale car. Death. Everything turned cold.

'Hell follows, John,' he said. 'Bad things follow Death and I don't want you to get hurt. Stay away from that car and tell me if you see it again.'

I looked at him, into his eyes, saw the warmth in them. He put his hand on my shoulder.

'Listen, son, you and your friends found something terrible in a place you thought of as sanctuary. You've all been touched by Death and at such a young age, it marks you out. But it is just a mark, a smudge that can be wiped away with honest prayer. God is with you, John. He will protect you and so will I.'

I nodded with him, smiled, but a crystal of ice settled in my chest, despite the blazing heater. Touched by Death. Haunted by him and his pale horse. With Hell and horror to follow. I was sure the pastor was right, my head told me that if anybody knew about this kind of thing, it was one of God's own.

Now, at least, the car, the strangeness, it had a name, a solidity that took away most of the fear. I felt lighter and smiled fully, honestly, when I called 'Gin' and laid out my four threes and run of clubs to beat him.

Over that winter and the months of gloom, that hour on a Tuesday was my home fire. The only thing I looked forward to. I'd race out of fourth period and get to the trailer five minutes early. The constant rain had turned the office dank, mould crept down from one corner and the air tasted musty. But it didn't matter. Frank, who I'd started to think of more as a father than a counsellor, and his roaring space heater chased away the cold, the damp, the bad memories. He listened when I spoke of the pale Ford and Rudy's arm and Mora and the way Jenny changed over summer, the obsession in her eyes, what she'd said, '*I wanted to see what would happen to me.*' He told me to be strong, stay the course, all would be well. And slowly, it was. The less we spoke of Mora, the more Jenny seemed like her old self, gabbing about fashion and flowers instead of dead girls and murder. She started to smile again.

February and Jenny's birthday came around. Momma forgot again and I tried to explain it away on drink and worry and the new man in Momma's life but I could see how much it hurt Jenny. All three of us could, so we had a party ourselves. Rudy charmed a coconut cake out of Didi at the Backhoe, Gloria gave Jenny a headscarf with blue stars on it and I got her the new Judy Blume with money I borrowed from Rudy who had stolen it from his brother. It was the first real fun we'd had since the previous summer.

Talk of Mora, our investigation and its sharp ending quickly faded. Whenever me or Rudy mentioned the car, its engine or speed, Gloria rolled her eyes and pretended to fall asleep, Rudy went quiet when we discussed his old man, unconsciously cradled his arm. Talk of the body, the lake, made me shrink away. So we talked about algebra problems and who was seen necking behind the football field or who wrote 'Larson Lions Are Pussies' on the scoreboard in red paint. The four of us settled into our normal rhythm but there was always something left unsaid. Averted eyes. Clipped tones. Some dark fog floating right in the middle of our circle. It faded over the winter but never disappeared. It was as if it were waiting for the sun to come back and ignite us all over again.

PART TWO

Summer, 1972

PART TWO

11

The rain carried on until May when it finally cleared and gave us a hot, clean summer. My worst and best summer. The weather changed just in time for the sunny photographs of the returning GIs to appear in the *Clarkesville Combine*. The newshounds loved it. The sun made the story come alive. After all, where was the triumph in a bronze star returning home in the rain, all soaked boots and dripping hair? Reporters and photographers from the *Larson Herald* and the *Combine* flocked to the bus stop to see them, snap them, hold out notebooks to get their quotes. How do you feel, son? How many slopes you kill over there? You're a goddamn American hero!

Those poor souls. Limping men in green. Day after day, the buses rolled in and deposited a few blinking, quiet GIs. Shades of the red-blooded boys who'd left a few years ago. The bus would blare its horn once or twice, bye kids, enjoy your ripped-up lives, then rumble on to the next town. They were the injured, the discharged, the too-messed-up-to-pull-a-trigger but still the vultures with their Pentaxes and flash bulbs circled, snapped, squawked.

Jenny and me sat on the bench outside Al Westin's grocery store licking ice cream cones. Jenny wore a sundress dotted with blue flowers, one of her favourites. A hand-me-down from some cousin we'd never met. Every year or two Momma would get a bag of clothes, all stained and full of holes, from a sister or brother she never talked about. Whatever fit, we'd keep. Whatever didn't, would be taken – still holey and unwashed – to the church. I wondered sometimes if they came from the goodwill donations bin and Momma just wouldn't admit it. It didn't really matter. Jenny found the gems when Momma only saw rubbish. Jenny would polish them, add to them, transform them, like she was transforming herself along with it. If I don't look like her, she'd say, meaning Momma, I'll never be her. Eric Lahane, our longest-running Pigeon Pa, knew how to sew and when he first appeared, helped Jenny re-hem a pair of denims, adding on a strip of flowery material to the flared bottoms. She loved him instantly.

Eric worked down at the Easton flour mill hauling sacks when he wasn't on our farm. He had a moustache that just about reached his chin and brown hair down to his shoulders. Momma said he was like a show pony at a Texas rodeo. He mostly wore mustard yellow shirts and flared-out blue jeans, hair all glossy brown waves like someone had taken a curling iron to it. Bit of a hippy, full of ideas and plans and dreams. He wanted the farm to turn a profit and bring in a good harvest but it had been so neglected it was up to him, Jenny and me to get it back. The chores filled my days and I loved it, having help, direction, someone to talk to about yields and soil and how we could best use our land. It felt like, for the first time, my dream of running the Royal farm was out of the pipe, free to soar and grow with the crop. The amount of work doubled and I spent all my spare time clearing fields, planting, hauling the good corn to Jenny to put through the sheller, hauling the bad stuff into a pile to be burned. From the ashes, John, Eric would say, will grow a mighty stalk and we will be showered in gold. Along with farming, he talked a lot about Vietnam and the draft, said he was going to Washington to tell the president to call it all off.

Eric greeted the vets as they came off the bus, thanking them, calling them heroes. Eric had pamphlets in the house talking about how bad the war was, how it was illegal and Nixon and LBJ screwed the pooch, killed a generation of American men and turned the survivors into murderers. Every night he'd sit glued to the TV set, watching those bombs fall in the jungle, hearing the justification from our side and snorting his disapproval. Before Eric, we'd all been aware of the war of course, not even Larson is that far under a rock, but he brought it dead centre and loud into our lives.

Eric wasn't the only one in Larson who didn't like the war. Across the road from the seven or eight GIs, four people held signs. 'Stop the War', 'No Baby Killers in Larson', 'My Lai Murderers, Get Out', 'If It's Dead and Vietnamese, It's VC', with a picture of a shot-up child beneath the words. They'd been protesting for years but now Eric was around, I found myself paying attention, caring.

Parents hugged their sons in disbelief and sorrow. A man wept on the sidewalk when he couldn't shake his boy's hand. Left it in 'Nam, Pa, I imagined him saying. Even

Frank was there, offering whatever comfort he could to the family whose boy didn't come off the bus.

'Johnny, your ice cream.' Jenny nudged me, took my attention from the man missing a leg and the other missing an eye, and brought it to a trickle of melted choc-chip.

I licked it up but it tasted foul in my mouth. It wasn't important. They were. Those men. Two years ago, Jenny and me sat on this bench and watched the smiling, healthy sons go off on that same bus. They hugged their mommas, they shook their daddies' hands, they saluted their coach and teachers, they drove away with fanfare and blown kisses. Jenny had been too young to notice, she'd kicked her feet, crunched on her waffle cone, but I couldn't stop staring at them. The story Momma told of our real pa heading off to war all those years ago was feeling thin and worn. The men who'd gone to the jungles either came home within a few years or a man in a uniform knocked on the door. We'd had neither.

Dozens went. A handful came back. They said you never know the reality until you're in your fatigues, on the battlefield, but their faces told the story clear enough. A man's memories can change and warp over time but the creases and scars on his face, the emptiness in his eyes, and quiver in his lips, they don't know how to lie.

I read them all like a book, saw their deeds writ large on their cheeks.

My choc-chip slumped and dropped onto the sidewalk.

'Those boys don't have much to look forward to.' Al Westin's voice from behind us. He leaned against the doorframe, arms crossed over his white apron.

'At least they're alive,' he carried on. 'But I ain't sure if that's a blessing or a curse.'

'What do you mean, Mr Westin?' Jenny said.

'They don't come back whole. When they seen what they seen, friends dead, bodies blown up, that breaks off a piece of your brain. It makes you see things different, maybe even see things that ain't there, can even make you think you're still out there in the jungle, still fighting and everyone around you is the enemy. Trauma like that, killing someone, breaks a man. Even the ones who didn't lose arms and legs left something of their mind out there. They ain't going to find this world easy any more. But we'll help them. Larson looks after its own. Some would rather be dead, I wager, and their parents think that too. Then they'd know and be able to put their boys to rest. That'd be something.'

The grocer smiled beneath his moustache, a thick grey thing like the end of a broom. The rest of his face, usually shaved close and smooth, had a blanket of rough stubble, a few days' growth at least.

'You okay, sir?' I asked. His eyes switched to me, sunken pieces of coal in a March snowman.

'Oh sure, sure. Just got to keep praying,' he said and something shone in his eye. 'Why don't you run over to the Backhoe, Scotty is over there.'

Then he gave me a dollar and told us to share a burger and shake. Jenny jumped up to say thank you but he'd backed into the store and closed the door.

'What's eating him?' Jenny asked and snatched the money from my fingers.

I stood up and dropped my empty ice cream cone in the trash.

'I'll have a cheeseburger, fully loaded, please, miss,' I grinned, pushing what joy I could through my face, into the world. Jenny wouldn't see the darkness behind it and that's how it should be.

I shouted at Eric, pointed to the diner to let him know where we were going. He waved back. We had to walk past the sign-holders to get to the Backhoe. One of them was Kendra Lyle, daughter of Mrs Lyle from the post office. Then two men I didn't know and, behind the last sign, the one with the photograph, I didn't quite believe it. I had to look twice.

'Miss Eaves?' I said too loud. Four-Misters Eaves, as Momma called her.

My geography teacher glanced at me, then, as if recognising me as part of her other life, lowered her sign. Red-faced, pale hair striking out at all angles from a loose ponytail, a dandelion shoved behind her ear. This wasn't my Miss Eaves.

'Hello, both of you,' she said, out of breath from shouting.

'What are you doing, miss?' Jenny asked.

Miss Eaves knelt down in front of us. 'Do you both remember where Vietnam is on the map?'

Jenny nodded. I didn't.

'It's the other side of the world,' she said, her voice urgent like she had to tell us this before it was too late. 'But that doesn't mean we shouldn't care about the people. I visited Vietnam once and it is . . .' she paused, found the words, 'it is the most beautiful country and the people, the most beautiful people. They have kindness as a first response and it just breaks my heart, all this. It has to stop.'

Eric had taught me to hate the war, hate the government, hate the soldiers, it's all wrong and illegal, bring our boys home. He'd never talked about the country they were destroying. The people they were killing. Nobody was. It was all America this, Yoo-Ess-Ay that.

'I'd like you to think about it,' Miss Eaves said. 'This world is a big, beautiful place. War only makes it smaller.'

Then she took up her sign and held it high and, for the first time, I felt like standing beside her, stone-faced and steadfast. It was what inspiration felt like. It is one thing to generate anger and fear to spur a person into action but it takes something much deeper to inspire them.

'I will, miss,' I said. 'I'll think about that for long time.'

I did too. In the Backhoe, with Scott Westin, I stayed mostly silent. I ate a few bites of cheeseburger, a fistful of fries and all Jenny's pickles because she hated them. I kept quiet all through Scott's chirping about his daddy making him do stock take this afternoon and about how miserable Al was at the moment. People had stopped coming into the store in favour of the 7-Eleven opened in the old laundromat on the other side of town. I didn't care, my thoughts were still with Miss Eaves. A few words from her drowned out months of Eric's speeches. It hit me how strange it was that my perspective on the war, the country, the people, could be shifted so quickly by another viewpoint. Two sides. Two points of view.

Two truths.

I glanced out the window to the protesters, their fervour dimmed now the returned soldiers had left with their families. I saw them differently. I thought of the GIs differently too and it felt dangerous, then, that just twenty minutes ago I hadn't. How can you be sure you're screaming the right words at the right people? Murderer. Killer. Hero. Saviour. They're all the same man and he is you and your brother and your dad and uncle and cousin. Maybe one day he'll be me.

'Dad's not been the same since Luke left,' Scott said.

Luke. His older brother. Drafted in '69 and not heard from since. I'd forgotten Al Westin even had another son and a wave of guilt soaked me.

'When's he coming home?' Jenny asked.

Scott shrugged, played with the straw in his milkshake.

A ding from the bell over the front door. Sheriff Samuels and Deputy Miller strolled in. Fat and thin. White and black.

Jenny tensed beside me. Neither of us had seen Samuels except in passing since he found us by Big Lake, wrapped in a dead woman, and questioned us in the station. His investigation, as well as ours, had fizzled out. No leads. No way to identify the woman. Clearly no one missed her enough to come looking in Larson. All those feelings I'd kept down over the last year came surging up inside me like I was a shaken-up Coke bottle with Samuels popping the cap.

We hadn't told him about the car Bung-Eye sold off, the clue, the lead. I hadn't thought of it in months. Rudy's injury broke everything. It showed our amateur detective club what we could expect if we dug further. It took Gloria away from us to some fancy summer camp. When she came back it was like Mora's body and Rudy's shattered bones never happened. But now the sun was back, and the Challenger, bright blue and gleaming chrome, smashed into the front of my memory.

Jenny leaned into me and whispered, 'We should talk to him. Maybe he knows something new about Mora.'

In her eyes, the strange hunger returned. I saw Jenny changing again under my nose, sliding back to that odd pale girl by the lake. If I could solve this goddamn murder, maybe she'd get over it, go back to normal for good. Her fingers raked the table like they'd raked at the hole in the cornfield, her nails and skin turned black with dirt. How could she change so much, so fast?

I took a long breath and tried to quell the growing rage. A woman's murder had gone a year unresolved. A million more went unpunished on the other side of the world. I wanted to go over there, tell Samuels all about the car and Bung-Eye, wanted to make the rumours I killed her stop for good, bring Jenny back to me.

'Stay put,' I said to Jenny and slid off my seat.

I walked up to Samuels and Miller. Both men slumped at the bar, each with a cup of coffee and a pile of eggs and hash even though it was far past breakfast time. Samuels shovelled nuggets of scrambled egg into his mouth. Half fell off his fork on the way, tumbled down the mountain of beef and potato onto the countertop. Every now and then Didi the waitress swept by to clear them.

'Sheriff Samuels, sir?' I said, keeping my voice low. 'I have to talk to you.'

'Come to the station on Monday.' He sprayed yellow specks as he spoke.

'It's about the dead girl we found last year. I need to tell you something,' I said.

Sausage fingers forced a toothpick between his back teeth. Whatever it dislodged, he ate.

'What is it? Have you been withholding evidence?'

Then he turned to Miller. 'Kids, huh?'

I felt eyes on my back. Dozens of them. I glanced back at Jenny, her mouth hanging open in disbelief then stretching into a smile. She nodded for me to keep going, her fingers scratching at the Formica.

'Can we go somewhere else?' I said.

Samuels huffed, dropped his fork. 'Like the station? Jesus, kid, I'm in the middle of my lunch and you want to talk about some year-old Jane Doe case right this minute instead of coming to the station on Monday, like I told you to not five goddamn seconds ago.'

I shuffled closer, lowered my voice so nobody else could hear and made a decision I knew would haunt me. 'I know who killed her.'

He laughed and whispered with me, humouring the kid. 'Who's that then?'

I was being stupid. Foolish. Stop talking, John, this is useless. Bung-Eye will find out and he'll kill you. What are you doing, boy?

'The previous owner of a new Dodge Challenger,' I said.

Samuels grabbed me by my collar and pulled me right up to his pig face. Forks clinked on plates, conversation hushed.

'How the hell could a little shit like you know something like that?' Samuels whispered. A crust of ketchup in the corner of his mouth opened and closed like a fresh wound.

'I–I . . .' but I didn't know what to say. There was nothing I could say. I'd done it, I'd killed myself and for what?

For Jenny.

'I thought so,' he sneered and threw me a foot backward. 'Lying to a sheriff is a crime, kid. One more word and you're spending the weekend in a cell. Get lost.'

Miller leaned backward so he could see me around his boss' bulk. Instead of playing the Officer Friendly card, he jerked his thumb toward the door.

'Piss off, you little freak.'

I stumbled back to my seat, stung and red-faced. I shook my head at Jenny's questions while Scott kept eating, oblivious.

What the hell had I accomplished by doing that? I glanced up to Samuels. He was still shovelling eggs and hash but now he had a deep frown creasing his forehead. He wasn't joining in the jokes between Didi and Miller any more. Maybe I'd got through. Maybe he'd go looking. Maybe he was just pissed that a kid knew more than him about all this.

'You did the right thing,' Jenny whispered to me and some of my panic eased. She offered me a French fry, one of the crispy thin ones she knows I like, and started talking about Mr Frome's biology class.

Scott laughed. 'You guys see how grossed out Rudy was by those sheep eyeballs Frome brought in?'

'He almost blew chunks into Maddie-May's book bag,' Jenny said and laughed too.

I grabbed a few more fries and smiled at the memory of Rudy gagging when Frome picked an eyeball out of the jar and pretended to eat it.

Then the sharp ding of the Backhoe doorbell and my smile drained away.

Darney Wills, chest first in his red-gold Lions letterman jacket, ginger hair cut to a flat-top with fenders, a style a decade out of date, walked into the diner trailing some dough-faced girl. Then the two darlings of Larson, Mark Easton and Tracy Meadows. Darney was the fullback to Mark's quarterback, *one helluva team* the pundits squawked. The Backhoe hushed. Eyes turned to plates, mugs of coffee, plastic tablecloths. Anywhere but them. Those shining smiles and loose swagger I remembered from Barks reservoir and my first session with Frank were gone. Mark had been drafted in February's pull, so had Darney but you wouldn't know it from his behaviour.

Mark was pale, still and silent. Tracy's eyes were red-rimmed. I felt for Mark then, the way his world had flipped from light to dark. So easy for that one moment, those far-away officials pulling out a blue capsule, those two or three words spelling out your birthday, to change your life. Samuels finding me and Jenny by Big Lake did the same. Our friends had thrown stones, turned us bloody. Mark's stones were disappointed glances, avoidance in the street, pity. By the look on his face, they hurt the same.

Darney dropped his fist on the bar, a fat grin on his face, and ordered four chocolate shakes and cheeseburgers, then slapped down a twenty-dollar bill.

'Coming right up.' Didi didn't hide her impatience.

A fog of distaste filled the diner, like everyone's meal turned rancid at once. A collective clink of set-down forks, a dozen nervous coughs and shifts on chairs. We all felt the same. Sorrow for the Eastons. Something else for the Wills. Those blue capsules didn't know good from bad, rich from poor, a star from a nobody. The Light of Larson was off to the jungle and Darney Wills was strutting around like a prize bull let in with the heifers.

Darney stood at the bar, a few feet from Samuels, waiting for Didi to ring up his change while Mark and the girls had taken the booth by the window. There was something about Darney I hated. Something instinctual like those zoo monkeys who have never seen a snake being dead scared of a plastic one thrown in their cage. Somewhere deep in their blood they know it's an age-old enemy they have to run from.

'What's the hold-up, Deeds?' Darney snapped his fingers at Didi. 'You having trouble counting such high numbers?' Then a sickening *hurr hurr* laugh.

Darney didn't have all that much spice in him. He wore
the smug smile of a bully with Daddy's money and position
to back him up. Carrot-topped and heavy-set, a covering of
fat over hard muscles that he could never shift. As soon as
he stopped playing football that muscle would turn to lard,
those pecs would sag and droop, the puffed-out chest would
turn into a paunched-out gut. I couldn't wait to see it, the
rolling mound of flesh he'd become, wheezing through
town in his truck with a wife he hated and who hated him.
He'd die young, diabetes or heart disease or swerving drunk
off the Talega Bridge.

Didi slapped the change on the counter. The nicest
woman in Larson, was Didi Hensher, so if she was pissed
at you, you know you've done something terrible. The diner
turned pin-drop silent.

'Oh come now, Deeds, you know I'm just playing with
you,' he said and held out his hand. 'Please may I have my
change?'

'Come on, Darney,' Mark called from their booth.

But Darney was the snake and Didi the mouse and he
wasn't done playing. Everyone in the diner, even Samuels
and Miller, kept their heads down. You don't go messing
with the mayor's boy.

Didi scooped up the money and put it in Darney's hand.
Thought I saw her flinch when her fingers brushed his skin.

'There now, that weren't so difficult was it?' he said, then
he teased a five-buck note from the tangle of coins and
handed it to her. 'There's your tip, beautiful.'

He air-kissed at her as she took the money. A five-buck
tip was worth the churning stomach any day. That was all
Darney was good for it seemed, money and mouth.

Darney made his way over to the booth and slid in next

to his girl. The diner breathed out, the chatter returned. February's draft had sent a bubble of joy through me. I'd thought Darney was going away, thought he would probably die out there and I hadn't felt a lick of guilt at being happy about it. Then a few weeks ago, the rumours began.

Scott Westin leaned close to me and I smelt onions on his breath. 'Heard Darney's dad got him out of it. Paid them off.'

'I heard it was Doc Wyndham who got paid off,' Jenny whispered, her eyes on Darney. 'His daddy gave the doc two hundred dollars to tell the army Darney was sick and couldn't sign up.'

It was heartbreak and fear and all kinds of anger when that news spread through Larson. Ours was a proud, close town. So many young men had gone, fought, never returned or come back broken, and we took care of them because they were brave, serving their country. Darney took a steaming shit on all of that but nobody dared call him out. Draft-dodger. Pussy. Traitor.

'He's a coward,' I said. A little too loud. A little too clear.

Darney's head snapped up and I wanted to shrink, disappear under the table. The word hung in the air, *coward*. I hadn't said his name but Darney knew, of course he did, a guilty conscience hears everything. He scanned the diner, dull brown eyes, twitching ruddy cheeks. He stood up, slamming both hands on the table, knocking over the sugar pot and sending a cascade of white over the floor.

'Someone got something to say to me?' he shouted, eyes darting, a sheen of spit around his mouth. Lips growing red and shiny like a two-cent drag queen.

'Calm it down, Darney,' Samuels said but he didn't even turn around, didn't get up.

'Who's got the problem? Huh? Who wants to say some-thing?' Darney didn't see the law, didn't acknowledge it. His life had no consequences.

Finally, excruciatingly, his empty eyes found me.

'A little pussy voice calling me a coward,' he sneered. 'Must have been the sissy.'

The diner looked at me as if 'the Sissy' was, and always had been, my real name. A cold blade of fear sliced through my stomach. The snake turned on me, a weak rodent, the runt of the colony. Yes, they were all silently urging, fall upon him and let us be spared.

I couldn't look at him as he swaggered over. My fists clenched and unclenched in my lap. My eyes picked out every nick and scratch on the table. There was no way I could take on Darney. He'd smash me to a pulp and leave me twitching on the sidewalk and yeah, you know what, I was scared of him. Shit scared of how far he might go if anyone ever stood up to him.

Darney reached my table. A mountain in a lettered jacket. My body wanted to move, put myself between him and Jenny, but I was rooted.

'You got something to say, sissy?' he said, slamming both hands on our table.

'No,' I said but I didn't hear my voice above the raging blood in my ears.

'Back off, Darney,' Jenny said, stood up, faced him down.

My mouth went dry and Scott's dropped open.

Jenny glared. 'I said *back off.*'

Darney straightened, raised his ginger eyebrows, and crossed his arms. 'Look at this, little pussy needs his sister to fight for him.'

'Leave her alone,' I said but I wasn't convincing anyone.

Darney's mouth widened into a gaping hole, a sour stink wafted over me. 'Oh. Oh. That's right. Ain't this them? Hey, Mark, this is them, right, Patty Royal's two? Heard you like sleeping with dead chicks, hey, boy? Heard you mighta even killed her, but I don't think a sissy boy like you's got the stones for that.'

'Stop it, Darney,' Mark's voice floated over from the other side of the diner.

Darney leaned close to me, ran his slug tongue over his lips, once, twice. I felt sick. 'That dead girl as good in bed as your momma?' He nudged me, laughed. Then he rounded on Jenny. 'Jenny Royal. What a woman you're turning out to be. Pretty, pretty, pretty.'

He slid closer, went to take her arm, but Mark came up behind him, slapped a hand on his shoulder and pulled him back. 'That's enough, Darney.'

A sting to the ego deflated him. 'Yeah, that's enough,' he said, raised his hands as if innocent and backed away. Then his eyes went to Jenny, up and down her body. His thick tongue licked a fresh sheen over his lips. 'Shame, me and Jenny were just getting acquainted, ain't that right, doll?'

Then he winked, another *hurr hurr* laugh, and sauntered off, back to his booth.

Mark met my eyes and gave a half smile. 'Sorry about him, he's not usually like this.'

Then he dug into his pocket and pulled out a handful of quarters, tipped them onto the table. 'Let me get your lunch, least I can do.'

I murmured thanks and Mark went back to his booth. Jenny picked up the coins.

'Time to go,' I said to her.

I had fury in me, filling me up, sharpening to a sword tip pointed right at Darney Wills. How dare he look at my sister, talk to her, insult her, insult my momma too. Fuck him. I wanted to rip the fat red lips off his face.

He watched us leave, not caring about me or Scott. All his attention was on Jenny. A new look on his face, like he was doing math in his head and coming up Grade A. The girl beside him, I thought then, with a sharp drop in my stomach, looked just like Mora. Dull blonde hair. Slim. Just his type? I shuddered, pushed Jenny toward the door.

The girl, narrow shoulders hunched under the weight of his arm, picked up her burger. Darney turned to her, yanked the burger out of her hands, and ripped out half of it in one bite, smiling while he chewed.

Jenny, Scott and me left the Backhoe quick as we could. It was Mark and Tracy though, who disappointed me most. A year ago, Mark would have shouted Darney down if he'd talked to anyone like that, now he was making excuses and paying off Darney's mistakes like everyone else. Mark was the lawkeeper of the senior class and everyone walked his line, even though there were only a few more weeks of school. But Mark did it kind. He did it good. Tables had been flipped since February. Mark was broken and beaten and Darney had stolen his shining crown.

Despite the blazing summer sun and unmarred skies, the colour and life had left Larson. Friends turned mean and petty and the speed of life slowed like we were all trudging through soft sand. School dragged and nobody remembered what we'd learned from one day to the next. My Tuesday sessions with Frank kept going. He called me sport and son and buddy. We played cards and went bird-spotting at Hackett Hill and Barks reservoir. He asked things like, *how's your momma, how's your sister, how's school and the farm and is Eric still in the picture?* Those sessions, a few evenings down at the Roost with the four of us, and the Saturday ice cream were the only things to give colour to my world, gave it landmarks and beats to mark time passing. They were the only things that didn't feel pointless, like the whole town was waiting for the bus and doing anything they could to pass the time, getting more tense, more irate, more volatile, the longer the wait went on.

It became clear that summer that I was failing school. I was trying but with all the work on the farm, I barely had time to study. I stayed up long after Jenny had gone to sleep after she'd spent all evening talking about Mora and what we should do next and why isn't Samuels doing anything and on and on into the night. Every day I was up before dawn, after only an hour or two of fretted sleep, dreams full of blue cars and dead bodies and the *snap* of Rudy's arm. I was too tired, my arms and legs and brain sore. I couldn't keep any information in my head that wasn't clearing, planting, harvest, chores, chores, chores.

I went to Frank, blubbing like a baby, and asked him for help. He said it was a brave man who could ask for help and suggested tutoring. An hour after school, twice a week for a month or two to get me in shape for the fall semester. Miss Eaves volunteered.

Frank came to my house to convince Momma. She scoffed at the talk. She was half-sauced but still clean enough to hear him out. School isn't for real men, she said, school makes soft heads and that's never done no one any good and that Eaves woman isn't hardly one to be telling my boy what to do, he's got work to do here. But nobody can refuse a pastor's plea for long. Go on, Mrs Royal, it'll be good for him, he's a good kid, just needs a little help.

'Fine,' Momma said, the whiskey doing most of the talking. 'It'll get him out from under my feet at least.'

At first, I was afraid I'd never be able to catch up with all the work on the farm by taking two hours away but as soon as I was out the yard, I felt lighter than I had in months. I loved the farm with every aching muscle but I was still a kid and, sometimes, I wanted to act like one.

After school on my first day of tutoring, I made sure Jenny knew she'd have to walk home by herself. Twice a week she would have to be with Momma and Eric without me there and Momma might not be in a friendly mood. Keep quiet, stay in our room, I'd said, just don't do anything to make her mad. Promise me, Jenny, promise me you'll be safe when I get home. She promised. Momma had been kinder, drinking less, since she met Eric but she could still strike out, a shout here, a pinch there. I hugged Jenny tight to me and told her I loved her and she said it back and kissed my cheek.

Jenny went home and I went to Miss Eaves' house on Cypress Drive. It wasn't far, one of the white houses with blue shutters near the middle of town. She opened the door with a 'Welcome!' and ushered me inside with a long sweep of her arm.

I'd only seen her a few days before, on the street with her dead baby sign, but that was a different Miss Eaves. The one leading me into her living room was the teacher I knew. All flowing skirts and bare shoulders showing off her arms, the skin, the folds, totally at ease.

'Would you like a glass of ice tea?' she said as we passed the kitchen.

'Please, miss.'

'Go on through then, just down the hall, your study buddy is waiting.'

The words stuck in my ear. Study buddy. Another person, here, in this house. Was it one of those kids who threw rocks at me, called me a murderer? My skin prickled and I wanted to turn and run back out the door. But as I entered the room, all the prickle heat disappeared and I smiled. Smiled and smiled, I couldn't control it. I must have looked like a clown, painted with a dopey rictus.

'Hi, John,' she said.

'Hi, Gloria.'

12

'What are you doing here?' Gloria asked as I sat on the couch beside her.

'Pastor Jacobs arranged it,' I said. 'You?'

She sighed. 'I slipped two grades in English Lit and History and my parents went mad at me, said I needed extra tutoring to make sure I kept my GPA. It hasn't exactly been easy this last year, since . . . you know.'

'I know.'

Gloria was different, more subdued than she used to be. We were never all that close, it was always Jenny and Gloria, me and Rudy, me and Jenny, Rudy and everyone. Never me and Gloria. She was quicksand, my momma always said, a red woman. Be careful of her, John Royal, she'll be the death of you.

Nerves fizzed inside me in the few minutes it took Miss Eaves to bring us the ice tea. Fear. Excitement. Something else.

'Are you going to summer camp this year?' I asked.

Gloria's forehead crinkled and she brushed a piece of red hair, proper rich red, not the harsh orange of Darney Wills, behind her ear. 'No. I didn't enjoy it that much. It was fine, I guess. Seems like so long ago I was even there.'

'What did you do there?'

Gloria shrugged. 'Swimming, canoeing, I don't remember.'

A few seconds of silence, then she said, 'I missed you guys though. A lot. I don't want to go back. You and Jenny doing okay? Your mom still with that guy?'

'We're good. Eric, yeah, he's nice. They seem happy enough.'

Then we trailed off. Fell into a fragile silence. We had shorthand, the four of us, a way of speaking that meant we never needed to say everything. Rudy used phrases like 'Bung-Eye lost at cards' to explain a beating, Jenny and me had all sorts of words for Momma: 'She'd had a long day', 'We were getting underfoot', 'She'd had a weekend at Gum's'. I only put it together later that we were making excuses for them. By not saying it out loud – Bung-Eye whipped me with his belt, Momma called Jenny a tramp and locked us in our room, Momma made Jenny sleep in the barn for back-talking and sass – we were excusing them. So many things the four of us didn't say out loud.

I'd never been alone with Gloria. Never had to make conversation with just her. We'd known each other since kindergarten, spent hours, days, weeks, together, and yet here I was, tongue-tied and awkward. It was a blessing then, hearing Miss Eaves' footsteps approaching and the clink of ice in glasses.

'Here you go, you two,' our teacher said. She set the tray down and took a chair opposite the couch. 'Where shall we start? Algebra?'

'You're a geography teacher,' Gloria said, 'how do you know algebra?'

Miss Eaves leant forward, rested her elbows on her knees and stared at Gloria. There was a flash, right in the corner of her eye, then Miss Eaves curled the corner of her mouth in a half smile.

'You caught me. I don't know algebra, at least not any better than you two do. But I do have a study plan with all the answers so I'm one up on you both.'

A strange, soft silence filled the room, same as it did in the classroom when the teacher made a joke and you weren't sure if you should laugh.

'Can we . . .' I began but couldn't finish. All day I'd thought about what I would talk to Miss Eaves about when we were alone. But we weren't alone and all my questions, the topics I'd memorised, stuck in my throat, too timid to come forward.

'What is it, John?' Miss Eaves said, her voice so kind that my nerves fled.

'Can we talk about Vietnam?'

Miss Eaves leant back as if my question pushed her.

'Yes.' Gloria perked up, that old fire in her voice. 'Can we? People never stop talking about it but they never seem to be telling us anything.'

Miss Eaves shook her head but in that way adults did when they were confused. She wasn't saying no.

'Gloria, you're behind in English Lit and, John, you're behind in everything,' she said, pursing her lips, clasping her hands. 'Neither of you need a lesson on the war.'

'I don't mean the war,' I said. 'The country. Like you talked about on Saturday.'

Her eyebrows and shoulders rose like God had pulled

her string. She slid the algebra study guide across the coffee table. 'I did, didn't I?'

Gloria raised her hand. 'Daddy says the zipperheads don't know what to do with their country anyway, we're helping them.'

'Wash your mouth out!' Miss Eaves snapped. 'Words like that are not welcome in my house.'

Gloria pushed herself back into the couch. 'Sorry, miss,' she said.

'Is this the wisdom being passed down to our children?' Miss Eaves said, calmer but I saw the same spark in her now as I did outside the Backhoe two days ago. 'Your father should know better than to sour you with his prejudices. Those men out there with their guns, they use words like that, words like *slope*, to describe the Vietnamese. Do you know why?'

Gloria, still buried in the couch cushions, shook her head.

'To make it easier to kill them.' Miss Eaves rubbed her forehead. 'In the Second World War, the British and Americans called the Germans *kraut*. It means cabbage. That name turned them from men serving their country, doing their duty and fighting for their cause, into nobodies. Our troops out in Vietnam are doing the same. If you come face to face with a human being in their home, a freshman private may take pity. He may let that mother and child live. If you come face to face with a *zipperhead*, the trigger is far easier to pull.'

'Are they cowards?' I asked.

Miss Eaves met my eyes. 'What do you mean?'

'I just . . .' My chest felt like caving in. 'I mean, cowards because they have to do that. They have to call them names and make them not real to do their jobs. It's like lying to yourself.'

'I suppose it is,' Miss Eaves said. 'But most of the men out there, our men, are not there by choice, they're boys like you, John, or good men like my husband Davey, and they are afraid. They are cowards.'

'Most of?' Gloria said, leaning forward now, out of the cushions.

'Yes. Most of. A few of them out there know exactly what they're doing.'

I didn't say it but it was those men I respected. To look your enemy in the eye and not be afraid, not make them into something inhuman but to know them, like you know yourself, that's what I wanted. I wanted to look Darney Wills in the eye and not be afraid.

'Why are you smiling, John?' Miss Eaves asked, with a deep frown.

The truth was usually the wrong thing to say. I couldn't say, you told me to face my enemies and pull the trigger. That kind of revelation would make its way back to Frank, it would be talked about in our Tuesday sessions, it would send fresh rumours about me around town and there were enough of those already.

So I said, 'You're a good teacher, miss.'

She smiled and I felt my chest puff up like a rooster.

The sun dipped low enough to shine gold through the front windows and fill the room with light. The tension fled and we settled into an easy quiet. The family room, without a family, was a chasm between basement and bedroom. Two full bookshelves, fat and bulging with trinkets and pamphlets stuffed between books, stood sentinel either side of the fireplace. Framed photographs covered the walls. A young

Miss Eaves smiled out from the top of a flat mountain. Her and one of her Misters, arms entwined, stood at the feet of a giant red Buddha. A dozen more photographs, beaches, palm trees, temples, a hundred new faces, friends, a husband or two, or three, all skin colours, all smiling beside my teacher. She painted the walls with her life so those visiting would ask where was this taken, who is that with you, and Miss Eaves could tell them, relive it again, and again. I thought, this is her way to escape Larson. Her way to still be the person she was, smiling in the photographs, instead of Four-Misters Eaves, a geography teacher in a backwater farming town.

Miss Eaves looked at her hands, gently rubbed the bright pale band of skin on her ring finger. Four-Misters Eaves with the tan line to prove it. Gloria scratched her pen around the edges of her notebook, drawing cubes and pyramids, diamonds and spheres, all three-dimensional, all pin-point accurate without a ruler. It made no sense she was failing anything.

Miss Eaves hadn't looked up from her ring finger in ages and her face had turned slack and pale.

'Miss?' I said. 'Are you all right?'

'I feel a headache coming on,' she said and picked up the tray of untouched ice tea. I thought she might cry. She'd said her husband went off to war, maybe she already knew he wasn't coming back and we'd hashed up all the memories.

'That's enough for today. Algebra next time. You can see yourselves out.' And she left, went into the kitchen and didn't return.

Gloria and I exchanged tight, uneasy smiles and repacked our book bags. We stepped silently down the hallway to the front door. The sunlight didn't reach the hall – it was cool and dim and dark faces filled the photographs on the walls. I imagined myself an intruder, walking through a tomb.

On the sidewalk, Gloria and I didn't know what to do. We had only been inside Miss Eaves' house for twenty minutes so our parents weren't expecting us for another forty at least.

'Got somewhere to be?' Gloria asked and I shook my head. 'Want to go up to Barks?'

'Sure. We can cut behind the church.'

The sun sliced down Main Street, turning the grey asphalt white. We left Cypress Drive and took Wilmore, past the post office, then Munroe toward the church, only stopping to stare at the flickering bank of televisions in the window of Merle's Kitchen and Electric. A brand new Emerson showed the news in full colour; green uniforms, blue sky, red blood. No matter what time or day of the week, you could always find the war if you went looking. It felt wrong now, after what Miss Eaves said, to watch what was happening over there as if it was *American Bandstand* with different music, bombs instead of bass. I heard some people kept the news channels on constantly. Mothers driven mad scanning the face of every grinning GI and row of bodies, lonely old veterans itching for a piece of the pie and shouting tactics at General Abrams like he was the coach at a football game. I couldn't watch any more. I turned away, back to Larson and Gloria and the low evening sun.

Somewhere behind, on one of the side streets, I heard a car engine rev up, a low rumble I'd heard before. I looked around but saw nothing.

'Do you ever think about it?' I asked and started toward the church. The sound of the engine faded as we walked away.

'What?' Gloria fell into step beside me.

'Last summer.'

The air thickened under my words and I saw, from the edge of my eye, Gloria hesitate.

'Sometimes,' she said. 'All the time.'

'Me too,' I said.

We walked the rest of the way to Barks reservoir without talking. At the back of the church, the tacked-on trailer office where I spent an hour of my Tuesdays was dark, the lights off, the door locked. Passing beside it now, empty and small, I saw how vulnerable the structure was. Those thin glass windows wouldn't stand up against a hurled stone. That plastic door would crack and swing wide with a good kick. It made my gut twitch to think of it, that someplace I loved could be undone so easily. But then, I realised, that's exactly what happened to the Roost.

'It's so ugly,' Gloria said, nodding to the trailer.

'Were you reading my mind?'

'That's on everyone's mind. It's just this horrible lump they put on the back of the church so the stupid pastor could have more privacy.'

I flinched at the word 'stupid' but tried not to let it show. 'Why does he need privacy?'

'Don't know. I asked my father once but he told me to mind my own business and not to question the pastor.'

Your father is dead right, I wanted to say but didn't. Gloria's father, a big-shot lawyer, richest man in three counties so they say, and college-educated no less, knows what he's talking about.

I smiled at Gloria. 'The pastor isn't so bad,' I said and left it at that.

I thought I heard that car engine again as we passed

behind the church but I put it down to the wind, or some far-away freight train rumbling on old tracks.

We got to Barks around fifteen minutes after leaving Miss Eaves' house on Cypress. Gloria's walk home from the beach wasn't too far but mine would take the better part of an hour. The place was deserted and the water low enough to reveal a few feet of sand. The sun beamed down gold on us and it felt like we were the only two people in the world and this lake was the only lake, this beach the only beach. The noise around us, insects, birds, rustling rabbits and mice in the brush, they were our music. Not one human sound but our breathing, in out, in time with the lapping water.

'Are you brave enough?' Gloria said, a wide smile on her lips.

I knew her well enough to know that I should be nervous at a question like that. That, no, I probably wasn't brave enough and we probably shouldn't do whatever it was she had in mind. But she was smiling and I realised then, I was a fool for that smile.

'Of course,' I said.

She laughed then kicked off her shoes and balled her hair into a bun with a band that seemed to come from nowhere. I took off my shoes, more out of reflex than choice. Then Gloria pulled her dress over her head, showing her white underwear. I'd seen Gloria do this a hundred times, swimming at Big Lake or Barks, but tonight was different. An electric shock ran through me when I saw the pale skin on her stomach and upper thighs, skin not even the sun got to see. She flung the dress in the grass, and ran screaming into the water. I had a second to breathe, to say, damn it, John Royal, get your shirt and slacks off and show her you're brave enough. I stripped to my under-wear and splashed into the lake.

'Just when I think I know you, Johnny, you go ahead and surprise me,' she laughed, standing up to her shoulders in the water.

I waded out to join her. She was taller than me, not by much, but enough to put the water to my neck. It was freezing but I wouldn't let it show.

'How do I surprise you?'

She sank so our faces were level. 'I don't know. I just always thought you were . . .'

'What?'

Her face reddened, she backed away sending ripples up to my chin and setting my teeth chattering.

'What?' I asked again, following her deeper into the lake.

She wouldn't answer, just swam further away, careful to keep her head up so her hair wouldn't get wet. I followed.

'Gloria, hey, not so fast.' I wasn't as strong a swimmer as her and I realised too late I was out of my depth.

The sludgy sand beneath my feet was gone, dropped away into an abyss. The water was black and empty but Gloria didn't notice. She kept swimming away, laughing. At me? Had she lured me in the water so she could watch me flounder? The opposite of a flapping fish on the beach but no less pathetic. Get a rock, put it out of its misery. Do the same to the boy. I went under.

Water filled my ears and nose and stung my eyes. But they were open. I could see nothing. Just ink black all around me. My lungs ached to breathe and my throat closed. My head said, breathe, you idiot, go on, take a deep breath, but my body was smarter. My open eyes blurred and I saw her. Coming toward me. A pale figure in the dark.

Gloria? No, someone else. Dull blonde hair floating like a halo up from the deep, her hand out, a gunshot hole in her stomach.

Take my hand, Johnny, Mora was saying, and I could hear it in my mind but not my ears. Help me. Find me. It's lonely here, so lonely and so cold.

She reached out, arms impossibly long, fingers stretched and gnarled like tree roots.

Pastor Frank's words hit me hard, blasted a stream of bubbles out my mouth. Touched by Death. You're touched by Death, John, and he's come to collect. That was the engine I'd heard on the way down here. The car. Death on his pale horse, he's come back for you, John, he's come back.

Her face changed and I was suddenly looking at my sister, pale and dead and reaching for me.

Fingers dug into my arm and pulled and my head broke the surface. My lungs reacted, pulled air into my body as Gloria hauled me out of the lake and onto the beach.

'Jesus. *Jesus,*' she kept saying between panicked breaths. 'Jesus, Johnny, I thought . . . *shit.*'

I put my head between my knees, coughed out foul-tasting water, tried to shake away the picture of Mora and Jenny. Help me, she said. I spat out the water and the words.

'I'm fine,' I said, voice hoarse. 'I guess I need to pay more attention in swim class.'

'What happened? You were just gone. I turned around and you were gone and I didn't know what to do.'

Her panic wasn't going away.

I looked up at her. Her hair was dripping wet and she was trembling. I put my hand on hers, gripped it.

'I'm fine, seriously. I just got out of my depth and went under for a minute.'

'I couldn't find you. I couldn't see you anywhere. You could have died.'

'I didn't though. Because you saved me.'

That calmed her. Her trembling eased and she let herself smile. I considered telling her what I'd seen, what Mora had said, but the idea of repeating it twisted my stomach. It was nonsense, a vision brought on by fear and lack of oxygen, nothing more.

Nothing more.

'What were you going to say before?' I asked. 'You always thought I was, what?'

She shook her head, fingered the sand and didn't look at me.

'You have to tell me now, I almost drowned.'

She winced, too raw and fresh for jokes.

'Come on, please?'

'I was going to say that I always thought you were a bit . . . a bit of a square. You never do anything crazy is all, but I don't think it really, I was just playing.'

I didn't hear much of what she said after that but she kept rambling, apologising. All I could think of was little Timmy Greer, the kid who threw the first stone at me and Jenny last year. Rudy always called him square, a wuss, a wimp, a boring little idiot who always went home to his mother and always did his homework and never talked back to teacher and was never, ever late for school. That's why that first rock was a shock. That's why it hurt so much and meant so much and that's why he did it. He wanted to break free of that cage everyone else had made for him. I won't be in a cage. A square? A boring, fit-in-the-box-perfectly square? No, sir, not me. Not John Royal.

Gloria was still talking when I kissed her. Right on the lips. My first kiss. Her first kiss. *Bam!* Who's square now?

It took her a second to register what I was doing but then she pressed her lips on mine. It was chaste. No tongue or anything like that but it jump-started something in me. I'd kissed her to prove a point but I forgot that in an instant. I was still kissing her because I wanted to, because she was pretty and nice and I liked her. All of a sudden, I liked her. Like, *liked* her. I'd never seen Gloria that way. She was always just Gloria, a friend who happened to be a girl, but now the tape turned over. Side B. She was a girl. Then she was my friend. And now I was kissing her. Holy *wow*, I was kissing her and she was kissing me back and I realised that I'd always wanted to kiss her, deep down, I really had. When our mouths parted, her cheeks were as red as her hair but she was smiling. Oh yes, was she ever smiling and so was I. I didn't think I'd ever stop smiling.

At this moment in the movie the boy would say, I'm so sorry, miss, I didn't mean to do that without your permission, you're just so gosh-darn beautiful that I couldn't help myself. Then she'd giggle and wave her hand at him.

I didn't apologise. Gloria didn't want me to. I could see that clear enough in the way she looked at me, the way she still held my hand. We didn't move for a moment. A freeze frame beside a calm lake, nothing to see us but the sun and crickets. We were two kids sharing something special, like a first cigarette. People ask, what was your first kiss like? I can tell them now. It was magic. And the longer I sat by that lake, beside Gloria in this strange hush we'd created for ourselves, the more that euphoria settled inside me, gained permanence.

Gloria murmured that we should get going. We collected our clothes and shoes and turned our backs as we dressed.

We walked mostly in silence until we got to the edge of the field bordering the back of the church. Her house was left, down the track that led to Gerrard Street. Mine was back past the church and through the centre of town.

'I'm sorry you got your hair wet,' was the only thing I could think of to say.

'I'll blame you,' Gloria said, biting her lip. The lip that I'd kissed. The one I wanted to kiss again.

'Bye John,' she said and smiled again. The euphoria blazed white at that smile.

'Bye Gloria,' I said. 'See you at school.'

Then she went left and I lingered, watching her. I told myself it was to make sure she was safe. I considered asking to walk her home but if her daddy saw us both wet and smiling, he'd run me off his porch. Besides, I wanted to get home. I wanted to see Jenny and make sure she and Momma were friendly and make sure Eric had cleared the weeds out of the west field.

But all that went to the back of my mind when I walked past the church and saw a light on in the pastor's trailer.

13

The sun was a few hours from setting but the trailer sat in the shadow of the church. It must be close to six o'clock and the pastor didn't open his office past five. At least, that's what he always told me.

'Five is our cut-off, John. Five is when I go home for prayer and privacy so let's wrap it up,' he said if our sessions went on too long.

The light in the back room of the trailer was on. It had been dark when we passed it on the way to Barks. The only room in the trailer with a lock on the door and a blind in the window. For darkness when I take my mid-morning nap, Frank told me once when I asked. My senses buzzed. Everything felt heightened. My wet hair and clinging t-shirt were suffocating while Gloria and the memory of kissing her were like brushing raw nerves, both exhilarating and uncomfortable. I wanted to tell someone, spill out the evening before the joy of it split me open.

I knocked on the trailer door.

'Who's there?' Frank shouted from inside.

'It's me. John.'

A few moments passed, footsteps moved inside. He opened the door but right away I could tell something was wrong. He seemed to look right through me, around me, anywhere but me.

'Come in, son,' he finally said.

Inside, the office smelt of bourbon. I knew the smell, could tell a bourbon from a brandy, a vodka from a gin, just from that sour prickle in the air. Momma taught me without her even knowing.

A single glass stood on the desk, a bead of gold on the rim. Frank, half turned away from me, reached down and placed his finger on the droplet, stuck his finger in his mouth.

The trailer was dark but for the light in the back room. It lit him up like a Halloween ghoul at the edge of the party.

'Is everything okay?' I asked.

'Oh yes,' he said, then saw me staring at the glass. 'Just something to warm the old bones.'

Then he frowned at me. 'Your hair's wet. What have you been doing?'

I blanked. The kiss with Gloria at Barks suddenly seemed like hours ago, the twenty minutes with Miss Eaves, yesterday.

'I had a lesson with Miss Eaves.'

He ran his finger over the rim of the glass again.

'Swimming lesson?' he smiled. 'How was it?'

'Fine, I guess. Algebra.' I watched that finger circle the empty glass, dip into it, streak up the side to pick up as much of the residue as it could.

'Ah, say no more,' he smiled, tapped his nose. 'You didn't knock on my door at this hour to talk lessons, did you?'

My cheeks warmed and the rest of the evening came hurtling back to me. His smile infected me. 'Not exactly.'

'Spill it, John. A fat grin like that usually means a girl's involved. Am I close?'

He flicked on the desk lamp and the room filled with warm yellow. All the initial strangeness fled with the gloom and the pastor smiled. It was as if the drink had pulled the cork out of the uptight churchman, let out all the hot air, left just your average Joe behind. He spoke to me like a man, not a pastor. Like a father might to his son.

My red cheeks blazed and all those excitements, the chest ache, the buzz in the back of my throat, tingle on my lips, all came surging. Red. All red. Everywhere. Love red. Gloria red. It was all I could see.

I told him. Every detail. First kiss, it was special, boy-oh-boy was it ever. All kinds of special. And the redness in my eyes and cheek and neck grew and I thought I was shining like a stoplight.

'Gloria Wakefield?' He sat back, arms crossed. 'That, I wouldn't have pegged.'

I couldn't tell his face, his tone. Was he impressed? Or shocked, because why would a girl like Gloria be interested in a guy like me? A tiny thorn worked its way into my temple.

But he read my worry and plucked out the thorn, like he always did. 'She's a lucky girl to have you,' then he patted the side of my arm, hard.

'This calls for a celebration,' the pastor launched himself from the desk. 'My boy has become a man and with the prettiest girl in town, no less.'

An ember glowed hot white in me when he called me

his boy. He opened one of the desk drawers, the deep lower one, and pulled out a bottle of Wild Turkey bourbon. The good stuff. Momma could only dream of a bottle like that. It was mostly full, just one or two glasses out of it. I would've bet a week's lunch money he'd opened it tonight.

'Been saving this one for a special occasion. This is one of them, that's for sure.'

The pastor uncorked the bottle and waved it under his nose. 'Nothing like that smell, huh, Johnny?'

Nothing like it, that's for damn sure. A hateful smell. The sour sting of Momma, her words and breath tainted with it and Jenny's tears stinging her eyes. Made me sad to see Frank taken in by it but not all those who enjoyed a good whiskey turned monster on it.

He poured a measure into the glass and handed it to me.

'No, thank you, sir.'

Jacobs frowned. 'This is a celebration, isn't it? A man's got to have a drink in his hand for that.'

A tiny change in his tone made me take the glass but couldn't make me drink. I'd promised long ago that I never would. Jenny couldn't live with two of us sodden. He shifted, became looser in his movements, like all his bones had come out of joint.

'What's the matter, John?' Frank took the bottle by the neck and raised it like he was giving a toast. 'Don't want to have a drink with an old man?'

I raised my glass to match him and as he took a mouthful right from the bottle, I mimed it. The smell alone twisted up my stomach. The fake-out worked and Jacobs patted my arm again.

'Ah, John. Nothing like your first kiss. You remember it, treasure it, you hear me?'

'I will.'

He went quiet for a while. Kept the bottle in hand, right up to his lips, but didn't drink again.

The trailer office felt strange to me for the first time. I had a distinct feeling I shouldn't be there, out of hours, in the dark. Felt like by closing the door, I'd closed off the world and this place had its own rules where a pastor could give a fourteen year old expensive bourbon and it was no big deal.

'Nothing like your first kiss,' Frank said again, fainter, to himself. He spoke over the bottle, voice turned hollow echo.

'I remember mine. Norma Fontaine. We were fifteen but she was a woman through and through. She was . . .' He shook his head, took a long suck on the bottle. 'She was a beauty, a top-of-the-pyramid girl, and she picked me. You know, every town has a make-out spot, from here to Virginia all the way across to California. Every town is a carbon goddamn copy. Our spot was called the Look Over. A craggy overhang in the forest that looked out over the town. We biked up there and we were so awkward.' He laughed and the bottle sang. 'Well I was. She knew exactly what she was doing. Girls at that age do. No idea how but they do. You'll see. They know exactly what they're doing way before us fellas do. Norma and I made out for about twenty minutes then she got cold and we rode home.'

He looked over me, past me to some other place, and ground his teeth against the bottle. The sound set the muscles up my neck twitching. The dark on the windows felt like a void, not night, and the streets and the town and the county were all gone. Just me and Frank left, standing in dim yellow light, smell of bourbon and damp corners, voices swaddled by narrow walls and low ceilings.

'I was on top of the world. I picked her a bunch of flowers from my neighbour's garden, risking my skin and good shorts with their nasty dog,' Jacobs said. 'I hid the flowers in my locker at school, planned this stupid romantic gesture at recess, figured I'd have an official girlfriend by last bell. But Norma, she really was a top-of-the-pyramid girl, she didn't see anyone below her. Norma acted like I didn't exist. Ignored me. When I spoke to her she pretended she didn't know who I was. But that's girls for you. Be careful, John. Gloria is lovely, beautiful, but she's still a girl. They know what they're doing. Us men, we're destined to play catch-up. It's only when you get to my age that you take a step ahead.'

The smell of the drink, the low light, his tone, all met and mingled and made my head and stomach ache. Momma got like this when she was on the strong stuff, maudlin and sour. He was no different. He just needs a bed and a strong Backhoe coffee in the morning. That'll right him.

'I'll be careful,' I said. All I could say. Gloria wasn't like his Norma. Gloria was my friend first and that made whatever we had all the more special. She'd never blank me. Ignore me. Make fun of me. She was Gloria.

'Good,' he said, took another mouthful of whiskey.

I waited for the quote from scripture to tell me to watch out for wicked women but nothing came. He hadn't spoken about God in all the time I'd been in the office. Not a verse or a lesson or a mention of Him Upstairs. The unease in my gut turned to outright discomfort. It's just the drink. Momma once said the devil was in the bottle and once the bottle is open you've got to drink it all down to banish him back to Hell. If anyone could take on the devil, it was Frank.

Outside, I heard a truck roar near the church.

The soft atmosphere shattered. Frank's back straightened and his eyes darted window to door to window like a rabbit spying a fox and wondering which way to run. He stood up and set the bottle on the desk so hastily it teetered for a horrible second before righting itself.

His frantic eyes found me, stared like he didn't realise I'd been there the whole time.

'You should be going.'

A heavy, pounding knock shook the trailer.

'It's getting late,' he said. 'You need to head home.'

He all but dragged me to the door, then stopped an inch from the handle. A wide shadow filled the small plastic window and I wondered how any man could be that big and broad.

Frank's hand trembled on my arm. I'd never seen him scared before.

'Who's out there?' I asked.

My voice snapped something in him and he pulled me away from the door, spoke to the room, not to me. 'Sorry, John. This visitor is sensitive. I need you to go out the back door.'

'There isn't a back door.'

He paused. 'There isn't. You're right. There isn't . . .'

He looked around as if this was new information and then ushered me into the back room, closed the door behind us.

'You'll have to use the window.'

He yanked up the sash on the wide back window as the man outside pounded the door a second time.

'What? Frank, what's going on? Who is that guy?'

'No one, no one.'

He strained against the sliding window but it wouldn't

budge. Sweat sheened his forehead and I didn't know where to look, where to stand, how to be. I'd never seen Frank like this, so out of sorts, like his mother had busted in on him with a dirty magazine.

Then he swore and unlocked the catch, slid the window open easily.

Another knock and a shout. 'Preach!'

Frank waved his hands at me. 'Go, go, come on, you're young and fit, you can climb out.'

'Yeah . . . but . . .'

'No buts, John, you have to go. That man is a private man and we have an appointment so he can't see anyone else here.' Then he stopped, eyes locked on mine. 'I'm not asking.'

The window wasn't big and I'd grown an inch or two this past year but Frank's blazing eyes scared me more than his words. I swung one leg out and almost broke my neck trying to bend it through the tiny square. I squeezed my body out the gap but lost my grip on the window frame. In one sickening moment of terror, flailing like a ragdoll, I fell backwards, landed in a butterfly bush.

When I looked up, Frank was gone, the light in the room switched off, and the window closed. He hadn't even waited to see if I was okay. Broken branches dug into my back and sides and I felt the sticky heat of blood on my shoulder. I struggled free, dragging half the bush behind me, but froze when I heard the man's voice again. Inside the trailer.

The knowledge that something in the pastor's office was wrong eclipsed the pain in my back. Was he okay? Did he need my help? He was acting so strange, so different to the person I knew so well.

I'd just wait, listen in, to make sure that man wasn't a danger to him. And if he was, I'd be there to call the sheriff or fight him off. I pressed my back against the rough plastic right below the back window. A sudden drop of guilt hit my stomach. Frank said the man was private and there I was eavesdropping. I shouldn't be here. It could just be some prayer or blessing that didn't take, it happened all the time. Some crazy old widower wants the pastor to pray his wife back from the dead then threatens with a shotgun when it doesn't happen, like he's some miracle worker. Fools. The pastor always soothed those people. Always talked to them calmly and explained God's magical plan. He had that way about him, that gentle tone that fixed an angry mind.

You should leave, John, the voice in my head said.

Just a few more seconds. I had to make sure he was okay. It only took a minute to tune my ears and I could hear every word.

'You shouldn't have come here,' Frank said.

'Oh come now, this is just a friendly visit, one neighbour to the other,' the man said. I knew his voice but couldn't place it. It was deeper than Frank's, rougher.

'Try picking up the phone.'

A bang, like a fist hitting a table. 'I don't 'preciate your tone, preacher.'

Silence. I felt my heartbeat in my throat. There was no calm in Frank tonight, no soothing Bible wisdom.

'You shouldn't have come here,' Frank said again like it would change the man's mind the more he said it.

'Oh calm down now, friend, we ain't gettin' rowdy. We just want to make sure you're still a man we can trust. I've dealt with one dead girl already, I don't want to deal with any more.'

A dead girl. The words hit me like a snowball to the face. The floor creaked as one of them moved.

'You need to leave. Now,' Frank said.

'I been hearing that some kids in town are flappin' gums about the Ridley girl. My employer ain't too happy on that, as you can well imagine. No one wants to be killin' kids, preach, but we got a business to run, *comprende?*'

The other man's deep voice filled with heat and I imagined his eyes blazing devil red.

Kids flappin' gums about the Ridley girl. Mora? A blast of heat scorched my cheeks. That was me. To the sheriff in the Backhoe. Oh shit, Johnny boy, what have you started with your idiot questions?

No one wants to be killin' kids. Your days are numbered if you carry on down this road, bucko. My heart thudded in my ears and my cheeks burned.

'For the last time,' Frank said, almost a growl. 'Get the hell out of my office.'

'I'm bedding down here, preach, till you give me my assurances. The terms of our arrangement ain't changed. You keep your mouth shut, we keep ours shut and we keep the supply coming.'

'Of course,' Jacobs said, barely audible.

That word stuck in my ear. Arrangement. What arrangement could Frank have with a man like this? Some arrangement to get him into Heaven? If that man was as nasty as his voice, it'd take more than greasing a pastor's palm to get him upstairs.

Another movement and the man's voice came closer to the window. 'Don't look so scared, preach. We're not going to incur the wrath of the almighty by hurting one of his chosen people but if we hear any more rumours, any more talk of dear, sweet Mary or a particular car . . .' he trailed off and my gut clenched.

The Dodge. Samuels must have listened to me that day, taken the information and started questioning the town's nastier residents. Mary Ridley. That was her name. Finally, she had a name.

'I get it. Now get out,' Frank all but shouted.

I'd never heard him speak like that, not in all the fire and brimstone sermons, not at kids breaking church windows, not at anyone, about anything. But I guessed this guy wasn't taking no for an answer.

My head throbbed and the rough plastic wall grated against my back. A small group of women carrying trays of food, probably on their way to a potluck, strolled down the street, talking, laughing. I shuffled deeper into the shadow and watched them pass.

The man whistled. 'Oh that's a nice bottle of brown lace you got. Wild Turkey soothes my aching chest, kind of you to give it to me.'

Footsteps shook the trailer and I heard the main door fly open.

'You take care now, father, I'll see you in church on Sunday. Save me a pew, right down at the front. Nice an' close, hey?'

The more I heard of the man's voice the more I recognised it but I still couldn't place it. It wasn't Bung-Eye or Perry Buchanan, wasn't old man Briggs or Al Westin or Gloria's father. I'd know their voices in a second. I gritted my teeth, tried to force the memory but nothing came.

The trailer creaked, like weight had been lifted, and I heard the soft thud of someone stepping onto grass. I didn't look. I didn't dare. It was no one I wanted to see and no one I wanted seeing me.

I listened for the man walking away. Soft steps on grass.

Then sharper, boots on the sidewalk. Fading. The sound of the crickets came back, the buzzing midges around the butterfly bushes.

The world came back into focus. The name, Mora's real name, vibrated inside my head. Mary Ridley. Mary Ridley. Get to Jenny, tell her everything. Find Rudy and Gloria, tell them too. Maybe it'd calm Jenny to know the girl's name, know the police are looking. I jumped up, ran out onto the street. My whole body shook. For a second I didn't know where I was. Too dark, too excited, I felt turned around, I stood in the road and all directions looked the same. A car horn startled me and I stumbled out of the traffic, onto the sidewalk.

I caught my breath and replayed every word of the conversation until I had it memorised. I had a name, the name of a dead girl from a year ago, and I'd made it happen, in a roundabout way. I also had Gloria's kiss still burning on my lips.

Today was a good day. Today was a fucking great day.

I turned around in the middle of the sidewalk, almost knocked into a man walking his dog. The dog yapped and snarled. The man, I recognised him from the Backhoe, sneered at me, said, watch where you're going, kid. I mumbled an apology and walked away but I heard the man mutter the word *freak*. It hung in the air, followed me, but I kept going, ran faster, tried to escape it, but there's no escaping the rumours in this town. Maybe if I went back to Samuels, told him that I have a good head on my shoulders, I can help, let me help, let me tell you about the car and what Bung-Eye said and what just happened in Frank's office. Maybe if I helped solve the murder, people would change my nickname to *hero*.

I couldn't go to Samuels without Jenny and Rudy and Gloria. They were in this as much as I was. We had all found her, we had to do this together.

I started toward home, a bundle of wires in my chest.

I cut through the fields behind town so fast I was flying, my legs retreated and my arms turned to wings, feathers, and I was up up up away from the Dodge and the gruff man in the trailer and toward Jenny and a better life, free of snide remarks and sideways glances, free of Jenny's pale fascination with death.

I crossed Three Points in two leaps, vaulted the fence into our resurrected farm. For the first time since I could remember, our fields bristled with good, fresh corn, green spikes stabbing up through the earth like a bed of nails at the circus. I watched the stalks inch taller by the day and with them grew a future for Jenny and me, a farm I could manage. There was life and vigour under our feet, pulsing around us, fattening the corn ears, making our faded white house a true home.

I burst through the back door into the kitchen. Momma was out with Eric – getting groceries, so said a note on the counter – but I expected they'd stopped at Gum's like usual. I ran up to mine and Jenny's room, through the door so loud she dropped the book she was reading, our second-hand illustrated encyclopaedia, onto the floor.

'What's wrong? Is it Eric?' She sprang up out of bed, bare feet on the floorboards.

'He's fine, fine, it's . . .' I heaved in breath after breath. 'It's Mora.'

'What . . .'

'I . . . found . . .' I stumbled to the bed, sat down to calm myself. 'I found out her name.'

Jenny went to say something, then thought again. She sat beside me. 'Start at the beginning.'

I raced through Miss Eaves and swimming in Barks. I faltered, didn't tell her about Gloria, I couldn't, the words snagged in my throat when I tried. I wanted to keep it mine for a little while longer. I told her about the drink with Frank, every word of the gruff man's threat and Mary Ridley.

Jenny fired up.

'We should go searching for her family, how many Ridleys could there be around here? The cops can't do everything, we have to help.' Jenny grabbed my shoulders. 'We can give the family answers. We found her after all. The sheriff can find her parents and where she was before she died and who was with her. They can find out who killed her. We have to tell them.'

'We will but—'

'But what? We have to help. They've had a whole year and all they've come up with is a name, that's bullshit. How did that man even find it out? Maybe he knows because he killed her? And why would he be telling the pastor unless the pastor has something to do with it?'

The words stung, all the more because they were true. I hadn't considered how Frank could be involved and why the name hadn't become public knowledge. I assumed Samuels had found out, told the man who had told Frank. But why wouldn't they tell everyone? Ask the public if they'd seen this girl last year? Ask anyone if they knew her? A fat worm of doubt wriggled in my stomach.

'Let's get Gloria and Rudy tomorrow and go to Big Lake after school,' Jenny said.

Just the mention of Gloria's name sent a tremor through me and I felt the kiss again.

I nodded. Kept my eyes away from my sister. My face bloomed red. Jenny shifted on the bed. I felt her stare, pressing into the side of my head.

'Is there something you're not telling me?'

I hated to lie but I wasn't ready for the truth. I didn't know yet what the kiss meant. Were me and Gloria going steady? Were we boyfriend–girlfriend? Or had it been a one-off moment of craziness like Frank and his Norma Fontaine?

'Course not. I told you everything,' But her stare didn't waver. Think faster, clearer, better.

'I got excited by the news but now . . . I don't know,' I let my voice sound uncertain. 'Maybe we should leave it to the experts. I guess I'm worried it'll bring up bad memories, you know? After what happened to Rudy . . .' I let the words hang, a note of accusation in my voice to make her feel guilty, steer her away from my secret.

'I suppose,' she said and her stare fell away.

Silence, for a second. Then Jenny said, 'Why is your hair wet?'

My heart skipped. Think, think, think.

'Miss Eaves,' I blurted out. 'She tripped. Spilled ice tea all over me. She let me have a shower.'

Jenny raised one eyebrow, just like Momma did. Today was the first time I'd outright lied to my sister. All because I went swimming and kissed a girl and couldn't bring myself to say it out loud. I hated myself right then. I'd let something, someone, come between me and my sister and I wanted to scream.

'Your shirt is clean though,' Jenny said. 'What's going on? What aren't you telling me?'

Thunder filled my ears, raging heart, raging blood. Stop lying, John Royal, lying never got you anywhere.

'She washed it,' I said. 'And put it in her dryer.'

Jenny took the hem of my t-shirt between her fingers, rubbed it. 'That was nice of her.'

I smiled, nodded, couldn't think of anything else to say.

I picked up the encyclopaedia from the floor and smoothed out the creased pages. 'It was good, though, the lesson. It helped.'

That was enough to take Jenny's interest down a peg. 'I should have asked. Sorry. What was it like?'

Easier, whiter lies came out of my mouth. Algebra and vocabulary, I said, boring really.

We settled into normalcy. I read my bird book while Jenny brushed her hair before bed. She said that one day she would go to a fancy salon and have her hair washed and cut and blow-dried big and bouffant and come out looking like Lana Turner.

I tried to listen while Jenny talked about school and our friends, but my mind kept going back to the kiss, to Gloria and what it felt like. I remembered the look on Gloria's face, the fear when she pulled me out of the water, the shock then shy happiness when our lips parted, the never-ending smile. The deep want and need to do it again and again. That was worth the lies to my sister, at least for tonight.

In the morning we went to school and Jenny and me hung out with Rudy, Gloria and Scott Westin. Everything was normal. Gloria and I occasionally caught each other's eye and tried to hide a smile. We talked about Rudy's stellar plan to be running back for the Lions, Gloria's useless piano lessons, Jenny's latest fashion experiment with one of the cousins' hand-me-down dresses. Gloria and I acted like friends who weren't that close. Rudy and me joked and he teased Scott. Jenny laughed, called Rudy names. When Scott wasn't around, and Rudy and Gloria were over the shock of learning her name, we finally talked about Mary Ridley and what we should do. We never came to an agreement.

Rudy wanted to handle it ourselves, not involve the cops. Gloria wanted more hard evidence so we could nail the guy first time. Jenny wanted to go to Samuels right this minute, and me, I wanted to leave it to the professionals and concentrate on keeping up my grades, keeping the farm going.

The four of us discussed it most days and soon the urgency waned except with Jenny. With her, Mary Ridley was like a best friend she had to save. Jenny spoke about her with such familiarity, I almost believed she knew the girl and it scared me. Jenny was slipping away again and this time, I didn't know how to keep her with me. I knew it would need all my attention but I couldn't give it to her.

No. Not couldn't. Wouldn't.

My heart overrode my head, pulled me away from my sister and toward my friend. Girlfriend? I still wasn't sure.

On Wednesday, after our second lesson with Miss Eaves, Gloria and I went to Fisher's Point. I kissed her again and I lied about it again. I hated myself for lying. I knew keeping something like this from Jenny would hurt her when she found out but I couldn't help it. I was swept up with Gloria, it was all so new and frightening, all raw nerves and electric shocks but oh so wonderful.

I kept putting off going to Samuels despite Jenny's demands, kept giving her reasons to delay, kept sneaking off to see Gloria and lying about it again and again, and not just to Jenny. To Rudy. To Momma. To Eric. Those lies became an endless stream rushing from one trickle. They soaked everything, fed into everything. They bore me along until I found myself in the middle of an ocean, my boat leaking, my oars broken. I felt the pressure building all around me. From below the water, Mary Ridley's phantom clawed for me, Death's icy hand reaching. From above, Jenny pushed me in one direction, Rudy in another, my conscience stuck between them, my nerves wrecked and shaking.

But Gloria sat with me in the boat and calmed the tide. I could ignore almost anything else. Her and me and nobody else, just for a little while longer.

14

That summer was like watching a car wreck in slow motion. First the minivan jack-knifed, then the motorcycle swerved and skidded onto its side, a truck screeched its brakes and slammed into the minivan, crushed the motorcycle, another car flipped, rolled and smashed, joined the metal fray. It was like a magnet pulled all these vehicles, these events, together into one big mess. Gasoline spilled, sparks flew, the glut of twisted steel became a fireball on the highway.

That was summer '72. The black smoke that wouldn't clear no matter the strength of the wind, the sallow faces and red-rimmed eyes of the townsfolk. It made all my secrets feel tiny, insignificant.

July 15th was the minivan, the week after my run-in with Darney Wills at the Backhoe. The first destruction that led to all the rest. Everyone in Larson remembers where they were that day. They say, 'I was cashing a cheque when . . .' and trail off before getting to the meat of it. There was never a need to say it outright, everyone knew. 'I was in the Backhoe when the sheriff came in . . .', 'I was making dinner when my husband rang to say . . .'

I was at home with Jenny. It was a Saturday and we were clearing up the plates after Eric made lunch. He was outside with Momma, having a smoke on the porch. When me and Jenny were done wiping down the dinner table, I said I needed to speak to Eric. Eric was like Superman to me back then. The way he fit so much into one day. It felt like he was always at home, always at the mill, always at a town meeting talking about a protest and then always looking after us when Momma was working or drinking or sleeping it off. He was the closest I ever got to a real father. Him and Frank. I thought I'd ask him to fix the tyre swing. Old man Briggs two farms over still had those tyres he promised us a few years back. I'd seen them piled up at the edge of his yard, higher than ever, and I was sure he wouldn't miss one or two.

'Eric would hang it,' I said to Jenny as I wrung out the dishcloth and draped it over the edge of the sink, just like Momma taught me to.

'Why are we even talking about this?' she said, absently twisting her hair into a single braid.

'What do you mean? We've wanted the swing back for ages.'

She shook her head, the exasperation in her movement made me flinch. 'That's kids' stuff. You can be a real idiot sometimes, John.'

She never called me John. It was always Johnny. Another flinch.

She came beside me, let the braid fall and unravel. She leaned in so her voice wouldn't carry outside. 'We have to go to Samuels.'

My heart dropped.

'You said we would,' she kept on. 'Right after your lesson with Miss Eaves, right after we talked it all through with Rudy and Gloria. I know they don't want to go yet but I do. You said we would. We know her name and we know about the car. We have to tell them.'

'But Samuels knows about the car and he must know her name by now.'

'But not the details! Not what Rudy's dad said. I thought you wanted to help Mary. She needs our help.' Her sweet voice was a harsh whisper, just like Momma's. 'I thought you wanted to help catch whoever hurt her.'

'I do but what can we do?'

'We can go and we can tell Sheriff Samuels what we know, everything we know. Now. What if he doesn't know her name? What if all that's stopping him from finding her parents or who killed her is *you*?'

'But the swing . . .'

'Who cares about the stupid swing?' Her whisper gone, her voice too loud. Momma's laugh filtered through the windows and walls. Eric always found a way to make her laugh.

That laugh was like a slap to Jenny. She hushed, calmed.

'What if it was me?' she asked.

I shot her a look.

'What if, huh?' she said. 'Would you wait all this time if it was me shot and dumped in Big Lake?'

Every word and the pictures they conjured were knives in my chest. Her golden hair turned grey, her skin bloated, her eyes milky. What had she said last year, when I asked why she went back to the body? *I wanted to see what would happen to me if a fight ever . . . if she drank too much . . .*

She leaned closer. 'I know you've got secrets. Something's been going on with you but you won't tell me. Don't you trust me? Don't you love me any more?'

'Of course. I love you more than anyone.'

How could she think otherwise? Had I neglected her that much? I tried to count like Frank taught me when I got upset. One-one-thousand . . . but Jenny's eyes were on me and I couldn't think of the numbers.

'So if Mary was me, would you go to Samuels?'

'In a second. I'd never stop until I found who hurt you.' My words came out in one fierce stream, my eyes on hers so she could see how much I meant it.

Then Jenny's arms were around me. My shoulders relaxed, my arms swept around her and hugged her back.

All would be fine. It was just a moment. A crazy horrible moment that she put in my head and then took away. The thought of someone hurting her, the image of her dead and rotting and nobody caring, the thought of her thinking I didn't love her, it was too much. The moment exploded and I wasn't her Johnny any more. Right then I was venge-ance. I was Death, all spiked feathers and dagger claws. Jenny brought me back, I didn't even need to count.

'Sorry,' I said again because it was all I could think of to say.

'Let's go to Samuels. Now.'

'Okay.'

If nothing else, a visit to Samuels could stem this growing darkness in my sister, end the obsession and bring back the sunshine girl she used to be.

Jenny put a flask of water and a handful of graham crackers wrapped in paper in her bag. We weren't stupid. One time last summer me and Jenny took a walk through the fields toward town when Momma sent us to post a letter and pick up eggs from Mrs Morton's hens. On the way back the track leading through Morton's back field was blocked, the old man was working the land, parked his tractor right on the path and hollered all sorts when he saw us coming. The detour took us a mile and a half out of the way. The sun was relentless. Worst summer heat in a hundred years so they said last year. It burned our scalps, dried us out, turned our blood to molasses, sluggish, thick. Jenny fainted right on the Three Points, that spit of no-man's-land between irrigation canals. She hit the ground and didn't get up. Impossibly still, unbearably silent. I shouted. I cried. I couldn't leave her, I couldn't help her. Old man Morton found us hours later. Momma, slurring and red-faced, hadn't even noticed we weren't back with the eggs.

We had a flask every day since then.

'Hand me that,' Jenny said, pointing to her scarf, the one with the blue stars, on the hook by the door.

I did. Watched her tie it neatly around her neck. So simple, so beautiful. Her fingertips brushed her throat, pale, barely touched by the sun.

I was invisible next to my sister, she the sun and I the moon. All I was, bright and gleaming in the dark, was because of her. Her light. Her attention. And when she shone, I happily faded.

'Shouldn't you dress smarter to see the sheriff? You look like a homeless person,' Jenny said, her eyes running up and down me.

A too-big white t-shirt and pair of old jeans cut off just above the knee. They weren't cool or stylish but Eric had given them to me and I liked them. It never seemed to

matter if I came home with mud or grass stains, the denim
was tough and cleaned right up.

I smiled.

'I think I'm handsome enough. Ready?' I said and took
the bag, which now, along with the crackers, contained two
squares of Eric's cornbread, my favourite, and slung it over
my shoulder.

I pushed open the screen door to the front porch. Like
startled rabbits, Momma and Eric sprang apart, their faces
all blush and bother. Momma's elbow knocked an Old
Milwaukee and sent it tumbling off the porch, spilling
frothing beer all over the ground.

'Damn it, John,' Momma said, wiping her lipstick,
straightening her blouse. 'Why do you sneak around?'

Eric adjusted his posture, rested both arms in his lap.
He wouldn't look right at me, rather his eyes traced the
shape of me, sticking to my edges.

'I'm sorry,' I said slowly, not at all sure what I'd interrupted. Jenny stood behind me, tense and ready to bolt.

'Can we go out?' I said.

A moment of hush as we waited, Jenny, Eric and me, to
see what Momma would say. The afternoon sun painted
this side of the house, turned the greying paint a brilliant
white for an hour or two a day. That's when Momma most
liked to sit outside, when her house looked the best.

'Where to?' Momma said, hard but not fierce.

'The Roost,' I said. The truth wouldn't sit well with
Momma. Any mention of Samuels or Mora's body would
send us to our room.

Momma glanced at Eric; her blush faded, his didn't.

'Have you done your chores?'

'Yes,' we both said.

'Come out here, let me look at you,' she said, grabbed my hand and pulled me out of the doorway, exposing Jenny.

Momma's eyes went from Jenny's sandals up to her hair, lingering on her legs and shoulders. 'Where did you get that dress?'

Jenny swallowed so loud I could hear her throat working. 'The cousins.'

Momma's mouth twisted. 'I'll bet it looked better on them.'

'Patty.' Eric put his hand on Momma's knee, then looked at Jenny. 'You look very pretty.'

Idiot. You idiot, why would you say that? Haven't you learned anything?

Momma threw Eric's hand away but kept her attention on Jenny. 'Pretty? She looks like a little girl trying to be a woman,' she sneered. 'Like she'd ride with any boy who asked and then say thank you when they're done with her.'

'Momma . . .' I tried but the monstrous moment passed.

'Get out of here, both of you,' she said and waved her hand.

Eric gave us a sad smile and we hurried off the porch before Momma could change her mind. I heard Eric say something like, 'You're too hard on them', and I thanked him in my head even though it was his fault the monster woke up and clawed its cage.

Jenny and me walked single-file through the cornfields, the stalks tall as my ears and still growing. She didn't speak and I knew enough not to push her. Momma had this searing, fizzing effect on Jenny, like when you burn your arm taking a pot roast from the oven. The initial contact with the hot metal is a shock, a gasp, a what-the-hell-just-happened moment. You inspect the wound and see a silver line, only hurts a little, it's not until afterwards, when your body has had time to react and defend itself, that the pain kicks in. Momma's words were the hot iron door and they were just starting to blister.

When we were halfway through the field and far enough away that nobody would hear us, Jenny let the pain out.

'Why does she do that?' she said and ripped a thick, green leaf from a stalk. The stalk swayed and creaked, sent its neighbours dancing with it.

'She's just trying to look out for you.'

'She's jealous of me.' Jenny ripped the leaf to pieces. 'I'm young, she's not. I'm pretty, she's not. She's an ugly old cow and she knows it.'

'You shouldn't talk about Momma like that.'

'Whose side are you on?' She turned on me, dropped the leaf scraps in the dirt.

'No one's. Yours.'

'Whatever, John. God, you're so annoying sometimes.' She shook her head and started walking again.

It pained me, deep in my chest, to hear harsh words about my mother. She was half my world and Jenny the rest. It was like swallowing giant pills, all dry and sticking to my throat, to listen and not scream in her defence. Momma is trying her best, she loves us both, I wanted to say, she's just protecting you, making sure you don't give out the wrong impression and get yourself in trouble like she did when she was young. It's all for you, Jenny, don't you see?

'She'll never change,' Jenny said. 'She doesn't know how. All this, it'll just get worse. We're leaving that house as soon as I turn sixteen, like we always said.'

'Mmhmm,' I said. It wasn't the gung-ho yes ma'am, we're

outta here answer she wanted. I had a worm in my gut at the thought of leaving Momma, leaving the farm and even leaving Larson. It was all I'd ever known, all I'd ever wanted. The farm was flourishing and this year I knew we'd have a corn crop to rival Briggs and Morton. It'd put the Royals on the map. Ours would be the biggest harvest, the best quality, all because of me and Eric. We'd be rolling in cash and soft white flour. How could I want anything else?

'John.' Jenny looked over her shoulder. 'As soon as I turn sixteen we leave, promise me.'

I met her eyes but couldn't hold them. I nodded a false promise and that seemed to be enough for her. Like Momma always said, a promise not spoken out, so both God and the devil can take note, ain't no promise at all.

15

Black clouds grew in the east, turning the edge of the sky dark as we walked into Larson. It made me nervous, the size of those clouds, the weight of them pressing down on us. I wanted to get back to the farm, protect the crop somehow. Maybe I could string up a dozen tarps, give the corn a raincoat. Rudy would help. Maybe Gloria would too. It might almost be fun. Soon as this business with Samuels was done, I'd beat the rain home and get started.

Me and Jenny talked about a handful of things, Mary Ridley, school, the farm, which she didn't care a stitch for, and Eric. He said he'd take Jenny, and me I suppose but he never said, to Washington DC to see the anti-war marches or to a Joni Mitchell concert in Chicago. He had a soft spot for Jenny, one that Momma liked to take a pin to. We discussed how we would tell Samuels about Mary Ridley and the car and if we should mention Pastor Jacobs. No, we decided at the edge of town, two streets from the sheriff's station, we'd just tell him that I overheard two men talking near the pastor's office and the girl's name was mentioned. We would remind Samuels about the Dodge and what Bung-Eye had said, *That cocksucker didn't have to kill her.* He could only be talking about Mary Ridley.

'Samuels can do whatever he wants with that information,' Jenny said. 'All I care about is finding Mary's parents. We should look them up, get a bus to them. She's what matters. Her family needs peace.'

'I hope he finds whoever did it. They deserve to hang.'

Jenny smiled and took my hand, held it as we walked. At the corner of Main and Wade Street, I noticed a group of women sitting outside the beauty parlour. They reminded me of a line of crows on a fence, screeching their business, oblivious to their volume or curious ears, but when Jenny and me passed, they hushed.

Watched.

The nail files slowed. The lipstick stalled halfway to their lips. The crow eyes followed us and the squawks turned to whispers.

'You two out for a pop an' ice cream?' one of the women said, the one with the puffiest hair who I recognised from school pick up.

Jenny smiled sweetly. 'Just a walk.'

'Yah, yah,' they said, nodding. And the school pick up lady continued. 'Careful now. Bad folks in town these days.'

Her eyes locked on me.

'Oh you betcha,' she said. 'All kinds of bad.'

The women tutted and shook heads and made squalling *mmhmm* noises.

I remembered the shouts and whispers in the school halls, the ones I thought had died away over the winter. *Murderer, killer, John Royal did it, didn't he?* And Darney Wills in the Backhoe, *Heard you mighta even killed her*. Half the town was in the diner that day. Half the town heard. They would have recounted the tale to the others, spread the infection. I remembered the man with his dog who called me a freak.

It's still happening, John, it'll never end. In the small minds of a small town, once a killer always a killer, no matter the truth.

'Come on,' I said and pulled Jenny on.

'Bye now,' I called to the women and the crows snapped away from us, on to more important topics. The lipstick finished its round. The nail files scraped away snags. The birds resumed their cacophony.

'What was that about?' Jenny asked as we got to the station.

'Gossips. You know what they're like.'

I pushed open the door to the sheriff's station and ushered her inside as the first spots of rain hit the sidewalk. I cast a quick glance over the street. A few people around, going about their Saturday. Nobody to notice me.

I slipped inside and joined Jenny in front of the reception desk. The station was almost empty, only one deputy and Mrs Drake, the receptionist, visible. It didn't feel right. The air smelt different, tense and full like a coming storm.

'He's not here,' the Drake said to Jenny. 'Come back on Monday.'

Jenny's jaw flexed, teeth clenched.

'Where is he? It's important,' I said.

The Drake, even more waspish and pinched than last year, stared at me over her glasses, all dried-out and crooked.

'Come back on Monday.'

Jenny looked at me. 'Tell her, Johnny.'

'We need to speak to Samuels,' I said. My voice gained power in the face of that cross. We were on the same side.

The Drake tilted her glasses down. 'The *sheriff*,' she paused, let the emphasis sink in, 'is not here.'

The phone rang. A sharp trill in the empty station.

Mrs Drake picked up the receiver, held it between shoulder and head. Done with us. Get out now. It doesn't matter how important it is, that a girl died, that a murderer is free, that the darkest parts of Larson, the Buchanans, are involved. No sir, that doesn't matter because the sheriff isn't here, probably at the Backhoe relieving Didi of half an apple pie. Come back on Monday.

We stood there, stuck, waited for Mrs Drake to be finished, but as we watched, her face changed. The hard lines on her forehead cracked, eyes widened, turned white.

She put down the phone with a trembling hand.

'What is it?' Jenny said, the anger and impatience gone, concern in their place.

She didn't say anything, just got up. Still shaking. Looked right through us. The air in the station, close and cloying from the summer heat and heavy clouds, turned electric. She took uncertain steps, like the ground had moved beneath her and she couldn't find her footing. Using the wall, then a desk, to keep herself upright, she crossed to the other side of the room, to the single deputy on duty.

'What do you think's happened?' Jenny whispered to me.

'Something bad,' I said. I could feel it, in the air, in my bones.

They say twins can sense when the other is hurt even when they're miles apart. Small towns are the same. When the town is rocked, everyone can sense it. Homely smells turn to garbage, favourite flavours turn bitter, the sidewalks, the roads, the floorboards, turn soft, uneven. Then the rumours begin.

I edged closer to the pair, caught the tail of the panic.

'Christ,' the deputy said, grabbed the back of his neck like it was going to explode.

'You have to go,' Mrs Drake said, tapping him on the arm.

His expression matched hers. A breath. A beat. Let it all sink in.

The deputy snatched a set of keys from a box on the wall, and ran to the exit. Right past us. Without a glance or word. His eyes were red. His body shaking. The receptionist stayed by the desk, fixed in place like she'd been hit with a freeze ray. Me and Jenny forgotten.

'Come on,' Jenny tugged at my shirt.

'Where?'

'Wherever he is going.'

But we heard the rumble of the Plymouth engine and the screech of hot tyres and knew it was too late to follow.

Curiosity burnt my insides. The news, whatever it was, would be all over Larson tomorrow, remoulded and warped to fit the speaker. But I wanted to know first, wanted to know the truth, the real story behind the inevitable rumours. Whatever it was had emptied the station. Samuels would be busy for days, even longer no doubt. That meant more time for Jenny to descend into her darkness, to talk and plan and obsess over Mary Ridley. Once she had her fist around an idea, she'd punch you with it until you gave up. At least I could say we tried to speak to Samuels. Maybe that would be enough for now.

We left the station and the sun disappeared behind a

heavy plume of cloud. Meagre rain struggled through hot air, turned the grey asphalt polka-dot black.

'What now?' Jenny asked, fidgeting on the sidewalk, wringing her hands, jumping from foot to foot.

'Go home, I guess.'

'I don't want to go back there. She'll be steaming drunk by now. Let's go to the Fort. Maybe Rudy will be there.'

Once we were out of town, on the long road home, the clouds let rip. The light rain turned heavy, streaming straight down in fat lines and the sharp musk of the earth rose all around us, sweeter and richer for the dry summer heat. On the road ahead, a few hundred feet past the turn-off to Briggs' farm track, I saw a shape in the streaking rain. A car waiting in the verge, two tyres on the road, two on the grass.

A Ford. *The* Ford. Even in the gloom, even squinting against the driving rain, I knew it, I'd recognise it anywhere.

'Death,' I whispered. My blood turned to ice inside me, the warm rain froze as it hit my skin, my hair, my face, the ground around me. I was marked. I was stalked.

'What?' Jenny said. 'What did you say?'

I grabbed Jenny back. Both her shoulders in my hands. 'Do you see it?' I shouted. 'Do you see Death? There! Look!'

'I don't see anything,' Jenny said, squinting against the glare and the rain.

'It's right there.' But the more I strained my eyes against the weather, the more the pale grey car seemed to fade into the rain.

'Come on,' Jenny said. 'We have to get under cover.'

I didn't take my eyes off the road, let Jenny drag me to Briggs' track until I almost tripped over a rock and had to pay attention. The car had been there, I knew it.

Just your mind playing tricks, Johnny boy.

I'd seen it. Hadn't I?

When I looked back, I saw only the dreary grey of heavy rain, the same grey as the car, as the pale horse. I was seeing things, had to be.

Jenny snapped at me. 'Earth to John! What's wrong with you?'

And the world was back in focus. The wheat bent under the deluge and the dry ground turned to slick, oily mud. But we were lightning through the fields, dodging raindrops and swaying corn stalks, and then we were at the pathway to the Roost, soaked through and out of breath. We slid down the slope and ran for the Fort. The rain beat against the leaves like a million tiny drums, turning the covered valley into a sweaty jungle. Finally inside the Fort, the fat drops rang from the tin roof, filled the shack with off-key music and, now out of the rain, my sister's laughter.

'It hasn't rained like this for years!' she said, wringing out her hair.

'It shouldn't last long.'

But it did. The rain kept up for the better part of an hour but the Fort was well built and kept everything out. I kept thinking about the corn, how it hated the rain, and how I would string up the tarps in time for the next storm. We sat in silence for a while, reading some of Rudy's super-hero comics and playing a few rounds of rummy. We didn't talk about what might have happened in town to set the sheriff's station so on edge and I didn't mention the pale car, what it meant. Jenny was fragile enough with all this Mary Ridley business, I couldn't throw a whole other heap of crazy into the mix.

I heard something outside and dropped my cards.

Wet, slapping footsteps, running toward us.

Then the door swung open and Rudy barrelled inside, slamming the door behind him.

'Oh man,' he said, panting, lying on his back on the wooden boards. 'Am I glad to see you two!'

'Why?' Jenny asked.

I reached down to pull Rudy up but he waved me away. 'Leave me! I'm drowning!'

'I'll throw you in Big Lake, that'll show you drowning, you fruit,' I said and a blush formed on my cheeks, the memory of Gloria pulling me out of Barks, the first kiss.

'Did you guys hear?' Rudy said, up on his elbows, blond hair flat and dripping. 'There's been a car wreck. A real bad one.'

Jenny straightened, shuffled closer to Rudy. 'Where? Did someone die?'

Rudy nodded. 'Two I think. Don't know who though. Samuels called Perry and the old man to bring out the tow truck to the trainyard.'

'The trainyard? The one near Gum's?' I asked.

'Uh-huh. They said someone parked on the tracks and *wham!*'

'Oh my God,' Jenny said, eyes blazing with curiosity, obsession. 'Who do you think it was?'

Rudy shrugged. 'Guess the ole Larson rumour mill will let on tomorrow. But the old man said Samuels thought the car was there on purpose, you know. Dad said, "What kind of retard parks on train tracks to take a nap, huh?"'

I swallowed. 'That's a real bad way to go.'

Rudy and Jenny kept talking but a stark, terrible thought hit me. Two people in Larson were dead. Momma and Eric went to Gum's all the time. It wasn't crazy to think they

went on a sauced-up joyride and ended up at the trainyard,
fell asleep in the truck like they sometimes did. I felt sick
deep in my gut and wanted to hurl up the nothing I'd
eaten since breakfast. Instead I grabbed the backpack and
wolfed down a square of cornbread, soggy in one corner
from the rain.

Jenny and Rudy both stopped to look at me.

'Hungry there, lardass?' Rudy, still lying down, kicked
my shin.

That's when I noticed the rain had stopped. Something
gnawed at my insides after seeing, or not seeing, the pale
Ford. Now, with this trainyard news, I felt lost, needed to
speak with someone who wasn't going to laugh at me.

'I've got to go,' I said, mouth full of cornbread. 'Got to
see the pastor and borrow a book off him.'

Right then, I didn't care that I was lying to my sister and
my best friend, I just wanted out.

'Jenny, you'll be home by dark, right?'

She nodded.

'Rudy, make sure she gets there?'

'You got it, chief.'

'I'm not a baby, John, I don't need a chaperone,' Jenny
whined.

'Please?' I said. 'Just let Rudy walk you home.'

Rudy swung his arm around my sister. 'Just you and me,
doll. I'll treat you right.' Then he winked at me and laughed.

'See you guys later,' I said and rushed out of the Fort.

The leaves still dripped and the clouds hung black in
the sky. My shirt and shorts stuck to my skin and a cold
prickle ran through my hair. Stiff-limbed and shivering, I
headed for the road. I came out of the trees, felt like I was
emerging into a new, different world. Toward town and off

to the right, the white Larson water tower rose and, between that and me, the peak of the church spire. To the far north of the church, the tip of the Easton mill's grain elevator, owned by Mark Easton's father. That grain elevator was part of Larson as much as the water tower, the church, the asphalt coating the roads, the pancakes in the Backhoe and it would endure, despite Mark's draft. Those high parts of town were my landmarks, my touchstones. I could never be lost. To me, Larson was a loop, you left on one end of Main Street but always found yourself at the other, no matter how far you walked. It comforted me to always be so close to home. Home is where the heart is, Momma always said, and where it's left unprotected. The best things always happen at home, she says, and the worst.

I kept an eye out for the pale Ford all the way to town but it never showed. Now, more than ever, I was convinced that car was not what it appeared. It was always there, right where Death touched down in our town. Mary Ridley. The two poor souls at the trainyard. Who else? Who next?

Finally, after it felt like I'd been walking for days, I reached the church. It was Saturday, late afternoon, so it was a long shot he'd be there, but I found Frank in his pulpit, practising his sermon for the day. He didn't see me at first as he boomed out the words, fist closed and shaking up at the heavens. It gave me a shiver to watch him, without him knowing I was there.

'Idle talk, like idle hands, are tools of Satan himself,' he cried, his powerful voice resounding off the walls. 'Proverbs teaches us to keep private matters private and I say to you, my good friends, do you want hands in your underwear drawers? Do you want hands pulling out your secrets and flashing them to the whole town? No you don't! No, ma'am, no sir, no child, you do not.' He stabbed at the air with one rigid finger.

He's talking about you, Johnny, my head said. All those shouts of 'freak' and 'killer'. He was talking about me, telling all those busybody townsfolk, all those cawing crows outside the beauty parlour, all the Darney Wills and gossiping kids at school, to stop it. Stop their chatter and their hurtful words. A swell of warmth grew in my stomach, up to my chest and cheeks, and I was smiling as he carried on.

'Rumours buzz around this town like flies on dung and I say to you, this must stop. Idle talk, people. The sin of the loose tongue. We are one people. We are a *community* and we must join hands, come on now,' he clasped his hands together, showing the empty pews what to do. 'Join hands with your neighbour beside you right now. Love thy neighbour, trust thy neighbour, for we are all God's children under this burning sun.'

Then he trailed off, read from his notes and recited a few words with different emphasis, clasped his hands together in a different way.

I coughed from the back of the room and he jumped.

'Good Lord, John!'

I walked up the aisle. 'Sorry, Frank. I didn't mean to intrude.'

He shook his head, a slight bloom of red on his cheeks. 'No, no. It's no intrusion. What are you doing here on a Saturday, shouldn't you be off with your friends?' As I got closer, he saw the state of me, t-shirt still damp in places, huge streaks of mud on my legs and shorts from sliding down to the Roost. 'What happened?'

'Oh nothing,' I said. 'You told me to tell you if I saw that car again. The grey Ford.'

His eyes burned into mine at the mention, and he stepped off his podium, came right up to me.

'Where did you see it?'

'Just outside town. Jenny and me were walking home and it was sat there on the side of the road, in the rain.'

'Did you see a driver this time?'

I shook my head and he put his arm around my shoulders.

'You were right about the car,' I said, the knowledge sat inside me like a stone, weighed me down. 'It is Death, I think. The first time I saw it was just after we found that woman, again today . . . I heard something happened at the trainyard.' *Momma and Eric might be cut to bloody shreds.* 'We moved the girl's body last year. It's like we let Death in. Opened a door and now he's following me. It always seems to be there when something happens. Something bad.'

'All right, John, calm down. I'm sure it's some joyrider. I heard about the trainyard, terrible, just terrible. Two kids, I heard.'

A great rush of air escaped my lungs. Kids. Not Momma. Not Eric. Thank you, God.

'I shouldn't have scared you with Revelations,' he said and guided me back up the aisle, toward the doors. 'Steer clear of the car, you hear me? You tell me when you see it, every time.'

'I will,' I said as we got to the exit. He patted me on the back and shook my hand.

'It's just a car, John, with a real person driving it. Nothing to worry about. Will I see you and your sister at tomorrow's service?'

I tensed. I didn't like sermons. Felt like I was being yelled at for no reason and I had chores on the farm to tend. With all that rain, I'd have to check the barn for leaks, clear out the drainage channels. All sorts.

'I'm not sure,' I said, voice weak with excuses. 'Jenny isn't feeling too good, you see, I think she's coming down with something rotten and I'll need to take care of her at home.'

Protect her from a sodden Momma more like. 'And I have chores, you know.'

Frank smiled. 'Of course. Give her my best.'

I said I would and left. As I walked back home, I was on high alert for the Ford. I wanted to confront it, storm up to the window and demand an answer, punch the guy right on the nose if he talked back. But the appeal of that plan quickly waned. What if it was truly Death and that's exactly what he wanted me to do? One touch from his bony hand and I'd be dead meat.

When I got back home, Momma's truck wasn't there. I went in through the back door, found a note from Eric on the counter. *Hey kiddos, heading out for a pair of frosties. My famous mac n' cheese is in the oven, you know what you do. Be good, peace, E.*

Nothing from Momma. Never anything from Momma. Jenny was in the family room and I called to her.

'There's mac n' cheese. You hungry?' I said.

Jenny trotted in, hair twisted up in a towel, wearing a clean t-shirt and the flared jeans she made with Eric.

I opened the oven and the smell of cold, melted cheese hit me. I smiled. 'Cold?'

There was something clandestine in the thought of eating dinner food differently, like we were in charge, we were the adults. In that one small act, we were deciding how to live our lives, just like grown-ups do.

Jenny joined my smile, my thought. 'With bread and butter.'

'Coming right up.'

I dished up the food, left enough for breakfast if Momma and Eric weren't home by then, and sat down to eat. It didn't take long for the atmosphere to sink. Jenny stopped eating halfway into her plate, forked at a glob of cheese.

'The sheriff won't care about Mary now, will he?'

'I doubt it.'

She sighed, eyes on her plate, pushing the lump of cheese around in circles. 'But I still care.'

'So do I.' *I care about you more and keeping you away from all this darkness.* 'Pastor Jacobs heard about the wreck, said it was kids in the car.'

'Oh God,' she said and fell silent for a moment. 'Why did you want to see him so bad? It wasn't to borrow a book because you didn't come home with one.'

Shit. Rookie mistake. I shrugged it off. 'I just had to talk to him about something.'

She glared at me. 'I don't know why you trust him. He creeps me out.'

I wanted to say, because he listens. Because he cares. You should give him a chance. But I didn't say that. Frank was my own, personal Pigeon Pa and I didn't want to lose that.

So I said, 'He's nice to me.'

She didn't say anything for a while, picked some more at her food, then stood up, came over to me and threw her arms around my shoulders. A surge went through me and I hugged her back, her head resting against my neck.

'Maybe it'll stop now,' she said. 'Now they have something

else to talk about. I don't want more people calling me a freak. I don't want them to throw stones again.'

Or thinking you killed someone. 'I hope so. I'm going to go out and check on the corn.'

Jenny nodded as if she'd expected it. Always out in the fields, John, she'd say, careful or I might think you liked it on this shitty farm.

I ducked into the barn to get my shovel but spotted a leak in the roof, even though the rain had stopped, dripping right onto our '55 corn picker. The picker was seized up, would need some love, but solid American-made underneath. The picker was left here when my real pa left, a vicious-looking three-pronged machine for cutting and shelling corn, green paint faded and peeling. I didn't have a tractor to run it but one day I'd buy Briggs' John Deere and then there'd be no stopping the Royals. But that's of course, if the damn thing didn't get rust from a leaky roof. I threw a tarp over the picker and climbed the ladder to the hay loft. I hadn't got halfway up when I heard Jenny calling from the barn door.

'Come quick,' she shouted up to me. 'It's Rudy!'

My heart leapt. Blood rushed all over me. Rudy, in trouble? Was he in that car wreck? No, of course he wasn't. Then what? I rushed down and back into the house to find the phone on the kitchen table, long cord strung across the room. I let out all my air and put my hands on my knees.

'Jesus, Jenny. I thought he was in trouble.'

'Just listen.' She picked up the phone, turned it so we could both hear.

A frantic Rudy shouted down the crackling line.

'You both there? Shit, guys, you'll never believe it,' he

said, out of breath from running up to the payphone at the end of Buchanan road. 'My dad and Perry just got home and man . . .' he paused and we heard him take giant gulps of air. 'The kids killed at the trainyard. Holy shit, guys, it's so messed up. The old man said they really had been there on purpose, the way the car was or something. Idiots parked right in the middle of the tracks and waited. Guys, *Jesus*, they know who it was, found ID or something. Fuck, guys.'

'Rudy, spit it out, who was it?'

Another wheezing breath. 'Mark Easton and Tracy Meadows.'

16

Mark and Tracy's deaths changed Larson. They were the spark running along the fuse. The storm that came on the day they died didn't leave. The heat waned as if the sun mourned along with the town and its absence let the rain come in sheets. More in six weeks than in the last six years. The town sank. The people with it. Corn maggots and blight invaded our fields, ruining any chance of a good harvest. No matter how hard I worked, how much my back burned from digging and re-digging drainage channels, no matter how sick I got from labouring in the pouring rain, I couldn't beat the weather.

Momma and Eric started arguing; the shouts and slammed doors shook the house and stopped us sleeping. I dreaded the mornings when the world would begin again, only a little bit worse. It felt like we were headed for a cliff with fraying brake cables.

The only bright spots were my sister, Rudy, and Gloria. Closer than ever, the four of us, arms linked, backs turned against the torrent.

We met up one Friday at the Roost, a week or so after Mark and Tracy's wreck. Rudy had called us all together. Waited for us after class and pulled us away, saying it was urgent, he had news about Mary Ridley and it couldn't wait, we had to go, now. Rain hung in the air, thick and unforgiving. It soaked us in seconds but we sat snug inside the Fort. Gloria beside me, elbows and thighs brushing each other, electric running all through me, more so because nobody else knew about us. We fed each other our warmth until the shivering stopped. We crackled, the two of us, shared a look, caught an eye, nothing to Jenny and Rudy but to us it was blaze after blaze. Each a tiny, addictive burn.

'Blame me if your folks give you shit about being late for dinner,' he said. 'I'm a Buchanan, got blame coming out my ears, bit more won't hurt.'

Rudy waited until we were quiet, listening, then started. 'This is going to sound crazy.'

'What doesn't these days . . .' Gloria said, voice heavy with Mark, Tracy, a Larson on the edge.

'Yeah but this really is fucking crazy.'

Rudy took a flattened, soggy pack of Camels from his back pocket and pulled out a joe. Lit it up with a Zippo, initials RB scratched in the silver side, and took a long drag. Blew out grey smoke.

He flicked off the first ash and said, 'I know who killed Mary Ridley.'

Spikes ran up my back, into my head, stuck themselves under my eyelids. I watched Jenny, saw her shift, brighten and darken at the same time.

Let him be right, my head said, let all this be over and Jenny be back to normal.

'What?' Gloria said but Rudy lingered, enjoyed the rising, boiling tension, turning the Fort to a steam room.

'Come on!' Jenny said.

'You guys *really* want to know?' Rudy's grin reached his ears and a bubble of anger rose in my throat.

Deep. Breaths. In. Out.

A drop of rain, from a pinhole in the roof, hit my forehead, ran down my nose, cheek, bypassed my lip, then hung on my chin. Rudy saw it, laughed.

'You needed a shower, Johnny!'

'Spill it, asshole,' I said. 'We're dying here.'

'Who is it?' Gloria grabbed his t-shirt and wrung it.

Gloria looked at me, but there were no butterflies in that look, no ruby-red hearts. Just pure, burning intrigue.

Rudy passed me the joe, caught my eyes and held them, something like defiance in his face. Are you making this up? Is this going to be a fake-out? A-ha! You guys are so easy, I got you so good. Got to be lying, got to be.

But if he's not?

'You can't just drop a bomb like that and then clam up,' Jenny said, plucked the joe from my fingers, took a lungful. None of the coughing, hacking up those lungs like last year, she smoked like a pro now. Made me sad to see it. My sister, growing up, right in front of my eyes.

'You're not going to like it,' Rudy said, looking right at me.

'What won't I like?'

'See, I thought it was nothing,' he said. 'Last year, when that old bastard broke my arm, I holed up at the church for a while. Our good pastor took me to get my arm fixed and said I could crash on the couch in the rec room for a few days while my dad calmed down.'

My night in the trailer with Frank came back, his conversation with that gruff man, the threat, the name. Black excitement inflated in my stomach, floated about, grew with every possible scenario. Maybe Rudy did know. Maybe he had found out some truth somewhere in Larson that pointed a finger squarely in one direction.

But he said I wasn't going to like it.

The bubble of anger stiffened, hardened into glass.

'I couldn't sleep one night,' Rudy said, pinched the Camel from Jenny and took a drag. 'My arm was killing me so I was sat up on the couch, watching one of those Bible story movies he's got on the projector for the little kids, you know? Noah's Ark, Moses in Egypt, one of them. Thinking it'd put me to sleep.'

'Does this story have a point?' Gloria waved at Rudy to pass her the joe. It was almost spent. She took the last few puffs for herself then stubbed it out on the floor.

'Yes, Miss Impatient, it does.'

'Hey,' I snapped, 'don't be a jerk. You're the one bringing us here in the rain, telling some cockamamie bullshit story. Get to the point.'

Three pairs of wide eyes. The outburst surprised me as much as them. Gloria gave my leg a nudge, the corner of her lip curved up. I wished I could kiss her.

'All right, boss,' Rudy said, sneer growing in his cheek. 'That night I saw your best bud the pastor through the window, in the middle of the night, meeting my bastard father behind his trailer, where they both thought nobody could see. A proper secret meeting.'

I almost laughed. 'That's it? Bung-Eye was probably there because you were there, dumbass.'

'No shit,' Rudy shot back.

'All right, all right,' Gloria said, arms out, patting down the air between us. 'Take it down a notch. Remember that a girl is dead,' she held that moment, let those words sink in. The tension eased. Then she turned to Rudy. 'What exactly are you saying?'

Rudy, full of sneer, knee bouncing, looked at us, one by one. 'I'm saying Pastor Jacobs killed Mary Ridley.'

This time I did laugh. 'Oh come on. You got that from one meeting?'

'Not just one.'

Jenny let out a tired sigh. 'John, be quiet. Go on, Rudy.'

'Of course it wasn't just that,' he said, suddenly losing the bravado, becoming Rudy again and deflating my anger at him. 'I didn't think anything of it at the time. Course it made sense for my dad to be there. But then about a month ago, I saw another meeting. This one with my dad and Mayor Wills. I got close and caught a bit of their conversation. The mayor said something like, "Is the matter resolved?" and my dad said, "Yes, back to business as usual."'

It stung me, right in the heart, that anyone would think that of the pastor. That anyone would even hear out the theory. But if a few meetings, a few words, were all Rudy had, then Frank, and me, didn't have anything to worry about.

'Not seeing the connection here,' I said.

Jenny slapped my arm. 'Shh, John.'

On his side, Jenny? After everything Frank had done for me? I retreated, shrank against the wall of the Fort. Listened to the rain.

'The mayor gave the old bastard a fat envelope,' Rudy said. 'Looked full of cash, a G easy, maybe two.'

'Why would the mayor be giving your father money like that?' Gloria said.

'And what's it got to do with Pastor Jacobs?' I asked. I didn't care about the mayor. If he was anything like his son, he was as downright dirty as they came, being involved with Bung-Eye was barely a surprise.

'That's the funny thing. I asked around a few people, folks my dad works with, even ran into Darney Wills. I tell you, trying to get a straight answer out of him is like getting sharp corners in wet dough. Ain't gonna happen.'

I heard the gruff man from that night with the pastor. *I been hearing that some kids in town are flappin' gums about the Ridley girl.* I'd thought it was just me. Rudy had been talking too. I swallowed, lump high in my throat that wouldn't go down.

'But then,' Rudy continued as my head began to throb. 'I saw my dad meet with the pastor *again* about two weeks ago, before all that shit went down at the trainyard. Jacobs came to our place, said he needed parts for an old car he was restoring and wanted to see if we had anything for a Caddy. Bung-Eye sold him a box of junk and the pastor handed over a stack. Fat as anything. All Lincolns. Ten times too much for what that crap was worth. I was sorting a box of washers just inside the barn, about ten feet away. Jacobs was all, "I hope this settles things", and my dad said, clear as glass like I wasn't even there, "For now. I won't cover for you a second time. No more mistakes. I won't have what happened last year happen again." Or something like it.'

As Rudy spoke, my insides twisted, like someone stuck a finger through my skin and twirled my guts. We all knew what happened last year. Mary Ridley was shot, dumped, and forgotten and nobody seemed to care. The trail we followed led to Bung-Eye Buchanan's property and a brand new blue Dodge Challenger that belonged to whoever killed her. *That cocksucker didn't have to kill her. Should have wrecked the fucker's car.*

My insides went cold and hard, frozen in a knot.

'I reckon,' Rudy went on, 'that the pastor had this girl back to his place, they got frisky, and one thing led to another, someone gets angry and *bang!* Shots fired.'

Bullshit. Bullshit. Bullshit.

One-one-thousand. Keep it together, Johnny. Two-one-thousand. Gloria's hand on my arm, soft and calming. Three-one-thousand. Rudy still talking shit about Frank. How dare he? Four . . . four-one-thousand. He's wrong. That's all it is. Plain and simple and wrong. Five-one-thousand. No point getting mad about it. No point lashing out and beating him to mush. Six-one-thousand. Let it play out. Let him spout off his wild theory, let's follow the bread-crumbs all the way and then we'll see. Seven-one-thousand. Then we'll prove that Frank isn't what Rudy thinks and is only trying to help. Eight-one-thousand. Then maybe I'll find out who really did it. The whole town will stop thinking I killed her. The whole town will pat me on the back. The whole town will call me Hero. Nine-one-thousand. And Jenny will be my sunshine girl again.

I didn't need to count to ten. Decision made.

'That's what I think.' Rudy leaned back, raised his hands behind his head. 'Pastor J got panicked and goes to the one guy in town who knows how to cover up a crime, pays him off with a pile of cash and a shiny new car, just like the one in that Dodge calendar he had up on his wall for months. Took that down quick after the body was found, you all notice that?'

The two girls nodded. And I did too. Go along with it, John, it won't take long for this stupid theory to fizzle out.

'We need more evidence,' Gloria said, her passion, her sense of justice, reignited. 'Hard evidence we can take to Samuels. No offence, Rudy, but a few meetings and some envelopes isn't enough. But we'll find it. We'll find who killed that poor girl and we'll make sure they get locked up.'

'Screw locked up,' Jenny said, back straight, eyes blazing. 'Whoever did that to Mary should get the chair.'

Rudy gave a hoot and I tried to keep the anger off my face. The thought of proving Rudy wrong, finding the real killer, made it easy.

'Let's do it,' I said and gave Rudy a 'Good work, bud' nod.

A moment of quiet. Rain tapped the sheet-iron roof and we all thought through this new information, next steps, possible outcomes. We bristled, the four of us, together, on a ledge, waiting for the right wind to lift our wings and send us soaring. We were galvanised but we had eyes on the wrong man. It didn't really matter. Our purpose had returned, our mission resolved, albeit with differing goals.

'We need to find the evidence,' Gloria said. 'There must be something in the pastor's office that proves he did something to her.'

'It wouldn't be in his office,' I said. Keep up the act, throw them a bone. 'Too many people go there, I'm there every week. He wouldn't risk it. But maybe in his house.'

'How do we get into his house?' Jenny asked.

We don't. And suddenly the plan grinds to a halt. I smiled but only a little.

Rudy flashed that movie-star grin. 'Leave that to me. We just have to find a time when he won't be home.'

'But he goes home for lunch,' Gloria said. 'We could try

after school but that doesn't give us much time before he gets back.'

'He's at the church half of Sunday,' Jenny said.

'But so are we, at least some of us,' Gloria sighed and rested her chin on her hands.

'We'll find a time, the right time.' Rudy put his arm around Gloria and a sharp ache hit my chest. She shrugged him off and met my eyes. I tried not to smile.

We spent another hour or so at the Fort, making plan As and plan Bs, running through wild theories about who the other man in the trailer was, what did it have to do with the mayor, the hows and whys of the murder itself, what Frank might have done. Did we all truly think he killed her? Really? He was a man of God, the caretaker of the whole town. He wasn't a killer, he just couldn't be. But something nagged at me. What if he was? He was involved with Bung-Eye somehow. With that gruff man who probably worked for Bung-Eye. And Bung-Eye knew who killed Mary Ridley. We had so many pieces but they all floated around inside my head, wouldn't come together to make a whole picture. We just saw parts, like those blind men with the elephant. Maybe in Frank's house there would be a piece that explained his corner of the puzzle.

We left the Fort and choppy waters of Big Lake, engorged and still growing from the rain, promising we would find a time to search the pastor's house. We'd keep our eyes open, watch him closely.

We didn't have to wait long.

On Wednesday the sky over Larson turned black and the second domino toppled.

17

The four of us were in biology class, last class before lunch, learning about the circulatory system, about blood and arteries and veins and all the chambers of the heart. Mr Frome, a precise, firm – if fat and lazy – teacher, kept slapping the diagram with his pointer, punctuating every name, *vena cava, carotid artery, aorta,* so they stuck in our heads.

'Nick one of these,' Mr Frome pointed to the web of red lines on the diagram. 'And you're kaput in seconds.'

I tried to memorise that diagram, imprint every tiny strand and finger of vessel on my brain. A cut here, a cut there, blood will seep or blood will rush. Under my eyes, my crude, copied diagram changed into Mary Ridley. A black dot appeared on her abdomen where she had been shot, where the eel had emerged. Right on the diamond shape of thick arteries running down the legs, and back up into the heart. She didn't stand a chance when that bullet ripped through. Whoever pulled the trigger must have known it. I thought of the pastor, a gun in his hand, watching a girl die at his feet and shuddered. I tore out the page and screwed it up.

I was deciding who to throw it at – Rudy or Scott – when the light changed.

Murmurs rose from the students. A shadow fell over the blackboard and obscured the chalk. Mr Frome told us to settle down and went to the window. I couldn't see his face but I heard his words.

'Jesus Christ.'

A giggle from the back of the room. He whipped around, a look of frenzy on his face. He told us to shut up and stay in our seats, he'd be back. He ran to the door, down the hall, leather shoes cracking on the floor.

Then we heard the sirens.

Rudy was the first to the window.

'Holy shit,' he called back. 'You've got to see this.'

The rest of the class surged forward, each boy and girl craning for a look at the black sky.

'Are those storm clouds?' Jenny asked beside me and I shook my head.

'That's smoke.' I swallowed the weight of my words. 'There's a fire.'

A tremor ran through the class.

'That's the Easton mill, isn't it?' someone shouted and we all knew she was right.

More sirens. More running in the halls. The classroom door burst open.

'Children.' Miss Eaves appeared at the threshold, her hair escaping its bun. 'You're all dismissed. Go straight home and, if your parents are there, tell them to get to the fire department. They'll need volunteers.'

Nobody moved. We were stunned cattle before slaughter. This was a trap. Go home in the middle of school? We ain't falling for that, miss.

Miss Eaves clapped her hands together. 'Now! Come on. Hustle, hustle, hustle.'

The corridor behind her filled with students and clamour, scared birds taking flight. That broke us out of the trance. This was real. This was happening. Get your bags and go go go.

Our class joined the stream of rushing bodies, through the halls, past the lockers, out into a midday twilight. I kept Jenny's hand in mine. Rudy and Gloria held onto the back of my t-shirt so we wouldn't be separated.

The sky, every blue inch, turned black and grey. The Easton grain elevator, a constant landmark stretching high above the streets, giving us our bearings, showing our way home, was gone. Nowhere. Obscured in smoke or destroyed, I didn't want to guess. The acrid smell of burning was everywhere, in every breath, blocking my nostrils, sticking to my clothes. The town coughed and sputtered, choked on itself. People rushed through the streets toward the mill. Police sirens, ambulance sirens, fire truck sirens, everything on fast-forward.

The four of us waded through the clot of staring students and onto the sidewalk.

'Oh God,' Jenny said and turned to me. 'Eric.'

My stomach turned to stone. Eric worked at the mill.

Dark thoughts filled my brain. He's dead. He's burned alive. He's trapped and suffocating.

'He'll be fine,' Gloria said. She stroked Jenny's arm and nodded to me. 'He'll be just fine.'

'Course he will,' Rudy joined in. 'He's probably on his lunch break in the Backhoe.'

Miss Eaves appeared at the top of the steps to the school doors. I told myself over and over that Eric would be fine, he's out to lunch, he's far away, but I didn't believe it. I squeezed Jenny's hand.

'We need to find Eric,' I said to her. 'We have to make sure he's okay.'

Miss Eaves clapped to get everyone's attention. 'Go home. Tell your parents Pastor Jacobs is organising the volunteers from the church. They need help. If your parents work at the mill, go to a friend's house and wait. Do not go anywhere near the mill, do you hear me?'

'We should go,' I said to Jenny. 'Eric might be hurt. Momma will be panicking.'

Jenny's expression soured at mention of Momma. 'Screw her. Eric is probably fine, like Rudy said. He goes for a walk every day with his lunch, right around this time.'

'But . . .' I tried but Jenny's face was stone.

Miss Eaves clapped again and shouted, 'The buses are pulling up. Get on them and go home. Tell your parents. Hustle!'

Rudy grinned, his eyebrows bounced on his forehead, and we all knew what he was thinking. Frank was in the church, would be for hours. Not in his office. Not at home.

Rudy said something but I didn't hear it.

A horrible sound, worse than thunder, worse than rage and fists, a crash, a bang, an explosion. A piercing cry from the crowd, people dropped to their hands and knees. The sound of breaking glass everywhere. The school windows shattered. Car windows shattered. Car alarms blared. The ground shook so violently I thought it would break apart, suck us all in. I grabbed Jenny, pulled her down, made myself her shield.

The twilight blazed orange and a pillowy mass of fire and black smoke bubbled up, up, up, impossibly high, impossibly huge. It hung for a second like Satan himself stood over our town, laughing, raising all Hell behind him. My stomach clenched, *and Hell followed with him.* Then the orange disappeared and fat belches of smoke joined the mass.

Nobody moved.

Miss Eaves held her hand over her heart, the other on the railing for support. Kids cried. The youngest screamed. Parents appeared, picking off their children and friends and whisking them away, eyes and heads sheltered from the sky, the smoke, the taste of ash.

We were statues, not moving, not breathing. I didn't know where to look. I'd catch the wide, white eyes of a classmate but there was nothing to say, we felt the same, we saw the same, then the contact broke in an instant. I clutched Jenny's hand, as tight as I could. I felt her shaking. I felt the whole world shaking.

Then Jenny turned, hugged me tight and whispered in my ear. 'There's no one at home for us. Momma won't volunteer and Eric will already be there. He's fine, John, I know he is because he has to be. He wasn't in the mill. I can feel it. Please, this is our chance.'

She pulled away and met my eyes, I saw the resolve. She would go to the pastor's house with or without me.

Gloria pulled us in close, her voice trembled as she spoke. 'If we're doing this we need to go now. Before Mandy gets here.'

Jenny and Rudy nodded, then Gloria turned to me, spoke just to me.

'He's okay,' she said, some of the power returned to her voice. Her strength transferred to me and I agreed. I didn't know what else to do.

We moved against the tide, away from the Easton mill, avoiding running men and women, ignoring those who tried to stop us. Feeling a stab of shame and guilt with every confused look. You're going the wrong way, those looks said. All the way through town my head kept repeating the words, Eric is fine, Eric is safe, until, as we got to Frank's street, I finally started to believe them.

Frank had a small place on the south side of town on a neat road, all square lawns and family cars. It didn't take us long to get there but, as we stood at the corner of his street, the reality hit.

I had a knot in my throat that wouldn't go away. Larson was bleeding, burning, and we were going the wrong way. People could be dead or dying, they could need help. Eric could need help. A needle pierced my chest. Momma's voice spoke in my head, What in God's good name could you do, John Royal? About all you could do is cry on them to soothe the burns but your salt would make it all the worse. She'd tell me I was soft for caring about people who called me a freak and a pervert. Eric is a grown man, she'd say, he knows not to stick around a burning building, he knows how to take care of himself. The knot in my throat unravelled. Momma was right. Momma was always right. The town could help itself, it was already, but nobody was helping Mary Ridley except us.

'Are we really going to break into a house?' I said.

'If we want to find out what happened to Mary Ridley we are,' Gloria said, firm and unwavering.

Jenny looked toward the source of the smoke. 'We have

to help her, John. Mary doesn't have anyone else, she needs us.'

'Shouldn't we be helping the fire department?' I tried, anything to stop them from snooping in my friend's house.

'They have enough help,' Rudy said. 'We'd get in the way.'

And the matter was resolved. We were going in.

The street was empty, abandoned. Only an eerie quiet. The dark smoke sky made it feel like the middle of the night. It was a dream world settled down like a blanket over the real one. We shuffled closer. The pastor's front door was mint green. The colour of hospitals, the colour you pick when you can't decide. I felt sick just being here, this close, without his permission, his invitation.

We walked straight past the house on Rudy's instruction, just four kids taking a stroll.

Rudy led us past two more identical homes, then we ducked down the side into the back yard. We crossed both yards, climbed over squat fences, and dropped into the pastor's.

'Watch and learn,' Rudy said and opened the screen door. He took two thin metal sticks out of his back pocket and knelt. It took less than five minutes for the lock to click open.

That wasn't the first time we'd seen him pick a lock. He was a Buchanan and that came with certain skills. The sick feeling in my belly grew. Frank hadn't done anything. He'd hate me for being here. Everything will be ruined.

Still kneeling, like the handsome prince in the stories, Rudy held out his hand and ushered Gloria and Jenny inside. I followed and Rudy closed the door behind us.

We stood in the pastor's kitchen and none of us knew what to say.

The dark outside made the inside feel like midnight. A single glass, single plate, single spoon and fork, beside the kitchen sink. White surfaces barely used, a floor barely walked on, a light covering of dust on everything but the sink and a square of countertop beside it. A prickle on the back of my neck. This wasn't a home, not like any I'd been in. My house was messy, Gloria's soft and warm, Miss Eaves' full of stories, Rudy's stank of engine oil. This was a copy of a home where the forger hadn't pressed hard enough on the carbon paper.

We were all hush and heartbeats, huddled together in the kitchen. Every throbbing pulse shook the dust, like a silent alarm. The cops know you're in there, they're coming for you, hell to the mill fire, you four are for the lash.

But they didn't come. We stood for so long, waiting, breathing in the pastor's must, until we realised no one knew, no sirens coming to arrest intruders. The four of us loosened.

'This feels so wrong. We shouldn't be here,' I said and folded my arms, afraid to touch anything, afraid to leave trace of myself.

Rudy ignored me. 'If I were a no-good, down-dirty pastor, where would I hide my stash?'

'Shut up, Rudy,' I said but he ignored me again.

'Where we looking first?' he asked.

'Maddie-May lives on this street,' Gloria said. 'I've been to hers a bunch of times. All these houses are the same. There's a family room through there.' She pointed down the hallway. 'Two or three bedrooms and bathroom upstairs.'

'Let's split up,' I said. Didn't want to be around Rudy

right now, too much enthusiasm for being here, betraying the pastor who had helped him, helped me.

'That's the spirit! Gloria and Johnny, you take downstairs.' Rudy winked at me as if he knew. Had Gloria told? A shiver went up my back.

'Me and the princess will check upstairs.'

Even in the gloom, I saw Jenny's cheeks flush. She nudged Rudy with her shoulder and called him charming. Twirled a bright blonde curl in her fingers. I felt a twinge in my chest, remembered some of Momma's harsher words about Jenny's dresses and boys. Momma would say Jenny shouldn't be looking at Rudy like that, blushing like that, flirting away with a boy like him.

This isn't the time, John, put it out of your head.

'Be careful,' Gloria said, 'put everything back *exactly* where you found it.'

We'd all watched enough cop shows to know what we were doing.

Rudy and Jenny crossed the kitchen, keeping their footsteps soft, passed through the hall and disappeared. A moment later, I heard the creak of stairs.

Alone with Gloria for the first time in ages. A tight flutter in my chest. In the close space of the pastor's kitchen, I smelt the smoke on her clothes mixed up with the smell of her, her skin, her hair, that underlying scent that would always be Gloria. That perfume pulled me to her like I had no choice in it. We looked at each other, smiled. Didn't touch. Suddenly sheepish. Since that first kiss in Barks reservoir there had been one more that week. I'd walked her halfway home after our lesson and chose a route that took us down a quiet lane. I did it on purpose, I'd wanted to know if it was a one-time crazy or something real. There was an awkward moment. She blushed, I blushed, she told me she liked me, I said it back. Then the kiss. Just as perfect and kick-in-the-gut as the last. Real as the birds in the sky.

'Family room?' she said.

I followed. This wasn't the time for kiss number three but oh my, did I want to. Here, in the pastor's house, with the world crumbling and burning around us, I couldn't think of a better or worse time.

No, John, the voice in my head said. How could you think it with Jenny and Rudy just upstairs? You and Gloria are meant to be a secret. Unless they already know. Rudy had winked at me. He knew, didn't he?

We entered the family room, just as empty as the kitchen. A single armchair facing the television set. Drawn curtains despite the hour. A fireplace full of display logs and dust. A Bible on the floor beside the chair. No other furniture except a lamp covered over with a thin red shawl. I switched it on and the room turned to blood.

'That's horrible,' Gloria said, her face and hair taking on the red and black shadows of a horror movie.

'Who would have this in their house?' she said, moved past me, switched off the lamp, picked up the Bible. 'Are you sure this is even the pastor's place?'

I nodded. 'He asked me to walk home with him once after a session, said we didn't have enough time together that day and the walk gave us extra.'

'There's nothing here,' she opened the Bible and flicked through, page after tissue-thin page.

A photograph fell out onto the carpet. A fuzzy Polaroid, taken in low light.

My throat dried like I'd swallowed salt.

It was a woman. Standing in a field or a park sometime near sunset. Smiling.

Upstairs, Rudy and Jenny laughed. Floorboards creaked as they moved from room to room, but it was like they were in a different house, a different time, on a different mission.

Gloria picked up the photograph and turned the lamp back on. She lifted the shawl enough to see the woman's face.

'It could be Mary Ridley,' she said.

'Doubt it.'

I took the picture, a blurred, half-turned-away woman, but same hair colour, same length. Plenty of women with hair like that but Gloria seemed sure. Seemed to have already decided.

'Pastor Jacobs told me he had a sister,' I lied. He'd never spoken about his family, except his dead father. 'It's probably her.'

I turned the picture over, half-expecting the pastor to have written the woman's name on the back, given us a clue at least, but it was blank. She wore a pale purple cardigan, trees and sky in the background as if the photograph was taken from below. The longer I stared, squinted at the blurred lines, the more I saw Mary Ridley's face.

'Put it back,' I said. I couldn't look. Not another second. It could be Mary, it could be someone entirely different, but I didn't want to know. If Frank wanted me to know who this woman was, he'd have told me. It was private and I wanted to keep it that way, especially if it meant Frank had something to do with a murder.

Gloria stuffed the Polaroid in the back of the Bible and set it on the floor. I nudged it with my foot into the right position.

As we stepped back toward the kitchen, I paused.

'What is it?' she asked.

'There's a door,' I said, nodding to the far side. Nobody noticed it when we came in, it was flat instead of panelled, and painted the same colour as the wall. As I reached it, my throat dried up a second time.

'What?' Gloria saw me tense. She joined me and saw it too.

A faint light came from beneath the door.

'I thought nobody was home.' I could barely speak.

Two voices in my head screamed open it, don't open it, open it, don't open it, over and over, louder and louder until my head wanted to crack apart, the sound and terror spilling out on the kitchen floor. All this sneaking around, all these accusations, all the snide remarks from Rudy, all got into my head and the guilt swept over me in great waves. It could be a light the pastor just left on when doing laundry or one on a timer to deter thieves. Or he could be down there. A knife stuck in my belly. He's here, he's home, he's going to find you and catch you snooping and then he's going to hate you, John, he'll hate you and you'll have lost another father. I closed my eyes and tried to count. One-one-thousand. Make the voices shut up, bring me silence.

'Two-one-thousand . . .' I breathed deeply. 'Three-one-thousand. Four-one-thousand.'

And slowly the fear and guilt faded. I felt frayed and raw around the edges and so tired of all this. I wanted to be back at the farm, trying to save what I could of the crop but no, I was here, in my friend's house, trying to prove he killed a girl.

'Five-one-thousand . . .'

'John.' Jenny's voice, my touchstone. She quietened

the world. She made the voices hush with just a few words.

I opened my eyes to my sister and two confused faces. Jenny and Rudy had come to the kitchen. Jenny's hands in mine, interlaced fingers. Gloria and Rudy stood back, watching me, their mouths wide like I was some carnival show.

'He's fine,' Jenny said, soft in the dark house. 'He can get a bit worked up sometimes, you know, worried. The pastor taught him this counting trick to calm him down.'

She smiled. 'It works real well.'

'You okay, John?' Gloria said, put her hand on my back. I felt its heat and its comfort and wanted to wrap my arms around her.

'Yeah. Thanks.'

'What happened?' Rudy asked.

I smoothed my hair. 'Nothing. I'm just . . . We shouldn't be in here, remember? Pastor Jacobs didn't do anything.'

'Yeah, yeah, Johnny, we all know you've got a stellar crush on the guy, want some time alone in his bedroom? You can cuddle his pillow or wear his jockeys,' Rudy said, wrapped his arms around himself and made fat smooching noises.

Something in me snapped.

I lunged for him.

The anger in me rose and rose and I almost got to him, almost had my hands on him, but Jenny grabbed me. Gloria grabbed me. Pulled me back. Rudy stared, back against the kitchen cabinets, over in a second. Wide-eyed rabbit boy. Rudy Buchanan shitting himself because of John Royal? Well ain't that a turn-up, folks?

'Do you boys want to go outside and cool off?' Gloria glared at us, let me go.

Rudy pushed away from the cabinets and his face, defiant

a moment ago, softened. 'Sorry, man, didn't mean anything by it. I know you and Jacobs are friends, he helps you. I get it. We good?'

I saw the sincerity in him. Saw the movie-star charm coming out. Saw the smile. Hard to stay mad at Rudy. It's not an untrained dog's fault if it bites, you should know better than to put your hand near its mouth. Frank would say, 'Lord, the boy knows not what he does.'

'Yeah,' I said. 'We're good. Sorry, man.'

A moment of quiet and calm. Let the dust settle. Then Rudy turned to Gloria. 'Is that a basement door?'

We were back on mission. Back to finding some dirt on the pastor, all because Rudy overheard a conversation or two.

Rudy held up his hands. 'What are we waiting for?'

Everyone looked at everyone else. They didn't want to say, of course, we're waiting for John to stop freaking out and we're waiting for you chumps to stop fighting.

Rudy stepped past me to the door, spotted the light but didn't comment. He grabbed the door handle.

Turned it.

My chest constricted.

'Wait,' he said and let the handle go. All the breath burst out of me.

'Goddamn it, Rudy.' Gloria ran her hands through her hair like she was pulling away the tension in strands.

He smiled and said, 'I think you two should stay up here. Me and John will go down. It could be dangerous after all.'

Gloria deflated but Jenny quickly agreed.

'Fine,' she huffed and shot Jenny a sour look.

'What do you think's down there?' Rudy said to me.

'A pile of junk probably.'

But that Polaroid had sent a flutter of unease through me, like my belly was full of tiny birds, all taking flight.

Rudy took the handle and opened the basement door. Enclosed wooden stairs led down. A bulb at the bottom gave off weak yellow light. Rudy went first. He told the girls to keep a look out for the pastor, they told us to be careful. There's nothing down there, my head told me. Junk. Storage. What else could it be? But the Polaroid. The girl. What if I was wrong?

My heart beat like rain on the window. Blood rushed all through me. I felt its movement in my toes, up my legs, through my gut and chest, into a whirlpool in my head. I didn't want to be here, I didn't want to take step after step down the stairs but I was. I saw myself doing it like I was still standing at the top and fake John was descending into the lion's den. Don't go, I shouted but I was shouting through soundproof glass. He can't hear me. He's taking another step. You idiot. Stop. You don't know what's down there.

The girls crowded the doorway like lookie-loos at a car wreck. At the bottom of the stairs, Rudy stopped dead, his attention fixed on something in the basement.

He shifted, his sneakers scraped the concrete floor.

'Rudy?' I said.

He shook, head to toe, then stared back up at me, stalled halfway down the stairs. His eyes gleamed bright beneath the naked bulb.

'Holy shit, John,' he whispered. The movie star turned terrified boy, eyes white and wet. 'Holy *shit.*'

'What is it?' I said, the wooden boards creaking beneath me.

'I don't . . . We were right, John . . .' his voice trembled, his eyes wild. My mind went to all the cop shows and spy comics and horror movies we'd watched and soaked up, all the terrible awful things in full Technicolor. Anyone could be down there in that basement, a wife, a child, a woman or man nobody knew was missing, they could be chained and gagged, weeping for a saviour.

My heart thundered. The rain grew to a storm. Rudy backed into the wall, shaking his head. 'Jesus, I don't believe it, *fuck.*'

Don't do it, John, the other me said. Turn around, leave, find the truth somewhere else.

But now I have to know. What if I'm wrong about Frank?

There is still time. Turn around. What if you're right?

I reached the bottom step.

Something moved, snapped free of the wall, grabbed my shoulders.

My heart exploded. No more breath, all white fire and fear. I screamed, fell, scrambled away. Hot blood filled my ears but I could hear only one thing. One thing that tore a strip of skin from my chest.

Rudy laughing.

He'd grabbed me. He'd scared me. He'd done it on purpose. The bastard. The fucking bastard. I could kill you, I could kill you right now. Hands around your throat until you stop fucking laughing.

'It's just a basement,' he said, doubling over, slapping his thigh. 'Full of junk, just like you said.'

At the top of the stairs, the girls sighed.

'Rudy, for Christ's sake,' Jenny said.

'Your face, man,' Rudy still laughing, ha-fucking-ha. 'If I could bottle that face and sell it for laughs, I'd be a millionaire.'

'You're an asshole,' I said, struggled to my feet.

Adrenalin ebbed and made my muscles shaky and weak.

Rudy held out his hand to help me up but I slapped it away.

'That was a really shitty thing to do,' I said.

I felt tears welling inside my cheeks, the tell-tale pull of my chin and ache in my jaw. I wouldn't cry, not in front of him, not after all this.

I stood and turned away from the still-grinning Rudy.

'Aw, come on, John, it was just a joke, you're wound so tight.'

'It wasn't funny.'

The basement was just a basement. No torture chamber. No cages. No guns. No blood. The storm inside my chest calmed and I could see the room clearly. In one corner, piles of papier-mâché animals from the church's nativity float, a few boxes labelled 'Books', a few pieces of broken furniture. On one wall, a rack of household tools, same ones Eric had in our woodshed, and a heavy wooden work-table with boxes underneath. At the top, a single narrow window looked out across the back yard.

To the left, almost behind the stairs, something caught my eye.

A bed beside the wall. One of those foldable ones with a metal frame.

'Look,' Rudy nodded, saw it too.

'You think he sleeps down here?' I asked. Forced Rudy's cruel joke to the back of my mind.

'No,' Rudy said. 'His bedroom was all messed up and all his clothes were there. Even half a glass of water.'

The bed was neatly made with a plain white blanket and thin pillow. The pillow had a dip in the centre as if it were slept on regularly.

'This is weird,' Rudy whispered behind me. 'Why would you keep a made bed in your basement?'

My head raced for an explanation, like the school librarian flicking through the card catalogue. Maybe the bed is for guests. Maybe when he's working he gets tired, takes a nap. Maybe.

The house was quiet but for the occasional footstep or murmur from Gloria or Jenny upstairs. I glanced around; something about the location of the bed confused me. I looked from the bed, around the room, floor to ceiling.

And then I realised. 'The window. You can't see the window from the bed.'

'So?'

'It's the only place in the basement where you can't see outside.'

Rudy let out an 'oooh' and said, 'Which means nobody can see inside either. The dirty bastard can do whatever he wants down here and nobody can see a dickie bird.'

I shook my head. 'What's he going to be doing, Rudy?'

My friend balled his fists and rocked his hips back and forth, humped the air. 'Anything the old perv wants.'

Then he laughed, saw the disgust on my face. 'See what I mean, Johnny? You're wound so tight.'

'Take a hike, Rudy. The pastor doesn't do that.'

Rudy threw up his hands. 'Whatever you say, Saint John-o.'

The bed turned sinister before my eyes. But it was Rudy's words. It was the smoke in the sky. It was the explosion, Mary's body, the meeting between Frank and Bung-Eye and the gruff man. It was all rumour. Thin white bones with no meat. No clue as to the animal they came from. I shoved any doubt down inside that dark part of me, the part where I shoved Momma's drunken fights, Jenny's tears, where I put the snide shouts of freak and killer and the thrown stones. That part would keep the doubt hidden. Keep it where it belonged.

I left Rudy by the bed. I didn't want to look at it.

I breathed in the smell of the basement, Frank's own den. I took in the rest of it, the piles of old moving boxes stacked by a wall, a dust sheet covering a large piece of furniture, splashes of green and red paint on the floor by the edge of the sheet like two cans had been knocked and splattered.

Green paint. My throat tightened. They'd found green paint on Mary Ridley's body.

Need more evidence than that, Johnny boy?

Yes. Did they find red paint on Mary Ridley's body? No, they didn't, so shut the hell up. Forget you ever saw it. With my foot, I slid the dust sheet over the paint.

On the far wall, beneath the strip of window, was the worktable. Craft supplies to match the papier-mâché animals, paint cans, jars of junk metal, full of washers, pennies, keys. A few boxes of car parts underneath. Normal stuff. Stuff we had in our barn, stuff Eric and a dozen past Pigeon Pas would tinker with. I ran my hand over the worktable. Frank sat here to make models or clean oil filters. Imagined sitting here with him, listening, learning.

A scraping noise made me turn. Rudy dragged a box from beneath the bed. He pulled out a light purple cardigan and my chest turned to stone.

Icy worms writhed in my gut. Same one as in the Polaroid? Don't be stupid. How many purple cardigans are there in the world? Thousands. Millions. Hell, Momma probably had something just like it. Wouldn't think she was involved in a murder just because of that, would you? Judge and jury'd laugh you right out of the courthouse.

'We should go,' I said. Rudy hadn't seen the Polaroid but he might want to look around the rest of the house. He might find it. He might search more of the basement and see the paint and then he'd put two and two together and get a hundred.

'Now,' I said, couldn't keep the shakes out of my voice. 'Let's go.'

Rudy dropped the cardigan back in the box. 'What's the matter with you?'

I had to get out. *We* had to get out.

'I just . . . I can't breathe down here.' I paced, flapped my hands, felt my face heat and turn red. 'I need air. I need air.'

Just go. Run. Now.

Rudy was back up the stairs just a second behind me. We burst into the kitchen as if we'd run a race, panting, bent over and leaning on our knees. He closed the door as Jenny and Gloria appeared from the living room.

Out of the house, John Royal, get out of the house.

I was past Gloria, to the back door, through the screen and into the yard. Fresh air, oh Lord, give me fresh air. I sucked it in but tasted smoke. Why was there smoke? I couldn't think. Why was it so dark? Then I remembered. My body turned to lead and I couldn't even lift my arm to wipe the sweat from my face.

I felt the others crowd around me. Jenny put her hand on my back. 'Johnny, what was down there?'

But I just shook my head, couldn't speak. I stood silent in the pastor's back yard, staring at the basement window, while Rudy told them.

'There's a bed down there. In the basement. And you can't see it from the window. That's fucked up, huh? The pastor has to be elbow deep in all this with a set-up like that. Bet you a thousand bucks he killed Mary Ridley down there.'

Hearing him talk like that pushed needles into my ears. Every word sharp but I didn't have the energy to bat them away. Rudy was wrong. Gloria was wrong. Jenny was wrong. I swallowed back bile.

'The bed frame was all scratched up in weird places too,' Rudy said. 'Deep scratches, you know, like metal on metal. Some on the wall too. And get this,' he made us lean in, 'the whole bed was bolted to the floor.'

Wings beat in my gut, grew into a storm.

'Bolted?' I said.

'Oh yeah,' Rudy nodded. 'Messed. Up.'

Why would anyone bolt down a bed? By the look on their faces we all asked ourselves the same question but none of us came up with an answer. Gloria told them about the Polaroid, the blurred girl who could be Mary Ridley or could be anyone else. She didn't mention the purple cardigan and I didn't either. Rudy knowing it was in the photo would be the last nail for Frank's coffin. I kept my mouth shut about the paint too. That was all we'd found, a neat bed and a photograph. The rest I'd put in that dark pit and there it would stay. Frank was a friend and I wouldn't have his name, his standing, his goodness, questioned any more.

Something inside me laughed. Something inside me stood up, cleared its throat and said, you don't really believe all that, do you, Johnny boy?

The sky darkened further, the sun sinking behind the

black smoke. The quiet was a heavy blanket on us, like the
tent pole collapsed, leaving us sprawling blind beneath
canvas. Rudy re-locked Frank's door. From the outside, the
house was as it had been, so simple and plain, like every
other on the street. Nothing special, nothing evil. But inside
those walls, inside my head, something stirred. Sinister
memories etched into the metal bed frame and faint
scratches on the wall, all invisible from the outside as if by
the devil's design.

'What now?' Jenny said.

Gloria looked at each of us. 'After the fires have been
put out and everyone has calmed down, we go to Samuels.'

'How long is that going to take?' Jenny asked.

Gloria narrowed her eyes. 'We'll give him two days, then
we make him listen.'

The four of us parted ways at the end of the pastor's street.
Gloria and Rudy went north, me and Jenny west. It was close
to six p.m., the rain had stopped but the sky was still heavy
with smoke. Any other day, it could have been just a regular
storm, clouds instead of smoke, the darkening before the
thunder crash, but it hung up there like some otherworldly
fog that wouldn't disperse. Walking beneath it, I felt its
weight pressing on my back, pushing me into the sidewalk,
into the dirt tracks, deep down into the earth itself.

Jenny and me crossed into the fields at the edge of town,
we cut northwest toward home, which took us through the
Hackett farm. At the top of the Island, the view, the vastness
of it, stopped us both.

'My God,' Jenny murmured.

The Easton mill was a piece of Larson so key and constant
that your eye glossed over it. Always just *there*, the multi-level

sheds, the top of the grain elevator, the twin silos by the road, the two dozen more out of view. Part of the landscape, white with snow in winter, grey with age in summer.

Not any more.

The Easton mill blazed and a black skeleton grew out of the smoke. A battalion of fire trucks shot useless jets of water. Cops and firemen only able to watch as the smoke streaked a fat funnel southeast for miles.

'They'll see that in St Louis. Maybe even further, down in Tennessee even,' Jenny said. 'I can't believe it. I hope Eric isn't hurt.'

Eric's fine, he has to be, we would know. We'd feel it, wouldn't we? Course we would. Eric didn't linger long in my mind; the pastor's house, that bed, the paint, the cardigan, the scratches, those memories swarmed over my brain, infected every thought.

Beneath the smoke sky, a flock of starlings launched, like the darkness itself had taken shape and started to dance. The devil was in the birds today, rejoicing at the destruction, weaving a gruesome ballet. A taunt to the town.

Jenny took my hand. 'It's all going to change now, isn't it? Everything will change.'

'Pastor Jacobs?'

'The *mill*. So many people work there, Eric, Maddie-May's mom in the office, the Lyle brothers, Timmy Greer's dad. Everyone,' her hand went to her mouth. 'God. They could all be dead. Eric could be dead. That explosion was terrible. Johnny, without the mill . . .'

There was no need for her to finish the thought. Without the mill, there would be no more Larson.

'They may as well have burned the whole town with it,' I said.

It would have been kinder, like shooting a sick dog before it had a chance to suffer. But people don't think that way about themselves. They'll strive and yearn and fight and they'll lose. They'll die anyway. Larson will die.

A feeling, like a piece of lead, hit my chest and stayed there. It said to me things were bad but they were going to get a lot worse.

We hurried home and found Momma sitting beside the blaring radio, rocking back and forth. When she saw us, she cried out, scooped us both up in her arms, squeezed us, breathed us in with a growl.

'You're safe, my babies, you're safe.'

Time seemed to have stopped while we were in Frank's house. The frenzy over the mill had gone from me and Jenny hours ago but it still blazed in Momma and the spark caught us too. Suddenly Frank didn't matter. His house didn't matter. We hadn't done it. It wasn't real. Only the mill was real, the fire, the smoke, the panic, the shattered school windows and wide, terrified eyes.

'Is Eric okay?' Jenny said, muffled by Momma's chest.

'He's fine, he's fine,' she kept saying. 'He's out there helping to put the fire out. Such a good man.'

Momma pulled away from us but kept hold of our arms. 'Where the hell have you been? School let out hours ago, I went to collect you. You weren't there. You can't just run off like that.'

I caught Jenny's eye, the tremor in it.

'We walked home through Hackett's,' I said. I didn't want to lie completely. 'We wanted to watch from the hill.'

Momma stroked my hair with a shaking hand. Her eyes were wet, bloodshot, but she didn't smell of whiskey. She wasn't drunk, all would be well. My shoulders relaxed.

'Good. Good,' she nodded and nodded, stroked and stroked.

'What happened?' Jenny asked.

Momma's attention snapped to her, I winced at the speed, waiting for the ferocity that usually came with it.

But Momma smiled, gently rubbed her thumb on Jenny's arm.

'Nobody is really sure,' Momma said. 'But when I went to the school, that fat maid – Mandy something – said Roy Easton, Mark's father, did it on purpose. Set fire to the whole thing.'

'Is Mr Easton okay?' Jenny said.

'No, I don't think so, baby. They say he was inside when the explosion went off.' Momma tried to smile but it wouldn't reach the corners.

Momma got up, said something about dinner then disappeared into the kitchen. The radio came back into focus, the rolling news update said nothing to report over and over again in different ways. It said there was a fire, an explosion, suspicious circumstances, no further updates, then back to the top.

I switched it off.

I was numb. I didn't know the right thing to say or do, the proper way to act during a crisis. Neither did Jenny. We stood straight and still in the family room, where Momma had hugged us. We were deflated balloons, fallen flat on the floor and unable to get up. We just lay there, waiting for the air to return.

What do you do when the world crumbles?

Frank, a man I trusted like a father, the leader of our community and the one person we would all need in this time of darkness, was under threat from my sister and my friends. The town, a flock of sheep lost in the field, would need their shepherd but he was fighting away wolves.

My mind twisted around itself and I didn't see anything in straight lines any more. There was something off about his house. The paint. The cardigan. The photograph. The bed. Put all together, it was hard to ignore. The pastor had secrets, he may have known Mary Ridley, done something to her. He may have even killed her, though the thought made me sick to my stomach. He probably did absolutely nothing and all those things we found were innocently explained but I didn't know for sure. One-hundred-per-cent, stake-my-Jenny's-life-on-it sure. I just didn't know. Tell me what to do, God, put me on the right path. Momma would know, but Momma couldn't know we'd gone snooping, it could wake a monster and Jenny would get the claws. My head ached and burned and the fire consumed my hair, my skin, cracked my skull.

I rushed outside, ignoring Momma and Jenny's questions, ran and ran to the back corner of the house. I flung away the lid of the rain barrel and dunked my head in the cold water. Sizzle, fizz, steam rose. The fire doused. I collapsed onto the dry grass, water streaming down my face, and searched the sky. Except for the streak of black smoke, it was empty, quiet, not even a bird. No answers for you John Royal, you're on your own. I didn't know what to do. Could I let my friends take away my sort-of father, the spiritual head of the town, even if that head was a serpent's?

I had two days to decide because once the fire and panic died down, Gloria, Rudy, Jenny and I were going to see Samuels. For, I hoped, the last time.

I wondered though, staring at the sky, if catching Mary Ridley's killer would even make a difference. Did it even matter in the long run? From that day, Larson changed to a place I barely recognised and it all came from Mark and Tracy, not Mary Ridley. Their stupid, selfish choice damned us all but it was my sister who suffered the worst.

18

The Easton mill explosion made the national news. It made the country wake up and talk reforms, heat sensors, safety precautions. Reporter vans topped with spindle antennas and plastered with initial decals – CBN, KNW, WNN – slithered around town like slugs to cabbage. Busybody curtain twitchers like Margo Hyland and Jennette Dawes became the voices of the tragedy. When poor Mrs Easton wouldn't talk, wanted to mourn in privacy, those two filled in the gaps. Mark and Tracy's suicide was exposed, dissected, judged. Even the Easton mill's accounts were pulled apart and pawed through like they were searching for a tick on a dog's back. All the Easton skeletons unearthed with a bulldozer.

It was the first time Larson was invaded by the big wide world, but it wouldn't be the last.

They found what was left of Roy Easton's body in his office slumped over the desk, so burned up they had to identify him by his teeth. Mrs Lyle at the post office said the fire ate him up right there, he didn't even try to get out, maybe he was already dead when the flames reached him. Thank the Lord, she said, nobody else was hurt. A firefighter was caught when a beam collapsed inside the grain elevator, burnt, scraped up bloody, but that's their choice isn't it, John, it's not like he died, Mrs Lyle said.

Rumours flew from corner to corner in Larson, changing, morphing as they bounced. A pinball machine of this and that and he said she said they said. Mrs Lyle told one tale. Al Westin another. Mayor Wills, Darney's father, gave an official account nobody believed.

The pinball kept jumping.

It was an electrical fault in the old wiring.

It was a revenge fire set by a driver Easton fired the week before.

It was a build-up of corn dust set off by a static charge.

It didn't matter. The result was the same. *Kaboom*.

The explosion blew the top off the main building and the fire spread, destroyed twenty silos and the grain elevator. All over town, windows broke in the shockwave and had to be boarded up. Me and Jenny drew the shape of it on a map. Right in the middle, the mill, then we marked all the damaged houses and stores. Almost a perfect circle. The force of it broke tree branches and they found shards of metal embedded in trunks half a mile away.

For a long time, Larson was beaten and closed off. Everyone said they were repairing, would be open again soon, come back in a couple of days, smiling through the lies. It didn't take long for us to realise that some of those window boards would never come down.

School was closed for a few days after, our classrooms full of broken glass and the acrid smell of smoke. Momma

wouldn't let us out of her sight so we stayed home. I helped
Eric clear the west field of the rotten corn. The wet summer
had brought maggots and blackfly, killed half the field. He
said we should clean and burn it before it got the other
half. Once she'd hung the sheets on the line, Jenny sorted
through the stalks, trying to find an ear or two to salvage,
but her collection was pitiful, the corn not worth the hulling.
We piled the debris high and Eric held the matches.

He stared at the brown tip and striker as if he didn't
know what they did. Half a minute later, he looked up, put
the match back in the box, and said, 'That's enough for
today.'

I glanced at Jenny but she was already on her feet, trailing
behind Eric into the house. The pile remained unburned,
the maggots writhed, the rot set in, right there on Royal
land. I wanted to burn it, watch those maggots hiss and
pop, punishment for killing half our harvest, but another
part of me wanted to see what would happen if the infection
stayed and ran its course. How far would it go? Would it
get the rest of the fields, would it reach the house, would
it get me and Jenny?

Inside the house, Eric wasn't himself. He was heavy and
slow, like his blood had been replaced with concrete. The
three of us sat in the family room, him in the armchair,
Jenny and me on the couch. Momma was upstairs in the
bath, soaking away one of her headaches. I wasn't paying
that much attention, my mind still on the pastor's basement,
what we would say to Samuels, what Samuels would say to
us. Then how Frank would look at me, how disappointed
he'd be, how hurt, when he found out I'd gone snooping.

Jenny shuffled closer to the edge of the couch, closer to
Eric. She tried to catch his eyes but he stared right through

her. He'd barely spoken these last few days, despite Jenny's endless questions about Roy and how they found him and what his body was like and how terrible he must have felt to do something like that. The wide-eyed obsession surged in her and he wasn't helping. He wasn't answering her questions and giving her peace of mind. He changed the subject or said he was tired or just flat out said stop asking. So the curiosity in Jenny started to burn, I saw it in her eyes, her movements, the jittering electricity in her bones. While Eric saw, and did, nothing. He just lay around the house, his long moustache turned ragged beard, show-pony hair dull and flat, constant smell of beer on his breath.

'Where will you work now? I heard from a girl at school that they're looking for farm hands in Bowmont. It's not that far,' Jenny said.

He looked away, tried to smile but his peace-and-love shell had cracked. Our Pigeon Pa hung his head, pressed his thumb and finger against the bridge of his nose. His knee bounced up and down like he was at one of his concerts, jumping to the beat.

Then he stood up, rubbed his hands together. 'You kids hungry? How about some pancakes, huh?'

I glanced at the clock on the mantle. 'It's nearly dinner time.'

Eric's head snapped back and forth, looking out into the hall, then to the clock, then to us. 'You can have pancakes for dinner, right? It's not like Patty's going to give a shit, huh.'

I flinched. That was the first time I ever heard Eric snipe at Momma. He was patience and calm beside her storm.

'She might.'

'You go without then,' Eric shot at me. Such venom in

his tone. I sat there with my mouth open, a helpless fish on the beach. I watched him, seeing a different man beneath the red flowery shirt and CND symbols.

Eric turned to Jenny. 'Come on, princess, you and me have a date with some chocolate chips.'

He held out his hand to my sister and she took it, smiling. Off to the kitchen together, left me in the family room. The sound of cupboards, the fridge, the tick-tick-*whoosh* of the gas stove. Eric said something, Jenny laughed and, just like that, I was in another world, another family, forgotten. I sat for a moment, stunned, until I heard it. Momma's gentle singing floated down through the floorboards and I found myself stepping, like a ghost, up the stairs.

'Momma,' I said, tapped on the bathroom door.

The singing, Patsy Cline's 'Crazy', Momma's favourite, stopped.

'Come on in, baby.'

I opened the door just wide enough to squeeze through then closed it behind me. Momma was private when she was bathing, no open doors, no prying eyes. This is my quiet time, she always said. Not even Eric was allowed in but I was.

The bathroom was a steaming blur, all soft edges and dull colours. The steam fogged the mirror, filled my mouth and nose with damp heat. The air tasted strawberry sweet from Momma's soap and I sucked it in, felt it seep through me. Our bathroom was small and tiled pale yellow with sunflowers. The bathtub was built into an alcove in front of the door so I could see only one part of Momma. Her glistening arm, dangling over the edge of the tub. Her fingers played the air to Patsy's tune and she began humming again.

'Momma . . .' I wanted to tell her what Eric said, the way he said it, but my mouth was empty, my throat closed up.

Her arm twisted, her palm opened up to me in a gesture that said, come closer, Johnny, take my hand. I did. The humming continued and my mind filled in the words.

'What is it, baby?' Momma said, her eyes closed, her head resting on a rolled-up towel.

I stood beside the bath, steam lifted off the white foam. It covered everything from her neck down except one knee raised out of the water like a mountain through clouds. The smell of soft fruit and Momma seeped into my head and blood, muddled me up like sipping the smoothest whiskey.

'Nothing,' I said, voice as warm and thick as the air.

She opened her eyes, perfect blue like Jenny's. 'You can tell your momma.'

'It's Eric, he's making Jenny pancakes and won't make any for me.'

'He shouldn't be giving either of you pancakes this time of day. Spoil your momma's dinner, wouldn't it?' she said, the soft heat in her voice sharpened. 'Why would Eric do a thing like that?'

I shrugged. 'He was acting strange. Jenny was telling him about a job in Bowmont and he just jumped up, said he'd make pancakes. I told him we shouldn't have pancakes for dinner, you wouldn't be happy, and he told me off. Said some other mean stuff.'

Momma's fingers tightened around mine. 'We can't have that.'

'He's changed,' I said.

No, Jenny has changed, Jenny is different. She's going down this dark, death-lined road and I don't know what to do. But I couldn't say that, it'd just make Momma mad at Jenny and I couldn't live with myself. Anger rose in me and I felt lies burning in my throat. This is all Eric's fault. I needed Momma to share my anger, to be mad at someone and it had to be Eric. The lies flowed from me like lava.

'He keeps saying he'll take her away to see Joni Mitchell and Jefferson Airplane,' I said. 'He says they'll go together, just them. He never asks me to go. He says all kinds of mean stuff about me and . . . and you and I don't like it. He looks at her different too, like he's only just met her, you know?'

Wheels turned behind Momma's dark eyes. In that last lie, I worried I'd gone too far and Momma would flip to blame Jenny instead of Eric but the wheels turned, the idea passed.

'Hush now, John,' Momma said and stroked my face. 'That girl isn't going anywhere, you can lay every dollar and dime on that. She isn't going anywhere with that man.'

Momma's voice didn't waver and I felt hot guilt for lying but maybe Momma would give Eric a stern talking to, make him get a new job or at least work on our farm if she thought he was making eyes at Jenny. Maybe she'd chuck him out. Would that be so bad?

'We don't need him any more. I can take care of you and Jenny. I can make pancakes and take her to concerts.'

'I know, baby,' Momma smiled, her hand lowered, stroked my neck. 'You have to keep an eye out for her, that's what a brother does. She's too pretty for her own good. That makes it all the easier for her to stray and men will snatch her up as soon as they see her. They can't help it, it's their nature.'

'I will, Momma.' I smiled too, my body felt lighter, my mind clearer. Eric didn't matter, he was a Pigeon Pa after all, he wasn't blood, wasn't ours.

Momma closed her eyes and straightened both legs in the tub. She let out a happy, warm sigh and reached for my hand without opening her eyes. She knew where all my parts were, as all mothers do.

I don't know how long we stayed like that, her holding my hand, humming Patsy. The next I remember was a knock at the bathroom door.

'Patty,' Eric, muffled through wood and steam. 'I'm going to Gum's. Don't wait up.'

Momma's eyes sprang open, her jaw set hard. I felt the muscles in her hand tense and I knew my lies had worked. Eric's footsteps sounded on the landing, then heavy and quick down the stairs.

'Off you go, John,' she said. 'See about fixing me a drink, will you?'

Momma dropped my hand and repeated her instruction. Drink. Now. Go. A glimpse of the beast in her eyes, before it sank back down into the bath.

'Yes, Momma,' I murmured.

Downstairs, Jenny sat at the kitchen table, her feet dangling, her toes brushing the linoleum, eating pancakes and smiling. Her blonde hair, so bright and straight, like a sunbeam tied up in a ponytail.

Momma always said some people need to be kept an eye on. Some people are tricky and wear masks. Frank had a mask, the one he showed his church tacked over his real face, the one he showed to me that night he offered me a drink and talked about first kisses, a normal man behind the white collar. Eric's mask of peace and love and justice was cracked and slipping. Maybe Jenny had one too.

'You want some?' Jenny said, holding up a fat triangle of pancake speared on her fork.

I shook my head and went to Momma's cupboard where she kept the whiskey.

19

The shouts woke me. The smash of breaking glass woke Jenny. Pitch black, sweating in the heat, we stared at each other, at the ceiling, at our bedroom door, and listened. Momma and Eric, raging drunk, him from Gum's, her from the bottle in the kitchen. My ears buzzed with every word, a hundred times louder for the darkness. The guilt hit me again. Had I caused this with my lies? Eric was a good guy, I liked him. What had I done?

Jenny's hand slid beneath our thin sheet and found mine. Fingers interlaced.

'I don't want Eric to leave,' she whispered.

'Me neither.'

I squeezed Jenny's hand. Another smash, a plate or bowl maybe. The floor shook as Eric stormed up the stairs, carrying the sharp din with him, getting closer, harsher. Momma screamed about work and money, Eric about death and compassion. Momma said he was lazy, Eric said she was heartless. Back and forth until Eric slammed their bedroom door and plunged the house into fevered silence.

My heart thrummed. I felt Momma downstairs, her presence and weight. I imagined her standing by the kitchen table, fists clenched, trembling and red-faced, then moving to the cabinet, fixing a last drink.

She never came upstairs.

Jenny and me found her the next morning asleep in the armchair, empty glass slack in her hand. Eric's snores tumbled down the stairs. We didn't wake them. With school still closed, Rudy and Gloria called for us and we went down to the Roost. I knew what they wanted. Go to Samuels. Tell him about Frank and the nothing we found in his house. It was time, despite my efforts to change their minds, despite my shouting that, no, you're wrong, Frank didn't do anything, you haven't got a stitch of proof. It fell on blocked-up ears. All three of them wanted to go. Every word they said was a sharp claw tight around my bones. Every raised voice, every 'Shut up, John, he's evil, he's a killer', were black wings in my chest, beating and buzzing and filling me up. We took a vote. Three to one. I couldn't argue any more, could barely speak through the humming in my head. Why would my friends do this? Was Mary Ridley more important than me? More guilt washed over me. It seemed to be all I felt these days.

I seized up, dug my sneakers into the mud by Big Lake. Eyes on the spot we found Mary, the cold, grey thing that started all this. They were headed in the wrong direction but I had to follow my sister, keep her safe. The birds quietened but never left. I felt them there, inside me, perched on my bones, ready to launch.

*

The four of us walked into town together. Smoke still lingered in the sky, almost disappearing against the heavy cloud. I trailed behind as we walked, didn't want to speak to them, didn't want to look at them. I felt wretched after what I'd said to Momma about Eric and Jenny, wished I could take it all back. Maybe she'd got so drunk she'd forgotten.

What kind of shitty hope is that, Johnny boy?

The only one I've got.

Gloria hung back as we turned on Main Street. 'You okay, John?'

'Fine.'

'Okay,' Gloria said, her eyebrows raised, surprised at my tone.

The four of us came together outside Al Westin's grocery store. One window and the glass door were boarded up, same as almost every other store in town. The mill explosion really did a number on this place.

'Got your stories straight?' Rudy asked and any patience I had left vanished.

'We can't do this,' I shouted. 'We'll be destroying his reputation.'

'Maybe he deserves it,' Rudy snapped. 'He's dirty, John. Deal with it.'

'And if he's not? Huh? Samuels is going to laugh at us and when we do find the real killer, he won't believe us. We're crying wolf here, you idiot.'

'What about the bed?' Rudy carried on. 'Only reason that's bolted to the floor, out of sight of the window, is 'cause that sick bastard does stuff to girls down there, and that . . .'

Rudy trailed off, his gaze followed something on the opposite sidewalk. The three of us looked.

Frank. My gut clenched. Strolling past the boarded-up barber shop on the other side of Main. A girl beside him. She was young. Our age. He was stooped, his hands clasped together behind him, speaking to her, nodding along when she replied.

I didn't recognise her, she wasn't in our school, but she had long, blonde hair just like Jenny. I wanted to race over there, grab him and tell him to run and never stop, my idiot friends are trying to get you arrested. We watched the pastor turn off Main Street, toward the church, the girl with him.

'Right out in the open like that.' Rudy spat on the sidewalk. 'What a fucking nerve that guy has.'

I balled my fists but held them by my sides. Rudy and I had got into plenty of scraps in the past but this, this was the first time I'd wanted to hurt him. Bloody up that pretty-boy nose of his.

Then something magic happened. Gloria turned to me, then to Rudy and said, 'Maybe John's right.'

'What?' Rudy shot at her.

Jenny stepped beside Rudy. 'Don't be stupid, Gloria. Of course the pastor did it.'

Gloria took a step toward me, by my side, close enough to smell her soap. Two against two. Heat in my cheeks and neck, another prickle of guilt.

'There's not much to go on,' Gloria said. 'We could keep looking and go to Samuels with something more concrete.'

'We're not wrong,' Rudy said, fist beating against his palm with each word. 'What other explanation is there for what was in his house? The picture? That bed? And what about the meetings with my dad?'

'It's your dad who's dirty,' I said.

'You're damn right! But that doesn't mean the dear old pastor's shit smells any better.'

'Can we just go?' Jenny sighed.

'I won't,' I said, folded my arms, planted my feet.

Rudy stepped forward, closed the gap between us. 'You won't? You're crazy, John. Why are you protecting him?'

'Because he's my friend and I know him. He wouldn't hurt anyone. You saw him buy a box of car parts from an auto yard. Shit, better call in the Feds,' my tone was changing, become cruel and hard, but I couldn't stop, the words kept coming. 'The only reason you think Pastor Jacobs is dirty is because he was buying those parts from your old man. If you took off your daddy's-boy blinkers for a second maybe you'd see how fucked up that is and be after Bung-Eye's blood.'

Rudy's face reddened. Fists tight. Jenny and Gloria tensed, tried to speak but I cut them off. I couldn't stop. Everything I'd wanted to say over the last few days vomited up and out, hit the sidewalk with a hiss.

'That bastard broke your arm and beat your ass on Christmas day,' I shouted. 'He grows Mary Jane by the ton behind those stacks of cars. You can smell it for a mile, think nobody knows that? He's been in prison more times than I've had hot baths and you're obsessed with a *pastor*? Can't face the truth about your dear daddy? You love your asshole of a father that much that you'd try to take away mine? That's pathetic. You're pathetic. Fuck—'

I saw his fist too late.

It cracked against my cheek and I stumbled back, more in shock than pain. Then the shock ebbed and an explosion tore through my face. I looked up at Rudy, shaking with rage, an animal in his eyes staring me down. Daring me to say something else. Gloria came to my side, took my arm to steady me, but Jenny didn't. That hurt worse than the punch.

Rudy, red-faced, pointed his finger. 'Don't you dare . . .' but his voice had no power. It was a voice on the verge of tears and I realised what I'd done.

I pulled back from Gloria and tried to look at my sister but she avoided my eyes. I saw the shame in her, mirroring my own.

All the bile emptied out of me, left a burning nausea in my stomach.

I turned, walked away. They didn't follow and I was glad for it.

The anger and shame sat inside me. It took shape and form and filled me up from the inside, wore me like a glove. When it moved, I moved but it wasn't me, it was something else using my skin and bones and muscles. It took me across town. Took me close to the church.

And there it was.

Parked across the street, a block from where I stood. That goddamn grey Ford. Clear as day. That shitty paint job. Those dirty windows. The shadow of a driver.

That's it. Last straw. Dead camel.

Steer clear, Frank had said, but I wasn't myself. My cheek throbbed from Rudy's fist, the pain surged into my head, into the back of my stinging, tearing eyes, made me see red. I was rage taken form and had no judgement. No fear.

I stormed to the car; right to the window before my good sense had a chance to talk me out of it. I'd had enough. Enough of being followed. Being haunted. Being afraid of the sound of a rumbling engine on the wind. Being afraid of what it all meant. I didn't care if it was Death himself behind the wheel, I'd have my say then punch his lights out.

I came up on the driver's side window from behind and banged on the glass. Up close, the grey paint job was rough, like they'd mixed sand into the base coat and left it. Nothing mystical. Nothing evil. Just shoddy work.

What are you doing, Johnny? What good can come of this?

Answers. Always better to face the monster.

Something inside the car shifted, the movement, the sound, unmistakable. The door opened.

Here we go. It's just you and me, horseman.

I balled my fists. Ready to take a swing. Ready to shout. Stop following me. Stop haunting me. I expected a glinting scythe growing out the door, bony hands on the wheel, a grinning skull. I expected smoke, or a ghost to scream and charge me.

I took a step back as a man stepped out. Barely out of his teens, maybe six or seven years older than me. Not some demon, not some biblical Death stalking me, causing all kinds of trouble in town. He was a man, just like Frank said.

Light brown hair flowed down past his ears, red-rimmed eyes and a look of guilt on him so deep his skin sunk around his cheeks. My rage dimmed but was still there, filling my body, overtaking my voice.

'Who the hell are you?' I shouted.

The man smiled, leant on his car and crossed his arms. Dirty blue jeans. A belt buckle with a horse's head stamped in the metal. Red and blue check shirt open over a stained white vest, like everyone else in this town. He looked familiar and it unsettled me. Like I'd seen parts of his face before but couldn't place where they came from.

'My name is Jack,' he said and his voice sounded strange, like I was hearing it as an echo. My ears wanted to pop but maybe that was just because of Rudy's right hook. My heart, my head, my face throbbed in unison.

Jack. JackJackJack. Who the fuck is Jack?

'What do you want?' I said. 'Why have you been following me?'

He lowered and splayed his hands, his movements too slow, like flowing oil. 'Mary Ridley was my sister. You know why I'm following you.'

I stepped back, stopped when I hit the wall of the boarded-up dress shop.

'What do you want?' I shouted. The street was empty. No one to see us or gossip or care.

Jack sighed, took a step toward me. 'Mary was all I had. Dad split, Ma died. Mary was my world, my sunshine.'

'What's this got to do with me?'

'You found her,' his voice seemed to throb, each word like the pulse in my ears, not quite clear, not quite real. 'You know what happened to her. You know who did it.'

Talons tightened around my bones. 'No. No, I don't.'

He slowly scratched his cheek, deep with stubble. I could hear the rasp of it across the sidewalk. The echoes in his voice made my head ache.

'You got a sister.'

'You stay away from her.'

Jack laughed and the sound ran through me like ice water.

'What do you want from me?' I asked. I had nothing. No information, no leads, just a name that this guy already knew and a hundred crazy accusations from my friends.

'Last I saw my Mary she was getting into a sweet ride with a man from Larson.'

A chill set in my bones.

'What kind of ride?' I asked but I knew the answer.

'Brand new Dodge Challenger. Mary never came home again. She was a good girl, you know.'

As he spoke, Jack's eyes darkened, the whites clouded red, almost demonic against the sun.

'You know who owns that car,' he said.

'I don't.' I knew I'd seen the car somewhere other than Bung-Eye's yard but I still didn't know where, and I wasn't about to let that slip to a stranger.

He stepped closer, his eyes boring into mine. I pictured his hand going for a gun in his belt, under that grimy shirt, tucked neatly against his skin. I slid sideways against the wall, planned an escape. Dash forward, surprise him, knock him off guard and sprint up toward the church, behind, up to Barks reservoir where cars couldn't follow.

'You'll remember.' Jack laughed again. A horrible, high-pitched sound.

'There's something rotten in this shitkicker town,' he said and the echoes grew louder, further apart, the movements of his mouth didn't match the sounds any more, the throb made my vision flicker in and out. 'Can't you feel it? You should get out of here. Take your sister because something is coming. Something real bad.'

I'd felt it. The coming storm. I'd thought the pale car was the harbinger, the sign of darkness, Death's own steed, but Jack was a man. A man trying to avenge his sister. What Jenny had said last year about Momma drinking too much, and what might happen, spun in my head and coalesced into one terrible thought. I could be Jack one day. Jenny could be the body in the lake and me the man stalking the streets, looking for answers.

I rushed away from him, my face and ears and jaw aching, my body sparking with electric rage. I looked back and Jack and his car were gone. Had I heard the engine? I must have. Anger blocked my ears, stopped me from hearing a truck rumble past the church. The anger ripped a handful of grass from the meadow. It kicked a peaceful anthill and sent the insects to war. It threw sharp stones into Barks reservoir and let me go at Fisher's Point. The high crag over the reservoir where seniors tested themselves. Everyone knew there were rocks in the water, just under the surface. Jump right and you plunge down into deep, cool water. Jump wrong and you break your leg, hit your head, drown screaming. The anger left me there, like it had run me right to the edge and fled before I fell.

I stared out across the water and the fields beyond. The clouds had cleared and the sun blistered the sky. The smoke from the Easton mill hung there still, grey-white now instead of black, and a hawk hovered over the empty beach. The world felt still for the first time in weeks. Larson felt like Larson. Jack Ridley's dark words of something wrong, something rotten, didn't feel right up here. If I tried, I could imagine that smoke as nothing but storm clouds, rolling in and rolling out again.

I found a flat rock and settled down in the sun. I hadn't realised how cold I was until then. My skin sucked in the heat and warmed the guilt. Maybe I could have helped Jack but I didn't know anything more than him. All I could have done was get his hopes up, maybe send him loaded and cocked in the wrong direction. I couldn't stand the thought of another death. Another body.

A weight lifted off me, then dropped back down when I thought of Rudy. I shouldn't have said those things to him. I was out of line but then so was he. We'd both said our piece, me with harsh words, him with a right hook. I forgave Rudy's fist and his doggedness, but when my mind turned to Jenny, I couldn't forgive. She was meant to be my back-up, my armour against the world as I was hers. But she just stood there. Watched him hit me and didn't even gasp, didn't cry out, didn't say, 'Johnny! Are you okay?' She'd just watched, with that horrible, Momma-smile in the corner of her mouth.

I think I cried. I remember hot eyes and the taste of salt. I stayed on Fisher's Point for hours. Didn't notice my hunger or thirst. Didn't notice the sun burning my skin and moving through the sky, sinking in the west. Didn't care much for any of it. I thought about jumping once or twice, testing my own courage and hoping for the rocks.

'John?' a sweet voice from the path behind me.

My shell cracked, light spilled in.

'That got out of hand,' Gloria said and sat down beside me on the flat rock. 'Rudy went to Samuels. We went together, the three of us.'

I looked at her then, flame hair catching the last of the sun, eyes on the water far below.

'What happened?'

'What you'd expect,' she said, shook her head. 'Samuels laughed us out of there.'

'Sorry to hear it.' I looked away, to the drop, and felt her smile.

'No you're not.'

'Do you really think Pastor Jacobs did something to Mary Ridley?' I asked.

Gloria slid her arm through mine and took my hand. At her touch, a sense of calm rushed through my body like a chemical. It was that moment, that second, I realised I might love her.

'I did for a while,' she said. 'But you're the one who sees him every week. If anyone knows whether the pastor has a hidden dark side, it's you. You trust him and, well, I trust you.'

I squeezed Gloria's hand. You trust me. A sudden surge of heat from my stomach went up my chest, neck, into my face. I felt it push up into my eyes. They wanted to look at her, take in all that beauty and see her speak those words all over again. What a feeling that was, to be trusted, I mean really *trusted*, by another person.

I kissed her cheek and said, 'Thank you.'

Then she kissed me properly and everything felt good again.

'I've always wanted to do the Fisher jump,' she said.

'Why don't you?'

She tossed a tiny stone over the edge and listened for the splash. She laughed. 'I don't want to die just yet.'

We were quiet for a while, heads together, watching the water. A fish snatched an insect from the surface, sent silent ripples over the lake. I realised how glad I was it was her who found me. Not Rudy, he would make a joke about the fight and make me feel stupid or try to push me off the Point. Jenny would judge me, make me feel useless, weak. It had to be Gloria. I still didn't understand why she liked me, why she could look at me and see something other people couldn't or didn't want to.

'How did you know I'd be here?' I said but I wanted to ask, why did you come here? Why do you care?

She smiled, looked down at her hands. 'Wild guess. It's nearly nine, you know. Rudy and Jenny went home. When you weren't there, Jenny called me. She's worried about you.'

'I don't care,' I said.

But I did. No I didn't. She hurt me. I'll hurt her back.

'If you don't want to go home you can always stay at mine,' Gloria said but her voice faltered.

'What about Mandy? Your parents?'

'Mandy has been useless since the mill, she's been at that roadhouse bar every night. I think she had a thing for Mr Easton. Mother is visiting her sister in Indianapolis and my dad is so distracted and busy with work these days I don't think he'd notice.'

I thought for a moment. Gloria's house would be empty, mine would be full. Full of Eric's rage, of Momma's scorn, of Jenny's sideways looks, cutting questions, that corner smile.

'Okay,' I said.

Gloria stood, brushed the dirt from the back of her dress and reached out her hand to me. I took it and stood.

Gloria pressed her lips together. 'You should know. I told Rudy about us. He kind of already knew and kept badgering me about it so I finally gave in and told him. I don't know if he's told Jenny. I certainly haven't. I guessed you'd want to tell her yourself and there's a reason you haven't.'

'The way she looked at me earlier, I think she has a good idea. It doesn't matter,' I said and it didn't. Larson had changed. People had died. A whole family had been destroyed, countless others ruined, by a single date some army guys pulled out of a barrel. The war didn't just destroy some far-away country, it was destroying my town, my Larson, turning it from a lively safe golden home into a bitter blot on the map. What was the point in hiding something good and bright like Gloria in all that darkness?

I went with Gloria back to her house. She snuck me in the back door and kept me hidden in the hall closet until she was sure nobody was home. Then she made me eggs and bacon. The eggs were too runny and the bacon not crispy like I like it but I didn't mind.

There was never silence with Gloria. Never a break in conversation that made me feel awkward or strange. We just talked. About school and lessons and Mary Ridley. She told me little Timmy Greer had tried to feel her up behind the bleachers last year and she'd punched him in the nose and kicked him in the balls. I told her next time I'd punch him for her but she didn't need me to. How wonderful it felt not to be needed but to just be allowed to *be*.

We picked over a jigsaw puzzle, a forest scene with a wolf howling on a rock. She found the edges and I made the wolf. We kissed a little. We laughed more.

We fell asleep sometime around midnight in Gloria's room. She was on her bed and I on the floor. She'd given me her pillow and a flowery pink blanket her grandma knitted. I'd never slept in a room with a girl who wasn't Jenny. It was odd, new, exciting. I fell asleep smiling.

I don't know what woke me but I woke cold and shivering despite the warmth.

I lay there, listening. Gloria breathed deeply in the bed but that wasn't what woke me. Something was alive in the house. There was no hollow emptiness any more. It was full, close, breathing.

I tried to sleep but the three glasses of grape juice sloshing in my gut made me get up. As I edged onto the landing to find the bathroom, I heard the voices.

Two men. In the hall at the foot of the stairs.

My heart seized, turned to rock inside my chest.

Their voices were muffled, trying to be quiet, but I recognised one as Mr Wakefield, Gloria's father. I looked back at her bedroom door, thought about going back in, closing my eyes and pretending to sleep. Then I told myself how stupid I was. If I made a single noise, clicked the door too loudly, creaked a floorboard, I'd be caught in there and God knows what he'd do.

My bladder ached but I couldn't risk going to the bathroom. I was fixed to the spot, my toes rucking up the carpet.

Then the other voice spoke, loud enough to hear and easy to recognise.

'You said there would be no trace,' Mayor Wills said. All-round snake in a cheap suit. Want to talk corruption in regional office? Wills is your poster boy. Beer gut bulging over his belt, blotchy red face. Darney's a chip off the old dough ball, that's for sure.

The risk of making a noise was worth it then, to get a closer look, make sure it was really them and not my ears playing tricks. I dropped to my knees, shuffled to the edge of the landing until I could see them both. Gloria's dad, tall, calm, with a thick black moustache and white shirt rolled up at the sleeves, and the mayor, frantic and haggard, sweating through his shirt, exchanging harsh whispers.

'There isn't a trace. It was a year ago,' Mr Wakefield said.

'Then why is Samuels asking questions? He's asking about Jacobs. He knows the girl's name for Christ's sake!' the mayor spat. He was a mess, his hair stuck out in all directions, his face round and covered in stubble, sunken eyes.

Then a footstep and a third voice. 'Come now, Mr Mayor, you're getting yourself all twisted up.'

I knew that voice. The one from Frank's trailer. The one full of threat and venom. I raised my head, stretched my neck to see over the edge of the landing, down into the hall. A man stood next to Wakefield. Small, bearded, built as if from stone, wearing a leather waistcoat covered in buttons. A feral dwarf, I thought, tattooed and missing teeth.

I knew him. All of Larson knew him. Charlie Meaney. One of Bung-Eye Buchanan's men. One of those figures who seem to persist in the town's consciousness without being seen, someone everyone had a story about.

'I warned you both,' he said. 'Didn't I do that? Didn't I say you keep your mouth shut, we'll keep ours. Huh? Well, who's been talking?'

'Nobody,' Mr Wakefield cut in. 'It doesn't matter. Samuels is a fool, he won't be any trouble.'

'He's a fool with a badge, rich boy,' Meaney said. 'A badge and a gun and now a name. You want to explain that to me? Or you want to explain that to my employer?'

Bung-Eye. I shrank back. Rudy. Gloria. Jenny. They'd gone to Samuels. They told him everything we found, including Mary Ridley's name. That meant Frank hadn't, despite knowing it before us. My throat tightened.

Mr Wakefield sighed. 'I'll take care of it.'

'What does that mean?' said Mayor Wills, pacing around the marble hall. 'I can't have this splashed on the news-stands, Leland. You assured me this business was taken care of a year ago. This cannot happen. Fuck. *Fuck.*'

Gloria's father lunged at the mayor, grabbed his shirt and pulled him close.

'Keep your goddamn voice down, Vern,' he said. 'I did take care of it. I always take care of it. I gave up my fucking car to keep the Ridley family quiet, didn't I? You know what that car was worth?'

He shoved the mayor away. And finally, a full year on, I remembered where I'd seen the car, why it was so familiar and yet not all at the same time. I'd fetched popsicles from the chest freezer in Mr Wakefield's garage last summer. The Dodge, newly waxed and gleaming, sitting proud on polished black tyres. Bright red, not blue. The Buchanans ran a chop shop and re-sprayed cars all the time. You idiot, John, red car, blue car, same damn car. No one else in Larson could afford a car like that, I knew it, always had. How could I have forgotten? How could I have missed it? Seeing it in the garage had been just a second, just a moment, then a week later we found Mora's body and she consumed everything. But wait . . . that meant . . .

Gloria.

I looked at her bedroom door. Pictured her sleeping behind it. Oh God.

'Money talks,' Mr Wakefield said. 'And it keeps people quiet too. Don't worry about Samuels. All he cares about is crullers, coffee, and a wide chair to park his ass. All three are cheap. It's taken care of. There's nothing to get in the way of our arrangement.'

'See that's true, or you and Mr Mayor here are out in the cold. If we go down, we're riding your asses down with us,' Meaney said. 'We got long arms in this town. Long, long arms, boys.'

Then he laughed and the front door opened, closed, and he was gone. The silence sunk down the stairwell and lay heavy on the two remaining men but their tension tore it up. I felt I could hear Wakefield's teeth grinding, taste the salt of the mayor's sweat.

'This is such a mess. Such a mess,' the mayor kept saying.

The grape juice stung my insides, pushing down and down, wanting to release but I couldn't let it. Not yet. Just a few more minutes. I couldn't breathe or move. Couldn't risk a sound.

'What she do, Leland?' the mayor asked, wretch in his voice.

Mr Wakefield stood, half turned away, obsessively flattening his moustache with two fingers. 'What?'

'I won't say anything, but I have to know. What did the girl do?'

I held my breath. Held every bone and muscle still. Told my blood to stop pumping.

I heard Mr Wakefield's leather shoes squeak on the marble, felt him tense even from way up here on the landing.

'Come on, Leland. Just tell me. Goddamn it, just spit it out!'

Mr Wakefield didn't say anything. It felt like the whole house squeezed me, squeezed the grape juice, squeezed the implications deep into my brain. My bladder, my head, my whole body ached and throbbed.

I still didn't know why or how any of it was tied up with Charlie Meaney and Bung-Eye Buchanan. What did Mary Ridley do to get killed? How did they know her? Frank had something to do with all this but what? Why would Gloria's dad help if he hadn't done anything? Oh, God, Gloria. She couldn't know, I couldn't tell her. God damn them for doing this. Why did they? Why, why, why? Still so many questions and no answers. Everything swam, too much had happened for me to make sense of. This was just the start, there was so much left to unscramble and piece back together. I couldn't look at them any more. The weight of it, that accusation, that confession, that . . . whatever that was, pushed me off my knees, onto my side. A floorboard creaked beneath my hand.

Mr Wakefield hissed at Mayor Wills to shut up.

I couldn't see them any more. My chest wanted to crack open, my heart the hammer.

'Gloria?' Wakefield's friendly father voice floated up the stairs.

I held my breath.

A step on the marble. 'Gloria, honey, is that you?'

A sharp pain in my groin and then, oh no, please, please. No, no, no. A river, a flood, a waterfall. Hot and wet and all over me. I clamped my hand over my mouth and my eyes filled with tears.

'Why, Leland?' the mayor tried again.

I couldn't see them but I heard Mr Wakefield move, maybe to the front door.

'Get the hell out, Vernon,' Mr Wakefield said. 'Don't make me remind you what'll happen if you run your mouth. I like our set-up and I know you do too.'

Everything muffled. My head roared. The front door opened and closed, the mayor gone. Mr Wakefield stood below me. I imagined him listening, waiting for the eaves-dropper to reveal himself.

Then his footsteps, a door somewhere, and silence.

I struggled up. Tears streaming from stinging eyes. My body shook, my legs could barely stand to support me. A dark patch on light carpet shouted my shame to the world. I didn't know what to do. I couldn't think. I was numb and wet and trembling all over. I couldn't go back to Gloria's room, not like this. She'd wake up and she'd see my pants and she'd see my face and she'd read my expressions and my eyes. She'd see that whole conversation with Mayor Wills and Charlie Meaney and she'd know her father was a killer. I couldn't do that to her.

I had to go. That's all I knew. Go. Get out. My body acted without my mind. I don't remember making decisions. I went down the stairs and out the front door in my bare feet and ruined pants. I walked through town. Through fields. Through muddy ditches. Nobody around at this hour to stop me.

Jenny found me lying naked outside our back door the next morning. My feet were bloody, a shard of glass in one so deep Eric had to take me to the doctor. I'd walked all the way home in the dark, stripped off at some point along the way. I didn't remember. I didn't remember anything after the mayor's words and Mr Wakefield's silence, after my body betrayed me. Jenny found my clothes. They were at the top of the pile of rotten corn, feeding the maggots, ready to be burnt.

20

For days, what I'd heard in Gloria's house swam around my head and never settled. Tell. Don't tell. Samuels wouldn't believe me, that ship had sailed and sunk, but my friends would. They'd listen.

But Gloria.

My chest ached at the thought of her face if I told her. She'd be broken. We'd all be broken. Pretend it didn't happen, Johnny boy, that's the safest way. What Gloria doesn't know can't crush her.

I went through those days in a fog, watching lives happen all around me but never quite living one myself. I thought if I was around people they'd see it on me, see the secrets scratched into my skin. It felt as if, as soon as you find something out, everybody knows you know it. All those bad men whose crimes I'd discovered were suddenly aware of me. They could see me, knew where to find me, what I might do or say, and they couldn't have that. They couldn't have a loose cannon like John Royal running around, shooting his mouth off.

I kept telling myself I was being stupid, they couldn't possibly know I'd heard them or I'd spoken to Jack Ridley about the car. I had to keep my cool. Keep my head on straight, Rudy would say. But God, I wanted to talk to them. I wanted to spill my guts to my friends and have them pat me on my back and say, shit, John, what a mess, let's sort it out together.

But I couldn't. I couldn't do that to Gloria. She needed her father. No matter what kind of monster he really was, he was still her father. Same as Momma, despite her own demons, was still our Momma.

I lay on my bed, staring at the ceiling, trying to put it all together but it was too much. Too many things had happened and my head ached, split open, when I thought too hard on it. Mary Ridley. Jack Ridley. Mayor Wills. Charlie Meaney. Bung-Eye Buchanan. Mr Wakefield. And Pastor Jacobs. Frank. My friend. I still couldn't imagine he was involved in whatever the others were. He must have listened to a confession, or overheard Wakefield and Bung-Eye, seen something he shouldn't have and was now in as deep as I was. Maybe they'd threatened him too. My mind kept circling back to that and the certainty that came with it was a comfort. I wanted to speak to him, tell him what I knew, and we could puzzle our way out together. But maybe that'd get him in deeper trouble with Meaney and Bung-Eye. Maybe it'd get me in more trouble. I didn't want to risk it. Didn't want to risk telling anyone what I knew in case it put them in danger too. So I lay on my bed, stared at the poster of Joni Mitchell and closed my eyes against the world.

Eric stuck around, for a while at least. He was a good man, deep down. Momma didn't know what she had but Jenny did. After the Easton mill explosion, the town sagged. Those broken windows, even with the glass replaced, the frames mended, remained broken. The heart's been ripped out, John Royal, Momma said, the heart and soul, torn up and stamped on. And what do men do, Momma asked me after dinner one night, when their lives are busted up? They drink, oh baby do they drink.

Business boomed at Gum's and Momma started tending bar five nights a week. Someone had to earn a living, she'd snipe at Eric. She heard the mill workers' stories over two fingers of bourbon then refilled and refilled, slid that last dollar out of their pockets for them. And it was their last, no more mill, no more money. Momma said they could spend it on a shot of whiskey or on a hamburger at the Backhoe, and better she get the tips than dried-up Didi Hensher.

Eric did odd jobs, earned a few bucks here and there, but it wasn't enough. All he had left to give was the little nest egg that would take him to Washington for the protests. He and Momma argued about it. He was holding out, she was gold-digging, the anti-war movement needed him, she and us kids needed him, and round and round it went, for weeks.

One night, in the final days of August, it ended.

'You go then,' Momma said. She was drunk, her tone rollercoastered up and down. I heard it through the floor-boards from our bedroom. Jenny beside me, kneeling on the floor over a book, hands clasped in her lap.

'We can all go,' Eric said, 'the four of us.'

Jenny's eyes widened and she turned to me, a smile growing. There it is, your get-out-of-Larson ticket, every corn kid's dream and my nightmare. What would become of the farm?

Momma laughed. A sick sound, no humour in it. 'To Washington? A one-bedroom hole in a block of fifty? What kind of man are you?'

'Patty, don't do that,' Eric said, weak, tired. I suddenly hated him, all mewling voice and sighs. What kind of man are you, Eric? Huh? No kind.

'Patty don't do that,' Momma whined back at him. 'Get some balls you *fuhking* pussy, you ain't a man. You ain't a man for me.'

'Patty, come on now.'

A harsh sound, like spitting. 'Patty, Patty, Patty. Get the hell out of my house. Go find some slut girl in Washington to bed. Not that she'll like it,' another laugh, full of bile. 'You don't know what the *fuhk* you're doing with that needle dick.'

Eric shouted something, something so full of rage I couldn't hear it. A smash. Glass or china. I'd have to clean it up in the morning. The shouting grew in power like a tornado touching down, roaring through the fields, coming right for us. I flinched at every word, the tremor reached up through the house, through the floorboards, through mine and Jenny's knees and into our chests. It was like being taken by the shoulders and shook and shook and shook until everything hurt and everything wanted to burst apart. I clamped my hands over my ears but it didn't help. The noise, the rage, was muffled but still there, even closer like I'd pushed the worst of it into my ears and held it there. My hands a cage, keeping a storm trapped inside my head.

I don't remember when it stopped. I don't remember climbing into bed or holding Jenny until she fell asleep.

Eric was gone when I woke up. I could tell from the way the house felt. His jacket was no longer on the hook, his boots gone from the door, his dozen records taken but for a Joni album he left for Jenny with a note. *For my favourite girl.* I tore it up before Momma saw and blamed Jenny for it.

They'd broken two plates in their fight the night before. Shards of white littered the kitchen. A spray of them by the fridge, another by the back door. A small scratch in the fridge told me the plate had been thrown high and hard, not dropped by accident. Momma had been aiming for his head.

When Jenny came downstairs, realised he was gone, she ran back up to our room and played the Joni Mitchell record over and over and cried. I couldn't comfort her. She wouldn't hear me. I left her for a while to calm as I made myself breakfast. I filled a plate with hot, thick-buttered toast and took it upstairs.

'I bet you're hungry,' I said but she wouldn't even look up at me. Her face buried in her pillow, her back heaving in time to the sobs.

'Come on, Jenny,' I said, set the plate down on the bedside table. 'We could go swimming in Big Lake.'

Big Lake wasn't what it used to be, since the body, since the cops churned it up, but anything would be better than this. Jenny didn't respond.

'How about milkshakes at the Backhoe? We could go for burgers too.'

'Go away!' she screamed into her pillow.

A sting but I brushed it away. I sat beside her on the bed. 'It'll be okay, Jenny. Maybe he's just cooling off somewhere and will be back for dinner. Meanwhile it's just me and you. Come on, sure you don't want ice cream? What about a slice of Didi's chocolate pie?'

'I don't want you! I don't want pie! I want Eric! Go away!'

The sting turned to a bite. A gash right through my chest. So much pain and venom in her voice. Her first touch of heartbreak and all I had to offer was ice cream.

You're an idiot, John.

I told her I'd fix her something else to eat when she was ready and left her alone, went back downstairs. Her words needled me, like thorn pricks too small to pull out. They'd burrow deeper, they'd swell my skin, they'd turn red and angry if I let them.

I cleaned up the kitchen with Momma's whiskey snores through the ceiling as my music.

I tidied the house alone.

I swept the front porch alone.

I washed the dishes and scrubbed the floors alone.

The house felt wrong, like I was living in a show home, one of those perfect snapshots of the life you could have if you lived here. Come on in, folks, look at that shiny linoleum, sign here and here and it's all yours. Everything was clean, in order, a big empty bowl on the table ready to be filled with fresh fruit or bread rolls but it never would be. It would be wax fruit, plastic bread, nothing beneath the surface but dust and air.

I edged upstairs to try to get Jenny out of bed when I realised she'd stopped crying. When I reached the top of the landing, I heard why.

She was speaking. To Eric. But the conversation was one-sided, like a phone call but there was no phone in our room. She'd speak, pause, then respond.

'Why didn't you take me with you?' she was saying. '. . . But I can help. I could get a job . . . I'm grown up enough . . . but . . . Oh, I love you too . . . Where did you go?'

A shiver ran down my neck and turned my blood to ice when she said, 'Mary would want me to be happy. She wants to go to Chicago too . . . but she's older and can take care of me . . .We're like sisters you know.'

I backed away, fear and disgust lodged deep in my throat, stopping my breath, making my pulse throb in my ears. She was talking to them? Out loud? I stumbled back down the stairs and her voice cut off at the sound. A few seconds later, she started playing a Joni record and called out my name. I didn't respond. I was too freaked to hear her out. What could she say? Oh, Johnny, sometimes I talk about dead strangers like they're my friends, I hold conversations with people who aren't there, nothing to get bent out of shape about.

With worry thrumming through me like blood and Momma still sleeping it off, I didn't want to be around when she or Jenny finally emerged. I left the house around nine thirty and headed through the west field, concentrated on the farm. I understood the farm. I could control the farm. Despite how terrible this year had been, I knew *why*, I knew *how*. Corn doesn't like rain. Rain causes blight and maggots, simple cause and effect.

We'd lost the whole crop of corn over the rest of this sick summer and it hurt to look at the barren earth. Needs weeding, needs turning, chaff needs burning, I told myself. That'd keep me busy over the next few days, my mind off Jenny and what I'd heard. But today, I couldn't bring myself to pick up a shovel, I wanted to walk, clear my head.

I took a loop, through a stand of stunted trees, and came out beside the narrow river that led down to Big Lake. But Big Lake wasn't sanctuary any more. I felt lonelier out here than I did at home. Without Jenny, or Rudy, or Gloria, there was no point in it. Who could I share with? Who could I swim with and smile with and laugh with?

I kept walking, right to town. I had a few nickels in my pocket, maybe I'd get a slice of that chocolate pie for myself and bring one back for Jenny, cheer her up a bit.

But as I passed the alley by the liquor store, a block away from Westin's, someone grabbed me by the collar, threw me into the alley wall.

I stumbled back. 'Hey . . .' I said, then looked up.

A sneering grin. Pink cheeks. Pink lips. Light ginger hair. Darney Wills.

A sharp stink of alcohol came off him, out of his skin, in his breath. The red of his letterman jacket was dark, stained, the threads fraying at the seams, the white sleeves now a dull grey. He'd graduated but still wore the letter. Look at me, it said, this rotten jacket means I Am Somebody.

'Little Johnny Royal,' he said, voice sharp, not slurring drunk like I'd expected. 'What's a freak like you doing here?'

'Leave me alone, Darney,' I said, stepped to the side to pass him, get out of the alley, into the relative safety of the street. He blocked me. A giant barrier of fat and muscle. I looked down, don't make eye contact, don't provoke it.

'You want a drink?' he said, held up a flat bottle of bourbon. He wasn't old enough to buy it, but when you're the mayor's son and the mayor's knee-deep in the filth of the town, not much is out of reach.

'No, thank you,' I said, sidestepped again. He did the same.

'How's your sister, freak?'

I looked up, met those glassy eyes, thought about clawing them out. I tried to push past him, but it was like pushing against a rotten tree. It gave a bit, a slight lean, then crack, snap, break, and I'm in splinters on the ground. Darney tripped me, caught the back of my neck and slammed me down onto the ground. Grit in my eyes, in my mouth, grinding against my cheek. I saw someone walk past the end of the alley, pause a second, then hurry along. I wanted to scream.

Darney pushed my head into the stone. His sweating fingers slithered in my hair.

'I'll go find out how your sister is. Pretty little bitch, really blossomed,' he said. I could hear the drool in his voice.

'Shut up,' was about all I could manage.

'She's a sweet piece though, ain't she?' He let out that thick *hurr hurr* laugh. 'She as easy as your ma? Ain't a dog in Larson not had his day on that.'

I'll kill you, I'll kill you. Rage, all over me, all through me, like hellfire swallowing up a Bible.

'Reason I asked you here for this meeting,' he said, his voice turned mock serious like when his father gave town speeches. 'I have a message for you.'

'What?'

'I have a friend, see, well more a . . . client, and you do not want to fuck with him, do you get me? You've been screwing around with his daughter and he ain't pleased. Little bitch wouldn't tell him at first who she'd been seeing and who'd been creeping around his house but he got it out of her, eventually. You know who I mean, freak?'

Mr Wakefield. Mr Wakefield knows about me and Gloria. That night, all I'd heard, all it meant, came screaming into the front of my mind. My body went rigid, cold. I tried to nod.

Darney's face lowered, a few inches from my ear. 'He knows you were there that night. Knows what you heard.'

Fear surged, made my bones, my muscles, my eyes ache.

'He told me to threaten you, say he'd break every bone in your pussy body, but I told him that wouldn't be enough for a freak like you. You'd piss your pants and cry it all out to Samuels or that whore mother. So we came up with a different motivator.'

His knee pressed down on my back, blasted all the air out of me. I sucked in dust and grit, felt my tears pooling against my nose, hot blood on my cheek.

'You tell anyone what you heard, you tell anyone about our visit today, and he'll rip you apart, freak. He'll wreck the one thing you love most in this whole crappy world. Your pretty piece-of-ass sister will be all his, and you saw what happened to the last girl he took a shine to. You say nothing and he won't touch a hair on her head. You get me, faggot? You understand what I'm saying to you?'

I was blind. White blind with hate and rage and fear and I couldn't move but to nod. Yes. I understand you. I understand Mr Wakefield. But my brain wouldn't process it, what it all meant. Gloria. Jenny. Mary Ridley. Inside me, the maelstrom howled and I couldn't breathe.

'He won't touch her if you keep your mouth shut, but I'll be keeping a close eye on Jenny from now on, you get me, freak?' Darney leaned closer to my ear so I could feel the heat in his breath, his stink on my cheek.

'Don't you worry,' he said. 'I'll break her in, gentle like. I'll even leave you some after I'm done. I know how close you two are.'

I found my voice. Some of it. This I could fight, this

threat of his, this disgusting image. This I could process and understand. Everything else disappeared.

'Leave her alone.' I strained against him, useless, weak, I couldn't move. 'Don't touch her! Don't you dare!'

He ground my face harder. 'Or what?'

A gob of his spit hit my temple. But it was acid, burning into my skin, through my bones into my brain. I thrashed and bucked, the birds filled my body and tried to lift me. Everything I had in every muscle unleashed and he, that fucker Darney Wills, just laughed. Laughed. Then I was free and he was standing and I was lying in the alley, yelling like a kid lost in a tantrum.

He kicked me in the side. All my screaming stopped. My vision filled with red and black and red again. My guts felt like they would erupt through my mouth if I only opened it.

'See you soon, freak,' he said, moving away, a sound like he was unscrewing the bottle of bourbon. 'Tell Jenny I said hello.'

I lay there for I don't know how long waiting for the pain, the nausea, to pass. Nobody helped. A kid just got beaten two foot off Main Street and nobody was helping. What had happened to my town?

Then arms around mine. Pulling. A soft voice I knew.

'You okay, John?' Frank said. 'What happened?'

I fell onto him, arms over his shoulders, hung there for a moment.

'All right, you're all right,' he said, warmth in his voice. Warmth I desperately needed. I pulled away from him, clutching my side, wiping my face of the spit. Frank pulled a handkerchief from his pocket and gave it to me.

Tell him, John. He can help.

No. Not him, not anyone. I was too afraid that I might
say the wrong thing, put Jenny at risk. So I told him Darney
jumped me, beat me up for calling him a draft-dodger.

'That little shit,' he said. 'Darney has always been a
mongrel, just like his father.'

I almost asked the questions squatting inside me. What
have you, Mr Wakefield and Mayor Wills got going on with
Bung-Eye Buchanan? Mr Wakefield killed Mary Ridley,
didn't he? Did you know? Did it happen in your basement?
What do they have over you?

But I didn't ask. I could've. Should've. But the way he
helped me, pulled me up, held me for just a moment like
a real father would, I couldn't say a word. I didn't want to
know the truth about him. It was all too much right now,
after Darney, after the threat, after what he said about
Wakefield. Oh God. Gloria. If she found out, it would kill
her.

I handed back the handkerchief.

'You keep it,' he said, smiled, checked the red graze on
my cheek. 'Don't worry about boys like that. They don't
grow up, they just get older. You're meant for better things
than this place, John, you mark my words. You'll get out
of this town one day.'

I matched his smile, felt a bubble of something grow up
inside my chest. Pride, maybe, that Frank thought so much
of me. He was a balm. A tonic. I felt my heart slow under
his gaze. Felt myself return to some degree of control.

'All I want is to make a good go of our farm,' I said, my
voice weak and strained. 'One day it'll be the biggest in
three counties.'

He nodded along. 'And how is Jenny? I hear she's doing
all right in school.'

I flinched at her name, Darney's words ringing in my ears. She's safe unless you talk, John, so keep it quiet.

But Wakefield killed Mary Ridley. He did it. He did it. What do I do with that information? What can I do?

Justice for Mary Ridley or safety for Jenny? That's an easy choice, when you boil it down, isn't it, Johnny boy?

'John?' Frank's calm voice cut through my panic. 'John, I asked after Jenny, she doing okay?'

'She's just fine,' I said. I think I said. I didn't hear my voice but he responded.

'Good,' he nodded, smile wide. 'Good, that's good.'

A few seconds of silence. Awkward and too long. I was screaming inside.

'Thank you, for helping me,' I said, then I laughed through the ache in my ribs. Laughing cures all ills, John Royal, my momma used to say, and turns prying eyes away from you when you need it.

I smiled, forced it through numb cheeks. 'Why is it you're always around just at the right time?'

'I suppose the good Lord sees to it you and I come together at times of need, which is fine by me. You'll always have this,' he patted his shoulder, 'should you need it.'

Then he clapped my arm. 'Watch out for Darney, okay? He's an ape but his father has clout. Just you and Jenny stay out of his way.'

'Yes, sir,' I said and my throat seized at her name. Enough clout to be involved in a murder and have no questions asked. Maybe even to cover one up. What could I do against that kind of power?

Frank said goodbye and made a joke about wishing him luck with the ladies of the Gardening Society, then he trotted down the street away from me.

I forgot all about the chocolate pie to cheer up Jenny. My cheek stung and my jaw ached from being pressed into the ground. I told myself I slipped, grazed my cheek and hit my side on a rock. Darney Wills never happened, the truth about Mary Ridley's killer never happened, the threat never happened. At least I knew Frank hadn't killed her. He did something but not that. Frank was still a good man. He'd soothed me, salve on a burn, but the damage and the hurt was still there, mixed in now with anger at Darney. The things he said about Jenny, the fear, oh God the fear, is she really safe? Will she ever be in this town? Then a different anger bubbled up at allowing Gloria's father to get away with murder, at this horrible sword hanging over Gloria's head, this secret I could never, ever tell.

But only Jenny mattered, keeping her safe, keeping her away from Darney and Mr Wakefield, and hoping to God nobody ever found out the truth about Mary's death, else it could all come back to me, back to Jenny.

I don't know what time it was when I got home but it couldn't have been much past noon. I passed the mound of rotten corn, buzzing with blackfly and wasps. My soiled clothes were under there somewhere, buried but still there, right outside my house. Shame coursed through me remembering that night at Gloria's. I'd burn it, today, I decided. Enough of the disease and infection, enough of the dead ground beneath being pocked and infested with maggots and beetles. I wanted to destroy something. I wanted to unleash all that anger Darney and Eric and Wakefield had put in me and seeing that mountain of rot was like the world holding up a mirror of my mind. I'd burn it out of me, burn out Darney's words, burn out the images they put in my head, burn out Wakefield's threat. That mound was the last thing Eric did, the last part of him remaining, and I'd clear it. That's what Jenny would need, remove all reminders, reset her home to a pre-Eric state, keep her mind free of everything else, free of that dagger hanging over our heads.

I strode inside to find the long kitchen matches Momma had for when the stove didn't light, but as soon as I stepped foot into the house, something felt wrong.

The pain in my side and cheek evaporated.

Silence. The record Jenny had been playing when I left had stopped. Joni wasn't wailing any more. Momma wasn't snoring any more. Then a hum came from the family room.

'Momma?' I said. She sat on the edge of her armchair, bent double in jeans and a yellow shirt, painting red onto her toenails.

She didn't look up. 'You and your sister will have to fix your own lunch. I'm going out.'

Her voice was thick and tired, I wasn't sure if from sadness or the drink, maybe both. Her hands trembled slightly but the nail polish was perfect.

'Where'd you two go?' she asked, dabbing a touch of scarlet onto her pinkie toe.

The word struck me. Two.

'I went to the west field to check the corn,' I lied. 'Jenny didn't come with me.'

Then Momma looked up.

She didn't register the graze on my cheek. Her eyes were red where they should have been white, her pupils blacker than I'd ever seen. The skin around her eyelids was dry and pinched, like the salt tears had sucked all the moisture out of her.

'She's not in your room,' Momma said, the sluggish tone sped up with worry, or anger.

A drop of red polish struck the floorboards, looked like blood.

I ran upstairs, flung open our door.

Bed unmade. Drawers open. Clothes thrown everywhere. My clothes. Hers were gone. I rushed to the bed, ducked to look beneath it. Her backpack was gone. Her shoes and coat and sunhat, gone. The record player turntable still spun, but it was bare. The Joni record nowhere.

'Momma!' I screamed.

That's what had felt wrong when I got back to the house, a new, horrible emptiness. He's got her, I thought, Darney beat me home and took her. Wakefield has her. But why would he pack her clothes? I didn't know. Couldn't figure it out. But it didn't matter. My sister was gone.

'Jenny's not here.' I ran downstairs. 'She's gone, Momma, Jenny's gone, where'd she go?'

I expected worry. I wanted her to spring into action, grab the keys, shout, let's scour the roads and ask everyone in Larson if they've seen Jenny. I expected a mother. But when it came to Jenny, Momma never acted like I wanted.

Her face changed. A deep, primal sneer came over her, in her eyes, in her lips, her cheeks, every part of her transformed.

'That little bitch,' she said, shook her head, clenched the bottle of polish so tight in her fist I thought it would shatter. Red spilled out onto the floor, across her foot, over her hands.

She stood, trod in the pool, walked bloody half-footprints toward me.

'You know what she's done, don't you?' Momma said, right up close.

Done? What could she have done? All I could think was, where, where, where, are you, Jenny?

'Her and Eric have run off together.' Momma's sneer grew, showed her teeth, stained yellow and black from whiskey and cigarettes. 'That little slut thinks she can steal my man. But I'll show her, oh my, oh yes, I'll show her what it means when a man takes notice.'

I thought of Darney Wills, of Wakefield, a man taking notice, and wanted to hurl. A monster, uncaged, unchained, rushed into the back of Momma's eyes.

'She might just be—'

'This is your fault,' she snapped. Her hand, painted red, shot to the back of my neck, pushed my head down. Her mouth was at my ear, the smell of stale bourbon in my nose, specks of spit on my cheek. Shock gripped me harder than her nails, she'd never grabbed me like that, spoken to me like that, I felt tears burn my eyes.

'You were meant to keep her clean,' she spat. 'That dirty girl needs to be kept clean and you were meant to do it. You're useless, John Royal, useless, just like your deadbeat father, just like that pussy Eric. You're no better than them.'

She let me go but I still felt her nails digging into my skin. I didn't know where to look, what to say, what to do. My heart galloped, thundering hooves kicked up panic and fear and left me gasping. Momma was speaking but the sound of my pulse was in my ears, blocking out everything else.

'Momma,' I said, a weak whimper. Too weak, I knew right after I said it.

The back of Momma's hand blasted across my cheek. I stumbled. Fell to my hands and knees. Then the pain and heat came, like a second hit, *bam!*

Momma was a hurricane of red polish and tight jeans, all rampage and chaos, spiked words and gnashing teeth. She spun away and I heard the metallic clink of keys, then the front door, then her bare feet on the hard, dry earth. The truck started up, roared out of the yard, screeching on the gravel road and then away.

I stayed on my knees. The sudden silence was foreign. It was what my house would be without Momma or Jenny and I hated it. I wanted to run outside, hear the birds, feel the wind, but I didn't dare move. What if Jenny came back and I wasn't here? What if she didn't?

Momma would find her. Momma had to.

But with Momma in this rage, I prayed she wouldn't, at least not until she calmed down.

Jenny could be on a bus to Washington by now, chasing Eric. Gone forever.

Impossible. Jenny's just upset, she's not thinking straight and, besides, where would she get that kind of cash?

My eyes went to the tacky, red footprints. Three toes and the ball of Momma's foot. They led from the chair to me, fading with each step. A mess around the armchair. I thought for a second how bad it would look if someone, anyone, walked in. A boy kneeling on the floor, a welt on his cheek, something like blood splashed and trodden across the boards.

21

Momma didn't come home for hours. I paced the house, never able to settle in one room. A thousand thoughts raced inside my head. Jenny's dead. Jenny's run away and gone for good. Jenny just wants attention. Jenny taken by Darney Wills to Gloria's father. Her *father*. My fault. All my fault. Dig too deep and you dig up bodies. You dig up danger.

Damn you, Jenny. Come home. She's at the Roost, hiding in the Fort, she's at the Backhoe, she got on a bus and could be anywhere, she's trapped and screaming. I tried to think of something else. Watch the sun, John Royal, that's the one thing you can count on, day in, day out, round and round the world it goes.

The sun rose to its late summer peak and fell over the west field, turning the sky to old gold. I stared at it through the kitchen window. A flock of starlings danced far off beneath the sunset. At this distance, they were one small cloud, not individual birds, just a swarm of darkness floating and pulsing somewhere else.

The night closed in, clouds obscured the stars and moon. No light touched the tops of the trees or swaying corn stalks. The world was black and there was only me. Then the rain began, soft and pattering at first, then a harsh drum beat. It made a cage of my home, made every wall and window vivid and tight around me.

I went about the house, switching on the lamps, listening to the hunger growl in my stomach. The weather turned the radio to white noise and the thought of staring at a book made my head ache. All I could think of was Jenny. Out alone in this weather.

Momma, please find her.

Momma, please don't.

The nail polish had set hard. Red and too bright in my plain house. It was a taunt, like God was telling me, heads up, kid, remember this picture, this is what you've got to look forward to. But it wouldn't be polish. It wouldn't be fake and shiny. It would be real and it would be Jenny's if Momma's rage found her.

I sat on the floor, chipping away at it with my fingernail when, over the beating rain, I heard the truck pull into the yard.

I'd been in a bubble but now the real world rushed upon me like waves on rock. Everything sped up. My body moved before my mind told it to. I was up the stairs and onto the landing, hiding behind the rails.

You're a coward, John, the voices said, but I had been in the path of the whirlwind already and I couldn't be sucked up into the gyre again. I'd be twisted and torn and pulled apart before I could help her. If she needed it. Maybe Momma had calmed and they needed time alone to talk. I'd listen and if things turned bad, I was only a staircase away.

See? You're a damn sissy.

No, I'm—

The front door crashed open.

My chest turned hot and spiked and I clutched the railings until my knuckles turned white.

Momma had Jenny by the arm and dragged her into the family room, slopping wet footprints and mud across the hall. Backpack nowhere, sunhat gone, but alive. Safe. And home. The spikes in my lungs softened to marshmallow.

But something didn't feel right.

Momma usually shouted, screamed, but she was dead silent.

I realised a beat later it was because she was sober. There was no fuel for her fire. It burned white-hot on its own and felt all the more dangerous for it.

They disappeared into the kitchen and I moved across the landing, to the top step, to see them.

The sound of a chair scraping the linoleum, then it came into view. Jenny's chair. Where she always sat around the table. Her faded butterfly sticker on the top rail.

'Sit down,' Momma said, so calm and cold it made me flinch.

Momma stood opposite Jenny, her back to me. My sister's face was not my sister's. It was streaked with tears or rain, eyes puffy and raw, and a bright red bruise grew on her cheek. My own swollen cheek ached at the sight. A small cut in the centre of Jenny's welt said Momma had turned her ring around before striking.

'Where did you think you were going?' Momma said. Her voice filled the empty house, quieting the rain and turning our home into a speaker box. Everything too loud, too close.

We were our own planet then. A rock sailing through the darkness. Just us, our farm, our whitewashed house. The dirt road no longer led to Larson, it cut off at the gate and fell into nothing.

Momma repeated her question.

No one would ever turn up at the door, break the moment apart, save Jenny from whatever Momma was going to do. Because she was going to do something. Something terrible. She had that coiled snake tension all over her. I felt it. Jenny felt it. And I couldn't move.

'Answer me!'

Jenny flinched, sank back as far as she could in her chair. Her fingers scratched at the seat, dug and dug and dug into wood. Her chin pressed into her chest, couldn't, wouldn't, look up into Momma's eyes. Those blue eyes that were Jenny's as well.

'I . . .' Jenny began but what could she say? 'I was just . . .'

The sound of my breathing, my heartbeat, clogged the landing. I want to be a bird, I want to swoop down these stairs and grab Jenny, fly her away. But I was rigid, stuck to my spot like I was a part of the house itself. Part of the prison.

'You . . . you were just?' Momma whined.

Then she rushed to Jenny, towered over her. 'You were running away with Eric, weren't you? Weren't you?'

'No, Momma,' Jenny tried but it was a lie. I saw it and it broke my heart. Momma saw it too. Momma can spot a lie like a hawk can spot a mouse.

'Don't lie to me, girl.'

Then Jenny looked up. Met Momma's eyes, met her ferocity. They had the same power in them, the same rage, only Jenny hadn't been destroyed by hers like Momma had. Not yet, anyway.

'We were going to Washington,' Jenny said.

She had been running after Eric, chasing him down to take her away to some better place. Tears spilled from my eyes and sizzled to steam on my cheeks. You would leave me, you would walk out the door and leave me and never look back?

'He wanted me. He said so,' Jenny carried on and I silently prayed for her to stop. 'He was sick of you, called you a withered old hag.'

'Don't you understand?' Momma said, her voice taut, a rubber band stretched to its limit. 'You are so stupid. I should have cut you out of me the second that no-good man put you in.'

Momma stood behind Jenny, her hands on my sister's shoulders. Those hands, fingers, so long and dark against Jenny's pale throat. They enveloped it, held it in a cage like the harrier held its prey. So gentle at first.

Momma bent down slightly, put her face closer to Jenny's head. 'Then you came out a girl and I thought, I can teach her, I can show her my mistakes and she won't make them herself.'

Momma's hands tightened around Jenny's neck and my body tensed, ready to fly down the stairs if she closed her fists. All Jenny's defiance ebbed away and she was so small in those hands. Her fierce eyes faded to a light blue and her lip and chin trembled.

'But you are making those mistakes,' Momma went on, her voice getting deeper, darker with every word. 'You're making them over and over. I wanted so much better for you but you just don't deserve it. You're dirt, you see that don't you? Head-to-toe filth and I ought to let those men do whatever they want, as much as they want, until they're all spent. I ought to charge them for it for all the grief you've cost me, but that dirty little cooch isn't worth a nickel. What's the point in you then? Huh? What's the *fuhking* point in you?'

I trembled on the steps. Rooted. Stuck between fear and shock and needing to help. Jenny had left me, the icy shard of that realisation pierced my chest. I felt the rubber band in Momma's voice stretched beyond its ability, I saw the white strain in its fibres. I waited. Any moment now. Any second.

'I didn't . . .' Jenny said. Tiny. Quietly defiant. Oh, Jenny. *Snap!*

Momma snatched up all of Jenny's hair in one hand. The chair toppled. My sister screamed, disappeared from view. A moment. A horrible moment of not knowing. What do I do? What the hell do I do? Then I heard her. Her voice reached up the stairs to me.

'Johnny!'

And I was on my feet. Down. Two, three steps at a time. Then I saw it and my blood, my bones, my limbs, every part of me froze and I stumbled.

Momma had pulled the carving knife from the kitchen drawer.

'This is for your own good,' she said, terribly soft against Jenny's struggles, her tears and pleas and please, Momma, please, stop, stop, stop.

Red-hot horror exploded in me. Momma wrapped her hand around Jenny's hair. Held Jenny tight against her side.

'Don't!' I shouted. A dozen pictures, possibilities, went through me, a dozen evil thoughts in my head. She's going to kill her. She's going to kill Jenny. It didn't matter what

Jenny did, what she didn't do, you can't hurt her. You can't hurt my sister.

Momma looked up. Saw me.

Run at her, Johnny, grab her arm, take the blade, take it in your chest if you have to, but I was too far and too slow. The floor was thick mud, the rug a tangleweed, the overturned chair a mountain in my path.

'Momma!' I shouted and shouted. The house filled with rage. Everyone roaring, crying, begging.

'Let me go!' Jenny dug deep scratches into Momma's arm but there wasn't a speck of Momma left. It was all monster and monsters don't feel pain.

Momma yanked Jenny's hair upward, ripped strands from her scalp with sickening *pop-pop* sounds.

In one long arc she brought the knife up and sliced.

It wasn't clean. The knife wasn't that sharp. She gripped Jenny's hair again, strands broke and split as Momma hacked and strained. A sheen of sweat on her neck, thin face red and boiling. Then she was finished.

Jenny fell to her knees. Suddenly released. Her kneecaps cracked on the floorboards and she cried out a new hurt.

I skidded down beside her, wrapped my arms around her shoulders. Too late. I was too late. I stared up at Momma and the length of Jenny's hair in her fist. A scattering of it on the linoleum, clumps of it matted with blood. Jenny's perfect hair, sunshine on her back, down to her waist, a beauty, a cascade. Now dull yellow in Momma's hand like Mary Ridley's after days dead in the water.

Jenny was stone in my arms. Her eyes wide, staring at the floor behind me. Her body rose and fell against mine, air scratched against her throat and lungs and came out in rasping breaths.

'They won't want you now.' Momma licked her lips, breathless. 'Don't worry, my baby girl, they won't want you any more. Momma fixed you.'

Momma took a step closer. Grip on the knife tightened, her knuckles bleached white around the handle. 'Well? Where's my thank you? I taught you better manners than that.'

I felt sick. Cut off her hair, make her cry, make her bleed, and make her say thank you for it? I wanted to scream.

Jenny shuddered in my arms, closed her eyes and said, 'Thank you, Momma.'

No fight, no sass, no life. Just *Thank you.* Dead words out of a dead mouth.

Momma murmured good girl, good girl, and let go of Jenny's ragged hair. It fell, splayed on the floor.

Momma tossed the knife onto the kitchen table and wiped her face with one hand.

'John, make your sister a sandwich,' then her eyes went to Jenny, her hair, her tears. 'She's had a long day.'

She kicked the hair. 'Clean this up too.'

When I didn't move, when I kept my sister in my arms, held her trembling body to mine, Momma grabbed me. Momma pulled me. Fingernails dug into my arm and I felt my skin rip. My muscles were nothing against hers and I was torn away, fell backward, Jenny left exposed, shivering.

'I said,' Momma bent right down to my ear, 'make your sister a sandwich.'

'Yes, Momma.'

I stood on uneven feet, my shoulders and back knotted up, waiting for another strike. This wasn't my mother, this wasn't the woman who'd bought me the bird book and taught us Euchre and braided Jenny's hair. This was some new horror and I was useless against it, tissue paper in a rain storm. The house buzzed around me. Darkness on both sides of the walls. The world outside was gone, the world inside changed forever.

The only thing I could focus on was the knife. The only tangible piece of the puzzle I could control. Get the knife, Johnny, get the knife before Momma changes her mind, does something worse. The blade lay on the table, facing me like it was choosing my hand to secure it. Go on, Johnny, before it's too late.

But my sister was on her feet. My sister was at the table. My sister snatched the knife and held it, shaking, arms straight out, blade tip pointed right at Momma's face.

My heart, my gut, sank straight to my feet. 'Jenny, give that to me . . .'

Did I even say that out loud? I heard it in my head but my throat was dry and tight.

Momma turned. A second. A beat. Then she laughed.

'Well, well,' she said, stepped past me, put herself between me and Jenny. 'Little bitch has teeth.'

Jenny's face, red and swollen, with a line of blood slicing through her skin from the wound on her cheek, and another from somewhere deep in her hairline, was not a face I knew. It was alien, ruined, a new thing taken shape in my kitchen. What was left of her hair fell choppy and uneven across her forehead and the bright blonde I loved was dimmed, like someone had thrown a shade over the sun. A house full of strangers. A family I no longer knew.

Fresh tears welled in Jenny's eyes. 'Why?'

'Why what?' Momma took another step to her.

'Why do you hate me?'

The tip of the knife wavered, lowered slightly. It was enough.

Momma lunged. Wrapped herself around Jenny, clutched both wrists until my sister screamed and the knife fell to the floor.

A moment of stillness. The house filled with Jenny's wails, Momma's breathing and my heartbeat and I couldn't move, didn't know how any more, feet and legs and back and arms were rock.

'I don't hate you, baby,' Momma whispered close to Jenny's ear. She pinned both of Jenny's hands across her chest and held onto her from behind. Momma eclipsed her, hunched over her until the sobs quietened. Momma murmured hushes and it's okay baby's into the top of Jenny's hair, kissing her and swaying her side to side. It felt like an hour, a day, a whole long, dark night, that the three of us stood frozen. My two monsters, calming each other, and me, paralysed at the side, just watching them, waiting for one to break.

Jenny squeezed her eyes shut, took a deep breath, and went slack in Momma's arms. Just like that, it was over. The monsters retreated, the air came back into the room and the darkness felt a few degrees brighter.

'I don't hate you, baby,' Momma said again. She let Jenny go and knelt down in front of her, pushed a few strands of shorn hair from her eyes.

Momma touched her forehead to Jenny's. 'I love you, my baby girl, can't you see that? Everything I do is because I love you so, so much.'

My eyes went from Momma's face to Jenny's. From triumph to defeat.

Still stroking Jenny's ruined hair, Momma turned to me. 'Where's that sandwich?'

So I made it, in a numb, mechanical haze. I don't even remember what was in it. One for Jenny. One for Momma. The thought of eating turned my stomach. They sat at opposite ends of the table. Neither would look at the other. Jenny barely ate. Momma smoked and drank can after can of Old Milwaukee.

I couldn't sit there, stand there, in their presence. Momma had taken a knife to Jenny but Jenny had taken it right back. They were my world, my life, and they were killing each other. I couldn't stand it. I wanted to cry so hard my face ached but I kept it in.

The light from the kitchen window reached the edge of the yard. The sky was clearing, allowing the moon to highlight the world's edges. I could finally see the answer to our ills, halfway across our field, fringed with silver light.

I gathered up Jenny's fallen hair and took it outside, grabbed the kitchen matches on my way. I tossed my sister's hair onto the pile. That's where our secrets went. Into the dirt with the maggots, ready for burning. The maggots writhed and pulsed and even in the dark, I could hear them moving. The tiny sounds their fat, white bodies made as they chewed and squirmed their way through our crops, our livelihood. They brought ruin on us. They drove Eric away. They knew my shame. They knew Jenny's hurt. The infection they brought to our farm had taken root, gone too far. It was time.

The rain had stopped but the pile would need help to burn. I went to the barn, found a gas can and started splashing the mound, all sides, as high up as I could throw. I struck a match, threw it, and the world lit up orange.

I saw them, then. The birds.

On the guttering. On the barn. On the fence line. On

every branch of the oak tree. They bristled at the flames but didn't fly away. Black marks on every surface, preening, shifting, watching.

'What do you want?' I said. 'Get out of here.'

I threw my arms up, shouted, 'Get', but they didn't move.

A thousand shining black eyes bored into me. A thousand talons flexed and tightened around my bones. A thousand wings beat in my chest. They were my birds, the ones inside me, the ones scratching under my skin. They were real and they were here. All around me, waiting for the maggots to hiss and burst, waiting for the fire.

I heard the screen door creak open behind me. Jenny's voice, dull and tired. 'John? What are you doing?'

'Do you see them? They won't go.'

I turned to her and flinched. Forgot.

She was a doll a child had taken a pair of scissors to. Her hair, no longer than her ears, stuck up and out and everywhere. Blood ran down her face from a nick in her scalp. A deep scratch flared red on the back of her neck, curling around to her ear. A curtain of dry, flaking blood touched her shoulder. She was broken. And I had to mend her.

'Do I see what?' she asked but her tone said she didn't care.

I turned away, back to the birds. The guttering, the oak, the fences, empty.

I felt the scratching under my skin, the feathers in my chest. Jenny stood beside me and the sensation stopped. My birds. My sister. Never in the same place.

'Nothing. It's all going to be okay,' I said and took her hand, interlaced our fingers. Her skin was cold.

'It'll grow back,' I said. 'The corn. Your hair. Even Larson. It'll all grow back and it'll be just like before.'

We watched the flames devour the corn. We couldn't
have known, either of us, how wrong I was in those few
words. The west field turned sour and acidic and wouldn't
take seed. Larson tried to drag itself out of the mire but a
few men wanted to keep it down, keep it desperate, and
they did it well.

PART THREE

Summer, 1973

22

The winter passed slowly, like the last old man in the corner of the bar refusing to leave at the end of the night. Drag him out by the collar and drag the world round on its axis. One thought gnawed at me all through the cold months. Jenny wasn't safe. Whether from Wakefield or from Momma or even from herself, she wasn't safe, but I didn't know how to fix it. The voices in my head told me to leave Larson, leave Momma, but that would mean leaving my farm and my future and my family. Besides, I had no money except for those few dollars I was saving to buy old man Briggs' tractor. How far away that possibility seemed now, barely more than a child's dream.

The snow was bad that year, heavy drifts, a blizzard a week. Jenny and me used to make snowmen every January. We'd throw snowballs, make angels, but not that year. The whiteout wasn't some magical wonderland, it wasn't glittering and pure. That year it was prison. A chain around our house and farm and lives. Everything too cold, too slippery, too dangerous to move. Everyday life was a heave and an ache, trudging through deep drifts, and nothing but an inch or two forward to show for the effort.

I kept my mouth shut about Mary Ridley and Wakefield. Kept that wolf at bay, at least for a while. But Momma, I couldn't stop her and I couldn't stop Jenny riling her. I lived that winter tense and waiting for the dagger to fall. I drew away from Gloria and Rudy, barely saw them for months. I couldn't risk Jenny by telling them the truth and if I couldn't tell them everything, I felt like I couldn't tell them anything.

By Christmas, they stopped trying to make me talk about it and we settled into a quiet distance. That hurt Gloria especially, I know it did because it hurt me too. I figured I'd hurt her less by ignoring it than ruining her whole family. It tore my heart to confetti to see her, staring at me across the school lunchroom, red eyes like mine, angry and missing each other.

Maybe one day, when all this Mary Ridley business was forgotten, I'd march up to Gloria Wakefield and sweep her up in one of those epic movie kisses like John Wayne and Coleen Gray in *Red River*. Rudy and me had snuck past Hell-on-Healey to see that in the Clarkesville picture house last summer, one of their old movie matinees. That movie made me think of Gloria, the way pretty Fen had said she was as strong as John Wayne any day, could handle anything the frontier could throw at them. I wished that were true of Gloria and me. I wanted to talk to her, be with her more than anything, but I couldn't. Not yet.

To distract myself, I volunteered to help Frank with the younger kids' Bible Study class on Sunday mornings. Most weekends I cleaned up the classroom in the back of the church and then Frank would buy me Coke or hot malt at the Backhoe as thank you. I wanted to tell him what Momma did that past summer to Jenny but I couldn't. I wanted to tell him about Mr Wakefield's threat but I couldn't. Those Sundays were my bright spots and as the year turned over to '73, I didn't have many to cling to.

The sun came back in April and melted the world to mud. I overheard Didi in the Backhoe one afternoon talking about how some folks in the next county found a dead man, soaking drunk, went missing as the snow started in December and wasn't found until the thaw. A secret held all winter long, like Jenny's hair and who and how and why it was all cut off. People looked, asked questions. Official story was Jenny did it to herself to spite her momma because she blamed her momma for Eric leaving and knew Momma loved her hair.

Don't you say a word about that day, John Royal, Momma told me, grabbed me by the shoulder, no one wants to hear your lies.

Solid ice all around me.

Jenny wasn't my Jenny any more. She was some angry thing living in my house, sleeping in my room, not talking, barely eating, never smiling. It was like that strange obsession with Mary Ridley had been kicked into overdrive. More than once I caught her talking to herself, to Mary, to Eric, even to Mark and Tracy, holding whole conversations with phantoms. Those were the only times I heard her laugh and it scared the shit out of me. Fear worse than when Darney attacked me, worse than hearing Wakefield talk about murder, worse than finding a girl's body. This was my sister, I loved her more than the sun, but I was losing her. I wanted to shake her awake, break through that hard coating and find my Jenny again, before it was too late.

One evening, sometime after Easter, Jenny and me sat in the family room, her reading, me pretending to. Her hair was up in its scarf, the one with little blue stars Gloria had given her for her birthday, and just a few yellow strands fell over her brow. The cut on the back of her neck from Momma's knife was healed up to a thin red curve. When her hair grows back, I thought, you'd never know it was there. That gave me a speck of hope. It would all be covered up, all the hurt and pain and blood and bad feeling. It'd be invisible again, forgotten though maybe not forgiven.

Momma was working the late shift at Gum's and we'd had two-days-ago meatloaf for dinner. We hadn't spoken all evening. Every moment spent with this Other Jenny was agony to me. I had to try harder to break the shell, bring her back.

But how?

Find a way.

Give her what she wants. If she gets what she wants she'll be happy. That's how it works with girls. Momma's always happy when I bring her whiskey or her Lucky Strikes.

'Jenny,' I said but she didn't look up from her book. 'Jenny, if you could have anything in the whole world, what would it be?'

She lowered the book and her eyes went to the window. 'Isn't it obvious?'

'Tell me anyway.'

'I want to get out of this house of course. I want to be away from *her*.' She swivelled around to me, lit up from the inside. 'I want to see the world and smell the ocean. I want to go to San Francisco and see the White House in Washington and join the protests, Eric tells me all about them. And New York City and Chicago and Paris, France.' Her hand went to the scarf and her tone darkened. 'It doesn't even matter where as long as it's not here.'

She stretched out her arms, a look of sadness all over her. 'I wish I was a bird. Wake up, fly away, and never look back.'

Then her gaze lost me, went through me, like she was talking to the distance. 'She'll kill me one day if I don't. I know it.'

I blinked, eyes suddenly hot. No, no way, not a chance, not ever. Momma wouldn't, couldn't, no but . . . but since Eric left . . . she was a different Momma, more drunk, more absent, more vicious. Then I saw the red curve on Jenny's neck. A few inches to the side, a little deeper, so easy to slip, and . . . But that was silly thinking, come on now, John. Momma would never hurt Jenny like that. But maybe she would keep chipping away at her until my sister was all gone and she wouldn't even want to see San Francisco or Washington or smell the ocean.

Darney Wills' terrible words came back. He'll destroy the one thing you love most in this whole world. Your pretty piece-of-ass sister will be all his, and you know what happened to the last girl he took a shine to.

Then I knew I had no other option.

It was the last thing I wanted to do but the only thing I could.

We had to leave Larson. At least for a while. Until all this Mary Ridley business died down.

My heart ached. I cast my eyes around the house and

out the window to our empty fields. Royal land. My land. My dream. Then my eyes found my sister, broken and bruised and not herself, and the ache diminished.

This isn't for you, John, this is for her. Keep her far away from Wakefield and Darney. Keep her clear of Momma. It'll hurt for a while, a sharp sting like ripping tape off your arm, but worth it. It doesn't have to be forever. It can't be. I knew I couldn't go the rest of my life without my mother and I didn't want to, no matter her faults she was blood and the only true parent I had. The thought of leaving her made me shudder.

They both needed distance from each other. Jenny will realise she plays her own part in riling up Momma, I'll make sure she sees that, and when she does, we'll come home. Momma doesn't mean it, it's not our real momma doing all those things, it's the drink, the anger, the fear of losing what she loves. Momma will learn to control it. She'll find a new Pigeon Pa to tame it. A Pigeon Pa who'll stick around this time.

Jenny went back to her book and I to mine, but my mind raced in circles and my chest hurt from sadness. I looked at her, the sharp angle of her jaw, the way she tied her scarf so neatly, the scar on the back of her neck, decided.

All I needed now was cash.

'Mr Westin?' I called out, standing in front of the empty counter in Al Westin's grocery store. The sound of boxes being moved in the back. A groaning huff from the old man. It was after school, when mothers would usually be buying their greens and potatoes for dinner but the store was empty, the collards wilted in their box.

'Mr Westin?' Louder. Craned my body over the counter, trying to see through the plastic curtain separating the light, bright store from the dark, cramped back.

'Coming,' came the reply, too gruff, too impatient for Al Westin.

I flinched. Sank back. Bad time. Come back later. He won't listen to you now.

Just as I was backing away, the old man swept through the curtain and rested his palms on the scratched wooden countertop. The frown set deep in his features eased when he recognised me.

'John Royal,' he said, half a smile. 'Haven't you shot up? Should call you Beanpole Royal now, ey, ey?'

A fat grin grew on my face. Four inches in the last three months but Momma and Jenny hadn't noticed. Frank had, when I saw him this past Sunday, and I'd beamed as much at him as I was at Al. I straightened my back, gained an extra half-inch. 'Yes, sir.'

'My Scott hasn't had his spurt yet, still a midget in short trousers, he is. He should be here soon, after practice, if you're looking for him. Anything I can do for you?'

I opened my mouth but my words stuck in my throat. On the way over here I'd run through a dozen scenarios, a dozen how-to-asks and a dozen possible replies, but now here, that dozen could have been a thousand for all it prepared me. How do you do it, ask for a job? Shouldn't Momma have taught me? Shouldn't school?

'John?' Mr Westin tilted his head to the side.

Just ask him, you idiot, he can only say no.

Ah, but if he says no you're screwed, you and Jenny, *royally* screwed.

A dark laugh inside my head.

'Yoo-hoo, John, come back down to earth, kid.' Mr Westin gently touched my shoulder.

'Sorry. I . . . uh . . . . I just wondered if you might need an extra pair of hands after school some days . . . you know . . . I could use some pocket money and . . . uh . . .'

Mr Westin's face fell. He rubbed the back of his neck. 'Ah, John. I'd love to help you out but I got Scotty helping me after school.'

I looked at the half-empty produce trays, the sad cabbage leaves and potatoes spotted with eyes. Mr Westin saw me looking.

'It's gone to hell, huh?' he said. 'Ever since that damn mill. My day kid, Billy-something, you remember?' I didn't but nodded anyway. 'He used to load the flour trucks for Easton when he wasn't working here. He had a girl in Clarkesville, heard he got her in the family way and you can't raise cats on the hourly I had him on. He ran off to Chicago with the girl, left me right up shit creek. Pardon my French.'

'So you only need someone during the day, when everyone is at school?' I said, a heavy stone sinking in my stomach.

'Sorry, son,' Mr Westin said, and I could see he meant it. 'You could talk to Didi, the Backhoe might need a weekend washboy.'

My cheek twitched at the thought. Too high a chance of Darney Wills seeing me, teasing me, holding my head under the brown sink water.

'Thank you, Mr Westin. I'll do that.'

'Hey, John, before you scoot,' he said, came around the counter and eyed the street outside. 'My Scott, you know, how's he doing?'

'Good, I guess, I don't really know.'

Mr Westin nodded. 'It's just, see, he's been roping around with the Buchanan boy, Rudy. That isn't really a kid you want hanging out with your son, if you catch my drift.'

It was everyone's drift when it came to Rudy and I'd had this conversation half a dozen times.

'You've got nothing to worry about, sir. Rudy's not like his family.'

'You sure? I heard he broke his arm that time falling out a window, they say he was stealing the church petty cash box.'

'That's a flat out lie,' I almost shouted. 'His father broke his arm. Rudy isn't a thief.'

Al Westin nodded but he wasn't convinced. For a second I hated this town, its people, for making up lies like that about my best friend. The same people who said I'd killed Mary Ridley. All the more reason to leave, Johnny boy. I took a deep breath. Al wasn't a bad guy, in fact, he was one of the only good ones left. I forced a smile.

'It's just gossip, sir. None of it's true.'

He smiled with me and nodded. 'All right. Well you better get on before Didi finds another washboy.'

I stepped out onto Main Street, into hot air and heavy silence. A few windows were still boarded, the wood scrawled with ugly words in garish paint. Pieces of litter and leaves, beer cans, fast food napkins, cigarette ends, caught up into a ball by the wind, swirled on the sidewalk, then dropped, scattered. A man, the only person I could see, walked right through the mess, didn't care, didn't want to see it. He kicked a can into the street like it was a game.

A sad ache in my chest. A year ago, that man would have stooped, picked up what he could and found a trash can.

A year ago, the chattering bird women outside the beauty parlour would have written a notice about our terrible litter problem and put it up on the church bulletin board for all to see, tut at, shame the perpetrators and clean up the town. Before Mark and Tracy. Before the Easton mill explosion. Before Eric left and Momma turned monster and Jenny changed.

I went through town, to Mrs Lyle at the post office, to Jimmy's auto shop, even the beauty parlour, but nobody was hiring. The chairs outside the parlour were empty of crow women in curlers. The post office was shuttered most days and the auto shop had turned chop shop to make up for the shortfall. Larson kids like me always used to get summer and weekend jobs in the mill stacking sacks of flour, breaking our backs for a buck a day. But not any more. There was nowhere left for us.

I considered the Backhoe but just couldn't bring myself to go inside. A washboy. Potscrubber. Kitchen rat. Cleaning up half-eaten plates of eggs and burgers in the swelter from the grill and the fryers, a thousand degrees hotter than the worst summer. Come home smelling of fry oil and meat sweat. Darney Wills would see me, wait for me after, beat me into a patty. Or maybe he would do nothing and that would be worse. Nothing for now, but just wait, let your blood boil at the thought, right up until you think you're safe, when you least expect it. Then *smash!* You're down. You're down, and you ain't getting up.

I was on my knees. In the dirt. Hot breath came out of me in quick blasts.

The sun was low, minutes from setting. Slowly, I realised where I was. The Three Points. The triangular, no-man's-land island made by irrigation canals, set adrift between farms.

'How did I . . .?' I said out loud like I expected someone to answer.

A blackout. I'd lost an hour or two, maybe more.

I stood. My sneakers were wet. A trail of damp footprints led behind me, toward Big Lake. I felt the scratching inside my body, on my bones, snagging at my veins.

I ran home as the starlings three fields over began their dusk dance. Always there, filling the sky, pulsing like my own heartbeat, mirroring the rush inside me.

When I got home, sweating and red-faced, it was dark but the house lights blazed. Jenny sat rigid at the kitchen table. Music, Patsy Cline, played through the house and then I saw Momma, dancing at the stove. Apron tied around her waist, spatula in her hand, hips swaying to the rhythm.

She spun around when she heard me. 'Here's my boy. My two babies are home. Just in time for dinner.'

The smell of fried chicken hit me and my stomach kicked. Momma's fried chicken was something special. Secret's in the spices, she always said.

'Get the plates, John,' Momma said, and started singing Patsy's chorus.

I took three plates from the cupboard.

'Ah!' Momma pointed the spatula at me. 'We'll need *four*, today.'

My chest tightened. 'Four? Someone else coming?'

'A special guest,' she said.

I glanced at Jenny, her eyes wide, her back rebar-straight, scarf around her hair.

'Who?' I asked, but the sound of a truck pulling into the yard cut above my question, above the music. Momma snatched the chicken pieces out the sizzling pan, rested

them, golden and crispy, on a paper towel, then pulled off
her apron.

'Put those on the table,' she said, smoothed and then
tousled her hair. 'How do I look?'

'Very pretty, Momma.'

I transferred the chicken to a bowl and set it on the table
beside a plate piled high with squares of cornbread. My
hands shook. I met Jenny's eyes. She shook too. Those eyes
pleaded. That was fear, pure and simple fear, right there
at the kitchen table.

The sound of a slamming truck door. Heavy footsteps
on the porch.

A booming knock.

Momma beamed at us like some giddy schoolgirl, but
through the smile her words were harsh. 'Best behaviour.
Don't you dare ruin this for me.'

She went to the door and I took my seat beside Jenny.

'Who is that? Why's she acting so strange?' I whispered
but Jenny just shook her head, watched for Momma to
reappear.

We heard soft giggling, a rough, low voice, then footsteps.
Momma came into the kitchen, holding a man's hand. I
knew him. Jenny knew him. Everyone in Larson knew him
and nobody wanted him as their dinner guest. I gripped
Jenny's hand under the table.

'Kids,' Momma said, like she was displaying a first prize
trophy. 'Say hello to Mr Buchanan.'

'Ain't this a glorious sight,' Bung-Eye said, pulled off his
jacket, old leather with denim patches. His armour. He
handed it to Momma without looking at her, without
speaking, with just an air of expectation that she knew, as
she should, what he wanted of her.

She took it, hung it in the hall and returned to his side. A horrible silence grew between us, no matter the music, no matter the sound of the fat still sizzling in the pan.

I squeezed Jenny's hand. Momma wasn't acting like Momma and it scared me more than any monster.

'Aw hell, Patty, these two can call me Eddie.' Bung-Eye winked that glass eye at me and Jenny. 'Or Dad, of course.'

Momma gestured for Bung-Eye to sit at the table. As he walked, heavy on our floorboards, his black boots made *chink-chink* sounds like he was fitted with spurs. He wore blue jeans, faded and worn in over decades, and a dark orange shirt with a tight chequered pattern. I'd never been this close to Bung-Eye Buchanan. Never seen him in full light, when I wasn't hiding or running or fearing for my life. His face was thin, dark hair flecked with grey, older than I expected, or at least, he looked it. Sunken, stubbled cheeks below one fierce blue eye. Small scar on his top lip. Another above his dead eye. Another curving around his left ear. He even wore an earring, a dull silver ball, nothing special but on him it was like a stud edging a leather trunk, practical, necessary.

The red-blue Dodge Challenger crashed into my memory. Gloria's father's car. A payment to keep Mary Ridley's family quiet. I know what you've done, Bung-Eye. I know what you are.

Jenny nudged me. Her hand. I was crushing it in mine. I relaxed but didn't let her go. Momma asked for best behaviour. Momma was smiling and happy and dancing and asked for best behaviour. Don't let your momma down, John Royal.

'Hello . . .' My throat closed up, filled with cement at the thought of calling him Eddie or, I flinched, Dad. '. . . Mr Buchanan.'

He nodded to me, cast his good eye over Jenny, lingered a moment too long, and took the chair at the head of the table, where Momma usually sat.

A flurry of black feathers in my chest.

Bung-Eye slowly pulled out the spare chair and put his feet up. Jenny and I watched, open-mouthed, terrified like standing on the tracks, watching the train come. Mud flaked off his boots onto the seat, onto the floor. And he stared. Right at me. His gaze was pressing against mine. He was waiting for me to speak, call him on it. Come on, man of the house, show me what you got. I didn't, couldn't. Best behaviour. He took a toothpick from the bowl on the table and started chewing on it, smiling, twisting the wood around his tongue, showing his tobacco-stained teeth, making himself right at home.

'We eating sometime today, doll?' he said, then leaned backward to Momma at the counter, spooning corn into a dish, and slapped her backside.

She laughed. A fake laugh, like the girls in those old movies when the man in the tuxedo says they're a real fox. I wanted to shout, who is this woman? What have you done with my Momma?

Then I remembered. A dangerous, beautiful man, she called him. They were high school sweethearts. The bad boy and the beauty queen, together again, together at last. I clenched my jaw, bit my tongue, forced the bile back down my throat.

She set down a bowl of mashed potato and the corn beside the chicken and danced back to the fridge for beer.

'Dig in, honey,' Momma said, twisted the cap off the bottle and handed it to him. He kept his eyes on me as he drank half in one breath.

Momma came to the table, to the spare chair, to Bung-Eye's footrest. She hovered a moment, waited, her smile cracking at the edges.

Move. Move your damn feet. I looked from him to her to him to her. Move, you son of a bitch.

'Eddie?' Momma said, her hand on the back of the chair, trying to keep the bright, light tone.

Bung-Eye looked up at her. A beat. A moment.

He looked down at his feet.

'Hmm, Patty-cake?' he said. He squinted up at her, sharp smile on his lips, his finger tap-tap-tapping on the bottle.

Momma's hand tightened around the chair.

My hand tightened around Jenny's. I felt her heartbeat in her wrist.

Another second. Two. Painful silence. Crackling air.

'Come on now, you waiting for a signed invitation?' Bung-Eye lifted his feet, dusted off the seat and pulled it out further so Momma could sit down. He even tucked it in behind her, like a real gentleman.

Then he leaned close to her, across the table, and planted a kiss on her cheek, hard, so her neck bent awkwardly under the force. Her smile returned, fuller, stronger, than before.

'It smells delicious, doll,' he said, sat back in the chair. Momma's chair. He flicked the toothpick on the floor like he was in a dive bar, then took the largest piece of chicken from the bowl. He ripped through the flesh with black teeth.

'Fine, fine chicken,' he said, mouth full of churning white meat. 'From a fine, fine woman. You always were made for the kitchen,' he licked chicken grease off his top lip, leaned closer to her. 'And the bedroom, ey? Ey?'

He winked his good eye at Momma and she flushed pink,

took a piece of chicken for herself and told us to do the same.

'Ain't this just picture perfect? The four of us, just like an *aw*-thentic, God-fearing, all-American family, ey, Patty-cake?' Bung-Eye grinned and finished off his beer.

He got up, went to the fridge and took out another. He popped the cap and tossed it onto the sideboard. It skipped and fell onto the floor. He sniffed at it. The good eye went to me, to Jenny, to Momma. The milk-white busted eye didn't move, but it was always looking. It was like a frosted window; blurred but it let me see the gears turning inside his head, setting all his pistons in motion. He looked at all of us again, whatever idea he had taking shape. I swallowed a mouthful of dry meat and waited, trembling, my pulse thumping like a countdown.

Finally, he sat back down and took a piece of cornbread.

'Patty, you getting that?' he said, tore a bite, crumbs scattered the table, the plate, his shirt.

Momma, halfway into a drumstick, said, 'Don't worry, hon, I'll get it later.'

Something changed in that moment. A shift in the air. Everything became electric, every movement, breath, chew and swallow, charged and ready to spark, set fire to the world.

Bung-Eye dropped the cornbread. It hit his plate and the noise jolted Momma away from her chicken.

I wanted to warn Momma and Jenny that Bung-Eye was coiled, ready to snap. That look on his face, that smug expression, it was the smile before the bite. I'd seen it before, right before he broke Rudy's arm. His own son. If he could do that to his blood, what could he do to my momma?

'It ain't nice to eat when there's garbage all over the linoleum, now is it?'

The cap, the toothpick – his garbage, his mess. Pick it up yourself, get on your hands and knees and clean our floor. All my muscles seized, my brain froze, stuck between actions. Shout at him. Don't shout at him.

Best goddamn behaviour.

'How about you, sport?' Bung-Eye turned to me. 'You gonna pick up that cap?'

I met my momma's eyes. A tiny, blinking nod. Not worth the fight, John Royal, that nod said. Go pick up the bottle cap. So I did, and the toothpick, and put them in the trash.

Bung-Eye grinned, shook his head. 'What a good lad you are, John, a good, good lad. You always do what you're told?'

Again, by reflex, I looked to Momma. 'Yes, sir.'

Bung-Eye scratched at the stubble on his cheek. 'Well ain't that something. Ain't that just something.'

I heard Rudy's screams in my head. I heard the sound of his bones snapping under those boots. Get me out of here. Get me and Jenny away from him, oh please, God, let us go.

'Jenny,' I said, straightened my back, gave myself the extra half-inch in height. 'You finished? We've got home-work.'

Jenny didn't need to look to Momma for her answer. She pushed away from the table and took her plate to the sink. I was about to do the same but something in Momma's expression made me stop. A crinkle in her forehead, slightly raised eyebrows, something in her eyes I didn't remember seeing before.

Sadness.

Disappointment.

The air rushed out of me.

'Of course, baby,' she said, soft, flat. 'You go on then. Was . . . was the chicken good, Johnny? You and your sister enjoy it?'

A special treat. Her own recipe. Secret's in the spices. It wasn't a treat for him, not really, it was for us. She'd made a special meal for her babies. She wanted us to like him, not the other way around. My chest cracked open as if by a hammer blow. My heart fractured with it.

Stay. Finish the meal. I looked at Jenny, waiting at the foot of the stairs, so timid and angry, her head wrapped in a scarf. Then to Momma, that sadness, that don't leave me with him, John, look in her eye.

Where do I go? Who do I choose?

I'm sorry, Momma.

I couldn't sit with Bung-Eye and play house, pretend he hadn't beaten my best friend on Christmas, broken his arm with his boot, looked at my sister like *that*. Couldn't pretend he wasn't involved in a girl's murder.

I went around the table to Momma and kissed her on the cheek, gently. 'It was wonderful, Momma. You're wonderful.'

I lingered, breathed her in. Camel cigarettes, the smell of the kitchen, the food, the beer, but something else, a deep scent, a body scent, underpinned it all. Strawberry bath soap, sweet, ripe corn, and sour, whiskey-tainted sweat. That was Momma. She was still there underneath it all.

'Night, Momma,' I said then took a deep breath. Best behaviour. 'Goodnight, Mr Buchanan.'

'Sweet dreams, sport,' he said, finishing off his second beer.

I didn't hide my distaste. His voice, his smell, his presence, were jagged in my home. He didn't fit. A puzzle piece that doesn't link up, no matter how hard you force it.

'And sweet dreams to you, princess.' Bung-Eye raised the bottle to Jenny, who flinched, took a step up the stairs away from him. His lip pulled up in a fishhook sneer and he winked at her. 'Yes, ma'am, sweet, sweet dreams.'

Then he laughed and I wished we had a gun because I would get it and load it and shoot him in that beautiful, dangerous face.

The house shook that night with their fucking. The moans, the banging, the shouts from him, from her, first in the family room, then later in Momma's bedroom, right below me and Jenny. It was never like that with Eric. Never so loud. So violent. We felt it through the floor, the rhythmic thud-thud-thud, every word, every grunt. I lay beside my sister, turned away from her, in the bed we shared and tried, God, I tried, to block it out. I tried not to feel it, like it was happening to me, by me.

My hand slipped downward. Gripped. I tried not to imagine it, tried not to let those feelings surge through me, into me, through the floor, the walls, the bed.

I bit my lip, clenched my fists, dug my nails deep into my palms. It was wrong. So fucking wrong. Larson called me freak, pervert. Maybe they were right.

'When?' Jenny said and her voice, its brightness, filled me with shame. My stomach, my chest, a rushing void. It sucked all the goodness out of me like an airlock opened in space. *Whoosh*, out into the blackness.

'When what?' I whispered. Too loud and she would hear the tremor in my voice, know its cause, call me freak too.

The noise below carried on, quicker, louder. Thunder inside me, thrumming in my blood.

The bed bounced, Jenny rolling over to face me. I knew her every movement, even in the dark. I dared not move, the growing shame turned my body to ice and her voice cut through it, melted it, took the dull ache in my groin away.

'When do we leave?' she said. 'You always said we would. Remember?'

She huffed over onto her back, made the bed frame creak. 'I can't stand it here. With her. I can't believe she'd go with Rudy's dad. He scares me. Did you see the way he looked at us over dinner? Ugh.'

She shook her whole body as if to throw off his gaze.

Their noise reached its crescendo, a great crash of voices and then nothing. Panting silence and a few seconds later a smell, smoky sweet, unmistakably marijuana, floated up through the boards. My blood cooled and slowed. The sick feeling eased.

'John?' Jenny sat up. I looked over my shoulder. Moonlight caught the white of her nightdress.

'We'll leave,' I said, still on my side, away from her. She'd see otherwise. She'd see my horror.

The room was an oven. Thick air, like breathing through steam, and it was only May. This summer would be the worst, I could tell. Maybe it would make history. Remember the '73 heatwave? How could I forget? Worse than '71 by a long shot. But we'd live through it. The heat, the new Pigeon Pa; we'd survive it, Jenny and me, but not by sitting still. Not by waiting it out.

'He's dangerous,' her voice changed, the defiance replaced with fear. 'I've heard stories. They say he's been to prison and he killed someone while he was there. I heard he did it with his hands but they let him out because the guards were too scared of him to keep him locked up.'

'Momma won't let him do anything to us. She'll protect us.'

Jenny's bitter laugh filled the room. 'She'll protect *you*. She'll ignore me then tell me I was asking for it if he hits me,' the laughter died. 'Or worse.'

I suspected she was right but it hurt to hear. Jenny always brought the devil out of Momma, made a tiny disagreement a hundred times worse with sass and back-talk, but Momma had gone too far when she cut off Jenny's hair.

I was tired of it and I had bigger fish frying on my grill. If living in Larson had taught me anything, it's that people talk, even when they've got nothing to talk about, they'll just go on and make it up. Keeping a secret is near impossible so it would only be a matter of time before the gossip mill churned and the truth about Wakefield and Mary Ridley flowed out. Then Jenny would suffer. I had to make sure we were long gone when that happened.

'I'll protect you. And we'll leave. Soon. I promise,' I said. 'Now go to sleep.'

23

The next morning Bung-Eye was gone and Momma looked tired. She moved slowly, like she was made of glass and afraid of breaking.

'Momma?' I sat beside her at the kitchen table. She sat in the spare chair, Bung-Eye's footrest.

'Yes, baby?'

She tapped a Camel from the packet on the table. Bung-Eye smoked Camels, Momma smoked Lucky Strikes. Rudy would steal one or two packs from his dad and we'd smoke them behind Gloria's house. We used to. That suddenly felt like a different person sucking on those joes. We hadn't done that for months. The picture in my head was sunshine through leaves, smiling, laughing faces, shared secrets, plumes of blue smoke rising into the sky. A lifetime gone, in just a year or two. Could I even count Rudy and Gloria as my best friends any more? We had barely spoken in months. If I did this, what I was about to do, what I was about to tell Momma, we might never speak again. But I had no choice. This was the only way I could think of to get Jenny away from Wakefield and Darney Wills.

'What is it?' Momma said.

'I . . . I've been thinking,' I faltered. Could I do this? Should I? You'll be back to take over the farm one day soon, Johnny, you don't need a college degree for that, just a strong back and a good head on your shoulders.

Momma snapped her fingers in front of my face. 'What's the matter with you?'

A flash of monster. The foreign smell of Camels in the house. The doubt receded.

'I want to quit school,' I said and Momma's eyebrows shot up her forehead.

'You do?'

I nodded.

She struck a kitchen match and lit the joe. 'Why?'

'To help with the farm and the bills. Al Westin has work for me and when I'm not there, I'll be here.' Stand firm, lie well. Your hands and eyes got to match what's coming out your mouth, Momma always said, and if you do it right, even you won't be able to tell the difference. I hated it but it wasn't bad lying, I told myself, it was burning the chaff to let the new seed take. All for the greater good.

'I want to be the man of the house,' I said. 'I want to look after you and Jenny so you don't need someone like Mr Buchanan, you'll just need me.'

Momma didn't slap me or tell me Bung-Eye was a good man and how dare you. She knew he was rotten. Momma sucked the cigarette down by half before she spoke.

'I always said school was no good for men. Makes their heads and hands soft. And we can't have that,' she said.

'Go on then, my man of the house. I'll tell the school if they ask.'

'Thank you, Momma,' I said, a speck of guilt about lying lodged in my chest but it was quickly obscured by relief. I kissed her on the cheek as Jenny came downstairs, ready for school.

She looked only at me, never at Momma, not any more. Jenny would think I was doing this to get her away from Momma. I'd never tell about Mr Wakefield and his threat against us. She'd go right to Samuels and then we'd be done for.

I walked with Jenny to school and told her my plan to quit.

'It's the only way,' I said. 'I can save everything I earn and then, when I've got enough, we can leave.'

Jenny just listened. I expected her to cry, no Johnny, you can't, what about your education, your future, don't do it, we'll think of something. But she didn't. And it stung.

'That's a big deal.'

'Yeah.'

'Are you sure?'

I nodded.

'I think it's a good idea.'

An invisible slap across the cheek. 'Good. Settled then.'

We were quiet for the rest of the walk. My stomach flipped over with every step. Was this the right thing? It was all happening so quickly, so easily. I'd set a ball rolling and now was running down the hill beside it wondering if I could catch it again. Momma didn't try to talk me out of it but I hadn't expected her to. Jenny from a year ago would have thrown up her arms and said, oh no, Johnny, you can't!

I didn't really understand until then how much she had

changed. I'd hoped the darkness was just on the surface and her insides were still the same but now I knew better. Now it was even more important to get her out of this dying town.

The sun, already strong despite how early it was, beat on the back of my neck. I looked sideways at Jenny. The wisps of gold-blonde hair escaped from her scarf, lifting gently in the breeze. The sun freckles on her cheeks. The blue eyes I loved so much.

As we reached the school, I stopped at the sidewalk. 'I'll wait for you after. Tell them I'm sick.'

She nodded, walked away. Halfway to the steps, she stopped, turned, and ran to me. Threw her arms around my neck. My heart, chest, blood, expanded and erupted in a wide smile.

'Thank you,' Jenny whispered against my neck. 'Thank you.'

All doubt vanished. All regret blazed and turned to ash. That was it. I was done with school, I had a higher calling. A larger purpose. Only Jenny mattered.

I watched her run up the steps and inside. I turned from school and my breath caught, eyes swam. A pale grey Ford crawled down the street, sun glaring across the windshield, heat haze shimmering against the tyres, bumpers, turning the metal to mercury.

As it drew level with the school it stopped, the window rolled down, and I expected to see Jack Ridley smiling at me.

But the door opened and a middle-aged man with a thick brown beard stepped out. My heart unclenched. The man lifted the seat and out jumped two kids, years younger than me, who ran into the school.

It wasn't the Ford. Wasn't Ridley. Wasn't Death on his pale horse.

You're seeing things, Johnny boy, keep it together.

I shook it off, told myself that was over, finished, and went about my mission.

I went directly to Westin's grocery store and convinced him to hire me. It was simple, he and I were desperate, and he never once asked me why I dropped out, why I needed the money. In a town like Larson, someone always needs the money. Every minute I wasn't in the grocery store or walking Jenny home from school, I was breaking my back in the fields. The school sent a few letters, made a phone call or two, then gave up, sent Momma a form to sign saying I'd gone and that was it. The day it arrived in the mail panic hit me. I'd made a huge mistake. I wanted to change my mind, go back to class, to chalkboards and spitballs and my friends, back to that sense of belonging and identity you get in school. But that was gone now and I'd be that kid, that drop-out nobody remembers.

One morning, at Westin's, I saw Mr Wakefield and Mayor Wills walking down Main toward the Backhoe. I froze, broom in hand, in the middle of the store.

They were the danger.

They were the killers.

And they had Jenny in their crosshairs.

All fragments of lingering doubt evaporated and I worked all the harder, all the longer. This was bigger than me and my dreams, bigger than Larson and its gossip, this was Jenny's life.

I didn't think about the lessons or the teachers, even Miss Eaves receded in my mind to some figure from the past, someone not quite there any more. Jenny, her safety and happiness, were all-consuming, a fire through dry corn.

It only took a few days of this change, and my first dollar earned, for the ice in Jenny to melt. She stopped wearing the scarf, showed off a short bob haircut, and started saying yes to Gloria and Rudy asking her to come out after school. Then I'd meet them at four when Scott Westin finished school and took over my job at his dad's store. For a month, the world turned for us, not against us. For a month, there was light, and hope, and the coming heatwave was exciting, not an oppressive spectre shimmering on the horizon. Summer meant swimming in Barks and reclaiming Big Lake from the memories. It meant rekindling cold friendships and freedom from sticky classrooms. For Jenny and me it meant our way out of Larson, away from Bung-Eye and Wakefield.

Everything changed one afternoon in June.

I'd finished restocking the fruit trays outside Westin's when I saw Jenny out of school. She was leaving the Backhoe, giggling in her white sundress, hand-in-hand with that fucker Darney Wills.

24

He said he wouldn't touch her.

He said he wouldn't touch her.

'He said he wouldn't fucking touch her!' I shouted. Burst into Frank's office. Our weekly sessions had stopped after the mill explosion and the basement, but he said he'd always make time for me.

He'd make time now.

The pastor wasn't alone. Some kid in my chair. I knew him, vaguely. Billy or Bobby something, a few grades below me. Kid was crying. Looked like he'd been crying for hours. There was a bruise on his eye but I didn't care. He was in *my* chair, in front of *my* desk, with *my* pastor.

Get out. Get out now.

That fucker Darney Wills said he wouldn't touch her. I stood in the doorway, chest heaving, fists clenched so hard the skin on my knuckles threatened to split and bleed all over the pastor's carpet. Frank stared at me, wide-eyed, mouth open like a gasping fish.

He stood up behind his desk, eyes on me, then he swallowed, finally he caught on, finally he saw my anger.

He looked at the boy. 'Bobby, let's pick this up again tomorrow. Off you go now.'

The kid frowned, head turned from me to Frank, about to speak up, about to say, hang on there, I need to talk. Just like I'd have done if some crazy person kicked their way into our session.

'Go on,' Frank urged, kind but impatient.

Go on. Get the hell out. My blood raged in my ears, a river swollen by rain, rushing over its banks, ripping up the soil.

The kid pushed past me out the trailer door, fresh tears welling, and I slammed it behind him. A sharp moment of silence fell between me and Frank.

My hair stuck to my face, cheeks red and burning with sweat. Fingernails cut divots in my palms. 'That fucker Darney Wills said he wouldn't touch her.'

The pastor sighed. Sat back down and gestured for me to take a seat. I did but I couldn't relax. My bones were clamped tight, my muscles strained and jittering.

'You're pushing it, John, barging in here like that,' he said and his tone was a bucket of ice water thrown over me. My fists unclenched. My palms throbbed.

'He said . . . that fucker . . .'

The pastor rubbed his forehead, sighed again. 'Back up. Tell me what's going on.'

And I did. Every word. Every beat. Every detail of Mary Ridley. Of what I overheard outside this office that night after Gloria and I had kissed. I worried, for a moment, Frank would be mad at me for eavesdropping but I had bigger fish. My sister's safety topped upsetting Frank, though that flicker of sadness, the disappointment in his expression when I told, made my heart flip. A nag in the back of my head kept chirping, don't do it, Johnny, you can't trust him, these secrets are made for the dark and he'll tell Wakefield, he'll tell Bung-Eye. But I pushed the nag away, clamped my hand over its mouth. The more I talked, the easier it was to say what I needed to. It felt so good to *speak*. To tell someone. And I couldn't stop once I'd started, despite the voice in my head screaming, 'He's involved, what are you doing?'

I told Frank all about Mr Wakefield, what he'd done to Mary Ridley, how he'd covered it all up, paid them off with the Dodge. All about Bung-Eye and Mayor Wills and Charlie Meaney and Darney's threat, the don't-tell-anyone sneering, spitting, kick-in-the-gut, he'll-wreck-what-I-love-most threat.

Despite my frantic head, I knew better than to talk about Frank's involvement, whatever that was. It would upset him, make him worry, maybe even put him in danger. He was a victim in all this too, he had to be, and I had to protect him best I could.

Darney Wills kept slamming back into the front of my head. He was out there in town, his fat, greasy hands on my sister. He was my rage taken bloated, glossy-lipped form, and I wanted to kill him.

'He said he wouldn't touch her,' I said and there were no more words. I was empty.

Frank stayed silent, never spoke up or butted in. Fingers steepled under his nose, deep frown between his eyes. All that confusion and fear and overwhelming weight I'd been carrying around with me melted. Eased off like shrugging away a rain-soaked coat. I'd handed it all to my pastor, my friend, my man of God, and said, help me, this is too much for me, you take it. Seeing Darney with my sister snapped something inside me. It was already happening, whatever darkness Wakefield had promised, Darney was making it happen, I could feel it. All I had left in my head, after spilling its contents over Frank's desk, was Jenny. Keep her safe. Get her out of town before the rope is cut, before the dagger falls.

'Are you sure about all this?' Frank dropped his hands, they hit the desk with a sharp thud that sent his pen rolling. He didn't stop it. The pen rolled to the edge, teetered for a second, and fell.

'I'm sure.'

'John, what you're saying . . .'

'It's true. It's all true. I swear it. Jenny is in danger.'

Frank shook his head, wouldn't look at me, and I turned cold inside.

'This was a mistake,' I said, stood up too quickly, swayed a step in the heat of the trailer. 'I shouldn't have told you. Darney said not to tell . . . oh God.'

Oh God. I've told. I've told. I leaned over the desk, palms on the wood. 'Please, don't say anything. They'll hurt her. I shouldn't have come here. It's my fault. All my fault.'

'Calm down,' Frank said. 'Remember what I taught you? Count, John. Count with me. One-one-thousand . . .'

Deep breath.

'Two-one-thousand,' I said along with him. 'Three-one-thousand. Four-one-thousand . . .'

By eight I was back in the chair. By ten I was close to calm. Frank stood and came around his desk, perched on its corner in front of me.

'These accusations are very serious, do you understand that? You're saying Leland Wakefield killed a woman, you found out, and now he's threatened Jenny if you say anything.' I nodded. 'It sounds crazy, John. Real crazy.'

'It's true. Darney Wills said—'

'Darney Wills is a thug,' he said. 'He's also a liar on his way to becoming a roaring drunk. He was no doubt just trying to scare you.'

'No! Gloria's dad killed Mary Ridley and now Darney Wills is going round with Jenny. He's going to hurt her.'

'John,' his voice turned soft, like a shag pile carpet you sink your feet into. 'You quit school.'

I flinched. 'So?'

'So, you're a good student, you get good grades now. Those tutoring sessions really turned things around. You seemed to truly enjoy learning. Why didn't you come to me to talk about your decision? What changed?'

'This! All I've been telling you. I have to get Jenny out of town, away from Mr Wakefield and Darney and . . .' Don't talk about Momma, I heard her voice in my head, that's family business. 'And I need money. Since the mill burned down there's no Saturday jobs any more so I didn't have a choice.'

He nodded, shifted on the edge of his desk. He went to speak but I cut him off.

'I'm not crazy, Frank. This is happening.'

The pastor shook his head. 'I just . . . I'm finding it all very hard to believe. Anyone could have killed that poor girl, a drifter, one of the transients that come in off the railroads. Your play den isn't all that far from the trainyard, you know. And why would a killer stick around? He's probably holed up in a cave in Canada by now.'

I stood up. I was almost as tall as him now but gangly where he was broad. It never occurred to me that he wouldn't believe me. 'You know this town is sick. A girl was murdered two years ago, I didn't make that up. Nobody cared. Nobody went looking for her killer except me and my friends and I found him. I found him right under our noses. It wasn't some hobo drifter. It was Mr Wakefield.'

I couldn't talk to anyone else about this, not Rudy, Jenny and especially not Gloria. I wanted to. God, how I wanted to. I hated keeping anything from them. My chest tightened, tears ached in my eyes. But Gloria. This couldn't get back to her from me, she'd hate me, more than she probably already did. In the movies, they always shoot the messenger, send him back headless on his horse. The ache moved south to my throat. Thoughts of last summer, of kisses and stolen glances and private laughter, swarmed in my brain like fire ants, nipping and stinging, a bite for each moment with her I'd lost.

'All right, John, all right. Let me . . . let me make some enquiries.' He raised his hand to stop my interruption. 'Careful ones, I won't let Jenny get hurt. Just . . .' He rubbed the back of his neck. 'Just keep your head down and stay quiet, okay?'

I nodded.

'You did the right thing coming to me with this,' he said, pushed off from the desk. 'We can't have this getting back to the wrong people, you understand?'

'Yes.'

'Leave it with me, John. I promise, I won't let anything happen to Jenny. But you have to keep your cool. Count, like I taught you, and don't do anything when you're hopped up like this.'

'I know. I'm sorry. I just . . . I'm sorry. I should go to Samuels, shouldn't I? That's the right thing to do. I should just tell him everything. Maybe the cops can protect Jenny better than me.'

But Gloria . . .

'No,' Frank snapped, then softened. 'If what you're saying is true, and this . . . whatever it is . . . involves so many prominent members of the town, then you have to be careful who you speak to. You can't go shooting your mouth off to anyone. Let me handle this. Everything will be okay.'

Then it hit me. A car smashing into the side of my head. A pale car.

'Jack!'

'Who?'

'Jack Ridley.' I waited for a sign of recognition but nothing showed in Frank's face. 'The pale car. The Ford. Remember? He's Mary Ridley's *brother*. I could tell him about Mr Wakefield. Jack could tell Samuels and I wouldn't be to blame. Jenny would be safe!'

'John! Stop it! Forget about that damn car.' Frank banged his fist on the table. Felt like the whole trailer shook. 'Someone is messing with you. Mary doesn't have a brother. You think if she did, he'd be following a kid around? Why wouldn't he be hounding Samuels every minute? He isn't, I know that for sure. Nobody is. Not even her parents.'

I shrank, curled my spine into the back of the chair. Don't be stupid, John, that guy is long gone. You haven't seen him for months. If you ever saw him at all. *Mary doesn't have a brother.* Who the hell was driving that car then?

Frank leaned forward, everything about him softened.

'I'm sorry. I'm sorry for shouting. Please, John,' he sighed, paused, picked his words. 'You and me, I like to think we're friends. Real friends. We went beyond pastor and congregant a long time ago, we're buddies, and you've got to trust me.

I want you and Jenny to be safe, more than anything on God's green, and you're both square in the scope of some pretty nasty guys. You've got to keep your head down else it's going to get shot off.'

He put his hand on my arm, his eyes fixed on mine. 'I will handle this, John. Trust me.'

I let myself smile, nod. The weight, the fear, the constant pain in the back of my head, was easing, drifting away on hot air. Frank would take care of it. Frank would make sure Jenny didn't get hurt. Just like a friend would. Just like a father would.

'Promise me,' he said, stared right into my eyes like he could tell if I lied. 'Promise me you won't go to Samuels or anyone else with this. Promise me you will keep your mouth shut.'

His gaze jackhammered into me. It was his pulpit stare, his stern sermon voice. I swallowed sharp bile and felt a flutter of doubt in my chest, like the birds inside me ruffled their wings.

You trust Frank, don't you?

But the paint and the photograph and the cardigan and the bed bolted to the floor and Charlie Meaney in his trailer and . . .

He's a victim too. He has to be.

'I promise,' I said, meant it.

I left his office lighter, the nagging dread replaced with a renewed purpose. I put aside the ache in my chest at leaving the farm, Momma, Rudy and, my throat caught, Gloria. I had one job now. Earn enough money to get Jenny out. Maybe we'd head to Washington and stay with Eric. Jenny would like that, though Momma wouldn't. Maybe west to San Francisco. Maybe northeast to Chicago, that wasn't at all far, less than four hundred miles, less than ten hours on a bus, but felt like another world. Maybe far, far southeast to Florida where I'd read in one of Momma's magazines that the beaches were blazing white sand with ocean water so clear you could see fish swimming around your feet. And they had pelicans and herons and all kinds of exotic birds in a thousand colours. So much world. So much to see.

When Jenny came home that evening I was waiting. It was one of Momma's nights at Gum's. She'd taken on more shifts in the last few months as the town realised life wasn't getting any better after the Easton mill explosion the year before. Desperate men drink, John Royal, Momma told me, they drink away their memories and they drink away hope. That's why Gum's and the liquor store will dance all over this shitkicker town. They'll dance until their feet ache and blister and I'll be right there, baby, Momma said, right there shaking my ass along with them.

Jenny came in around nine. I'd eaten dinner and left her a plate warming in the oven. More mac n' cheese, Eric's famous recipe, one of the only things he left behind, just like my real pa had left his belt. Since Momma had taken more nights, it was mac n' cheese or nothing. Despite the free vegetables Mr Westin gave me, I didn't know how to cook anything else. I heard Jenny in the hall kick off her shoes, stumble, then drop her book bag with a sharp bang that echoed through the house.

A prickly heat crawled up the back of my neck, around the curve of my skull, deep into my hair. I wanted to be happy she was home, I wanted to ask about school and borrow her textbooks to keep up with her learning. But

Darney Wills was in my head. That *hurr hurr* laugh. Those red lips like pieces of raw meat. Those words. *I'll break her in, gentle like.*

The prickle swarmed over my head and into my cheeks, my neck, my chest, down into my arms and hands. It pulsed and gained power and I felt like I was glowing, the Human Torch ready to explode, just call me Johnny Storm.

Jenny stepped into the family room where I was sat, tense and burning, in Momma's armchair.

'Hi,' she said, smooth and easy and cold. 'Is there dinner? I'm starved.'

Maybe I was wrong. Maybe it was perfectly innocent. Maybe Jenny had a free period and went to the Backhoe for a milkshake and Darney just walked her back to school. Maybe she'd been with Gloria or Maddie-May, or any of those girls, for the last five hours.

A long, dark laugh inside my head. Stupid, stupid Johnny Royal.

'John?' Jenny said, still in the doorway, her eyebrows up. 'Is there food?'

'In the oven,' I murmured and she huffed, shook her head, and stomped to the kitchen.

As she passed me I smelt it. The tang. The sharp, unmistakable sourness.

I followed her to the table. 'You've been drinking.'

She bent to open the oven and sighed. 'Mac n' cheese again?'

'Who gave it to you?'

Jenny took the plate from the oven and set it on the table with a fork. She didn't look at me. I was an irritant to her then, a blackfly buzzing in her ear.

'You could learn to cook something else now you have

all this free time,' she said as she took a mouthful. 'Something not out of a packet.'

The burning in me grew, the rage taking form under my skin. I clenched my fist around the back of the spare chair. Felt like the wood would scorch and catch and blaze up under me.

'Was it Darney Wills?'

She looked up then. Stopped chewing a moment. Her eyes on mine, reading between my lines and finding her answer quickly. Eyes tinged red like Momma's after a few cans. A flicker of a smile. Then she went back to her dinner.

'So what if it was?' she said.

'What did he give you?'

The wood creaked beneath my fist.

'It was just a beer. Jesus, can you back off?'

Her tone was cold water on my fire. Hiss and spit and reduced to steam and smoulder. Momma's drunken temper reared in my sister, a paler version but still vicious.

I pulled out the chair and sat. Told my voice and body to soften, to loosen up and listen to her, not berate her.

'He's not a good guy,' I said.

She shrugged. 'People say bad stuff about him but he's actually sweet. Once you get to know him.'

'How long have you been getting to know him?'

But I wanted to say, how long has he been touching you and holding your hand and making you laugh? What have you done with him? Have you let him do it? I'll kill him if he put those filthy fat hands on you.

'It doesn't matter,' she said. 'Not long.'

Then she saw my thoughts through my eyes, my face, my clamped jaw.

'Oh, John,' she said. 'He hasn't done anything to me.'

But I didn't believe her and she could see it.

She dropped her fork onto her plate. 'He is a gentleman, okay? He hasn't touched me. You really think I would do that? Is that what you think of me?'

'I don't . . .' but I did and I hated that I did.

She surged up, knocking over the chair. The noise shook the house, shook us both. Her face set in a sneer, deep and dark. It was Momma's sneer. On Jenny's sunshine face it didn't fit but it did at the same time.

'Darney Wills is bad news. Remember that time in the Backhoe? What he said to us?'

Jenny almost laughed. 'That was years ago and it was just a joke. He apologised to me for that, anyway. He was in a really bad place what with Mark being drafted. We got talking about Mark. When he died, Darney had a breakdown, did you know that? His best friend killed himself. He's a good guy, really. He's kind.'

I dug my nails into the back of my neck. Pain brings clarity, Momma always said. Start at the beginning.

'When did this start?'

Jenny's expression softened. 'A couple of weeks ago. I ran into him outside school. We started talking and he walked me home.'

Every word was a sharp jab in my chest. I remembered the feeling of Darney's spit on my face. Of his weight on my back, pushing me against the sidewalk.

'He's too old for you,' I said.

'I'm not a kid,' Jenny said, the sneer returned. 'I'm a woman. I can make my own decisions. Momma doesn't care and you're not my father. It's none of your business who I see.'

I felt Darney grinding my cheek into the gritty concrete.

I felt the explosion in my gut when he kicked me. I felt the fear of his threat all over again.

'Please,' I said. 'He's dangerous. Anyone but him. You're skipping school to see him, aren't you? You can't do that. What about your grades?'

'I skipped a few classes, so what?' She straightened up, crossed her arms, scent of beer on her words. 'I'm not going to flunk out like you did.'

Those jabs turned into a spike and pierced me right through. This was not Jenny. Jenny was bright and kind. This was someone else in her skin, her very own monster come to the surface.

I stood up. Sadness overtook me and I just wanted to be alone. I'd never wanted to be away from my sister but now I needed to be, in case I said something I didn't mean. I couldn't stand up to Momma, I was too weak and her monster was strong and ancient. After so many years, I knew its patterns and could avoid it. But Jenny, hers was volatile and brash and lashed out at me with such force and cruelty that all I wanted to do was bite back.

But I wouldn't bite. Not at her. It would just send her further away from me.

'Jenny,' I said, slowly. 'I quit school to earn us money so we could leave. Remember that?'

'I'm sorry I said that. I'm grateful you quit, really I am, but I never asked you to.'

Anger flashed inside me.

She met my eyes. 'You have to trust me. You're my brother and I love you but I can take care of myself.'

I bit down on my tongue to stop me screaming at her. I told myself it was just the beer. Told myself it wasn't really

Jenny same as it wasn't really Momma. Over and over again I said it while the voices in my head laughed.

'Why are you being like this?' I could barely look at her.

She let out a long sigh, threw up her arms. 'Like what? John, just chill out and let me live my life. I don't give you lectures about shacking up with Gloria.'

Those words were a spear to my chest. Right through my heart and lungs and out my back. She'd killed me with those words. Killed my anger and righteousness and energy. *I gave up Gloria for you,* I wanted to scream but knew I couldn't. It wasn't Jenny's fault. She didn't know about Wakefield. It was more important than ever that we leave but I didn't have enough saved for two bus tickets. I needed a little more time.

'Promise me,' I said, my voice weak. 'You won't let him . . . do it . . . to you. Okay?'

Disgust came over her and I knew then I'd crossed a line.

'I won't open my legs for the first boy who asks. I'm not like *her.*'

Momma. You're more like her than you realise.

I'd never say it. That was the worst thing I could ever say to Jenny.

'I know,' I said. 'Please stop seeing him. Please.'

'I'm going to bed now,' she said, arms still crossed, chin tilted up. 'I think it's time we stopped sharing a room. We're not kids any more. You should sleep on the couch from now on.'

My jaw went slack and the sadness in me grew too big for my body. I didn't have the will to fight it any more. Not after what she said.

'If that's what you want,' I said.

'I do.'

She went upstairs, didn't look back, and when I heard the slam of our – her – bedroom door, my legs buckled and I fell onto the chair. I don't know how long I sat there, still, silent, shocked into immobility.

She'll get better. The anger will calm and fade and the real Jenny will come back.

Or it will get worse and she'll go steady with Darney and Wakefield will get his hands on her.

'No,' I murmured. 'I won't let that happen.'

The sadness solidified into new purpose. Work harder. Save more money. Get Jenny away from Larson.

I curled up on the couch but couldn't sleep. I always found it hard to sleep when Jenny wasn't in the room. When she was at sleepovers with Gloria or Maddie-May I'd stay up all night reading or make an early start on the day's chores, anything but sleep. Jenny's rhythms and breathing, her fidgeting and warmth, they were a part of me. Without them I was lost, uncomfortable. For hours, the old couch springs dug in my back and side, the house made different creaks and groans, the air smelled of cold, cooked cheese and cigarette smoke. I could hear the rats in the crawlspace gnawing at our joists, skittering along the bricks.

I stared at the spots and smears of red nail polish still bright on the dark floorboards. Blood that would never fade to brown. Bright scarlet like Darney Wills' slug lips. I imagined those lips on Jenny's and my stomach turned to stone. I started off the couch, my knees hit the boards but I didn't feel the pain. I was on my feet, in the hall, pulling on my shoes. I took a flashlight from the kitchen and swung open the back door.

The night air smelled sweet, like the woodsmoke from

a far-away fire had found its way here, leaving its acrid taint somewhere behind. The heat was coming. Spring was already dead and waiting to be turned to cinders, the winter so distant it was as if it existed in some other world.

I switched on the flashlight and lit up a circle of dirty, whitewashed wall. I crouched and pulled away a board covering the entrance to the crawlspace. Rats scattered in the light. The loose earth sucked back worms and beetles and the spiders retreated to their corners. The smell of cool soil and stale air hit me. My body ached from tiredness, from hauling potato sacks, from weeding fields, from the uncomfortable couch, but I got on my hands and knees and crawled beneath the house.

I found the brick. Prised it free. Pulled out the knife. RB scratched into the handle. I pressed the small silver button and the blade sprung free. The years hidden in the wall hadn't slowed the mechanism and, but for the layer of dust, it was as good as the day Rudy bought it. As good as the day Gloria threw it in Big Lake and I fished it out and made it mine.

I closed the blade and put the knife in my pocket, where I kept it every day from then on, ready for anything Darney Wills could do. I closed up the crawlspace and sat on the back steps to watch the sunrise.

Jenny and me lived in a tense rhythm for the next two weeks. Her hair was just brushing her shoulders now but as that got longer, the hem of her dresses crept higher. I saw her with Darney, when she should have been in school, a few more times. Throwing it in my face. She knew where I'd be at what times and she'd parade herself before the big windows of Westin's grocery store on purpose. I'd turn away. Close my ears to their laughter. Push my anger and sadness down into the dark pit of my stomach.

The heat hit hard and turned the county humid, like we were all sat in a steamer basket. With only me caring for the farm, I planted about half the west field before the season closed up. But I had rushed and the stalks sprouted in mismatched, uneven rows. They wouldn't grow right or tall or golden, I knew it from those first tiny spits of green from the earth. They were gnarled and twisted, stunted stalks, clustered and overlapping, leaves a sick brown colour.

The humidity only lasted a few weeks before the sun dried us out. This will be a broken year, Momma told me one night, it'll snap right in two and people won't remember it right. Momma said they'll forget about those short, hot months and talk about it as the time before the heatwave and the time after, nobody will remember what happened in between.

The sun scorched the air and dried the mud and made every breath burn the inside of my lungs, filled them with pale dust. We breathed out shimmering heat and the side-walks, asphalt, truck hoods, and rooftops turned to liquid glass. That heat, that awful heat, drove Larson deeper into madness. Drove calm men to pull their guns over a spilt drink, drove them to fists and fury over the wrong look.

Then that madness showed itself in my home. I heard the sandy crunch of Momma's truck in the yard. Too early. The sun wasn't half set and she was due at Gum's until the last drunk stumbled out into the parking lot. Momma burst through the front door, ragged panic all through her, a long cut on her forearm. Bung-Eye with her. Blood on him. Blood on her.

'What happened?' I jumped up as she came through the family room, holding her arm above her head, blood trickling, dripping onto the floor, joining the stark, red nail polish.

'Ain't that sweet? He's all worried about his ma,' Bung-Eye drawled, drunk and grinning. He went straight to the fridge for a Budweiser. Since Bung-Eye became our Pigeon Pa, Momma had to buy Buds instead of Old Milwaukees. Four times the price on Momma's pay cheque but Bung-Eye wouldn't drink cheap.

My mouth dropped open. He'd left my momma hissing and bleeding to get himself a drink. The bastard. Didn't even get one for her. Didn't even offer. Momma likes to drink to calm her nerves, don't you know that? Don't you care, you son of a bitch?

I went to Momma and guided her to the kitchen, set the water running, and got some towels to clean her up.

'Who did this?' I leaned close to her. 'Did he . . .?'

Momma shot me a look that said, don't you say another word. Her eyes were red and raw. There was fear and pain deep inside them and all I wanted in that moment was to take it away, heal her, save her.

'Just a fight at Gum's,' she said, loud, the official story for Bung-Eye's ears and mine.

'We ran out of ice,' she said and flinched as I wiped the edges of the cut.

'What's a bar expect when they can't keep their drinks cold?' Bung-Eye said, leaning against the fridge, one arm up, over his head. A crooked lothario. 'Ain't reasonable to ask a man to drink warm suds. Might as well ask him to drink warm piss.'

'It was a broken glass,' Momma said. 'No real harm done.'

But her voice trembled, either from the shock or from Bung-Eye's attitude to it. Maybe it was his broken glass, his warm drink. I tried to keep my eyes on Momma, tending her, but they kept straying to him. A wolf in my house, appearing tame, appearing soft, but on the inside, its veins boiled with rabid blood.

'Where's your sweet sister?' Bung-Eye pushed away from the fridge, didn't stumble despite the slur in his words. As he spoke, he prodded his tongue around the inside of his mouth.

'Upstairs. Studying,' I said, didn't try to keep the hate out of my voice.

'Mmhmm,' he said and finished off his beer. 'I need to drain the snake.'

His hand adjusted his crotch and started toward the stairs, up to the bathroom. I listened for every step as I got the medical box from under the kitchen sink. Momma's cut wasn't that deep and had almost stopped bleeding.

'You think I'll live, Dr Royal?' Momma smiled and squeezed my hand.

'Yes, ma'am. But this is going to hurt.' I doused the wound with Bactine and Momma swore like a mill-hand.

As I bandaged up the cut, I noticed the footsteps upstairs. They went to the bathroom but then weren't coming back down. Not going into Momma's room. The footsteps went up to my room. Jenny's room. Where Jenny was right now. Alone.

Momma grabbed my hand.

We both knew every sound of the house, every breath and stretch and ache of it, and we knew when something didn't belong. Her eyes blazed into mine but I couldn't read them.

'Don't,' she said. 'It's not what you think.'

'What does that mean?'

But she wouldn't say. The footsteps stopped, their desti-
nation reached. No sound but my thundering heart.

'What is he doing?'

Momma took a pack of Camels from the pocket in her
jeans and lit one up. She wouldn't look at me any more
but kept her attention on her arm.

'What a good job you've done,' she said, too bright, too
breezy.

I wanted to scream, overturn the table, rage and rage
until she gave me my answers.

'What is he doing?' I asked again, and again, she said
nothing.

My bones began to itch.

'Momma?'

Then his footsteps. One heavy, plodding boot after the
next.

Momma blew a plume of smoke high into the air, like
steam from a kettle spout.

The footsteps came down the stairs. It was a few seconds,
really, a few horrible, haunting seconds he was up there
with Jenny.

'What's going on, Momma?'

'Nothing, baby, he's just saying hello.'

She stood up, took a beer from the fridge, no doubt for
Bung-Eye, pre-empting him, keeping him always calm and
wanting for nothing. She'd stopped drinking as much at
home when he was around. There'd been a half-full jar of
whiskey in the cupboard for a month. Maybe we couldn't
afford the Buds for both of them. Maybe she wanted to
keep herself sharp.

'Tell me the truth,' I said, eyes darting to the bottom of the stairs. What had he done to her? What had he said? If he touched her – my head fizzed with anger, and I couldn't finish the thought.

'I am, baby.' Momma's voice was thin, dazed. 'Nothing is going on. Now what do you want for dinner?'

'How about some of that fine chicken, Patty-cake?' I flinched. Bung-Eye's voice from behind me, booming, full of malice.

I turned to him. Wanted to rip his throat out. Dig my nails into his flesh. I felt the weight of Rudy's flick knife in my pocket. One press of the button, one swipe, and Bung-Eye would be gone. Jenny would be safe. Momma would be safe. Even Rudy would be safe.

Bung-Eye stood a foot away from me. Tilted his head. Sized me up. 'You got something to say, sport?'

'Yes, sir, I have. There's a whole lot I want to say.'

Bung-Eye arched his eyebrow and a wide grin peeled apart his lips.

The words burned inside my throat. I want to say fuck you. I want to say get the hell out of my house. I want to take my knife and show you who's the man here, who's protecting Momma and Jenny and if you touched my sister I'll kill you, I'll kill you where you stand.

'Well, sport?'

'John,' Momma said behind me and I faltered.

'You don't call out a man like that,' Bung-Eye said, 'and not have the cojones to throw the first punch.'

That dead, milk-white eye saw my insides and saw their squirming cowardice. It could see my soul and it was laughing at me. Weeks of hauling vegetable sacks alongside my chores had strengthened my back, turned my skinny arms to thick muscle and broadened my chest, but I wasn't a man when I stood next to Bung-Eye Buchanan. Nobody in Larson was.

He moved close to me, whispered right in my ear. 'What you want to say, John? Come now, your momma can't hear you.'

'If you ever hurt them,' I said, my voice shaking, 'I'll kill you.'

The grin widened, puckered his eyes. He slapped me gently on the cheek and laughed. 'Atta boy, Johnny.'

Then he pulled back, stared me right in the eye. All my anger withered under his gaze and I was suddenly the weedy runt sizing up the alpha male.

'Atta boy,' he repeated and spat a glob of brown saliva at my feet. He sniffed, wiped his nose with the back of his hand, and swaggered into the family room, still grinning, still laughing.

I was weak and angry and full of shame. How could I protect Jenny from this? What was I compared to him? I retreated to the table as Momma busied herself with dinner. Bung-Eye lounged in Momma's armchair watching football on the TV set, only speaking to ask for another beer.

'Do you need help? Does your arm hurt?' I asked Momma.

'No, baby, you go on now and check on your sister. Tell her dinner's coming but she doesn't have to come down if she's got homework.'

She met my eyes, nodded, and I didn't question it.

Bung-Eye let out a hacking cough then shouted, 'You two must have something mighty important to talk about if you're gabbing all over the first quarter.'

'Go,' Momma whispered to me, then called to Bung-Eye.

'Sorry, hon. Fat's just heating up for the chicken, be there soon.'

'What did I just say, woman?' he yelled back, wet gravel in his voice. 'Shut your damn mouth.'

Momma tipped her chin toward the stairs. I didn't want to leave her, not with him, not hurting and bandaged over a spitting fry pan. But then she smiled at me. Small, but enough. My momma had a core of steel running through her. Don't fret over me, those eyes said, no man would dare touch Patty Royal.

'Yes, Momma,' I said, too low for Bung-Eye to hear.

At the top of the stairs, I stopped. I could still smell him. Leather. Camels. Sweat. All over the air, the walls, invading our home. I pressed my ear against my bedroom door and there, beneath the muffled sounds of the TV downstairs, beneath the hot summer wind groaning at the windows, my sister was crying.

'Jenny?' I tapped on the door.

She didn't open it. 'Go away.'

'What did he do?'

The crying turned into a long sigh. 'Nothing. Go away.'

But her voice lacked energy. She really said, come in, I need my brother. I heard it in the tremor and the quiet.

I turned the handle and closed the door silently behind me. There she was, sitting on our bed. She'd taken down my poster of the Stones, replaced it with Janis Joplin, the dead-too-young rocker woman. She'd laid her favourite bedspread, the one stitched with fat, gaudy sunflowers, over my side of the bed as well as hers. She knew that blanket made me itch. She knew the weather was too hot for it. It was a tiny act of spite but her tears and her puffy cheeks and her red eyes took the sting away. Keep the nasty bedspread, I thought, just please stop crying, please don't be sad any more.

'What happened?' I said and sat beside her. Her math homework lay untouched on the floor, the answer boxes empty.

As I sat down, she grabbed one of my t-shirts from the floor and pulled it on over her sundress. The shirt drowned her, took her shape away, as if she was trying to fade into the pale colours of the world, turn invisible in plain white cotton. With her shorter hair, she could have been one of those feral children from Paradise Hill, the trailer park outside town. One of those girls who don't know how to be a girl. They only know dirt and swearing and ratty hair. They run like their brothers, throw like them, fight like them, look like them. No sunshine and fluttering eyelashes, no dresses or flowers or playing tea party.

'Talk to me,' I tried but it felt like talking to a block of ice. 'What did he do?'

Jenny sighed again and wiped her cheeks on the t-shirt. 'He didn't do anything, just said hello.'

'Then why are you crying?'

'I don't know.'

'Is it that Darney Wills? Did he try something with you?'

'No, nothing like that.'

I put my arm around her shoulders but she flinched away from me. That was a whip crack on my hand. She stood up, crossed her arms tightly over her stomach. Wouldn't look at me.

'Jenny,' I said, my arm still hovering in the air where she had been as if holding a ghost. 'What's going on? Please, tell me.'

'Oh, John. What can you do?' She shook her head, eyes on her feet. 'We're all trapped in this town, you, me, Gloria, Rudy. Even Momma.'

'I have money,' I said. 'I've been saving everything. Soon I'll have enough for two bus tickets.'

Jenny's raw eyes met mine. The pink bloodshot dulled the blue, made her seem far away. Disconnected. They weren't her eyes. I hated them.

'How soon?' she asked. 'Sooner than tonight? Sooner than ten minutes ago when that man came in here? Sooner than last week? Or last year when she cut off my hair? How soon, Johnny?'

I opened my mouth but had no answer.

'It's already too late.' She leant against the wall and tried to smile. 'But you should go, get on a bus and get as far away from here as you can.'

'What did he say to you?' I wanted to shake the answer from her. Tell me, tell me, tell me, and I'll fix it. I'll fix everything.

'He said . . .' She shook her head and her eyes glistened. 'He just asked me if I had a good day at school. That's all. Now please leave me alone, I have homework.'

'Jenny . . .'

'Go!' she screamed suddenly, out of nowhere, out of nothing.

The calm sadness in her a second ago now blazed white-hot. 'Get out!'

Her eyes, first red from tears, were now red with anger. Her voice a banshee's, not my sister's. What was this creature, standing in the corner of our bedroom? Jenny flashed before my eyes, sweet sunshine in a yellow dress into gnashing teeth and nails.

I blinked it away. Rubbed my eyes. She was Jenny again, in my clothes, tired and upset but still telling me to go. She screamed it at me again and again until I got up, opened the door, left her.

I stood outside our bedroom, her voice ringing in my ears, muting every other sound. The smell of fried chicken reached up through the house but it turned my stomach. I saw Bung-Eye mashing that tender white meat between tobacco-stained teeth. I saw him smiling, staring me down, walking into Jenny's room. I heard him and my momma and their fucking. Smelt the pot. Smelt the stench of him everywhere. He was an infection in our house, the maggoty corn pile all over again, and he had done something to Jenny to make her cry.

I turned to go back into the bedroom, confront her, make her tell me, but I heard her voice in my head again. *Go. Get out.*

I stumbled down the stairs, through the kitchen. Momma asked if I was okay and I said I was going out but I don't remember saying it. I heard it inside my head as if it was a question she would ask, and the answer I would give. All my edges were fuzzy, all the noises muffled, the memories blurred.

Dry grass sliced against my shins. The summer turned everything to husks, every sound was a snap or a crack, every smell hot and sweet as smoke. There was tension in the air, like the sky was a balloon blown too large. It stretched and paled and any day, any second, would explode, fling us wide and clear and into nothing.

I wanted comfort. Familiarity. A place where I could breathe and sit and pretend everything was as it had been when Jenny was normal, just my sister, before Mary Ridley and her obsession, when she called me Johnny and asked me to go fishing, when she held my hand and didn't shout and didn't cry and looked at me like I was her big brother, not some annoyance, a jagged stone in her shoe.

As soon as I stepped over the low rise from the fields into the trees leading down to the Roost, Big Lake and our Fort, I felt a sharp prick of guilt. This place had been our world, the four of us. My sister. My best friends. Our home that we built for ourselves. But circumstances and time and all kinds of horror had left it to wither and grow distant inside my head. Jenny and Momma and Bung-Eye took up all my space, shouted for my attention. Big Lake, Rudy, Gloria, they shrank into my corners, tiny chirps in a nest of screaming cuckoos.

Big Lake wasn't as big as I remembered it. Even in the half-light of the evening, my eyes took in the whole body of water. Maybe the sun had dried up the stream that fed it, maybe it had sucked up the surface water and I was only seeing half of what it used to be. But there were no dark lines around its edge to show its depth. No grey leaves or patches of mud once submerged and now revealed. It was as it always had been but to me, then, it was little more than a pond. Pointless. Childish.

I hated it. Hated the memories it brought. The nameless girl, tangled up in that sycamore. The one who became Mary Ridley, the one killed by Gloria's father with Frank and Bung-Eye and Mayor Wills all involved. Nobody had been punished except me and Jenny and Rudy and Gloria. We were suffering for finding her, for caring, for wanting justice. I was out of school and going to leave the home I loved. Jenny was changing into something harsh and unkind. Gloria and I were friends but not more. No more kissing down at Barks. No more stolen smiles and blushing cheeks. Rudy was mostly his normal self. We talked, we laughed, we hung out, but there was a new desperation to him. He and Jenny only ever spoke of Mary, of leaving Larson, of what next, what next. And I couldn't join in. I had too many secrets squatting inside me. They trapped my tongue and seized my brain, threatened to spill out if I opened my mouth to say, 'Hello.' So I was silent, distant, and they didn't know how to fill that kind of quiet. Now Bung-Eye had his claws in Momma and Jenny, and I couldn't pull them free. Everything was dying and rotting away because of that girl and the men who put her in the water.

Deep breaths, Johnny. One-one-thousand. Two-one-thousand. That was Frank's technique but now his words felt hollow, after what we found in his basement, after that terrible conversation with Charlie Meaney. Was he still my pastor, my almost father?

Count, the voices scoffed, count to a thousand and it won't change what's happened.

I thought of Jenny. Of two-years-ago Jenny when the sun cascaded down her back, through her hair and when she still smiled, no matter Momma's words. That stilled my heart, more than numbers ever could.

I turned away from Big Lake. Spotted our Fort further down the valley. A new, gleaming piece of sheet iron for a roof. As I got closer, I saw new boards patching up the walls and a strong door with a lock.

I heard voices. Soft, each word murmured close, as if within an embrace. Two people. Together. A quiet, warm laugh.

I knew the laugh. Knew the voices.

I stepped between dry leaves, dead giveaways Rudy called them, to a crack in the boards. In the light from an old storm lantern, I saw them. Rudy and Scott Westin. Tangled up together in a nest of blankets. Speaking sweet words, laughing sweet laughs. Rudy must have patched up the walls, fixed the roof, made himself a hidden place.

I didn't know what I was seeing, not really. They were boys, but they were kissing. They were touching. They were acting like girls and boys act and I didn't know why. Rudy the charmer. Rudy the boy with a hundred hearts carved in trees. Rudy the ladies' man.

Rudy the queer?

I turned away, left silent as I'd arrived, ashamed I'd even been looking. But as I got further away, I realised I was annoyed at Rudy. Really damn annoyed. The feeling scratched around my guts like rats in a dumpster. Why hadn't he told me? Why had he flirted with all the girls when all the time he wanted something else? All those times he'd spoken about us running off to LA together. You write the movies, Johnny, and I'll star in them. I felt tears on my cheeks, angry burning salt tears, why didn't you tell me? We're best buds, aren't we?

Oh boy, oh boy. My chest tightened. Bung-Eye'll put Rudy in hospital again if he finds out, or maybe this time it'd be six feet under. He's good as dead, Johnny, and you know it.

I wanted to rip out the voice in my head, pitch it into Big Lake and watch it disintegrate.

I'd wanted somewhere to sit and think and clear the fog from my brain but Big Lake, the Fort, it was not that place any more. It wasn't what I'd remembered, where we'd gone fishing and swung on a rope and smoked a Camel between the four of us and dreamed and made all kinds of plans. I'm going to be a model. I'm going to be a movie star. I'm going to be an astronaut.

No.

It was where we met Death for the first time, sitting on the banks of our lake. It was where kids go to fool around with sex and stolen beer.

My head filled with pictures of Rudy and Scott. I slammed my fist against the side of my skull. Each hit changed the picture.

Rudy and me.

Smack.

Rudy and Jenny.

Smack.

Jenny and that fucker Darney Wills.

Smack. Smack. Smack.

The side of my face blazed, hot and tender, like hellfire itself had risen up inside me. Everything was going wrong. If anyone found out about Rudy and Scott, they'd be run out of town. If Bung-Eye found out . . . The thought made my stomach spasm. Our lives hung by one arm off the edge of a cliff. Something dark had overtaken my sister and was grinding its boot against her fingers. Soon she'd fall and I didn't know if I could catch her.

I walked home slower, trying to cool myself. It wouldn't be long now until I had the money to get me and Jenny away but with so much darkness in our town, so much darkness already in my sister, it might be too late.

When I got home, stepped through the back door into the kitchen, a cold mite of fear burrowed itself into my gut. I knew my home, knew its air and smell and weight, and I knew when something had shifted, like when Jenny ran away.

Bung-Eye was gone, his stink fading. No sound from upstairs.

On the couch in the family room, Momma snored, blood soaking through the bandage on her arm. On the kitchen table, her once-hidden, half-full jar of whiskey was empty. Upstairs, Jenny was gone.

25

Jenny never told me where she had gone that night but she came back changed. She stopped brushing her hair and ate like the end of the world was at her heels. I should have known then that it had started, that unstoppable force that I set in motion with my anger, my loose tongue, my misplaced trust.

I found her one evening, in our – her – bedroom, taking a pair of scissors to her favourite sundress, the one with the yellow flowers. The door was open an inch and she didn't see me. She tore the dress to ribbons then started on another, and another, until the floor disappeared beneath shredded cotton. All the while she was babbling to Mary, to Eric, to Mark and Tracy.

Inside my head, I screamed at her. Tell me what's going on. Let me help.

I counted the money that night. Ninety-four dollars and a handful of pennies. Enough for bus tickets but not much else. Another two weeks and I'd have cash for a place to stay, a few days' food. That was it. Just two short weeks and no more Bung-Eye, no more crying and fear and secrets.

I kept the money in a matchbox toy carton Eric had given me before he left. I'd lost the car, a lurid green AMX Javelin, but somehow kept the box. I hid it behind the loose baseboard in the family room, beneath a cabinet full of books and ornaments nobody even glanced at any more. The weight of the box and the heavy slosh of coins inside kept my spirits up as I went into another day hauling sacks at the grocery store.

'John,' Al Westin called from the back room when I was cleaning out the onion trays. A moment later he appeared through the plastic curtain, pulling off his apron.

'I've got to bust out for a few hours,' he said. 'That numbskull Del, the fruit guy, he's gone and got his truck stuck in Early Creek. Arches deep he said on the phone. Damn idiot.'

'Want me to come and help?' I said. It was Thursday afternoon and we hadn't had a customer in over four hours.

He ducked down behind the counter and reappeared with a jangle of keys. 'Del's got his boy with him. You stay here. Stay open. Fix up those onions and then take stock on the tates.'

'All right.'

He clapped my shoulder as he went past me to the door. 'If Scotty comes by, give him a dollar out the register and tell him to fix his own dinner.'

My gut twisted. Scotty Westin and Rudy Buchanan, wrapped up in each other, hidden away in our nowhere valley.

'Will do, Mr Westin,' I said, forcing the words through the images of his son and my friend. Al rushed out and let the door slam behind him. I wondered what Al would think, how he would react if he found out. Couldn't be worse than what Bung-Eye would do, that's for sure.

I was paralysed, holding a handful of onions by the stalks. Is that really what I saw the other night? I'd seen couples making out at Barks reservoir, on the beach, in the trees. I knew the movements and sounds and small, private looks they shared. I'd had the same with Gloria, so long ago now. The Fort that night was full of that passion, maybe even love. Bung-Eye would kill Rudy if he found out. Mr Wakefield wanted to kill me when he found out about Gloria and me. It didn't matter who you were kissing, there would always be someone wanting to kill you for it.

I desperately wanted to see Rudy, talk to him, tell him I knew and it was okay, I'd never tell Bung-Eye or Perry or anyone, no matter what. But I couldn't leave the store and we were hours from closing.

Straight after work, I told myself, the second the lock clicked in that door, I'd find him. I'd run all over Larson if I needed to. Every minute in the shop from then made me itch. I couldn't stay busy enough, couldn't count enough apples or cauliflowers or tates. Couldn't clean enough trays or sweep enough floors and not one person came in.

Until four. The bell dinged on the door when I was in the back, sorting and restacking boxes of oranges.

'Just a minute,' I shouted and a voice I knew called back.

'John, we need to talk,' Gloria said, with a tone of seriousness I barely recognised.

I left the boxes in the middle of the floor, suddenly nervous, suddenly feeling all those feelings for her again. Seeing Rudy with someone had made me want my own fumbles, my own secret, hidden embraces. And there she was, Gloria, the girl I used to love. Still loved.

I came out of the storeroom expecting her to be alone but Rudy stood beside her. Stone-faced and cold, the both of them, and my nerves crackled, scratched against my bones. What have I done? What have you done? Did Rudy see me that night? Will you call me 'freak' too? I still wanted to talk to him but not with Gloria there.

'Hello,' I said. I didn't know where to look.

'Hey,' Rudy said, smiled that movie-star smile. 'How are things? Your mom okay?'

He gave me a look that said he knew about Bung-Eye and Momma, he knew and he was sorry about it.

'She's fine,' I said, tried to smile back. 'She knows where the knives are.'

Rudy laughed. 'Thank God for that.'

But the levity quickly died and we fell silent for a while.

'I don't know how to say this,' Gloria started, faltered, looked down to her red shoes.

'Something is going on with Jenny,' Rudy said. He had a calmness about him that he never used to. Rudy used to jitter and buzz but now he was still, like he'd finally settled into his skin. Seeing that made my insides settle too.

'What is it?' I said.

'She's . . .' Gloria looked at Rudy, then back to me. 'She's been drinking and smoking at school. She hasn't been going to class for weeks. She's failing, John.'

Failing. Drinking. Smoking. My body throbbed.

'I didn't realise it had gotten so bad,' I murmured.

'That's not the part we're worried about,' Rudy said.

'What are you talking about?'

Gloria met my eyes. 'She's been going with that ape

Darney Wills and she wouldn't talk to us. I tried everything but she kept blanking me. She's been dressing differently too, wearing thick sweaters, t-shirts and baggy denims. She's not looking after herself. I don't know the last time she brushed her hair. Since you quit school it got worse.'

A sharp stab of guilt in my gut.

Gloria kept going. 'The other day we got into an argument. She hadn't been herself for so long. I missed my friend, you know? Well, we both said some things and it got heated and she hit me. Really goddamn hard.'

Gloria turned her head and pointed to a scratch below her left eye. Then I noticed the dark shadow of a bruise on her cheekbone.

'That isn't our Jenny,' Rudy said. 'Something is wrong.'

I couldn't look at them. I was failing my sister. She had this other life I couldn't be a part of. So many hours we spent apart now, so many days I went with barely speaking to her except over tense meals or a hasty goodnight. Suddenly all this working, saving money, all my promises seemed as much use as chasing dust.

The three of us stood, awkward and in silence, until Gloria finally spoke again.

'We followed her.'

'What?'

'Today,' she said. 'It was just after Miss Eaves' class. Darney Wills was waiting for her on the corner and we followed them.'

I looked to Rudy but his face held no trace of apology.

'Where did they go?'

I expected Barks. Or Darney's house. Or even the old warehouse on the way out of town, the place seniors went to shack up, full of mattresses and cardboard partitions. It made me shiver to think of Jenny there. Some disgusting place he could put his filthy hands all over her, ply her with beer or stronger. She'd never be able to fight him off. I felt my pocket, traced the shape of Rudy's flick knife. I'd go there now, wherever they were, and I'd cut Darney's throat. The oily black wings inside me woke, rushed, beat a hundred times a second.

'Where?'

Gloria and Rudy didn't answer, just looked at each other, unsure of the door they'd opened, the beast they'd unleashed.

The black birds grew and raged and they were all I could hear. 'Where are they?'

'We'll show you,' Rudy said. 'Just, stay calm, yeah? It might even be a good thing.'

A good thing? With Darney Wills? I wanted to punch Rudy then, smash the stupidity out of him.

'Now. Let's go,' I said, forgot about the shop, about Al Westin and his trust and his 'good boy, Johnny'. They were smoke in a storm.

I couldn't get out of there fast enough. I didn't lock the front door. I didn't hide the cash tray. My mind was consumed by Jenny and what she was doing, what Darney was doing to her. It was fire through paper, all-powerful and rampant. I'd only find out later that the store was robbed, trashed, and the week's take stolen. Westin's Groceries soon went under. But to me, then, nothing mattered but Jenny.

I was so distracted, I didn't hear Rudy and Gloria making small talk and I didn't realise where we were going until we turned onto a familiar street.

'We followed her and Darney here,' Gloria said. 'He left

her with *him* and hung around outside for a while then wandered off.'

Five doors down from where I stood was Frank's house. The last time I'd been on this street, the sky was black with smoke from the Easton mill. Today the sun blazed and it looked like just a street. All my panic suddenly seemed absurd.

I stopped on the sidewalk, looked at them both. 'Are you sure?'

'Yes.' Rudy put his hand on my shoulder but I didn't quite understand why.

'It could be nothing,' Gloria tried. 'She's been having problems, right? He could be being a good pastor, giving her advice and . . . you know, spiritual guidance.

'John,' she said, grabbed my arm. 'It's probably totally innocent. He's a pastor.'

I laughed, all the fear and tension drained right out of me. 'Are you kidding? She's with Pastor Jacobs?'

Gloria frowned. 'We're not kidding.'

I wanted to shake them both. 'So we're back to this. How many times do I have to say it? You both still think he killed Mary Ridley but . . . ' *your dad killed her, Gloria*; the words caught and I couldn't breathe '. . . he didn't and now, you think Frank's going to hurt Jenny? He never would. You're both saying some big black evil is happening in this quiet street with its mown lawns and drawn curtains and perfect fucking flowerbeds. Give it up.'

But there was some evil. I felt it under the bright summer sky, the creeping uncertainty of Frank's involvement in all this mess.

Rudy folded his arms, straightened his back. 'If you're so sure about all that then let's go take a peek.'

'Fine. And when there's nothing going on, will you drop it? Finally? Will you leave Pastor Jacobs alone?'

Rudy and Gloria glanced at each other.

'Yes,' Rudy said and Gloria nodded.

'Then let's go.'

I ducked down the side of the nearest house, Rudy and Gloria behind me, and crossed the back yards until we reached Frank's. We hid in a bush, crept as close as we could.

I saw them through the kitchen window. With the blazing sun, we could see right through his house, through the kitchen, hallway, and out through those wide front windows in the family room. Jenny sat at the kitchen table. She wore my old t-shirt, hair rough and ragged but tied up as best she could with a scarf, the one with blue stars, the birthday present from Gloria. I thought she'd stopped wearing it.

She sat opposite Frank. Two glasses of half-empty ice tea between them.

There you go, I wanted to shout. Enjoying a cool glass of ice tea, nothing more. Jenny wasn't screaming or crying or scratching for escape. She just looked sad, her eyes down, all attention on her glass, like she needed someone to listen.

'See?' I said to them both.

'They're just talking,' Gloria said, sighing out her relief. I nodded.

Rudy shook his head. 'But why would Darney Wills bring her here?'

'Maybe he was doing something nice for her, taking her for counselling,' Gloria said, but I could tell it pained her to say it. Pained me to hear it.

Frank reached out across the table and Jenny flinched away. Just like she'd flinched away from me. Through the house, on the street, a family of four passed the window. I heard them laughing in the quiet afternoon. Just a normal neighbourhood on a normal day.

'Maybe,' I said.

'Sorry, John. You were right,' Gloria said, put her hand on my hand, met my eyes. Felt a hot ache in my chest. All the things that could have been, right there in one look.

'We should go,' Gloria said and started to move off. Rudy did the same. The absence I felt when Gloria took her hand away cracked something inside me.

'I'm staying,' I said. 'I'll wait for her, walk her home.'

'All right,' Rudy said and put his hand on my shoulder again. 'We'll keep an eye on Jenny at school, yeah? She'll be fine.'

Gloria smiled at me. 'Don't be a stranger, Johnny.'

'Thanks, guys,' I said. 'Let's do something next week, after school, maybe go to Clarkesville and see a movie or something.'

They smiled, agreed, said goodbye, see you soon. But I knew they wouldn't. Me and Jenny would be long gone by then. Off to San Francisco or the Florida beaches, safe and free.

The weight on my back dispersed but I was seized by something else, some sharp ache in my chest as I watched Rudy help Gloria over the fence.

'Wait,' I said to him as she dropped down the other side and we were alone. I grabbed his arm, and pulled him a few steps away, back into the shelter of the bushes.

'What?' Rudy said, yanked his arm from my grip.

'Get out of this town,' I said. 'Get out and never look back.'

His eyes locked on mine. Wide and confused.

'What are you talking about?' he said.

'You're too good for this place. Take your savings, get on a bus and go,' I faltered, should I? Shouldn't I?

Yes. Say it.

'Before Bung-Eye finds out, because he will. You know he will.'

His eyes, with the slightest shift, showed a glimmer of fear. He blinked it away, broke the connection. Despite the distance of the last year or so, he was and would ever be, my best friend. I remembered the snapping sound his arm made when Bung-Eye caught him, I remembered the black eye and the wincing and crying at Christmas. I wanted him to know I'd never be the cause of his hurt. I'd never tell a soul about him and Scott. His eyes shone, the beginnings of tears maybe, then he hugged me.

'See you soon, yeah?' he said and I smiled.

He climbed over the fence and he and Gloria ran out of my life. Still smiling, I turned back to Jenny. We'll go, first thing in the morning. Ninety-four bucks was just enough for two tickets and I'd get odd jobs down in San Francisco or Chicago or wherever to pay for food and a nice place to stay for a while. Jenny could finish school by the ocean, breathing in the freshest air, far away from Darney Wills and Bung-Eye and, for now at least until the monster was tamed, from Momma. I'd write to Momma every week and make sure she knew we were okay and why we had to leave and that we'd be back when she promised to treat Jenny right and say sorry for cutting her hair and everything else. Then I'd take over the farm. We'd be a real family again, and I'd take care of everything. For the first time in a long time I felt hopeful. We'd be happy.

I kept my eyes on Jenny. The window glass and the glaring

sun obscured her details but I knew her shape, her tiniest movements, what they meant, what they looked like in full glorious resolution. Her shoulders were relaxed, her breathing calm.

She's fine, Johnny, she's doing just fine. Frank is doing his thing, being a pastor, tending a lost sheep. That's what he did, for me and now for her. Me and Jenny had a brand new future waiting at dawn, that's all that mattered. My body filled with light, bright joy. I was a birthday balloon on a string, tugging at a child's hand. Let me go, let me float away and see the wide world. Larson is just a speck, one drop of paint on a giant splatter canvas. I'd miss Frank but I promised myself I'd write to him, he could come visit, we would take trips. It'd be a new life for all of us.

I felt like rushing into the house and carrying Jenny away, starting that new life right now, but I stopped myself. Let her finish, let her get her troubles off her chest.

I saw us boarding a Greyhound and riding it until the endless, stifling cornfields transformed into forests, mountains, lakes, sweeping plains, and finally, beautifully, the great blue ocean.

I shifted in my hidden place and the golden reflection from the sun on the pastor's windows moved with me, removing the glare, allowing me a clear view.

The instant my eyes locked on Jenny, I knew something was terribly wrong with my sister.

Frank had stopped talking. His lips weren't moving any more and he was staring at Jenny.

Her eyelids drooped. Her head lolled then jerked up like she was falling asleep.

Frank slid the now empty glass out of Jenny's hand.

The picture of the ocean, the beach, the sun, turned grey in my mind.

Jenny's head dropped again and she looked up at Jacobs, her face slack, her eyes half-closed. Something in his expression changed. Through the distance, the angle, the warp of the glass, it was there on Frank's face – a sneering, nervous impatience. A traitorous prince waiting for his poisoned king to die.

But Jenny wasn't dead and she wasn't asleep, not yet. Frank said something, called over his shoulder, and stood up. Everything happened in slow motion but I couldn't react. I was coiled steel, tense and waiting for the release.

A man walked into the kitchen from another room. Grey slacks, a white shirt open at the collar and rolled-up sleeves. A thick moustache.

Mr Wakefield.

Every bone in my body felt like it broke at once. A sharp *snap* in my head, under my skin, all over me under me inside me.

Mr Wakefield. Gloria's father. Right there.

Frank lowered his head, shook it, and rubbed his cheek. A look on him I'd never seen. Was that shame? Was it fear? What the hell was going on?

Wakefield took Jenny by the shoulders and pulled her to her feet. She was loose and slumped against him. He led her across the kitchen. I remembered the exact layout of his home. But I couldn't put the pieces together. Nothing added up in my head. This can't be happening. No, it mustn't. That's my sister. Where are you taking her?

The basement.

The bed, bolted to the floor.

Darney Wills had said, *Your pretty piece-of-ass sister will be all his, and you saw what happened to the last girl he took a shine to.*

I remembered the green paint on the basement floor and on Mary Ridley's skin. The purple cardigan under the bed. The Polaroid of a girl who could be Mary, could be any number of girls, stuffed in a Bible. The last girl Wakefield took a shine to ended up dead. In that house. Where my sister was right now.

I surged forward, broke through the bushes, my hand in my pocket, on the flick knife. The world turned red and black and I saw only him and my sister. His daughter's friend. What kind of man? What kind of father?

I reached for the back door. I'd rip the screen away. I'd kick the door to splinters. I'd paint his house with his own black blood.

I didn't hear the footsteps behind me.

I didn't see the fist until it cracked the side of my face.

And I was on the grass. I don't remember falling. My ears and skull and teeth and jaw all throbbed, wanted to shatter in my head.

A great weight landed on my back. My ribs and spine joined the screeching choir. Everything hurt, nothing was clear, my mind tangled and knotted itself and there was only pain and Jenny and Mr Wakefield and Frank and me, unable to move, unable to get to her.

'Hush, hush, Johnny boy,' Darney Wills breathed in my ear, ground his knee into my back. 'Just in time for the show.'

But he'd gone, hadn't he? Darney had left. Gloria and Rudy said so and they wouldn't lie. Darney had brought Jenny here for a counselling session. He was misunderstood. He was good deep down. That's what she'd said.

No. There's not a hair, a cell, a nail, of good about him. He's that fucker Darney Wills and he's betrayed her. And me. And the whole town. He hadn't left. He'd wandered off but he'd come back. He was watching, waiting. He knew what was going on and he was making sure nothing and no one interrupted it.

'Get off me!'

I don't know if I shouted it or just thought it. I couldn't breathe or lift my head. I tasted blood and felt it trickling out of my mouth into the grass.

But I could see.

Right in front of me, the window to the basement.

'Stop. Get off.' I strained but I was a mouse against a bear.

'Shut the fuck up, freak,' Darney whispered in my ear. The stink of his sweat and breath was all over me.

'I'll kill you,' I said. 'I'll kill both of you. You fuck . . . you fucking bastard.'

He pushed my head into the dry grass, needle spikes in my eyes. 'Big words for such a baby. Calm down, freak. I haven't touched your slut sister. I'm just the delivery boy. Someone's got to make sure the stock gets to the buyer. He warned you, freak. I warned you and you didn't listen. You went running your big mouth and look what happened. Nice going, pussy boy.'

Hurr hurr.

Sour bile rose up in my throat and I thrashed and bolted under him. He lifted off me long enough for my lungs to fill then drove his ham fist into my kidney.

'Here comes the fun bit.' He grabbed my hair and wrenched my head up, toward the basement window.

Wakefield appeared, carrying my sister in his arms, still

awake, her hand pawing at his chest, her head unable to carry its own weight. He had a serene look on his face like he was carrying his daughter to her room after she fell asleep on the couch. His daughter. Gloria was his daughter. Jenny was a year younger. Jenny was fourteen. I felt sick. Felt my stomach swell.

Wakefield reached the bottom of the stairs and turned, toward the back wall of the basement. He paused and looked over his shoulder, out the window, right at me. Our eyes met and he smiled. The bastard smiled.

I see you, the voices screamed, I see what you're doing and I won't let you get away with it.

Then he, and my sister, disappeared behind the stairwell. Into the blindspot.

The bed.

No, no, no. Not Jenny. Don't you dare. *NO*.

It's all my fault. I spilled my guts like Darney warned me not to. I told.

Frank. My gut seized. I told Frank.

I strained my eyes to see into the kitchen and there he was, standing by the sink, washing up glasses as if he'd had guests. Why aren't you stopping this? Why aren't you doing anything?

Because he's a part of it. He knew about Mary Ridley because Mary was in his house. He knew what Wakefield had done because it was in his basement. He knew he killed her. He always knew. And he fucking *helped*.

They were right. Rudy and Gloria. They were right about him and I'd defended him and said he was a good man. The thought stuck in my throat and I wanted to throw up all those good words I'd said. I thought I was screaming but no one came, no neighbour pulled Darney off me or raced into the house to save my sister. I was pinned and useless and my face was exploding and my head was on fire and I wasn't me, I wasn't John. I was nothing. Nobody.

Tears blinded me and burned my cheeks. I raged beneath Darney and I felt him give. His great heft no match for my anger. God or the devil or pure, unfiltered hate or all three at once filled me, from my heart, radiating out through my bones, my muscles, my tendons and veins. The rage wore me like a skin. I was on my knees and rising, up, up, up, my wings spreading, lifting me. My hand was free and it held the knife, pulled it from my pocket. Everything coalesced into one brilliant moment as my finger found the button.

Darney smashed his boot into my side and my ribs crunched.

Acid hit the back of my throat. The wings turned to glass on my back.

'Time to sleep, freak,' he said and kicked me again, harder, and in the face.

My neck snapped back, my brain bounced inside my skull. The glass wings shattered. A moment of searing pain. A flash of bright white. And a terrible fall. The only thought was that I couldn't protect her. I said sorry over and over as darkness swept me up and my body hit the dirt.

26

I opened my eyes to the end of the world. Blood in my mouth and crusted on my cheek. The smell of dusty grass swam around me like gas, raised me from the unconscious blur. I lifted my head and a shockwave went through my brain, blinded me, pressed me back down into the dirt. A prickling sting grew on the back of my neck, the side of my head, backs of my arms and legs. My skin was sucked dry and taut, sunburnt and red, maybe blistered or would be soon.

When the pain eased, I slowly, agonisingly, pushed myself onto my knees. The vulnerable skin in the creases of my knees felt like it was ripping apart, itching from the dust, burning from the sun.

I brought shaking fingers to my face, felt for my features, found only swell and flaking blood. I was alien, not myself. One cheek was puffed up double, one was too painful and raw to touch. I rolled my jaw, heard a creaking, grinding sound, as the bones in my face reset themselves, then a sharp pop in my ears followed by ringing.

I heard myself sobbing, felt the quick breath in my chest, but couldn't connect to the emotion. I was hovering above myself, the hawk above the mouse, feeling only pain, only confusion.

I remembered where I was, why I was. It hit me harder than Darney's boot in the gut and the anger resurfaced. Frank's garden. Not where I'd fallen, I realised, not where Darney had beaten me. I'd been dragged behind a bush, out of view of the kitchen windows, inches from the shade that would have saved my skin.

The stars emerged from the black and a sliver of moon shone pitifully, lighting nothing, helping nothing. The pastor's house was dark, like every other I could see. I was in a ghost town. Except for the weak, distant orange of streetlamps, the only lights I saw twinkled on the Larson water tower. The small spots illuminated the town name, the white curves of the tank and nothing else. It was alone in the dark now after its brother, the Easton mill grain elevator, burned down a year ago. I couldn't look at the tower, so stark against the black, a constant, looming reminder of the mill's absence. They were a pair, like me and Jenny, and the sky, the town, the whole world, was not complete without them both.

My sight adjusted to the dark and a chill crept through me, sending shivers up and down my legs and back. It wasn't cold, the undamaged parts of me knew that, but still I shivered, still I hugged myself, my skin stretching, threatening to split.

I limped to Frank's window but saw nothing inside. Then I struggled down to my knees, checked the basement.

Darkness and silence. No sign of Wakefield. Somehow I knew Jenny was not in that house. I spotted Rudy's flick knife on the ground. I'd been so close until that fucker Darney Wills caught me. I would have smashed the window. Crawled through it. Let the glass slice me up. I wouldn't have cared as long as I got to Wakefield before he got to her.

But I'd failed. A tremor went through my stomach. I'd failed. And he'd done whatever he wanted with my sister while my pastor, my *father*, let it happen right beneath his God-fearing feet.

I picked up the knife, put it back in my pocket and stood. A part of me wanted to sneak inside the house, find Frank's bedroom, find him sleeping like a babe, dreaming all kinds of dreams, and cut those dreams out of his head, cut that lying tongue out of his mouth, watch him choke and try to scream, let him know that I, John Royal, his buddy, his son, his sport, knew exactly what he'd done. Then I'd go after Wakefield.

My chest seized. I couldn't go after him. I couldn't take him away from Gloria. I loved her. I knew I did from the first kiss at Barks. I couldn't hurt her. Never hurt her like I'd never hurt Jenny.

Jenny. God, I wanted to see Jenny. To hold her and make sure she was unhurt and take her far, far away as soon as dawn broke. If I killed the pastor right here, right now, I'd never be able to keep her safe and she'd be left with Momma and Bung-Eye and Darney Wills. I'd never stand beside her by the ocean, shrieking in and out of the surf, kicking the sand into clouds.

I turned away from Frank's house, from the man who I thought better than all of them, and made my slow, aching way home.

I don't know how long it took to get back. I shuffled one foot in front of the other in a daze, clutching my side. My left ear rang and a cut on my cheek itched. I was numb to what he'd done. What they'd both done. To her. To me. To the whole town.

When I got home, the house was dark and quiet. I went in through the back door, it made less noise than the front, then straight up the stairs to the bathroom to set the water running. I would be clean when I saw my sister. I wanted to sink into a steaming bath and let all the grime and blood dissolve, float away from me from tip to toe so in the morning I could leave Larson, and all that had happened here, scrubbed and gleaming.

I climbed up the second set of steps to the attic room, to our bedroom. I eased open the door without making the hinges creak and half-stepped inside. On the bed, covered head to toe in that ugly blanket, was my sister. Sleeping. Safe. The unease inside me faded but didn't disappear. I closed the door and made my way back to the bathroom.

Jenny and me would escape the dark seed grown up to vines strangling the town. That creeper with roots and tendrils reaching through Gloria's father, Bung-Eye Buchanan, Charlie Meaney, Darney Wills and his corrupt mayor of a father, into the incompetent sheriffs and Samuels turning a blind eye to a girl's murder, all the way to Frank, the godly heart of Larson. It was a snake eating itself. The town fed on its own misery and it was fattened up for slaughter. But I vowed, in that bathroom, that Jenny and me would be gone before the final stroke of the blade, before the guts and blood of Larson spilled into the hot dirt.

After I'd seen what I'd seen in Jacobs' house, felt what

I'd felt when Darney's boot struck my face, heard what he'd said, after calling me a freak, after saying it was my fault, he'd warned me, he'd said, *Someone's got to make sure the stock gets to the buyer*. It all came together in my head. Wakefield had bought Mary Ridley, then killed her. Maybe it was an accident. Maybe that's what he paid for. And now he'd *bought* Jenny. I felt like laughing if only to stop me screaming. Their 'arrangement'. You pays your money and you takes your choice, right? Had the mayor paid too? What about Frank? Of course they did, John, you don't even need to ask. All those puzzle pieces clicked together, finally, two years after we found Mary Ridley's body. All those pillars of the Larson community were covering it up and which bastard was pulling the strings and taking the cash? The bastard sharing my momma's bed. I wasn't even surprised. If anyone would look to make a buck out of a girl's pain and misery, it was Bung-Eye Buchanan. The anger had become so absolute and a part of me that I barely felt its sharpness. I gripped the edge of the bath until it hurt. Then let go. I couldn't hurt them. I couldn't stop them. All I could do was take Jenny away, protect her, and I would, until the day I died.

But I was wrong. About so much. Found out too late how wrong. Wakefield had taken his revenge on me. My pastor had let him. But that was nothing, that was just dust kicked up on the road.

As the water ran and the bath began to fill, something felt strange. I couldn't quite explain it, maybe it was my brain tired and full of pain, but deep in my chest, something gnawed at me. I left the bath running and stepped out onto the landing. A voice.

'Baby, that you?'

Momma. In the family room.

I ducked into the bathroom; the bath was barely half full, so I went to the top of the stairs.

'Momma?' I whispered so not to stir Jenny. 'I'm sorry for waking you. It's late, you should go back to sleep.'

'Baby . . . Johnny . . .' her voice floated away on a sea of whiskey.

Had she been down there the whole time? Asleep on her armchair maybe? I hadn't checked when I came in.

I went downstairs and found her standing, barefoot in the dark, between the kitchen and family room. She wore a robe tied tight at her waist. She had the lapels in her fist, drawn right up to her neck showing not an inch of skin from chin down or shin up.

I went to her, the sound of the slow-running water upstairs in my ears, and took her gently by the upper arm. 'Momma, let's get you to bed.'

'Do you know what time it is?' she said, her voice suddenly strong and hers again. She pulled away from me and switched on a lamp.

In the light, she saw me fully, and her heavy eyes widened, whitened, took in my injuries. 'Jesus John, what happened to your face?'

Tell her.

Don't tell her. Don't tell her about Bung-Eye, she'll hate you for it. Don't you ruin this for me, John Royal, she'd said all those weeks ago. The truth would ruin everything.

But tell her something. She's your mother, Johnny boy, she loves you.

'I had a run-in with Darney Wills,' I said.

Momma moved past me to the couch, switched on

another lamp, and beckoned me to sit beside her. She
didn't acknowledge the name, or the bastard behind it. She
shook her head, an expression on her face saying, to my
throbbing mind, the fight was my fault. Darney Wills is a
big guy, those drunk eyes said, why would you go and tussle
with him? He sure put you in your place, John Royal, right
under his boot.

'Momma?'

'Bring the medicine box and sit down,' she said. 'I'm
always patching you up. Why do you get into so many fights?'

I went to the kitchen where we kept the box and something caught my eye. The knife drawer was open an inch
and I knew Momma didn't like that, she'd caught her
side once on a drawer Jenny left open and had a bruise
for weeks. I closed it before going back into the family
room.

'Is Bung-Eye here?' I asked, pushed the name through
a mouthful of bile.

No answer. Upstairs the bath filled, the sound of the
water slowly changing as the level rose.

'Momma? Is he here?' I'd kill him if he was, I thought,
felt the knife in my pocket.

I sat down beside her. I put the medicine box between
us. She ran her finger over the red cross on the lid, her
other hand still clutching the collar of her bathrobe.

'Hmm? No, he's not, he's gone for a while, about a week,
on a job . . . somewhere.' She shuffled closer to me, started
tugging on my t-shirt. Once white, now splattered with blood
and dirt. 'Let me see.'

I lifted my t-shirt. Momma gave a sharp hiss when she
saw me. From my hipbone, halfway to my armpit, a bruise,
ringed with black, seemed to grow before my eyes. In the

hot red centre of it, a few distinct shapes spoke of Darney's boot tread.

We were silent. I let my shirt drop. Momma didn't open the medicine box, she didn't tend my wounds, didn't look in my eyes. I took her hand. Her skin felt different, cold and thin, like a grandmother's. I thought if I pinched it the fold would stand tall.

'Why are you with him?' I asked. 'Bung-Eye, I mean.'

'Bung-Eye . . . he hates that name you know.' Momma smiled. 'Eddie isn't so bad, not really.'

The voice in my head raged. He sells young girls to old men. He sold Jenny. My sister. Your daughter. He did that and if I see him I'll kill him, Momma, I'll kill him.

Don't ruin it. A war raged in my head and I knew I wouldn't survive it. Not in one piece. I couldn't say what I wanted, so I said a smaller truth, one just as terrible.

'He broke Rudy's arm, snapped it right in front of me.'

'Rudy broke his arm,' Momma said, a sharp edge in her voice. 'Eddie didn't break it for him. Don't be so stupid, John.'

Her words clipped my ear and shamed me. My eyes counted the scratches in the floorboards, the knots in the wood, anything but look up at Momma. Then I saw dirt on the floor, a smear of dust and mud. The smear led to Momma's bare feet. In the dim lamplight, I hadn't noticed the dark mud between her toes, caking the edges of her feet, black spots splashed up her ankles.

'Momma, did you go outside? It must be past three in the morning.'

She leant over to look down to her feet, kept her robe tight to her neck. 'Took out some trash.'

But that was mud, not dry dust. Wet mud. And the sun

had dried up our land as far out as the irrigation channels around Three Points Island. Maybe she knocked the water tank in the dark, sent a river running through our back yard and trod it into the house.

The water tank is nowhere near the trashcans. You know that, Johnny.

Put it out of your head. It's nothing.

It's something. It is. You know it deep down. You felt it in the bathroom, something is wrong.

It doesn't matter. All that matters is Jenny. Maybe if Momma knew what was going on with Bung-Eye and Jenny and Pastor Jacobs she'd reach her arms around us both and draw us in. We'd stay beneath her wide, all-encompassing embrace, safe from Pigeon Pas and Darney Wills. But that was little more than wishful thinking. Jenny and me would leave Momma tomorrow, get on a bus, and give her enough time to tie up all her business before sending for her. She'd finish Bung-Eye, quit that dive bar, stop drinking, and come be our momma somewhere new.

You just have to tell her, Johnny, and you know Jenny doesn't like you talking to Momma about her.

Jenny's upstairs. Asleep. It can't go on. She won't spend another minute with Jacobs or Darney or Wakefield or the mayor.

'Momma, I think something has happened to Jenny.' She flinched as I spoke the name but I carried on. 'Tonight . . . earlier, I saw . . .'

Momma put her free hand on my leg. It felt cold through my shorts and I saw crescents of brownish-red grime beneath her fingernails.

'Did I ever tell you about when I was queen of this town?'

'Momma, please, listen to me.'

'Hush!' she snapped. 'Did I tell you the story?'

She had, a hundred times, but I knew she loved the telling. Knew it made her happy. I was tired and aching, my eyes stung and my cheek throbbed and my side burned but I'd hear the story again. I'd hear it as many times as Momma wanted to tell it. A few more minutes of her happiness, before I told her all about Jenny and the pastor and Wakefield and us leaving, wouldn't hurt.

'They crowned me Cornflower Queen when I was sixteen,' Momma said, a whiskey smile on her lips. 'All the boys went wild for me, they ran alongside that float all the way down Main Street, howling and baying at me like dogs. I could've had any of them. I could've picked them up one by one and then thrown them away and they still would've loved me.

'There was your daddy of course. He was a blocker for the Lions, nice enough, handsome enough. He was a good boy, everyone said so. He did his homework and he said his pleases and thank yous and he went to church every Sunday with his ma and pa.'

This wasn't the story she usually told. My real pa, she'd said, was a quarterback and his mother died while Pa was still a baby. Some dark feeling squirmed in my gut.

Momma kept her eyes down, kept her hand tight on her collar. 'He figured he'd get out of high school and get a job doing drywall or filling sacks at that god-awful flour mill until he could afford to buy us a farm. He'd marry me and I'd pop out two brats and get fat and make him his dinner every night like a good farmer's wife. That was all he wanted and back then, that was exactly what was expected of a woman,' She lost her smile and her face contracted into a sneer. A voice needled in my head, that's the life you wanted, John, a farm, a wife, a family. The life your mother hated.

'If there's one thing your daddy was good at, John Royal, it was lying. He told me all the things I wanted to hear. He said he'd take me to Paris, France, and he'd kiss me on top of the Eiffel tower. He said we'd go to Mexico and California and we'd lie on beaches and swim in that clear blue ocean water. He said he loved me and he'd give me everything and anything if I would be his lady. All those promises just to get my panties off and have his way. He wasn't a man . . .'

She trailed off, as if the memory caught her up and swept her away. A second later she returned, eyes brighter, smiling again.

'None of them were men. Except my bad boy. He made the Buchanan name mean something in this town. He was the only one who didn't come to the parade and see me. Eddie Buchanan. Nineteen and raw. He was beautiful. He was movie-star-James-Dean beautiful, and my God, he wasn't like any of those other boys. Eddie was real man.'

Momma's eyes went glassy, lost in the past, while here, in the present, the squirming feeling in my gut kept getting worse. This wasn't the story she told. This wasn't the way she told it.

'Momma,' I said, 'why are you telling me this?'

'You've got to know, John,' she said. 'You've got to know why it is what it is.'

'Why what is?'

The house was silent but for the sound of running water. The bath would be nearly full now but I didn't want it any more. I forgot about the pain in my face, my side, the ringing in my left ear. My skin was chilled despite the heat.

Momma's words, her tone, the mud on her feet, it all put maggots in my belly.

'I tried to get Eddie to notice me back then but he never even looked my way,' Momma carried on. 'I thought, there's a man who wants more out of this town than any of those football boys. There's a man who can make good on all his promises. Eddie didn't go to pep rallies or homecoming or the prom. He went to car shows and cattle auctions and he watched people. He figured out what made them open their money clips and handed it to them at a good price. I thought, if I'm going to hitch my wagon to any man in Larson, it should be the man who one day is going to run the place.'

Momma raised her free hand in a slow flourish, the sleeve of her robe slipped down, showed a faint red smear on her wrist.

'And now I have. It only took me seventeen years,' she said, and brought her hand back down to her lap, the smear covered.

Red lipstick?

You know it's blood, Johnny. Maybe Momma caught the cut on her arm.

Maybe.

I hated the way she spoke about Bung-Eye like he was a good man. It didn't sound right coming from her mouth. This woman was some other mother, some new form of monster I'd never seen and it terrified me.

'He doesn't run the town,' I said, tried to put that red mark out of my head. 'Sheriff Samuels, he's in charge.'

Momma laughed. 'Bless you, baby. I raised a simple boy, didn't I? You could learn something from Eddie about people. Eddie's got all of Larson's big boys over a barrel.

The mayor, Samuels, the pastor, even pompous Wakefield. Roy Easton too. Boy, I could tell you stories about all of them that'd turn your hair white. Especially Wakefield.' She whistled and shook her head. 'That man's a snake in a linen suit, a slithering eel, always has been, even in high school. But they're all scum. You know it wasn't just Roy's son parking on the tracks that sent that man over the edge. He had a mountain of debt to my Eddie and the price of corn wasn't what it used to be.'

My Eddie. That hurt worse than a boot to the face.

'Eddie's got to make sure all those rich sons of bitches get what they want and keep coming back for more. It's all secrets in this town and those men have dark ones they want to keep hidden. First they pay Eddie for their pleasures, then they pay him to keep their wives, their voters, their congregants from finding out. It's been going on for years. I told you, Eddie knows people.'

My head swam, dizzy, sick. I stood up, ignored the pain shooting through my side. 'Stop it.'

My ears buzzed from her words. My vision blurred. Did she know about Wakefield? About Mary Ridley? Did she know it was me who caused that bastard to take Jenny? Did he pay for the privilege? Did he pay Momma? Too many pieces. Too much horror. My head couldn't put it all together so it focused on something else. The house. Too quiet except for the running water. The bath would be full now, I should turn the tap off, lift the plug, but I didn't move. Jenny was a fitful sleeper. All these nights I'd spent in the family room I'd heard her moving around, but now there was only quiet, only my heartbeat fierce in my ears and Momma's cruel tone. It was as if Jenny wasn't even here. But I'd seen her, asleep in our bed. Hadn't I?

Momma reached out to me, caught my wrist. 'Please, baby. You have to understand why it had to happen this way.'

My breath ached in my lungs. 'It doesn't matter. I'm leaving, Momma. I'm leaving this town and I'm taking Jenny so you and Bung-Eye can do what you want if you like him that much. Jenny's not happy here.'

'That little bitch wouldn't be happy anywhere,' Momma snapped. The monster surged forward, forcing her to her feet, her face a finger-length from mine. 'You know what she told me tonight? That ungrateful bitch, after all I've done for her. She said, "Momma, I'm not staying here another minute. I'm going to Washington to find Eric and you can't stop me."'

Momma laughed like the devil was sat in her throat.

'Then she went over there.' Her hand shot out, pointing to the cabinet.

The baseboard was loose. I went to it, pulled it free, reached my hand under and found nothing. No matchbox. No ninety-four dollars.

'Where is it?' I rose to my feet, red heat pulsing through me. 'Where is it, Momma?'

'She took it. She wanted to leave you here, John. She wanted to leave us both to be with that man.'

My heart hurt, as if a hand was reaching into my chest and wrenching, twisting. Leave me? Jenny was going to leave me? She took all that money I earned for us both and left me.

I couldn't make sense of the words. It couldn't be true. Yet I knew, in the deep, dark pit of me, that it was. She'd left. She'd abandoned me. My sister. The person I loved more than all other people. My head split, ached, like shards of bone were lodged in my brain.

I looked at Momma. Wanted her to tell me it wasn't true, that she'd gone after her like she did last year and brought her home. She stood there on her muddy feet, clutching her robe together. Sweat sheened her forehead. Why was she holding that robe right up to her neck? It wasn't to keep a chill off. She looked so small then. Her hair loose and wild, a shade of dull blonde she hated. Her hair was nothing compared to Jenny's vibrant gold.

Jenny's gone.

But she's asleep upstairs.

Go and see, Johnny boy. You know what you're going to find.

I rushed upstairs, two, three at a time, my legs and side screaming at me to stop. Water pooled on the landing but I didn't slow. I splashed to the attic steps and left wet foot-prints on the wood. Without stopping, I barged in the room, went right for that ugly blanket and pulled it clear.

Pillows. Cushions.

No Jenny.

Inside me, a tornado of black birds raged from my centre, outward, pulsing, swarming, bigger and bigger. I ran back downstairs and found Momma standing by the cabinet, my AMX Javelin matchbox in her hands.

'I wouldn't let her take this from you,' Momma said and handed me the box, still full. 'You earned this, baby.'

I took it in my shaking hands. The wings beat a cacophony in my ears. 'Momma, where's Jenny?'

'She's done her part for this family and that's the end of it.'

'What part? What are you talking about? Did she run away again? Where did she go?'

Momma tilted her head, looked at me like I was an idiot.

'Do you have any idea what a girl like her, with those wide puppy eyes and skinny hips, is worth in this town?'

Momma stroked my arm but I didn't feel it. She smiled, and there in her eyes, pride. I wanted to vomit. Spill all my insides over the floorboards.

She lifted my chin, made me look in her eyes, and said, 'Eddie knew what they would pay for her. He'd had offers. And when he told me how much . . . well. Who can say no to that? Finally, I thought, something that girl is good for. She wanted it, you know, she said as much with those short dresses and bare legs, running all over town.'

My gut clenched, the maggots writhed in my stomach and the birds began to feast. The ringing in my left ear turned to white noise, as if muting the world, a defence against what I was about to hear.

'You knew?'

Momma stroked my swollen cheek and I felt my tears beneath her palm. 'Oh, baby. My beautiful boy.' She leaned in and kissed my forehead. The monster, the darkness, flickered in her eyes and showed Momma again for the briefest moment.

She let out a sharp gasp as if the real Momma knew what was going on. Knew, and couldn't believe it.

'I wish I could have given you more,' she said. 'I wish your sister were more like you, than like me. You're so sensible, so strong, not like her. But I did my best, John, only ever my best for you both.'

'Momma,' I couldn't speak more than a whisper. 'Where's Jenny?'

Her other hand slipped from her robe. It fell open at the collar.

I closed my eyes and let the tears fall over my raw cheeks. I rested my forehead on Momma's and let her hold me. I cried out the pain in my chest. A low, animal noise I didn't believe came from my throat. I reached for her robe, pulled the belt loose and saw it all.

From her neck to her knees, the white nightgown was soaked with blood.

'What did you do?'

My throat and chest and lungs and all my muscles tightened and all I could do was stand there and cry and oh God, oh God, why is there so much blood, Momma? Why is there so much blood?

'I had to baby, for us.' She took my face in both hands. She kissed my cheeks and pressed her head to mine.

'Jenny was going to go to Clarkesville and tell the sheriffs there about Eddie and then she was going to run off. She was being so selfish, don't you see that? She didn't care what it would do to me. It was only a few times with Wakefield and, from what I hear, he was a gentleman about it. I was surprised he even asked for her, she was young for him, but who can tell with men like that? She'd have made us good money and learned a lesson. Besides, the way she carried on with Darney, Eddie said she was enjoying herself. Made for the work, he said.'

The smell of the blood, of the whiskey on her skin, of the mud on her feet, it made my head swirl and throb. 'You didn't . . . oh God . . . please, Momma . . .'

Momma stroked the back of my neck, her rough hands scratched at the sunburn. 'If I'd let her tell anyone, they would have taken him away. I've waited seventeen years for Eddie Buchanan and that little *slut*,' the sharpness in her voice cleared the fog from my head, 'would have taken him from me. Like she took my beauty, my body. She took my life. She wasn't going to take my Eddie too.'

I pushed away. She'd let the monster win. She'd given up and done something so terrible that my real Momma couldn't face. Real Momma would never have hurt Jenny.

My eyes scanned the family room, the kitchen, searching for anything that would tell me what to do, just tell me what to do. There. On the floor, a thin line of blood led through the kitchen, and out of the back door.

'Where's my sister?' I almost shouted.

Momma looked down to her feet. Black mud. The nearest water. Three Points.

I ran.

I didn't care about the pain in my cheek or my side. I was flying through the corn, through the brush and dry grass. All around me, darkness, but I knew my way. No stars or moon shone above now, they were dead, their life snuffed out. But I saw through the blackness, through my momma's words. Those words weren't real. They were all lies and Jenny would be standing on the island, waiting for me to take her to the ocean. That was it. It had to be it. The monster was dangerous, hurtful, a liar, but not a killer.

My legs and arms worked like pistons, pushing me on and on. My lungs, my muscles, my heart burned with the effort. I was fire. I was streaming flame through the fields and all I could think was please, please let it be lies, please let the blood be nail polish like it was before. Please, please, don't let her be gone.

I passed a stand of trees, the last barrier between me and the island and saw them. The birds. Black and ragged on every branch and fence line. The world bristled with them and they were here for me. I skidded, fell, felt a rush of quiet. They waited, watched. Their wings didn't move, not like when I'd burnt the rotten corn. Then they'd twitched and cawed and scratched their claws as the maggots and rot were consumed. Now they perched like statues, terrible gargoyles staring down at the scene.

I walked those last few steps to the irrigation channel, through the water, the mud, up onto the island. Saw what they saw.

A shape in the dark.

Still and silent as the birds.

'Jenny?' I said. 'Jenny? Don't be Jenny. Don't be Jenny.'

The tears came again and I screamed into the night. My body wasn't mine any more. It was fire, it was dynamite about to blow. This couldn't be real so I couldn't be real. I was a bird. Oh God, make me a bird, let me fly away from this, let me soar and forget.

I dropped to my knees, pressed my face against the dirt. Breathed out a cloud of dust. Tasted earth. Make it not real. It's not real. Nothing is real. For a brief, wonderful moment I didn't know where I was, why I was. Then I looked up. Saw her. There's her shape. There's her hair.

My heart shattered. My mind shattered. I was pieces, fragments, seeing all of it and none of it at the same time.

I knelt beside my sister. Ignored the red blackness pooling around her, ignored the flies buzzing around her. I held her. Felt her weight. Felt the wetness of her blood soak into my t-shirt. Told her that it would all be okay.

'I'll protect you, keep you safe forever,' I said into her hair, the smell of her lingered in my nose, my mouth, I could taste her.

Her eyes were closed and with my fingertips, I lifted the lids. Even in the starless night, they shone blue and brilliant.

Such beauty in her eyes and it was still there. Momma hadn't found that. Hadn't stolen it. They were her last beauty. I closed my sister's eyes and she was sleeping.

I don't know how long I knelt there. For seconds. For hours. Forever.

Light. Soft, glowing, like sunrise, but it couldn't be. I looked up or down, I don't know which way but I saw her. Jenny. There she was, standing over herself. I'd closed her eyes and let her go and she'd come back to me. A bright, golden light emanating from her skin like she'd captured the sun and swallowed it whole. I blinked at her in the dark, asked her if she was real and she said she was. I remember taking her hand and walking back to our house. The body on the points was not my sister and so I left it, for the birds, for the insects, for the sun to dry and turn to tinder. My sunshine, my sister, walking with me in the cornfields, said she'd wait for me in our room. Jenny told me to be quiet when I came in because she was so tired and wanted to sleep for a week. I said I wouldn't make a sound and she smiled, and kissed me on the cheek.

Her light left me at the back door.

The house felt empty and full at the same time. It felt like the world outside was gone, fallen away into the abyss and there was just me and there would always be just me. I knew the sun wouldn't rise again in my house.

Only one sound found my ears. A humming. A tune. From the bathroom. 'Crazy', by Patsy Cline. My momma's favourite song.

A river ran down the staircase but I didn't care. The wood might warp but it would dry and everything would go back to normal. And that's what I wanted. Everything back to normal. Me and Jenny and our momma, all together, all safe as houses. That's all I want, all I've ever wanted.

At the top of the stairs, Momma's tune became clearer and she sang the words with it. The bathroom door was open and I went in.

The tune stopped and Momma, in the steaming tub, looked around at me and smiled.

'Hey, baby,' she said and reached out for me.

I let myself go to her. I knelt beside the tub like I was taking communion. Oh, Holy Father, forgive me. Forgive us all.

I wanted to ask why she'd done it, why she'd done that to Jenny. But I knew any answer would be too hard for me to hear. I was broken. She had broken me. I couldn't feel anything. I was kneeling beside her, her hand playing in my hair, and I was trying to pray. But there was no God in this house any more. She'd driven Him away and replaced Him with Bung-Eye Buchanan. A man she loved and hated and would do anything for.

I raised my eyes to her. The water tinged pink from my sister's blood. The smell of strawberries.

'You're so quiet, John. And what a mess you are, we'll have to throw that shirt out. That stain will never clean,' Momma said, but it wasn't Momma. The words were soft and kind and I always longed for that tone but it was the monster saying them, trying to trick me. She closed her eyes, began to hum.

My hand rose by my side, dipped into the water, found Momma's chest. My mind didn't understand what it was doing, my body followed primal orders. The skin felt different than it used to, it was tough and hard beneath my touch. The monster made flesh. It had finally done what it always wanted to do. It had taken Jenny from me and here it was, right in front of me, tired and weak and beneath my hands.

'John,' the monster spoke but I chose not to hear it. 'John, what are you doing?'

The monster's claws grabbed my arm but I was stronger.

'John! John! Stop!'

Then the water swallowed it up, cut the voice out of its throat.

I pressed hard on its chest until I felt it hit the bottom of the tub. Both hands pushing, straining, keeping it under.

Its arms and legs thrashed and soaked my t-shirt. The bloody water splashed on the floor, joined the lake on the landing, the river on the stairs. I moved one hand to its throat, squeezed and stood and bore down with all my weight.

My foot slipped on the tile. The monster raged against me, sensing weakness, but I held firm. Its eyes bulged and red spider veins appeared in the whites.

A few more seconds and it will be gone and Jenny will be safe forever.

I heard my sister's voice in my head. 'You're my hero, Johnny, you're the best brother in the world. You always know what to do.'

The thrashing slowed. Stopped.

Arms and legs slackened, slipped back under the water. No bubbles rose from the mouth. I held on for a few more seconds. Just to make sure. The monster in the movies always comes back right at the end but I wouldn't let it. Not this time. This is a John Royal picture show.

I dried my hands and left the bathroom. It was done. The evil dead, the house ours. I couldn't hear anything but my heart and its dull thunder. My home, finally silent, finally safe for Jenny. We wouldn't need to leave any more. We could stay forever. I went up to our bedroom.

My sister, glowing golden from the inside, opened the door for me, took my hand. The throb in my head, arms, legs, chest, slowed, turned warm like early morning sun on my back. I took a long breath, filled my lungs to their edges. The room smelled different. Clear, fresh, as if a storm had raged in the night and left the air thin, scrubbed clean of dust and heat. The kind of air you suck down in gulps. The kind that tastes sweet and urges you to bite it. The kind that eases you into heavy, empty sleep.

Jenny let go of my hand and twirled, spun around with her arms out and laughed. I didn't hear the laugh, not exactly, not with my ears but inside my head, so much closer than I'd ever heard before. She lit up the room. I blinked, rubbed my eye, and she was not twirling any more. She was in bed, sitting up under the scratchy yellow blanket. The light dimmed but I knew the way. I'd know it in the dark, my eyes squeezed shut. I'd always know where to find my sister.

I set a Joni Mitchell record playing, Jenny's favourite. Then I crawled into bed where my shining sister lay and I said, 'We're safe now.'

She smiled and asked me to tell her a story.

27

Muted. As if the land, the birds, the wind itself, were treading softly, barefoot on thick carpet, afraid to make a noise and disturb the calm.

Ears rang.

Hands, skin raw like fresh sunburn, flinched against the rough blanket.

Arms, legs, back ached.

Eyes wouldn't focus. Everything soft edges and jittery, a TV with a broken aerial.

I moved but my muscles begged me not to.

The bed was empty beside me. Jenny already up. Making breakfast?

But I heard nothing in the kitchen.

The house didn't feel like mine. Like I'd wandered into someone else's, crawled into their bed.

Maybe Jenny is reading on the couch. Maybe Momma is sleeping sound.

You know different, Johnny.

All I could think was how tired I was last night. Tired down
to the marrow. Everything heavy and thick in my head. Sleep
stole me away before I got to the end of 'once upon a time'.
Jenny had asked for a story. She always asked for a story.

Maybe her and Momma went out.

They're not out, Johnny.

Sunlight speared through my bedroom window, lit up the
dust, highlighted a square of floor near the door. Footprints.
Mine. Shaped in mud.

Fresh air drifted in. Tasted like far-off smoke. And somewhere in the distance, a low rumble, a sound I couldn't
place. My mind lost in the afterlight, empty of memory.

I pushed the scratchy yellow blanket away. Smell of strawberry bath soap wafted up. Momma's bath soap.

Sickly sweet.

Felt the mud on my feet, flaking between my toes.

Every movement took a lifetime. I was in water, in sand,
in treacle, my body and my mind, slowed down to a snail.
Everything an effort. Everything a hurt.

I watched my finger rub a line of mud from my foot. Let
the dirt fall into the bed. Momma would be mad.

My stomach twisted. Momma. Suddenly dizzy. White spots
sparked in my eyes.

I got out of bed, still dressed in yesterday's clothes. Jenny
would call me a hobo for that.

My t-shirt felt odd. Stiff against me, like it'd got wet with
something and dried wrong. But I couldn't look down.
Couldn't see. Wouldn't.

The world was all blur. The ringing in my ears got worse.
The rumble on the air grew louder. Only one clear thought
rang out in my head.

Don't go in the bathroom, John.

I trailed dry mud. Walked in my own footprints. Down the attic stairs. Past the closed bathroom door.

Don't go in.

From behind the door, a sound. Dripping. Constant, rhythmic *plink, plink, plink*. Water into water. Tap into bath.

Don't go in.

The floor, the wood of the upstairs hallway, felt strange under my feet. Soaked and swollen. Still damp. All the way down the stairs into the family room.

My AMX Javelin matchbox sat on the cabinet. Coins and bills spilled out and onto the floor. *She took it. She wanted to leave you here.* The voice, like a dying echo, faded.

Mud everywhere. Footprints. Smears. And something else. A line of dark brown. I followed it, dazed and unthinking into the kitchen, to the back door. Flecks of brown on the screen. Not mud. I knew it wasn't mud.

The sun beat through the windows but barely lit the room. Outside, birds began their morning song but did nothing to drown out that distant rumble. I knew the sound now, as if from another life, the life I had before all this. And the smell. Mud and smoke and strawberry and something else. A cold butcher-shop smell

In the kitchen sink, one of Momma's knives. The blade dark red. Almost black. I stared at it. My fingers went to my pocket and felt the flick knife there. The handle initialled RB. Rudy. My friend. And Gloria.

Aching sobbing agony flared in my chest and I couldn't breathe

*

Out the front door, into the yard. Past Momma's truck with
a dent in the side. Past the frayed rope hanging off the oak
tree. Used to have a tyre on it. We meant to hang a new
one, Jenny and me, meant to swing on it and play. But we
never did.

Out of the yard, onto the track. Sharp spikes of gravel
drove into my bare feet. I passed the mailbox at the end
of our track with 'Royal' in red paint on the side. Faded
and chipped but in Momma's curled hand.

My name. Jenny's name. Momma's name.

I felt the tears. Pouring down my cheeks. Falling like
rain. Spotting on the dried blood on my white t-shirt, flaring
it red again. Jenny's blood. An ocean of it. Covered me
shoulder to waist, diluted by bath water, smelling like strawberries

A mile in bare feet. A car stopped, a man spoke to me and
I spoke back but I don't remember . . .

I killed her.

The moment faded, a dream, never really there.

I walked down the centre of Main Street. Something sticky
on the asphalt and I looked down to see fresh blood. A
cut on the sole of my foot left red smears on the black. In
my chest, sharp wings stirred. I felt vibrations through the
road, like a giant engine revving up beneath my feet. The
smell of smoke stronger here. The rumble louder. I saw
shapes in the corner of my eyes. People. The good townsfolk
of Larson. Heard a gasp. A shout. Someone said my name.
But nobody stopped me. Maybe someone tried but my brain
wouldn't see them. The blur and daze clouded everything.

I walked bloody footprints over the grass to the church. My
legs had taken me here, spurred on by something I didn't
understand. A lost dog returning to a master who beat it.
A lost dog. Me.

On the church steps, a figure. A shadow. A man, barely
there, the sun shone through him. A man I knew. A man
who wasn't a man. Old blue jeans, faded now to grey, rips
in the knees. Red chequered shirt. Light brown hair. A
horse on his belt buckle. The rumble. The sound, like an
idling engine, grew in my ears. The pale man smoked a
cigarette. He raised his hand and smiled. His face suddenly
my face. A cloud passed over the sun. The man was gone
and I trod blood on the church steps.

Had he even been there? Had he ever?

I pushed the door open. Felt its weight against my aching
arm. The same arm. Skin burning from the hot water.
Scratch marks near my elbow.

An image of the Three Points burst into my head. A
shape lay on the dusty island.

As quickly as it came, the picture disappeared, like a
movie-show flicker reel. Two seconds and gone

The booming sermon voice of my pastor addressing empty
benches. Saw him in his pulpit as he saw me. He stopped
mid-verse. Was that my name he said? It was like trying to
hear through water. Then he was away from his pulpit,
running down the aisle to me. My pastor. My friend. My
father. He'll help. He'll know what to do. But the closer
he came, the clearer I saw his face. The face I'd seen in
his house, sitting beside my sister. The last time I'd seen
Jenny.

With him.

With Wakefield.

He'll not help. He's not good. My heart hammered, shook the world. And I was crying. I was screaming. Inside my head. Outside my head. Too much. It was too much. Wings beat, stripped my insides raw, threatened to break me apart. Hot white pain seared through my brain. And the smell. My God. The smell of burning and fire everywhere and the engine rumble, the drone, filled up my ears, shook my bones, no escape, I couldn't drown it out, couldn't scream it away. Hell was coming for me. The devil riding out to claim me for what I'd done. What have I done? What have I done? I saw the devil running at me, arms out, fingers, claws reaching, white collar blazing, blinding. Here he comes, here he is, he's got you, Johnny boy, he's got you good. The birds raged. My eyes went dark. Blackness rushed me from all sides and I fell.

28

'Open your eyes, John.'

I knew the voice. Swimming in the dark.

Open your eyes, John. Different voice. Jenny's. Shining in the black. Open your eyes.

Other voices floated down into my pit.

'. . . he was mumbling . . . his sister, his mother . . .'

'. . . the blood on his shirt . . .'

'. . . keep it quiet . . .'

Two men. Frank and someone else.

In the dark, Jenny took my hand, turned up the volume.

'Go and check his house,' Frank said.

Footsteps. A door. Silence. More darkness. More sleep.

I stirred when Jenny's hand squeezed mine. Her light brought me to the surface and then she was gone. I opened my eyes to moving shapes. Fish. In all colours, hanging from a mobile on the ceiling. Kindergarteners made them during Sunday Bible Study. I remembered hanging them during a session with Frank.

I shook my head. Didn't want to hear it. Couldn't. 'I saw you. I know what you are.'

'John—'

'No! I saw you with Jenny.'

My voice broke at her name. Confusion on his face, I wanted to rip it off. 'In your house. With *him*.'

The confusion changed to something else. Anger? Shame? His brow, usually calm and open, was dark, drawn, his eyes down. He crossed his arms over his chest and leant back on the craft table.

'You don't understand anything, John.'

'I understand enough. Wakefield threatened my sister. I tell you and he makes good on his threat. You ratted me out. You . . . helped him do that to her.'

It hurt to speak. Talking about something made it real. I wasn't ready for it to be real. To face . . . her . . . what I'd done to her . . . oh God, Momma. Where's my momma I want my momma.

Keep going. But the hurt rose in my body, aching against my bones, forcing tears out of my eyes.

'You lied to me,' I said. 'You were meant to protect me and her and you let this . . . you made it happen. Why?'

Frank bit his bottom lip, twisted his face into a sneer. I wondered if the costume he wore burnt him, like sunlight burns a vampire. Is that white collar too tight? Does it mean anything to you any more?

He was quiet for a long time. Outside, the ladies from the Gardening Society passed by. Only twenty feet away. Might as well have been twenty miles. On the wall, the clock ticked to eleven. At eleven oh-three, he spoke.

'It's my job to help people,' he said, keeping his gaze to the left of me, at the brightly coloured pin board collages of church activities. 'I have the whole town to consider. A pastor tends his flock the best way he can. The men . . . there is an arrangement. They have certain requirements, which have to be met in order for them to live happy, productive lives. These needs are met with company from out of town. Girls in the oldest profession already or those who would probably fall into it no matter what. They are well paid by the men they see, far better than if they were walking the streets, I insist on that.'

I felt my blood heat, felt the rage boil.

Hear him out, Johnny, keep it together a little longer, then decide.

'It's not their fault,' he carried on. 'These men are sick. They're weak. Weak of body and weak of mind. But they are Larson's leaders and the town needs them so we turn the other cheek like the Bible tells us. Their souls need to be saved, just like everyone else. I help them.' He held up his hands, looked at me for the first time. 'I don't participate, John, you have to know that. I . . . I just *facilitate*. I keep the process under control and quiet. It happens in my house where people won't look twice at those men coming and going. It's safer all round.'

I laughed. Laughed so hard it hurt my throat. Laughed so hard tears flowed freely and my cheeks turned red and the sound drowned out everything else.

'Mary Ridley wasn't safe. What does the Bible say about her?'

Frank nodded. 'That was a mistake. Leland knows what he did, he's prayed for forgiveness, he's working through his problems, and he's compensated Mary's family. Her mother and her father are working through their grief.'

Mother and father. My chest clenched. Jack said they

were gone. I remembered the spectre on the church steps, the words of my once-friend Frank, Death rides a pale horse. Mary didn't have a brother. Was Jack ever really there? I tried to remember, to push through the fog in my head, if anyone else had seen the car or Jack. I knew they hadn't. But I had. They were real. I'd touched them. Hadn't I?

No, John, you didn't. You know you didn't.

I felt dizzy and sick and my head hurt. Is this what going crazy feels like?

The pastor kept talking. 'And you kids finding her, well, I'm sorry about that, John. I'm sorry you ever became involved in this. And Jenny . . . Jesus, that was not meant to happen but Ed and Leland, well, they said it was agreed and you can't exactly argue with Ed . . . I . . .'

I turned away. Couldn't look at him any more. I was made of glass and I was cracking. I had a raging monster caged in my memory and I'd turned my back on that too. I touched the scratches on my arm. The scent of strawberries faded now but I still heard the *plink, plink, plink* of the dripping tap. What had I done?

The right thing.

The pastor sat beside me on the couch.

'Do you know how long you've been here?' he asked, didn't wait for me to answer. 'Two nights. You collapsed and have been in and out of consciousness since. Samuels sent officers to your house. They know what happened.'

'Do they know why it happened?'

'No. They think your mother killed Jenny, then got drunk and drowned in the bath.'

Momma. Oh God. My momma was all alone. My hand, the hand that pressed down on the monster's chest, shook and ached. I had to do it. I had to slay the monster once and for all.

'That's not what happened,' I said. 'I did it . . . to Momma . . . the bath. I held her until it stopped.'

He shifted, the bed groaned. 'I had a feeling.'

'Will I go to prison? They'll put me in the electric chair.'

'You're not going to prison.'

I shuffled around, stared at his hunched-over back. 'I should. I deserve to.'

'No, you don't. It's been decided. You'll go home and you'll forget about all of this.' He spoke like he was delivering a verdict on a cop show, all level and matter-of-fact. 'You'll grieve for your mother and your sister but you won't talk about anything else. None of it ever happened. It was all I could do to stop those men from putting a bullet in your head. I told them you were a smart kid who could keep his mouth shut. You have to. Your mother killed your sister and drowned by accident. Do you understand?'

They don't want you in front of lawyers and cameras and reporters, the voice said, and it was Jenny's voice, her tone, her rhythm. They don't want you to throw their dirty laundry all over the six o'clock news.

What should I do?

You don't want to go to prison, do you, Johnny?

I don't want to go to prison.

But Momma. I remembered her face, under the water, so afraid. Of me. Her eyes were Momma's eyes, the monster fled in that last moment and it was her. She was Momma deep down inside and I loved her and she loved me and I killed her. I killed her. I held her under the water until she stopped breathing.

Because she killed me, my sister said.

The monster did. Momma didn't. Momma didn't. She never would. She loved us both. Oh God. I can't breathe. What have I done? What have I done? Take it back. I want to take it all back. Press rewind on it. Go back in time, they do it in the movies, why can't I?

'Do you understand me, John?'

'What about Wakefield? He's a murderer.'

'He deeply regrets it. He's working through his guilt.'

'Why did he do it? What did Mary Ridley ever do to him?'

Frank's jaw clenched and I heard his teeth grind. 'She was pregnant.'

Of course. I closed my eyes, saw the eel squirm out of Mary Ridley's stomach. Out of a bullet hole. It was all right there. A great wave of nausea rushed up my throat, left me gasping for breath, clutching my gut.

'He'll never go to prison, will he?' I choked out the words. 'Not for murder. Not for . . . Jenny . . . She's fourteen, Frank. Younger than his own daughter.'

'This is the deal.' Frank's tone hardened and he stood up. 'You keep your mouth shut and you stay out of prison, you get to have some kind of life.' Then he sighed. 'Besides, who would believe you?'

I let out a long, shaking breath and knew he was right.

'Now,' he said, 'do you understand?'

'I understand. But it's not right.'

'It doesn't have to be right. You just have to do what they say. You know how dangerous they are.'

'I thought you were a good man,' I said as he crossed the room to the door.

He turned, finally looked me in the eye. I remembered the man I'd played cards with, the one who'd saved us from Samuels, the one I'd thought of as a father.

'So did I,' he said.

He looked broken. Defeated. A man so deep in his own shame, no act of kindness could ever pull him out. I hated him. But I loved him. And I didn't know what to do any more. I had no guiding hand but my own and that hand had killed my mother.

Frank shook off the sorrow and his voice brightened. 'Your house is still a crime scene so you can stay here tonight. Samuels wants to take your statement. I'll take you over there later and I'll drive you home tomorrow. Sit tight.'

'Did you care about me? Or Jenny?' I asked, fresh tears straining against my eyes. 'Did you ever really care?'

Frank tried to smile but it just twisted his face further, turned him darker. 'More than you know.'

Then he was gone, the door closed softly behind him.

29

Pastor Jacobs dropped me at the end of my farm track and drove away as soon as the car door closed. I watched his car disappear, obscured by a cloud of dust, and I knew I wouldn't see him again. My home, my farm, was a mile from town in an ocean of silent cornfields. Just the wind and the birds for company.

My mailbox had been knocked over. Maybe by the police, maybe by kids who'd heard what had happened in my house. The faded red 'Royal' was dented, coated in dust, the wooden post freshly splintered. We'd gone to Samuels yesterday but I'd barely spoken. Frank did all the talking and I nodded along. Signed papers, made it official. Samuels was almost kind. He gave me a brown evidence bag full of cash, said the AMX matchbox was evidence but the money wasn't. I didn't count it. It didn't seem to matter any more.

My clothes went into evidence bags and they took my fingerprints. Frank let me pick out what I wanted from the church's goodwill jumble. A blue and yellow striped t-shirt, a pair of short denims and Keds with the sole flapping loose on the right heel. The sneakers pinched my toes as I walked the track to my house, half a size too small but better than opening up the cuts on my feet again. I kept my eyes on the ground, didn't want to look up, didn't want to see my home, my farm. What would I find there?

The smell of burning, just like the morning after that terrible night, still filled the air. It was the corn stalks, they had a particular flavour I could taste a mile off. To the north, in the distance, a wall of white smoke drifted south. Someone nearby was burning the stubble in his field. It was too early for harvest, which meant his crop must have been lost. The fire would do its work, cleanse the ground, kill the rot and make it ready for next year. Good as new.

I stopped when I reached the yard. Momma's truck stood where it always had. The frayed rope was still despite the breeze. All just the same, but for the torn-up grass, all tyre tracks that didn't belong. A ripped piece of police tape fluttered, still nailed to the front door like a flag signalling my arrival. Vivid yellow against the brown door, like army banners after the battle, I thought with a dim smile.

My sister's voice filled my head. Why do they always make such a mess?

I can't go inside.

You don't have to.

I watched the rope and was suddenly sick of it. I couldn't stand it any more. I started walking. Past the house, through the west field, toward old man Briggs' farm. I took a route to Briggs that went nowhere near Three Points. I couldn't face that. Not now, not ever.

I found a good-sized tyre on Briggs' pile and rolled it back home. I replaced the rotten, grey rope with one from our barn and hung the new tyre. When I was done, I sat back, felt the sun on my shoulders and closed my eyes.

I heard the rope creak. Heard a soft laugh. Opened my eyes.

Jenny swung on the tyre, giggling with every sway. Her voice was distant, an echo inside my head. She was blurred at the edges, not quite there but at the same time so real, so perfect, I was suddenly crying. She's here. She's back with me and I laughed. I laughed with her through hot tears, through a deep ache in my chest.

She's not really there, you know that, the old voice in my head said. This is what going crazy looks like.

Then let me be crazy. Maybe I always have been.

I sat on the ground and watched. Joy leapt from my sister, burst from her smile and shining eyes, real or not I couldn't take my eyes off her. It was how I always imagined she'd play and laugh if the swing was ever fixed. Maybe that's why she was there. I'd changed the landscape of our lives and she'd come back to me but I should have done it months ago, years even, maybe that would have made a difference. The yard, at least, would not look the same any more. It wouldn't be the same yard that existed when my family existed. Even if replacing the swing would have changed nothing, it was a small mercy that I wouldn't have to look at the rope any more and remember my real pa hanging it, or Eric promising he would fix it, or the way Momma flicked it with her finger when she passed, her little ritual. Its swing told us she was home and though it brought me happiness, it brought Jenny fear.

Never again.

I sat watching Jenny until the sun sank and the dusk midges swarmed. They bit me and I let them. There were no night birds singing. No rustle in the trees. No starlings pulsing in the orange sky. As darkness came and Jenny quietened, her laughter faded, her shine dimmed, a crushing weight lowered onto my shoulders.

I was alone. A different, absolute kind of alone that made my stomach drop and my breath catch if I thought too long on it. It was like the time Jenny ran away and Momma went after her and the house felt, sounded, smelled wrong. This time she and Momma would never come back, and that emptiness was all the deeper, all the darker, a black chasm opening between hip and heart.

The house behind me was full of them both. How could I go in there? Into the bathroom? Into mine and Jenny's bedroom? Into the kitchen where I saw the carving knife? So I slept in the crawlspace, in the dirt, with my back against the brickwork, Rudy's flick knife in my hands, opening and closing it, over and over. Once I pressed the blade against my wrist. Pressed hard and dragged. A shot of pain ran up my arm but the knife wasn't that sharp. It was as if Rudy himself was in the blade and refused to hurt me. I kept it in my pocket.

I dreamed of Momma. Of playing Euchre and gorging on a quart of mint-choc-chip. Of her calling me 'baby', holding me, even in the heatwave summers, her arms around me, her murmurs of 'I love you, I love you'. The bird book she'd given me just because.

I love you, Momma. I'm sorry. I'm so sorry.

I woke up at dawn, my cheeks wet with salt tears, my eyes raw.

I don't remember much of that day. Twice a reporter van snuck up the track like a slug sliding to lettuce. I hid in the crawlspace and watched two men get out. They started poking around, knocked and shouted but left when no one responded. The second time, they brought a crowbar and prised open the front door, went inside my house. I followed their movements from the crawlspace, heard the shutter snap on their camera. In the family room, *snapsnap*. In the kitchen, *snapsnap*. Then up the stairs to the bathroom, *snapsnapsnap*. Mumbled exchanges between them, something about the front page, but I didn't care enough to listen.

Other people came around and I kept hidden. Some I recognised. Mrs Lyle from the post office. Miss Eaves. Al Westin. Even the gossipy curtain-twitchers Margo Hyland and Jennette Dawes. I never answered, just watched through the gaps beneath the porch. They left dishes covered in tinfoil, usually with a note about heating at three hundred for twenty minutes. I ate it all cold.

I wondered for a while if Pastor Jacobs would ever think to check on me. Wondered whether all this would become part of his sermons. Wondered too if everyone in town knew the full truth of what happened. Probably. Keeping secrets in small towns was like holding ants in your hands. They'll always find a gap, a way out, even if they have to bite you to do it. I expected most of the town knew what Mayor Wills, Bung-Eye, and the rest of them were doing, which meant they probably knew how Momma was involved and how the mess spiralled from there. Guilt visits. Guilt casseroles and pies and mac n' cheese. Easier to say nothing and pretend it's all roses and cream than speak up, blow that whistle and call down the dogs. Easier. Safer. The quiet life is all these people want. Larson was a Cyclops with one big blind eye.

You're being cynical, Johnny, Jenny's voice in my head,

her hand on my arm. When tragedy hits a small town, they close ranks around their own and look after each other. Haven't you noticed that? When the Easton mill exploded, every man in Larson took up a bucket and hauled water. When Mark and Tracy died, the town mourned together. Larson may be rotten at the core but some of the fruit is still good.

Nothing feels good any more, I told her, took her hand in mine. Except this. Except us.

30

The next morning I sat on the porch steps with my sister, eating cold mashed potatoes Mrs Ponderosa from the Gardening Society had left me, when I heard them. They rode into my yard on bikes. Rudy's rusted-up Schwinn finally fixed but still looking like a piece of junk. Gloria on her Raleigh, basket on the front, the garish pink frame covered with green and blue stickers. They jumped off the bikes without braking, let them clatter into the dust, and ran to me. In a second their arms were around me and mine around them and I felt life in my body. Life and heat and grasping hands and tight, tight embraces. My friends had come and I couldn't let them go, I'd never let them go. Jenny, apart from us, watched, smiled, and I felt her absence in my arms so keenly I almost cried out.

'What took you guys so long to come round?' I asked.

Gloria shook her head. 'My mom and dad said it was too dangerous for me to be out by myself after . . . you know . . . so I finally snuck out.'

'Same,' Rudy said. 'My old man's away and Perry is just as much of a bastard. He locked me in my room the other night, kept giving me these crazy chores, threatened a hell of a beating if I left the yard. If I didn't know better, bud, I'd say our folks don't want us hanging around you.'

Bung-Eye. Wakefield. Of course they didn't want me around their kids. I knew all their dirty secrets.

'I don't blame them,' I said.

The three of us were mostly quiet. There wasn't much to say and I'd done enough talking, enough thinking about what happened. I couldn't bring myself to tell Gloria the truth about her father. It did no good to ruin another family. So we told stories about Jenny. When she tried a cigarette for the first time and coughed up a lung. When she caught her first fish in Big Lake and screamed so loud we couldn't get near her, then demanded we set the perch back in the pool. When she got an A minus on the history test she'd been dreading, all about Gettysburg, and it was the highest grade of all of us. When she laughed and the world seemed at once brighter.

With true friends, like with family, there are things you don't need to say, they are known from the tiniest expression, the simplest word. We had a secret language, the four of us, one that existed in moments and looks and silence. We cried together. I held Gloria as she wept. Rudy too. And they held me. All the while, my Jenny, my shining sister, watched us from the other side of the porch, a look of serenity on her face like saints in church paintings. I knew not to tell them I could see her. I knew this was something special, some gift from God that allowed me to keep her with me. God's way of apologising for one of His pastors, for His failure to this town and to my family. He'd given me an angel.

We were talking about the Roost when Gloria started, as if bitten by a rattler. She jumped up, ran over to her bike to get something from the bag in her basket. She handed me a photograph.

My heart stopped, then beat all the harder.

There we were. All four of us. Standing outside our Fort after we'd finished building it. It was black and white but I knew every colour and detail of that day. I smelt the summer again, tasted the air. Gloria had taken the picture on a timer and set the camera on a tree stump. Me, Rudy and her were twelve and Jenny was eleven. It was the summer before the body and the police and the darkness. Rudy was just the same, but with less weariness in his eyes. A movie star. Blond hair and wide smile. His arms raised and flexed, showing his biceps like a strong man. Gloria in a light green dress, her red hair puffed out wild, standing next to Rudy with her arms crossed, grinning.

Then me on the other side of him, three inches shorter, skin and bone to his muscle. Halfway to mimicking his pose, the camera caught my arms out wide, blurred, all loose fists and an awkward, incomplete smile on my face.

And Jenny. Next to me, arms clasped behind her back in her sundress. The one dotted with yellow flowers. Her hair long and straight and flowing in a frozen breeze. I ran my finger over her face.

'I thought you'd like to have it,' Gloria said.

Sadness choked my words. 'Thank you.'

'You know, Johnny,' Rudy said. 'You should come crash with me. You can't stay here alone.'

I winced at the thought of being anywhere near Bung-Eye. 'It's okay. I'm fine here.'

'Sleeping in the crawlspace is not fine,' Gloria said.

I panicked for a moment that she'd offer to put me up too. She didn't but she wouldn't look at me either. She kept her eyes down, shuffled her feet, something she did when she was uncomfortable. I felt, with a cold drop in my stomach, she was hiding something.

'Serious, man.' Rudy stood in front of me and stooped, made me meet his eyes. 'If you need me, I'm there. Blow a whistle or ring a bell and I'll come running.'

I nodded. I trusted him more than almost anyone and knew he would sprint down the track in the middle of the night if I needed him. Rudy gave me a bear-hug and said he'd be back tomorrow morning with a surprise and I'd better like it. Before he left I gave him back his flick knife. With my friends back, with Jenny safe, I didn't need it any more.

Gloria stayed. We returned to the porch and watched the sun dip. The air chilled.

'Have you been inside yet?' Gloria asked.

I shook my head.

'Would you like me to go in?'

'Okay.'

She came back with a pair of Cokes, a packet of saltines I didn't know we had, and a blanket. The one from the back of the couch for when Momma fell asleep in front of the TV or stumbled in after a night at Gum's. I held it to my chest. Breathed it in. Her smell. The real smell, not mud or blood or hate. It was whiskey and strawberries and Lucky Strike smoke and that heady, body scent behind it all. That was Momma. And it was all that was left. I cried again.

Gloria held me until the sun was gone and the night was full. I apologised for not being good company and she told me to shut up. Being so close to her again after so long, something sparked in my chest and warmed me from the inside. I held her hand and she stroked my thumb with hers. A tiny, absent-minded movement that sent shocks of heat through me.

When the night chill came Gloria led me into my house. I kept my head down, face buried in the blanket so I wouldn't have to see what had happened to my home, and followed her upstairs. I knew the way even with my eyes closed, felt the swollen boards under my feet outside the bathroom, the creak on the fourth step up to our attic room. Nothing had changed but everything had.

Gloria and me lay side by side in mine and Jenny's bed, wrapped in the blanket despite the summer heat. The windows were open, letting in a sweet, smoky breeze that made me think of chestnuts at Christmas. We stayed like this, not talking, just breathing, being, for a long time. Gloria's fingers played in my hair and her other hand held mine. For the first time in days, I felt the pieces of me come back together. I knew I'd never be fixed, how could I be without my heart, without my soul? I was a glass smashed against a wall, some pieces gone, some turned to dust, but a few shards still intact enough to try to repair. Rudy was my steady hand. Gloria was my glue.

I woke beside Gloria. She was sat upright on the bed, knees drawn to her chest under her dress, staring at the poster of Joni Mitchell. She didn't realise I was awake and for a blissful minute, I watched her. Gloria's face, usually bright, cheeks plumped by a smile, was slack and sad. She scratched at her knee, picked at a scab from a graze I didn't recognise. Empty eyes. Staring but not looking, the same darkness across her expression she had last night. It looked like she was fighting with herself, rocking slightly, frowning, troubled. A year ago, with Gloria in my bed, I'd have been a wreck. Shaking and nervous and babbling about being caught, what would Momma do, what would Jenny think, but that worry seemed so distant now. So small.

There is something raw, stripped, in someone who doesn't know they're being seen. People change when they notice. A mask slips on. It gets thinner, more transparent the longer you know someone but it's always there, always will be. A barrier. A lie – white and harmless, but a lie all the same. Except in those moments between glances when the mask is gone and a kind of truth, unfiltered and free and open, shines out. Watching her made me think of something Momma said once, an old saying about a tree in the woods. If it falls with no one to hear it, does it make noise? Does a person, when there is no one to see them and their mask is fallen away, still exist? Did I still exist in those days I hid in the crawlspace? And now?

'Hey,' I said, startled her. The mask eased over her face. 'Hey.'

I sat beside her, knees up like hers, and tried not to look at my room. Jenny wasn't here and I was suddenly afraid she was gone. Really gone. But the fear was short. I felt her, everywhere.

'I have something to tell you,' Gloria said. 'I wanted to tell you last night but I couldn't.'

'What is it?'

From the pocket of her dress she pulled out a thin scarf. My insides went cold. A white scarf with blue stars. I knew it. Gloria knew it. She had given it to Jenny for her birthday. My throat squeezed.

I took it between trembling fingers. It felt wrong, like

it'd been washed in new detergent, and it smelt of smoke. Not Momma's Strikes or Rudy's Camels but cigar smoke. Mr Wakefield smoked cigars.

'Where did . . .'

'I found it in my father's jacket.'

A fresh wave of hate crashed over me. He'd kept a souvenir, as if that bastard hadn't taken enough. I wanted to scream. I screwed the scarf in my fist and closed my eyes, tried to keep calm.

'I found it the night before Jenny . . .' Gloria said, voice caught and it took her a moment to recover. 'I didn't know she was gone at the time. That morning, I came round here to find you, see if Jenny was all right. But the sheriffs were already going through your house and we couldn't find you. Oh God, John, I can't imagine . . . I wish I'd been here, helped, I'm sorry. I'm so sorry.'

'It's okay,' I said and she took a deep, shuddering breath.

'I called on Rudy,' she said. 'His brother had heard someone in town talking about Jenny and your mom. He said people had seen you walking barefoot, covered in blood, but that you were okay. Rudy and I went up to Barks and sat on Fisher's Point and talked it all through, all the way back to Mary Ridley. It all felt connected somehow, her and Jenny, but I didn't know how or what it meant that my father had her scarf stuffed in his jacket pocket.'

Gloria's lip and chin shook, losing a battle against her tears.

'Then I remembered the blue car that you and Rudy saw that day at Rudy's place and what Bung-Eye said about it. I'd seen a car like that before but in a bright red, same as the shutters on our house. For a long time I thought it had to be someone else's. I never put the pieces together before or maybe I did and just didn't want to believe it. Rudy didn't know who the car belonged to until I told him.'

'Your father.'

'My father. He must have had Bung-Eye repaint it. Rudy said that what you both heard made it pretty clear that the person who owned the car killed Mary Ridley. And then I find that scarf and hear that Jenny . . .'

'He didn't kill Jenny.'

'But he did kill Mary Ridley. And he did something to Jenny. Something bad.'

I swallowed acid. Gloria's face, so beautiful, was pale, like she'd painted her skin with chalk. It looked all the whiter against her red hair. I took her hand.

'Did Jenny find something? Did she find something out about my dad and that's why . . .?'

'She didn't find out. I did.'

'And your mother?'

I shook my head. Wings crackled inside me for the first time in days. Don't talk about Momma. I can't think about Momma. Her skin under my palm, soft and leathery from the sun, the warm water, the smell of strawberries.

'You knew all this, didn't you?' she asked.

'Yes.'

Her face cracked. 'You've been carrying this around. Why didn't you tell anyone?'

'I didn't think you'd have believed me. You'd have been angry with me. Hated me.'

She interlaced her fingers with mine. 'You're probably right.'

We sat in silence for a long time. A square of sunlight on the floor stretched and shifted before we spoke again. There was too much for our minds to work out, talking about it only did so much. Gloria cried once or twice and I held her. I'd lost my family and she'd lost hers too. Two great betrayals – my momma and her father – and now here we were together, orphans adrift.

'What about your mother?' I asked, softly in the quiet.

Gloria gave a half-hearted smile. 'I tried to talk to her about it. I told her that Father had seen other women, girls my age. She slapped me and told me to stop telling lies. My mother has always treated me like a princess. Act a certain way, look a certain way, perform on cue, curtsey and twirl in your pretty, pretty dresses in front of Daddy's senior partners.' She sighed, tugged on a piece of her hair like she wanted to pull it out, destroy that prettiness to spite her mother. 'As long as the apple is shiny and red, it doesn't matter if it's rotten.'

'What about Mandy?'

She laughed. 'And have it all over town by dinner time? No thank you.'

Jenny stood in the sunbeam arching across the floor. First time I'd seen her since waking and I almost jumped up, greeted her with a hug and a where have you been, when I remembered Gloria didn't see her. Jenny looked at me with an answer written across her face but I couldn't read it. I didn't have the code to crack it. It said, you know what to do, but I didn't. I had no idea. I was swimming through a black pit of grief and Gloria had just dived in behind me. I felt a pull on my legs and saw the dead white hand of Mary Ridley, of Jenny, of Momma, and then the shark-like face of Mr Wakefield.

'What are we supposed to do now?' Gloria said and her voice cut through the dark. The tug on my ankle disappeared.

'School starts in a few weeks,' she said. 'God, can you imagine going to school? Sitting in those classrooms, everyone staring. It doesn't seem real.'

Nothing seemed real any more.

'Everything's changed. Ever since that day at the Roost. Then when Mark and Tracy . . . and the mill.' She let out a bitter laugh. 'You know, my dad said a few months ago that the war was winding down and he'd bet a month's salary that Mark would never even have been called up to serve. How awful, huh? They died for nothing. Sometimes I wonder why him and Tracy didn't just run away, you know, Canada or someplace. I guess they didn't have the money.'

Because Bung-Eye was bleeding Roy Easton dry. A dull, inevitable darkness lodged in my belly. There was no escaping that man's reach, nothing he didn't have some hand in, however indirect. You may not see the claws but you'll still feel the scratch.

And he'll never suffer for it. It made me want to scream.

Gloria shifted, a floorboard creaked. 'What is this town any more? It doesn't feel like home. Doesn't feel safe. What's left now?' she asked.

My farm.

What farm? Dead soil and an empty house, no money for food let alone a tractor or seed or fertiliser. And what would be the point now? Without them?

'I should go but I'll see you later for Rudy's big surprise,' Gloria said and slid off my bed. She didn't look at me, just flattened down her dress and went to the door.

She stopped. 'I wish we'd never found that body. I wish we'd never gone looking. I made us, I know I did, and I'm sorry. I'll always be sorry.'

Gloria walked back to me, kissed me on the cheek, then left.

I heard every movement. The landing, a pause outside the bathroom, then her flight down the stairs, through the family room and outside. I went to the window and watched her pick up her bike, stop for a moment, look from the house to the track, as if she was deciding which route to take, which future to pick. After another minute, she got on her Raleigh and pedalled away.

Jenny, on the bed now, smiled at me. The world was so quiet. The heat didn't bother me any more. I didn't even hear the buzz of insects. I saw birds, the occasional hawk, mostly blackbirds, but I never heard their calls. There was a haze over my world, like I was trapped in a glass case watching and hearing only muffles. Endless golden corn-fields stretched out on all sides, stabbed with clumps of trees and strung about with telephone wires and barbed fences. To the west, the land dipped into our valley, our Roost, where we made Big Lake and where all this hurt began. In between the Roost and my home, out there somewhere, in a place my mind knew but tried to block out, was that triangle of no-man's-land, the Three Points.

It was known, a town legend, that you could say or do anything on the Points. It didn't belong to anyone. Maybe Jenny thought she would be safe there. It hurt to think about so I turned away from the outside and toward my angel of a sister, sitting on our bed with my book of North American birds in her hands. A gift from Momma. One of my favourite things.

It's okay to love her, Jenny said, and I cried into the pages.

Jenny tapped me on the shoulder and I realised I'd fallen

asleep, the book splayed open on my chest. The light dimmer but still there. Mid-afternoon. That strange expression on her face again, the one with the answer, the one I couldn't understand.

She looked to the left, toward the landing. A second later, someone knocked on the front door.

There's your answer, she said and urged me out of bed.

Rudy stood on the porch with a duffel bag slung over his shoulder. Big movie-star grin on his face. He wore blue jeans and a black t-shirt, a pack of cigarettes folded into the sleeve, with a denim jacket threaded through the handles on the bag. He hopped about, that smile reaching past his mouth, into his eyes and all through his body.

'It's time,' he said, voice jumpy like the rest of him. 'It's finally time, Johnny.'

'What are you on about?'

He dug into his back pocket, gave me a piece of card. 'Surprise!'

A bus ticket. A ringing sound in my ears, piercing like feedback on speakers. Then it passed and I heard the birds, chattering in the trees. And the wind through the corn, the familiar rustle of the dried husks. And the creaking of the house, breathing in and out, just like it always had.

'A bus ticket?' was all I could think of to say.

'St Louis then down to Kansas City, then all the way to San Francisco.'

'You're leaving?'

'We're all leaving, man. There's one for you, one for me and one for Gloria.'

Jenny swung on the tyre in the yard. That expression on her face had changed. I knew the answer now. I could read it clear in her smile, wide enough to match Rudy's.

You can't stay here, Johnny, she said. This isn't home any more.

I knew she was right. Could I really walk through town again, see all those faces who knew every detail of what happened to my family?

Every inch of Larson was drenched in memories of Jenny and Momma and the life we had. The Backhoe where we'd shared shakes and hamburgers and Didi's blueberry pie. Al Westin's where we'd bought ice creams and exchanged Coke bottles for spare cash. Barks reservoir where we'd gone swimming and dared each other to jump Fisher's. The school where we'd cheered on the Lions to playoffs. The woods behind Gloria's house where we'd learned to smoke and made such grand plans. The Roost. Big Lake. Three Points. My house where Momma danced around the kitchen in her bare feet, where she painted her toes cherry red, where she sang and used a wooden spoon as a microphone, where she played dress up with Jenny when we were little, made her a flower, a princess, Carmen Miranda with the fruit bowl on her head. Where she carried me upstairs when I was five when I fell asleep after chores, where she held me in her arms and called me her special boy. Where she loved us. Where she destroyed us.

Could I look at all that every day? For the rest of my life? Could I walk past that church and hear the echoed sermons of Frank Jacobs and not run in there and shoot him dead? What about that gurning monster Darney Wills? And when his mayor father comes up for re-election and promises to 'Clean up the town' and pledges family values? Could I keep my tongue? And what if I saw Gloria's father on the street? How would I stop myself grabbing him, squeezing my hands around his throat until the kicking stopped? I suddenly wished the pastor and Sheriff Samuels had locked me up, that would be a lesser punishment than living here with all this. I'd never truly wanted to leave my home, my town, until right then.

'What do you say?' Rudy nudged me, dropped the duffel onto the porch.

'I don't have much money,' I said. The ninety-four dollars from the AMX matchbox was still in the evidence bag, in the crawlspace. 'Just a little.'

'I got you covered. I've been sneaking change from my old man for months and then I found Perry's stash. Dumbass kept it all under his mattress. Every cent is in here now.' He kicked the duffel bag. 'Gloria and me have been planning it all week. She tell you about her dad?'

I nodded. He went quiet for a moment, as if in respect.

'It's time to go,' he said. 'Perry and the old man are at a car show in Bowmont, they'll be back tonight and I got to be three states clear by the time they find all this missing. Bus is in an hour. Then we get the red-eye from St Louis. Besides, what you said . . . before . . . about them finding out about me and . . . and Scott . . . You were right. I got to leave. They'll kill me if I stay and this town has had enough of that.'

I bit my lip. Stared down at the ticket. Then to Jenny, on the tyre swing, lit up gold in the afternoon sun. All their lives, they'd wanted this ticket when I never had. Everything they did, they did for this thin piece of card. Everything Jenny did. Now it was in my hands and it was like holding a baby bird. Too afraid to grip it tight that I might hurt it and yet scared to hold it too loose that it might fly away.

'Is this for real?' I asked.

'Yeah. Bought them yesterday. Had to tell the old goat

at the ticket office they were for me and my mommy and my daddy and they were waiting in the Backhoe for me to hurry back. Last man in Larson who don't know who my old man is, thank God. You in?'

'I don't . . .' I shook my head. Good memories washed over the bad, flooded me inside and out. I'd be leaving them too but at least I'd have Jenny with me. On the swing, she smiled, nodded, shimmered in the sun.

'What's left here for you?' he said. 'What's left for any of us?'

I met his eyes. My best friend who I trusted more than anything. Jenny would be with me, no matter where I went. This would be my chance to finally do what I promised, to get her out of Larson. To show her the world and I would. I'd show her everything. Behind me, the house was just a house, the fields just fields. It would all decay and wilt and break. I could stay there, wilting and breaking along with it, or I could follow my friends, have a brand new life.

Rudy asked his question again.

'Nothing,' I said and felt Jenny's hand in mine. 'Nothing is left that I can't take with me.'

Rudy whooped and pulled me into a fierce hug, slapping my back and shouting, right into my ear, to get packed.

I found a rucksack in Momma's closet, covered in sewn-on peace badges, faint smell of pot inside. Eric's. It was perfect. I lingered there for a moment, in amongst her clothes, her scent. I found a shawl she wore sometimes in the winter. I remember her wrapping me up in it with her while we watched *Family Circus* one time. It was soft and held onto her perfume. I put it in the bag then went to mine and Jenny's room. I folded up the scarf with the blue stars and put it in my pocket. Then I packed clothes and my bird book and a few other bits and pieces. I went down to the crawlspace and shoved the evidence bag in the rucksack. I took a jacket from the hook, my warm one with a red chequered pattern, and forced that in too.

'Are you ready, Buff?' Rudy said in his best John Wayne cowboy voice.

I smiled. We'd snuck into the Clarkesville movie theatre a few years back to see the Duke in *Hondo*.

'I was born ready,' I said and Rudy winked at me, slung his duffel over his shoulder.

Gloria met us at the bus stop opposite Al Westin's grocery store with her suitcase and two fat rolls of cash she'd taken from a box in her father's closet. It was the same stop where they'd dropped off the army boys fresh back from the jungle. Back then, people had been holding protest signs across the street, now the sidewalks were empty, half the shops still boarded up after the Easton mill explosion. This town wasn't my town any more. That darkness, like a mushroom spore, had taken root and spread. Now poison popped up on every corner, infecting everyone who walked close. The sun still shone, the birds still chirped, but the people walked with hunched shoulders and grim eyes.

Jenny linked her arm in mine and rested her head on my shoulder. Gloria seemed nervous, fighting with herself over her decision to come with us, but I took her hand with my free one, told her everything would be okay, and she seemed to calm. Rudy whistled at us both and made smooching noises but it didn't bother me like it would have last year. I was different. They were different. Everything was different. My world had altered its axis and spun in a new rhythm. On my back I carried the only important pieces of my old life. In my hands, by my side, were all the pieces to build my new one. My Jenny. My best friend Rudy. And Gloria. The girl I loved.

We had money. We had tickets. We had nobody stopping us. It was all so easy. A cold fear came over me.

'Are you guys sure this is for real?' I said and they both turned to me. 'You're not playing a prank on me, are you?'

'Yeah, sure we are, John. We'll get all the way to San Fran then yell, only kidding!' Rudy scoffed. 'We're *that* kind of buds.'

'But, you know, this isn't like a dream and I'm going to wake up in the crawlspace with spiders all over me?'

Gloria made a disgusted face. 'God, I hope not.'

Rudy stepped to me and punched me hard in the arm.

'Jesus! What the hell was that for?'

He grinned, popped a piece of gum in his mouth. 'In the movies they say, "Pinch me, I'm dreaming", figured this would be a more fun way to tell.'

'Jerk,' I said.

On the other side of town, the church bells signalled the hour and a few moments later, the bus, a rusted hulk from the fifties, rolled up. We boarded, showed our tickets to the driver, then took seats on the long bench at the back of the bus. Rudy at one window, Gloria beside him, then me and Jenny by the other window. A few other people were sat nearer the front, including a young man in army uniform. He was missing an arm. He smiled at me as I passed, nodded like he'd seen a fellow soldier, then turned back to the window. Nobody else paid us any attention. We were just four kids taking a trip, nobody knew the truth and that relaxed me. Nobody else need ever know the truth. But that meant those terrible men would never see the inside of a jail cell, at least not for this. That wasn't right.

None of this is right, Jenny said, but leaving, starting fresh someplace new, where nobody knows us, is the best we can hope for.

'Last chance to turn back,' Rudy said, eyes glued to the window, waiting for the bus to take off.

Finally, Gloria smiled and any lingering doubts vanished.

'No way,' she said. 'We're a flock, remember, and we have to fly away together. Where you idiots go, I have to follow to make sure you don't do anything stupid. Besides, this is what Jenny would want for us,' she paused, let herself smile. 'We'll see the world for her.'

The bus juddered forward. We slid open the windows and let the cool air rush over us. Jenny leaned her head and arm out of the bus and rode the wind, squinting against the sun. Gloria and Rudy play-fought on the seats and laughed and I looked back, at the town we were leaving. We passed the sheriff's station and school and the road to the old warehouse. Through the dust, the white Larson water tower and the church spire receded. Once they were so important, my landmarks for the town, that I could never imagine a sky without them. Within a few miles, I couldn't see them any more.

The road turned to liquid glass in the heat and I caught a car following us. A pale grey Ford with a bad paint job that seemed to absorb the light and didn't have a driver. I closed my eyes.

When I opened my eyes, we were far out of town, past the places I recognised by name, but the car was still there, way back, but there. I caught Jenny's eye. I see it too, she said inside my head. She put her hand on my arm and I understood. Marked by Death, from the day we found the girl in the sycamore roots to today and every day from now on. I knew I'd see that car wherever I went. It was a warning, a sign, not a danger. It was my albatross.

I pressed my hand to the glass and realised I wasn't afraid any more. Not of that car, not of what it meant. I was free, like the birds I loved, and I was flying away.

I looked forward now, as we roared down the interstate. Sunlight streamed into the bus, painted the four of us in warm gold. The heavy, hollow feeling of grief and fear I'd carried for months, which had spiked in this last, terrible week and stabbed into my heart so deep I thought I would die from it, eased from my chest. Lifted off me as if all those horrors were tethered to the town and the further we drove, the more of it pulled away. It was the past and I was leaving it on the road behind me, like a rope unspooling on the asphalt.

I had my best friend, fogging up the window and drawing stupid faces in his breath. I had my shining sister beside me and nobody could take her away again. And I had Gloria, my beautiful quicksand girl. I met her smiling eyes and saw the spark of excitement in them to match mine.

I relaxed into the journey for the first time and let my eyes wander. We rolled through a town I didn't know, with people I'd never seen, a diner I'd never eaten in, and I smiled at its newness. We passed a road sign saying thirty miles to St Louis and at the same time, to the west over cornfields I didn't know, beside trees I'd never climbed, a cloud of starlings began their dance.

ACKNOWLEDGEMENTS

I'm not supposed to say this, but this book was not easy to write. It was an emotional marathon and ended, as marathons do, in exhaustion and an overwhelming sense of accomplishment. I am extremely proud of this book, but it wouldn't have been possible without the help and support of a few key people. Sarah Hodgson, with her patience and stern editorial hand, guided this book through countless drafts and never let me give anything but my best. Thanks also to my agent Euan Thorneycroft for his keen eye and sage advice, and to the whole team at A. M. Heath for their support.

Special thanks to my mum who read early versions of John's story and never shied away from telling me exactly what was wrong with it.

And my eternal, constant thanks to my wife, Neen, for everything else.